Houses with a Story

Seiji Yoshida

translated by

Jan Mitsuko Cash

A Dragon's Den, a Ghostly Mansion, a Library of Lost Books,
and 30 More Amazing Places to Explore

AMULET BOOKS • NEW YORK

CONTENTS

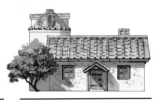

Cacao Tree Houses
57

A Timid Ogre's Hideout
59

A Tower House Near
the Border
61

An Outbuilding Inhabited
by a Poltergeist
63

A Shepherd's Hut
65

An Eccentric Botanist's
Laboratory
67

A Wanted Man's Sod House
69

The Seven Dwarves' House
71

House with a Dragon
73

A Lonely Ghost's Mansion
75

A Young Inventor's
Windmill
77

A Ronin's Tenement House
79

The House of a Woman
Fascinated by Dolls
81

A Man in an Abandoned
Subway Station
83

A Miner's Engine House
85

SIDEBARS

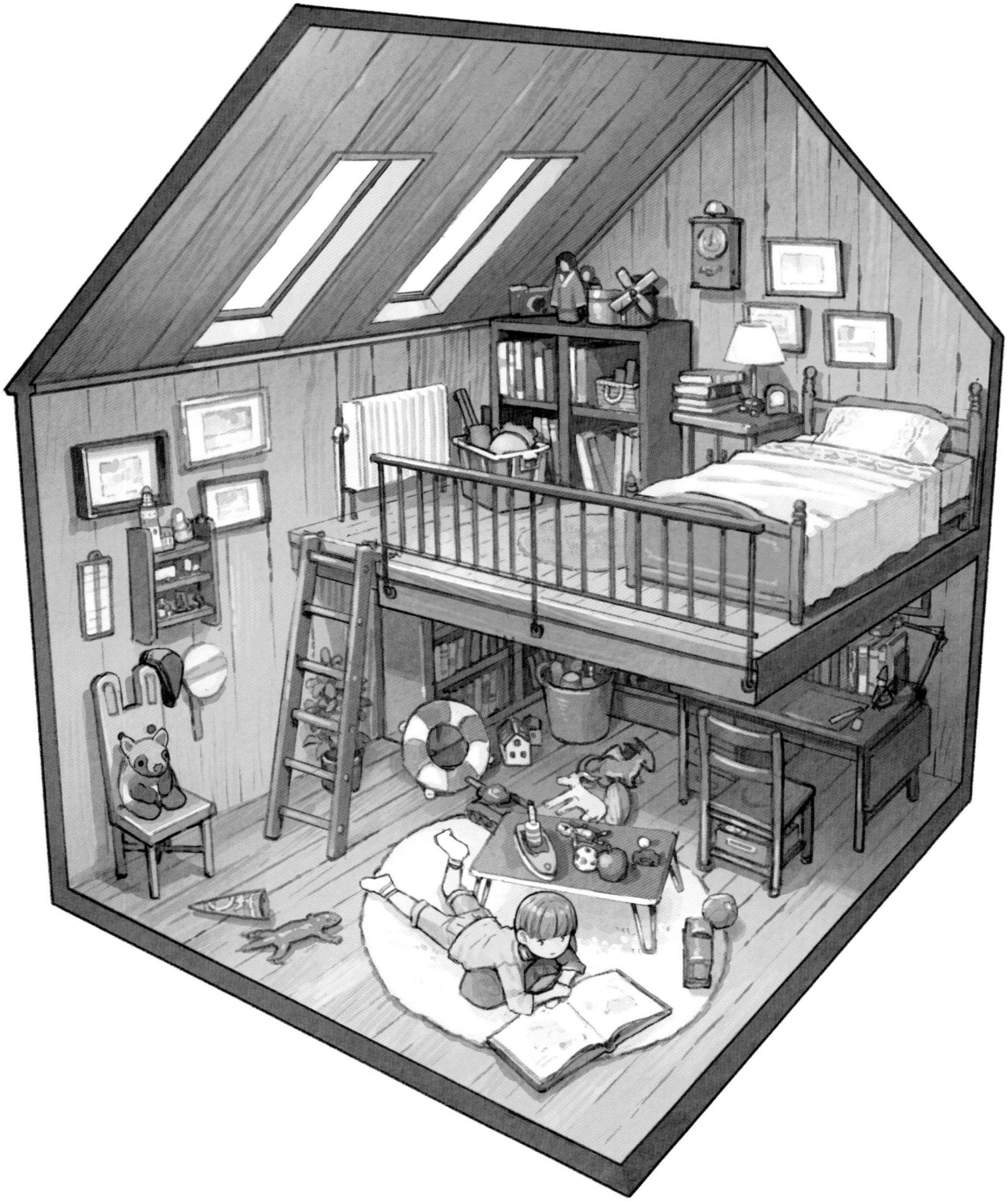

FOREWORD

From picture books to novels, the stories I've encountered since my childhood have almost always featured buildings that left impressions: the hideout in *The Adventures of Huckleberry Finn*, the hut in the Alps from *Heidi*, the Nowhere House of Master Hora in *Momo*, and so many others. I would read the stories and look at the illustrations over and over, dreaming about the details of those worlds.

To re-create my childhood self's delight, I introduce unique homes within this book, all of which could easily turn up in stories of their own. Since the location and time period of each house is different and I've drawn from a broad range of genres, you'll encounter an entirely new story with each turn of the page. Every dwelling should feel as though it has an entirely different origin from the others—you should be able to sense how the owner of each home came to live there, what types of foods they eat, and even where they sleep.

You may find houses that feel as though they've come straight from certain books you've read in the past, while other abodes may be so peculiar that you've never encountered anything like them before, even in your own imagination. The tale you weave for each house is entirely up to you, and nothing would give me greater pleasure than you finding yourself immersed in a wonderful story.

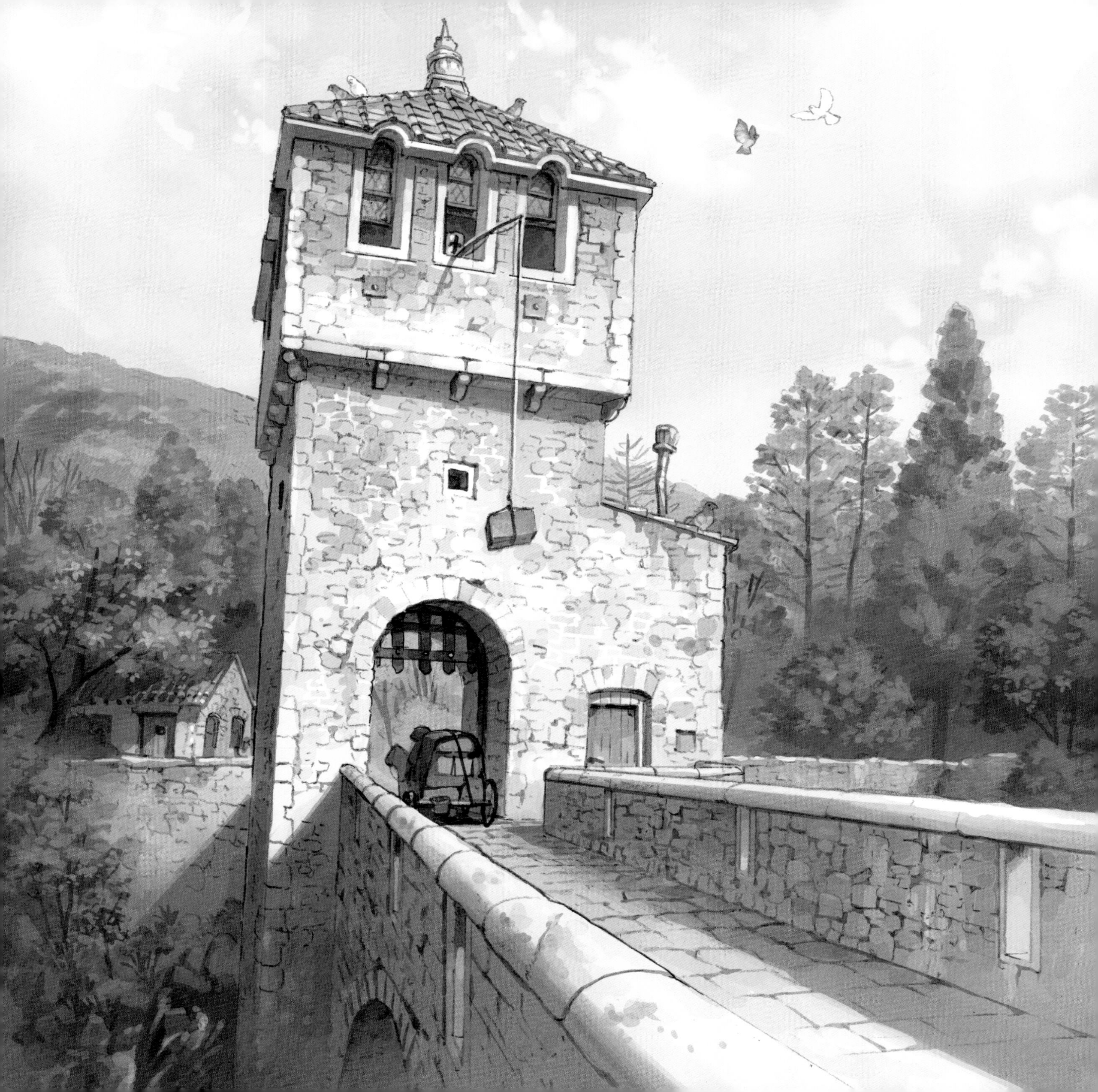

Mischievous Bridge Tower Keeper

A bridge tower is a type of gate built at a bridge's entrance to protect a city or fortress. However, it appears the original guard is no longer living in this tower and that an outlaw from somewhere or other has taken up residence.

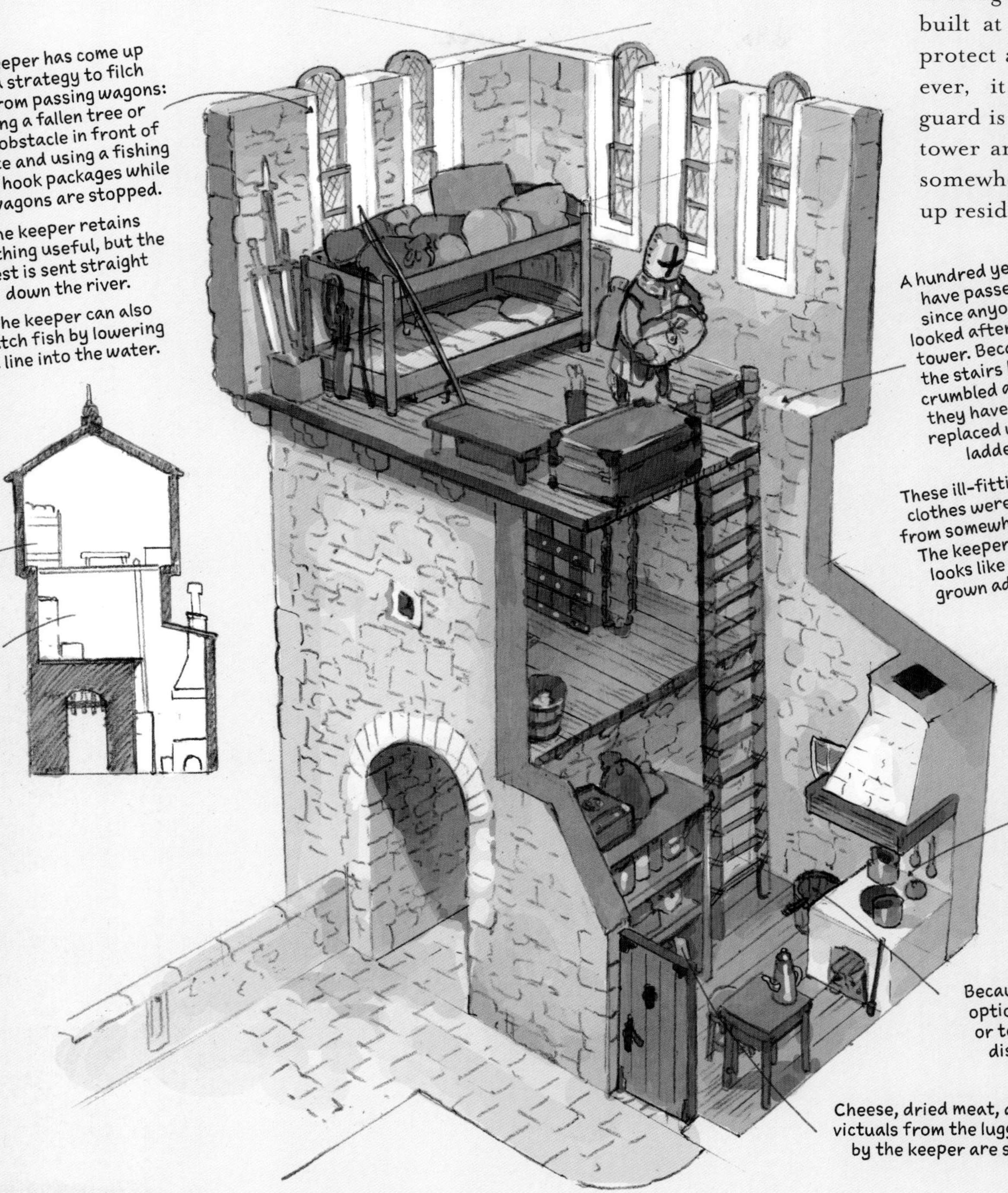

The keeper has come up with a strategy to filch goods from passing wagons: leaving a fallen tree or other obstacle in front of the gate and using a fishing rod to hook packages while the wagons are stopped.
The keeper retains anything useful, but the rest is sent straight down the river.
The keeper can also catch fish by lowering a line into the water.
A hundred years have passed since anyone looked after the tower. Because the stairs have crumbled away, they have been replaced with a ladder.
Though the stove rarely gets any use, the keeper occasionally uses it to cook meat or boil water.
Because there is no toilet, the only options are to use the river below or to use this bucket and then to dispose of the waste outside.
Cheese, dried meat, and any other victuals from the luggage acquired by the keeper are stored here.
Bed
Storage

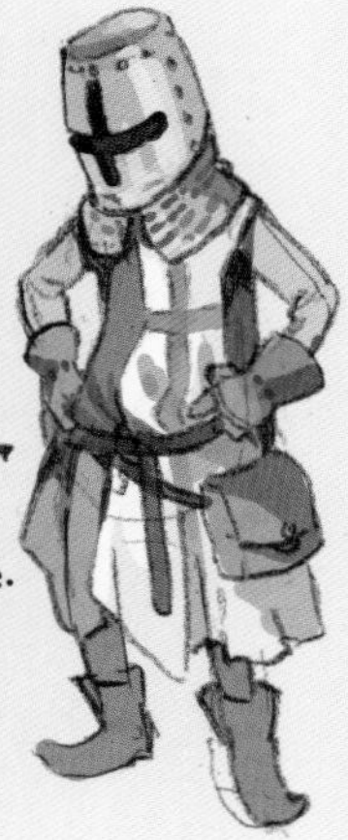

These ill-fitting clothes were stolen from somewhere else. The keeper hardly looks like a full-grown adult . . .

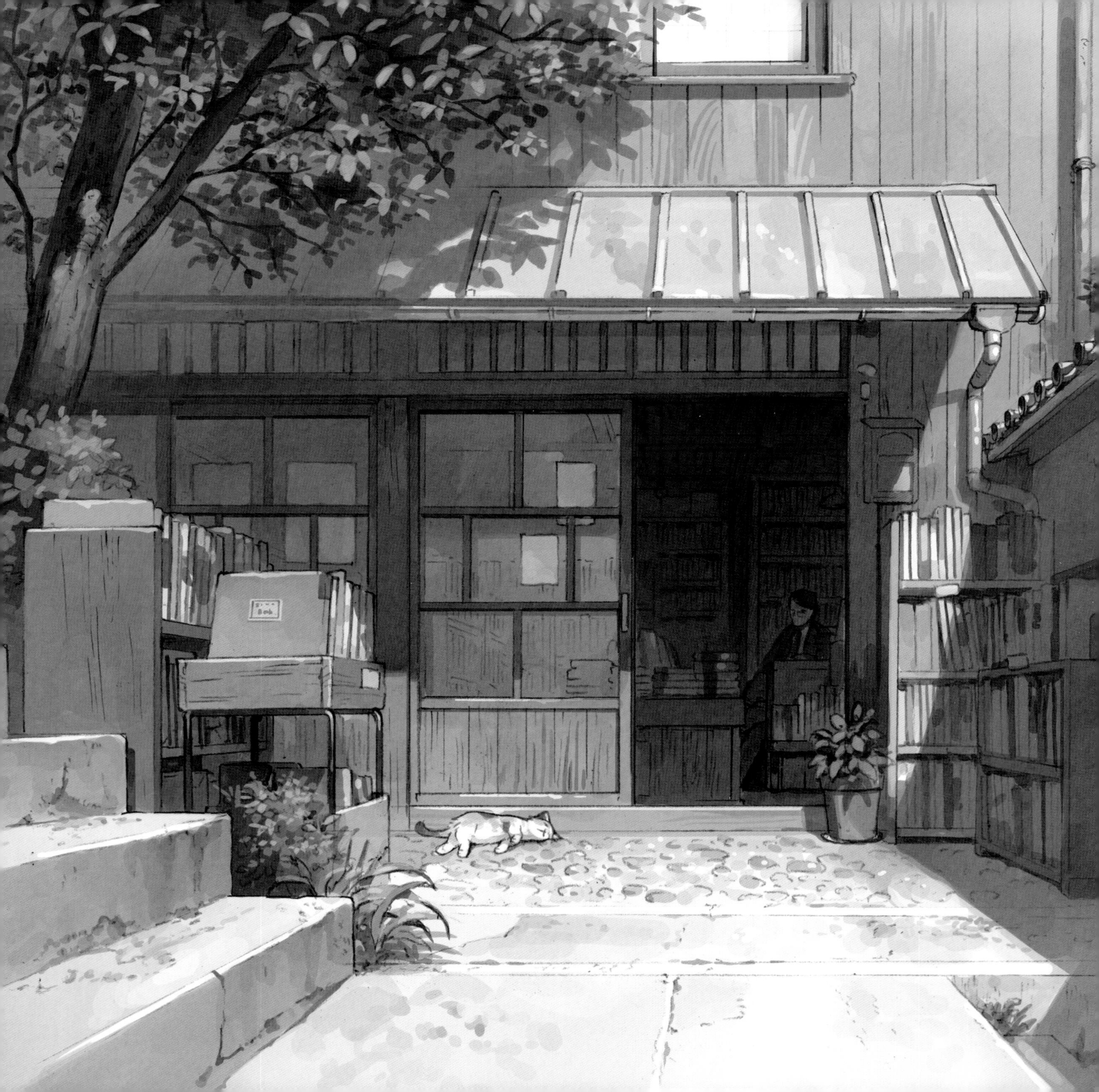

Kaidan-Do Bookstore

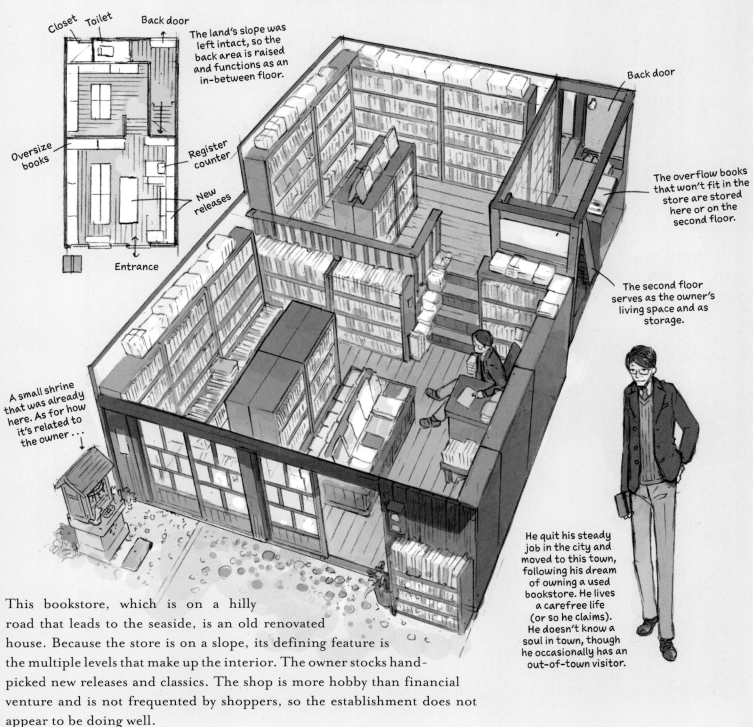

Closet   Toilet   Back door

The land's slope was left intact, so the back area is raised and functions as an in-between floor.

Oversize books

Register counter

New releases

Entrance

Back door

The overflow books that won't fit in the store are stored here or on the second floor.

The second floor serves as the owner's living space and as storage.

A small shrine that was already here. As for how it's related to the owner . . .

He quit his steady job in the city and moved to this town, following his dream of owning a used bookstore. He lives a carefree life (or so he claims). He doesn't know a soul in town, though he occasionally has an out-of-town visitor.

This bookstore, which is on a hilly road that leads to the seaside, is an old renovated house. Because the store is on a slope, its defining feature is the multiple levels that make up the interior. The owner stocks hand-picked new releases and classics. The shop is more hobby than financial venture and is not frequented by shoppers, so the establishment does not appear to be doing well.

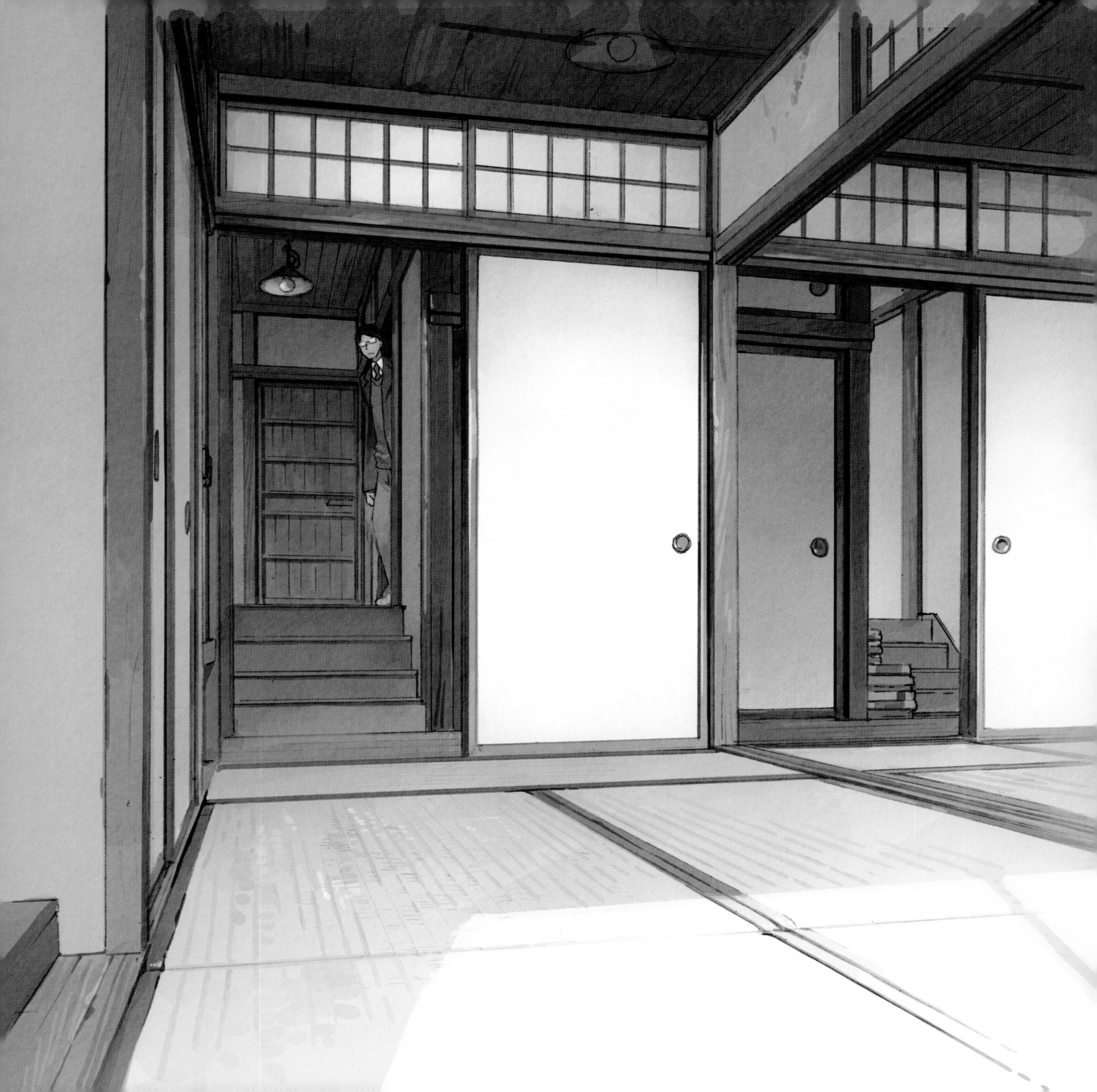

Kaidan-Do Bookstore

SECOND FLOOR

The second floor is a living area, so it has a living room, kitchen, bathroom, and platform for drying laundry. As with the ground level, the topography requires steps in the middle.

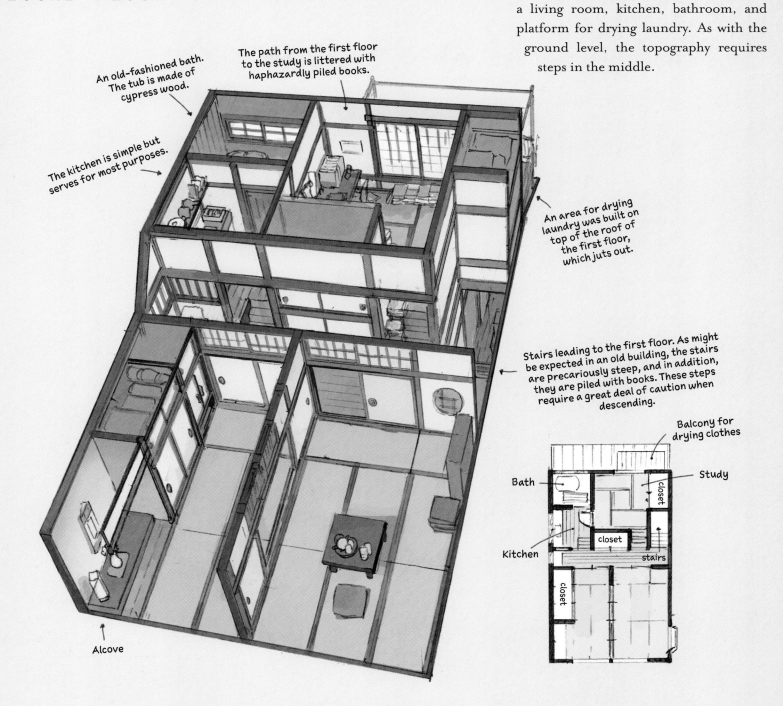

An old-fashioned bath. The tub is made of cypress wood.
The path from the first floor to the study is littered with haphazardly piled books.
The kitchen is simple but serves for most purposes.
An area for drying laundry was built on top of the roof of the first floor, which juts out.
Stairs leading to the first floor. As might be expected in an old building, the stairs are precariously steep, and in addition, they are piled with books. These steps require a great deal of caution when descending.
Alcove

Balcony for drying clothes
Bath
Study
closet
closet
Kitchen
stairs
closet

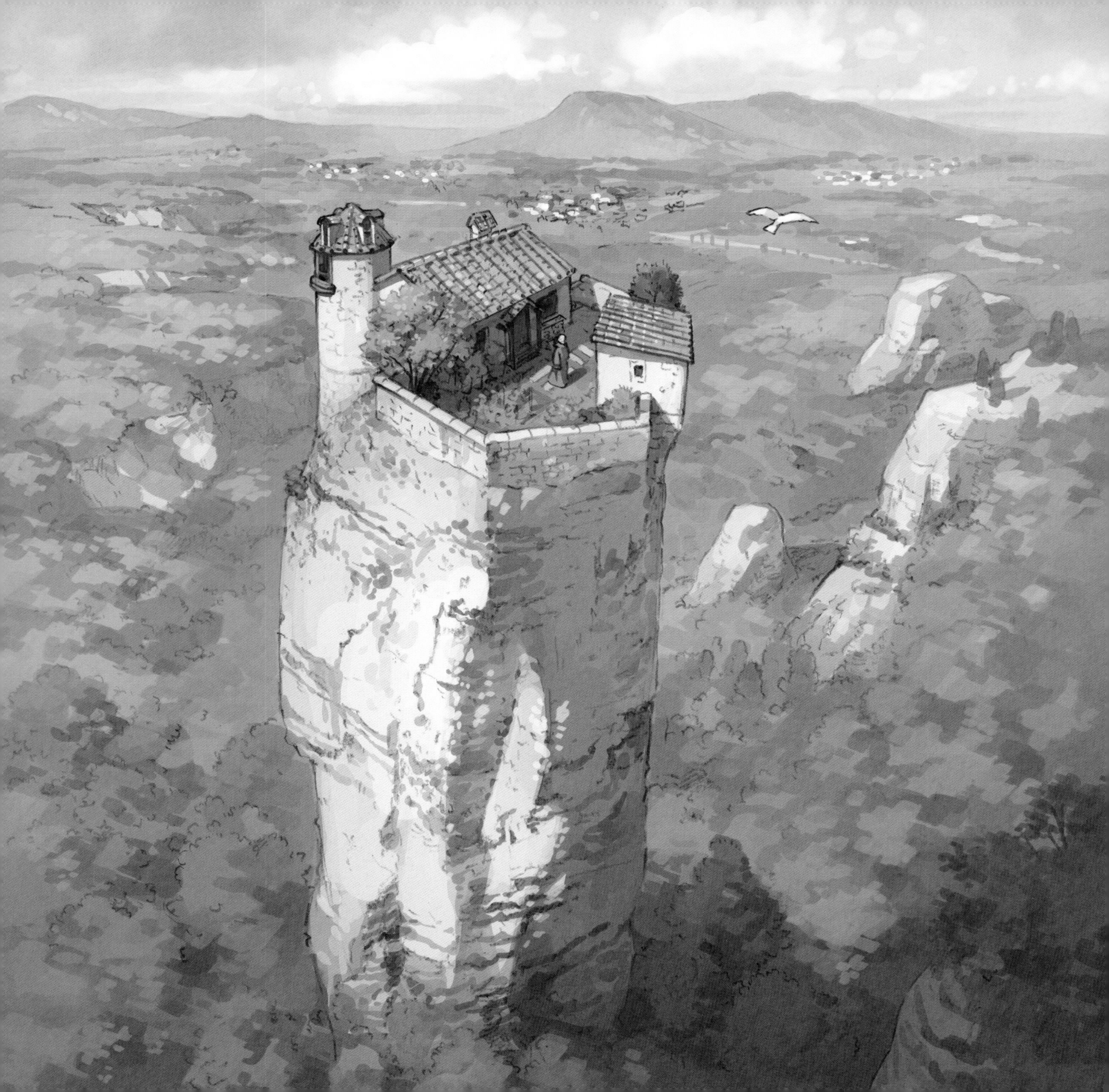

World-Weary Astronomer's Residence

The hermit-like owner of this home has developed an intense interest in the night sky and spends his evenings stargazing from atop a secluded rock formation. Though people might call the man an astrologer, his studies are extremely advanced for his time, and he would more fittingly be called an astronomer.

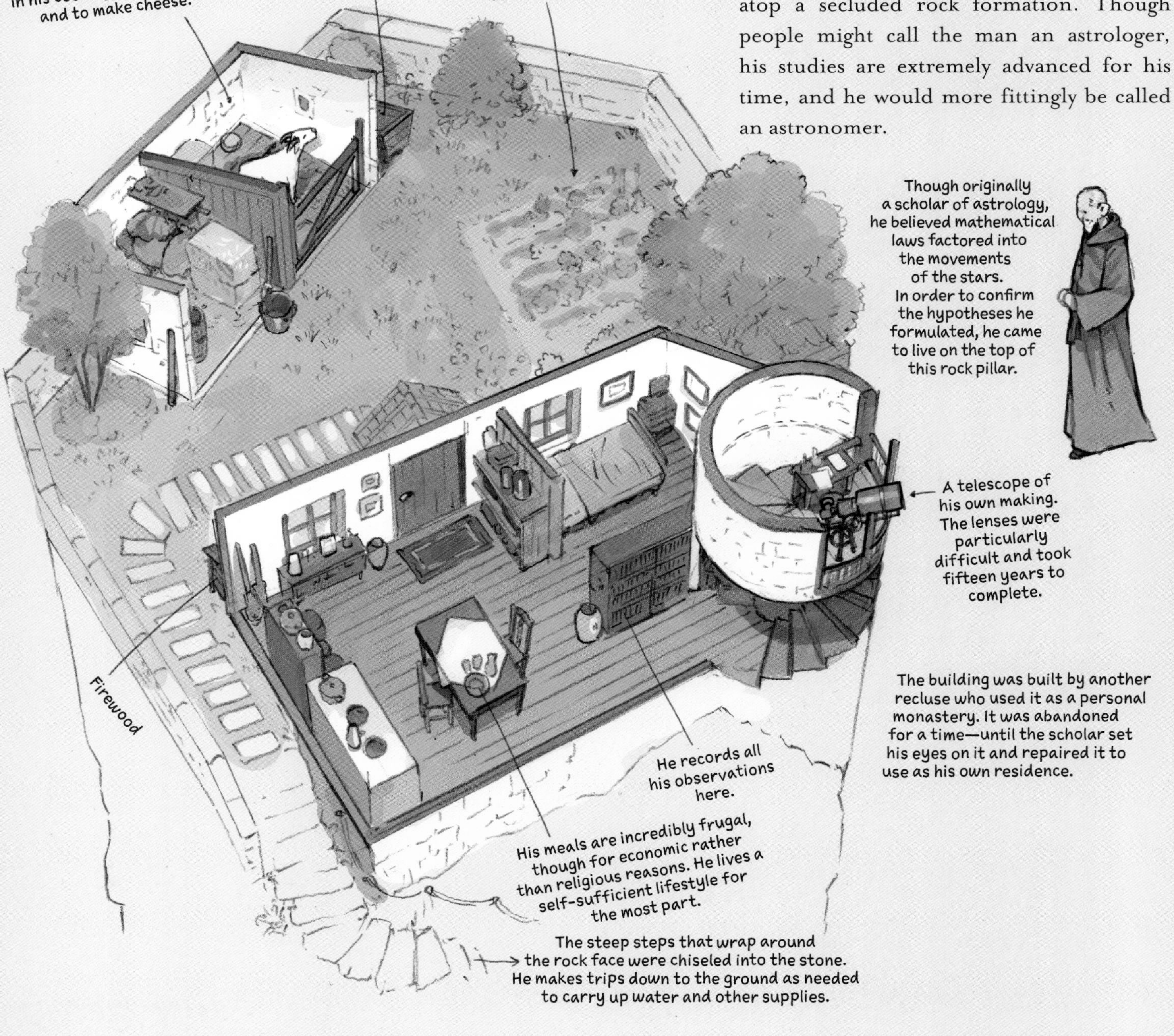
He carried the goat up while she was still young and reared her at the top. He uses her milk in his cooking, for drinking, and to make cheese.
Cistern
He cultivates vegetables, beans, and other food-stuffs here.
Though originally a scholar of astrology, he believed mathematical laws factored into the movements of the stars. In order to confirm the hypotheses he formulated, he came to live on the top of this rock pillar.
A telescope of his own making. The lenses were particularly difficult and took fifteen years to complete.
Firewood
The building was built by another recluse who used it as a personal monastery. It was abandoned for a time—until the scholar set his eyes on it and repaired it to use as his own residence.
He records all his observations here.
His meals are incredibly frugal, though for economic rather than religious reasons. He lives a self-sufficient lifestyle for the most part.
The steep steps that wrap around the rock face were chiseled into the stone. He makes trips down to the ground as needed to carry up water and other supplies.

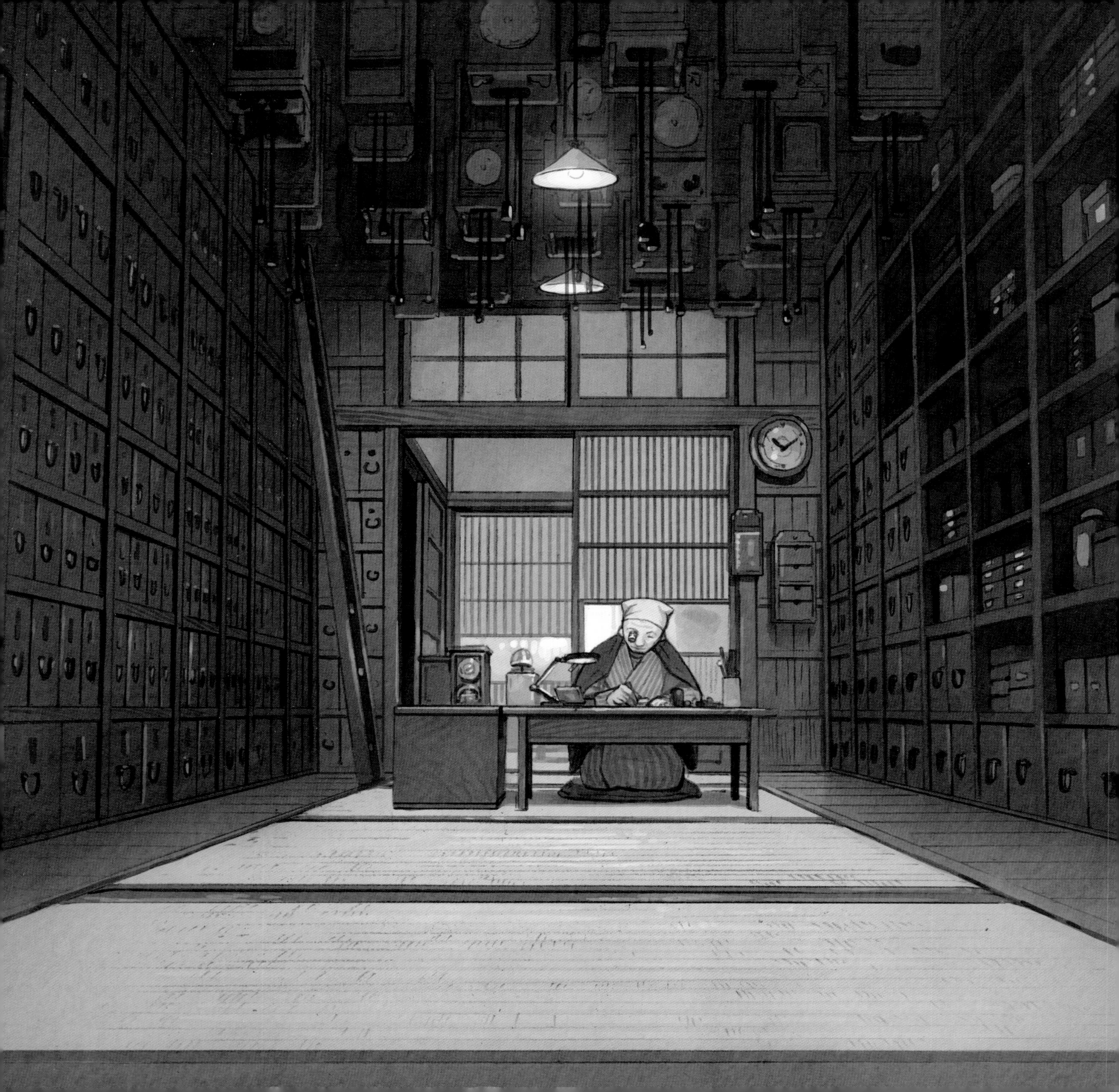

Meticulous Clockmaker

Once a pharmacist who opened his business during the Edo period (1603–1867 CE), this homeowner took up clock repair as a hobby, and at some point it became his main occupation. Naturally, our clockmaker can repair Western-style timepieces, and though Japanese-style timekeeping was rendered obsolete when fixed-increment time practices were adopted, he is able to repair Japanese timepieces as well.

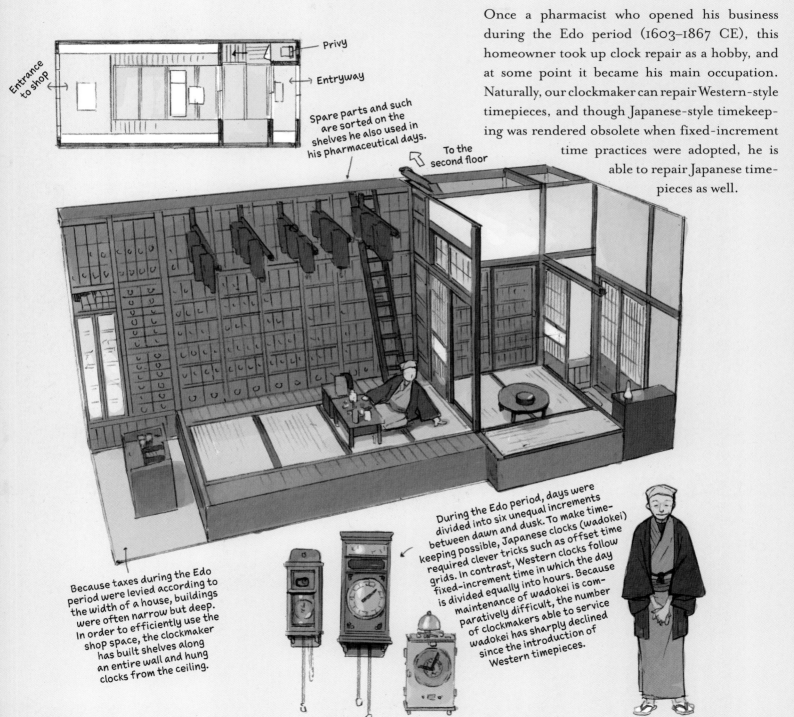

Entrance to shop
Privy
Entryway

Spare parts and such are sorted on the shelves he also used in his pharmaceutical days.
To the second floor

Because taxes during the Edo period were levied according to the width of a house, buildings were often narrow but deep. In order to efficiently use the shop space, the clockmaker has built shelves along an entire wall and hung clocks from the ceiling.

During the Edo period, days were divided into six unequal increments between dawn and dusk. To make timekeeping possible, Japanese clocks (wadokei) required clever tricks such as offset time grids. In contrast, Western clocks follow fixed-increment time in which the day is divided equally into hours. Because maintenance of wadokei is comparatively difficult, the number of clockmakers able to service wadokei has sharply declined since the introduction of Western timepieces.

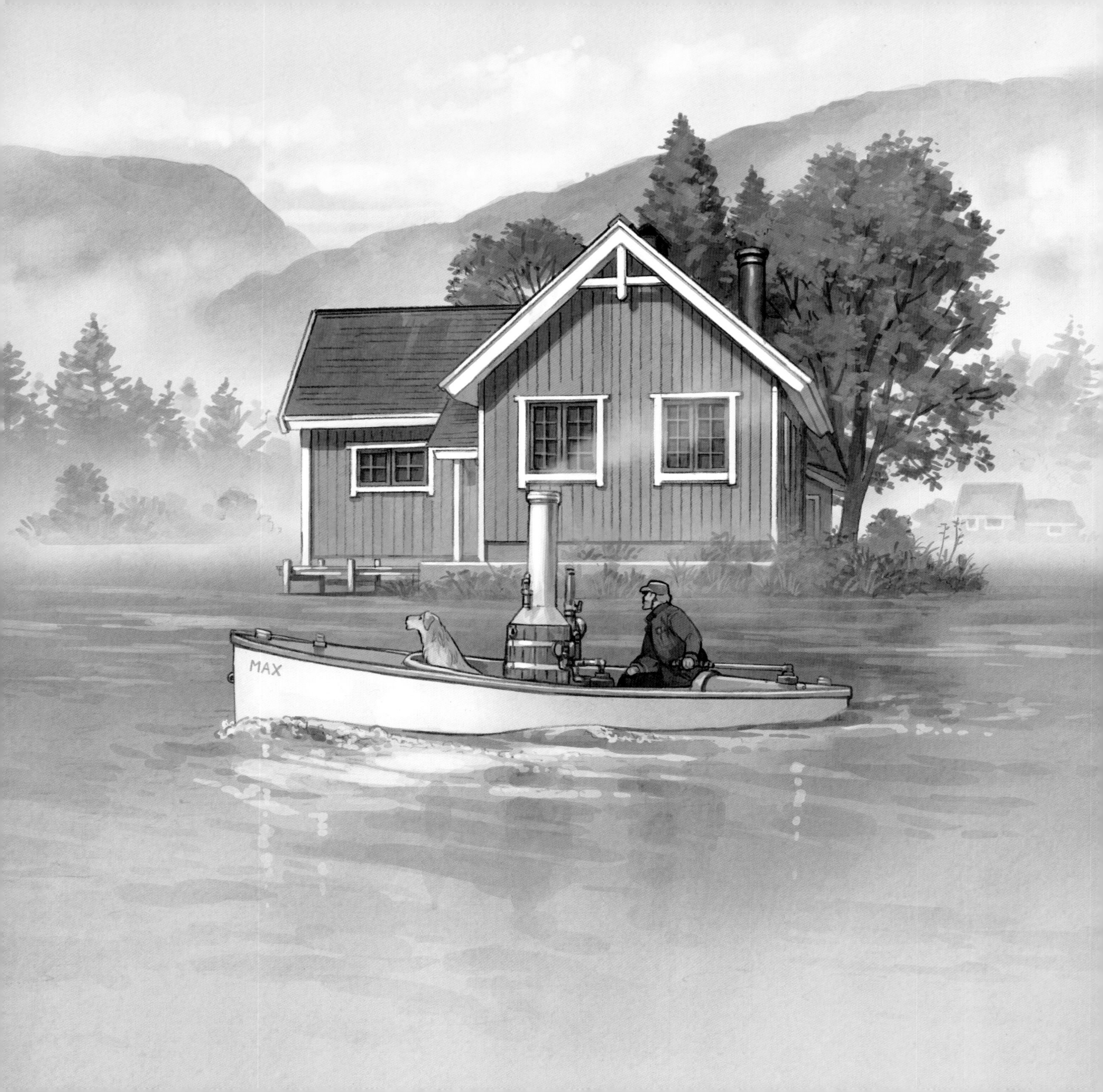
MAX

Reserved Mechanic's Cottage

The owner of this home works as a tireless automechanic most days. During long vacations, he visits the lake. He feels most at home when he's tinkering with machinery, so while staying at the cottage, he enjoys nothing more than working on his steamboat or riding in it.

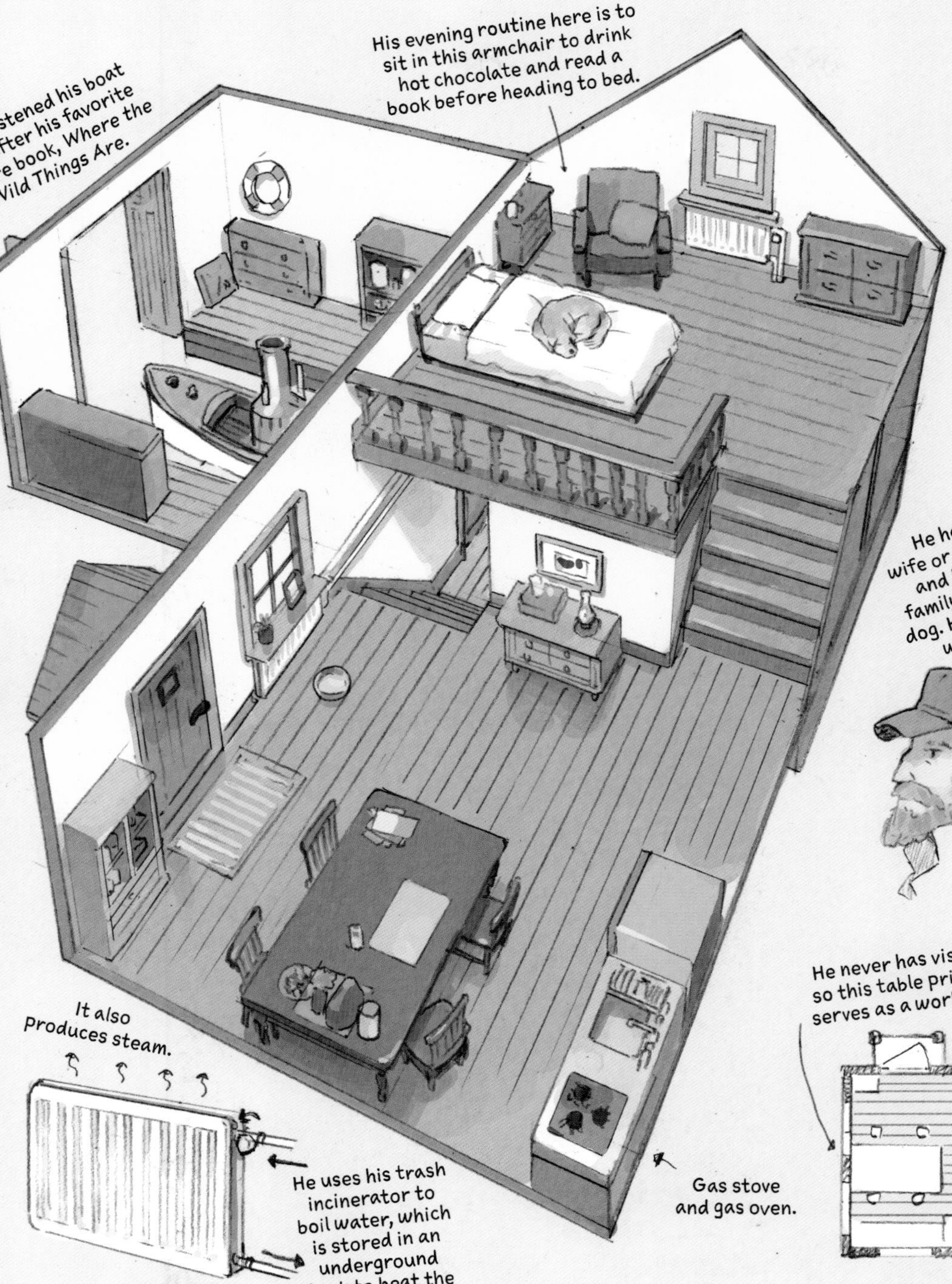
He christened his boat Max after his favorite picture book, Where the Wild Things Are.
His evening routine here is to sit in this armchair to drink hot chocolate and read a book before heading to bed.
Gas stove and gas oven.
It also produces steam.
He uses his trash incinerator to boil water, which is stored in an underground tank to heat the room.

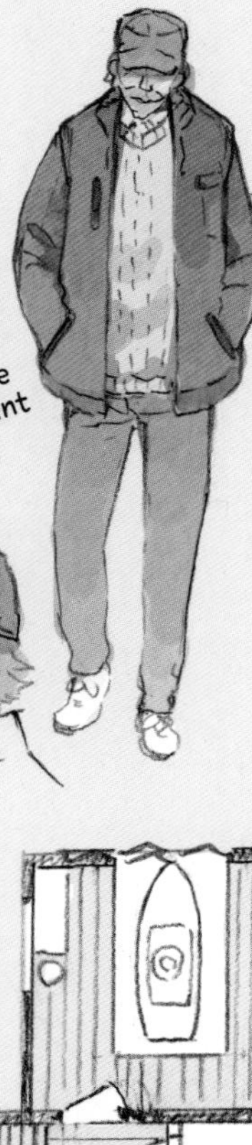
He has no wife or children, and his only family is a large dog. He's content with that.

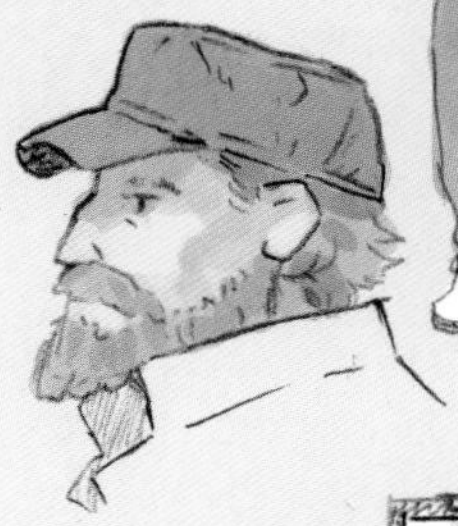

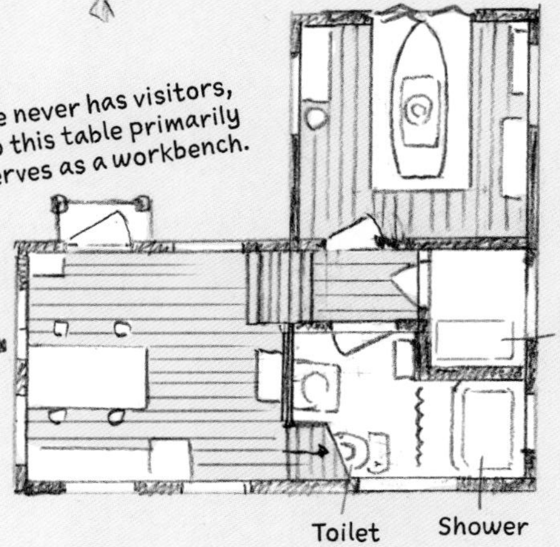
He never has visitors, so this table primarily serves as a workbench.
Hot water tank
Toilet
Shower

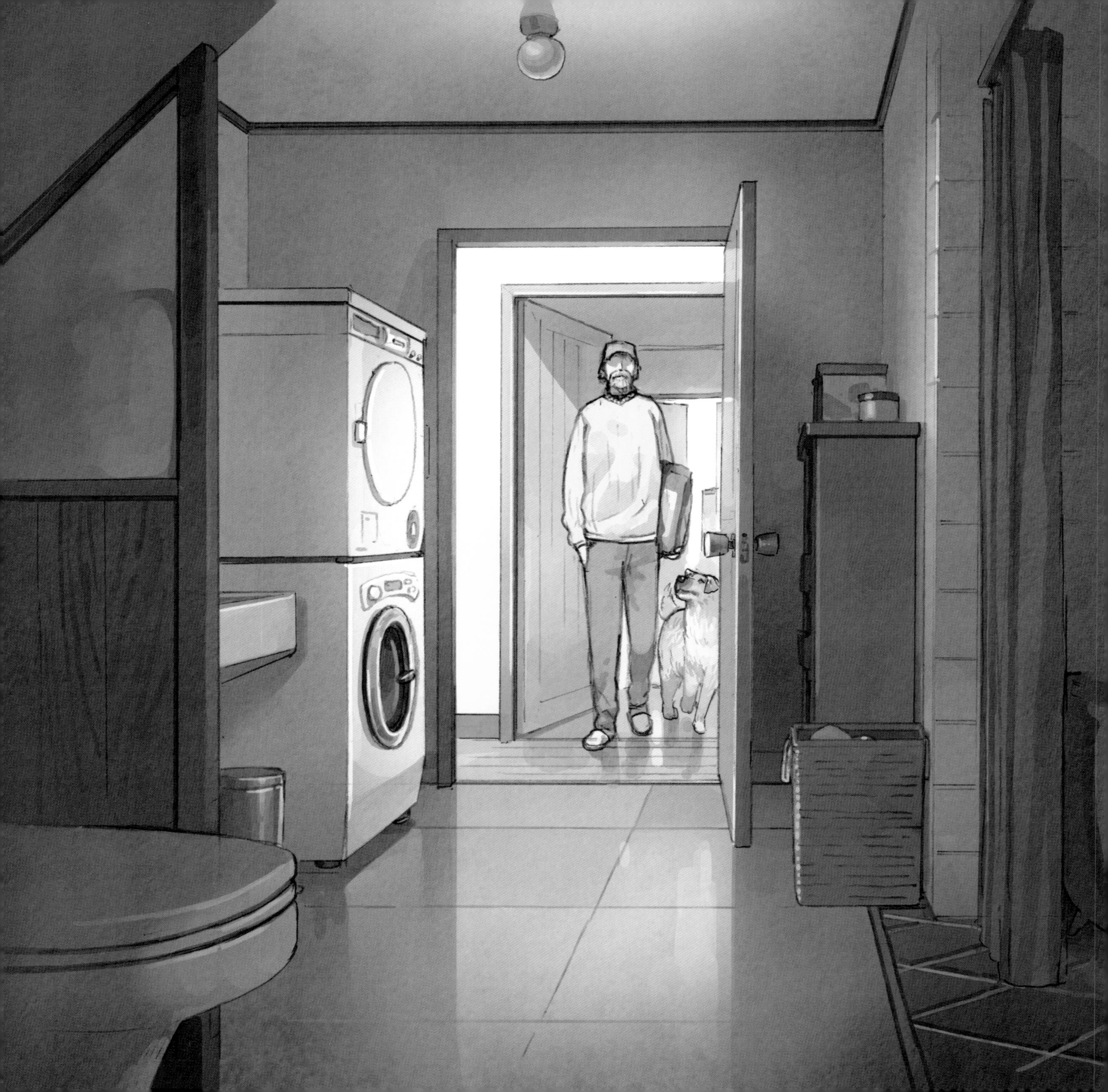

Reserved Mechanic's Cottage

DOCK

The cottage has a basement level furnished with a bathroom, hot water tank, and boathouse.

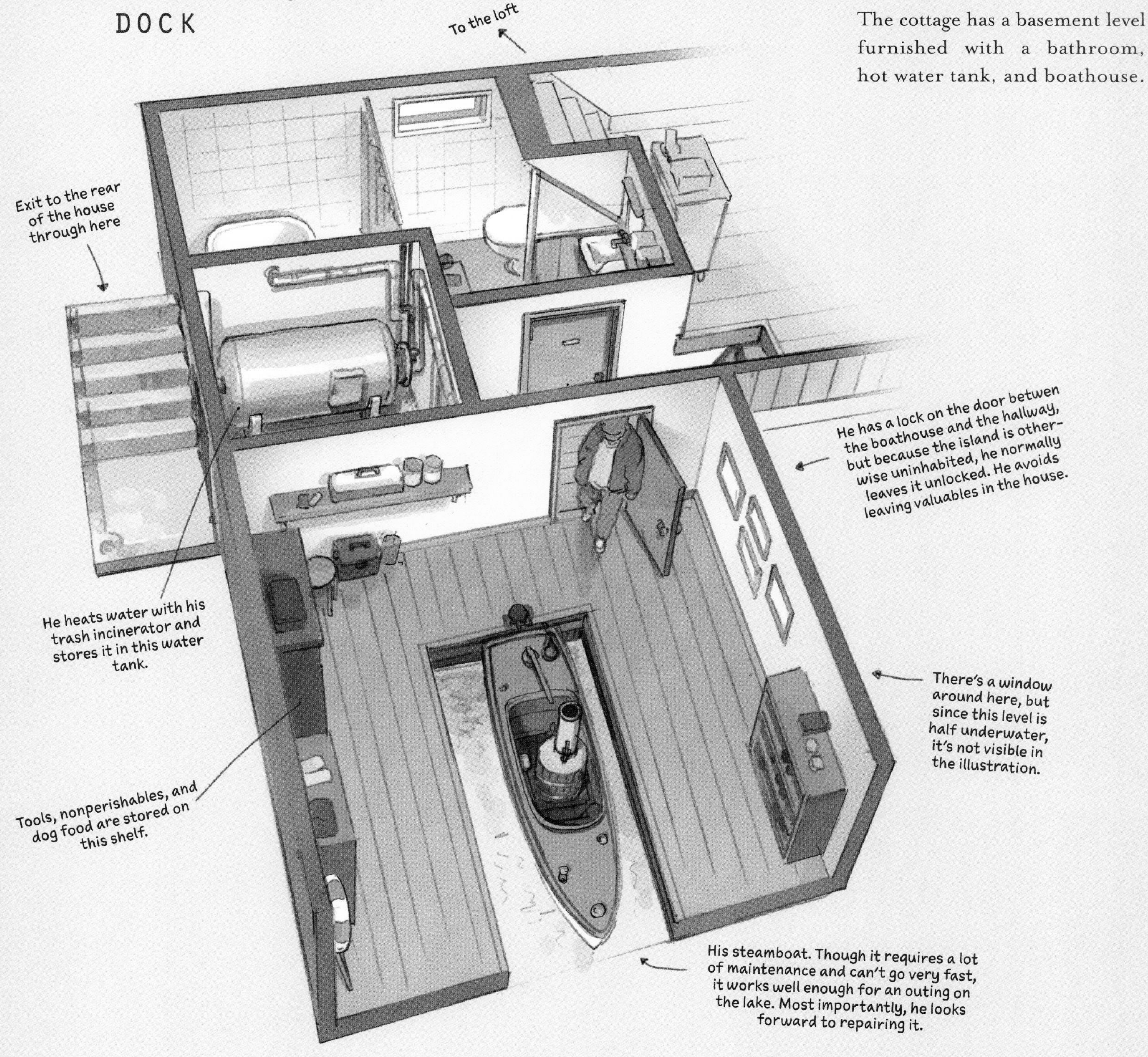

To the loft
Exit to the rear of the house through here
He has a lock on the door betwen the boathouse and the hallway, but because the island is other-wise uninhabited, he normally leaves it unlocked. He avoids leaving valuables in the house.
He heats water with his trash incinerator and stores it in this water tank.
There's a window around here, but since this level is half underwater, it's not visible in the illustration.
Tools, nonperishables, and dog food are stored on this shelf.
His steamboat. Though it requires a lot of maintenance and can't go very fast, it works well enough for an outing on the lake. Most importantly, he looks forward to repairing it.

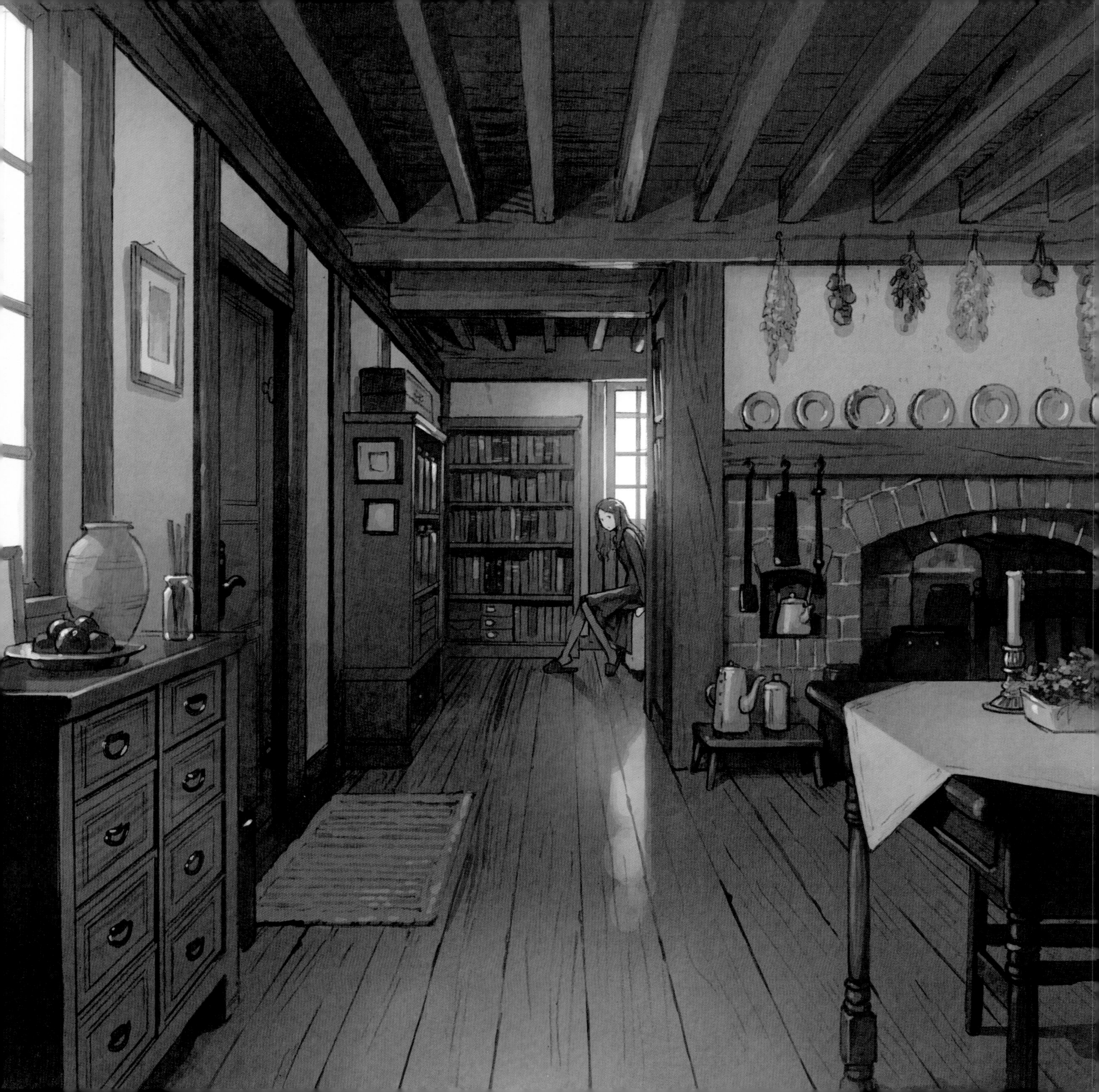

Methodical Witch's House

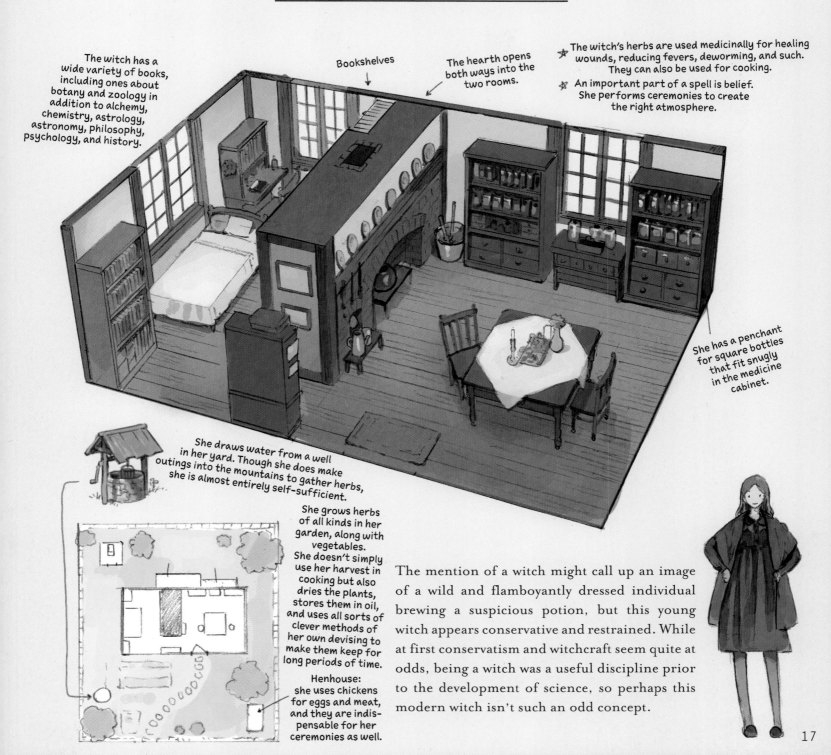

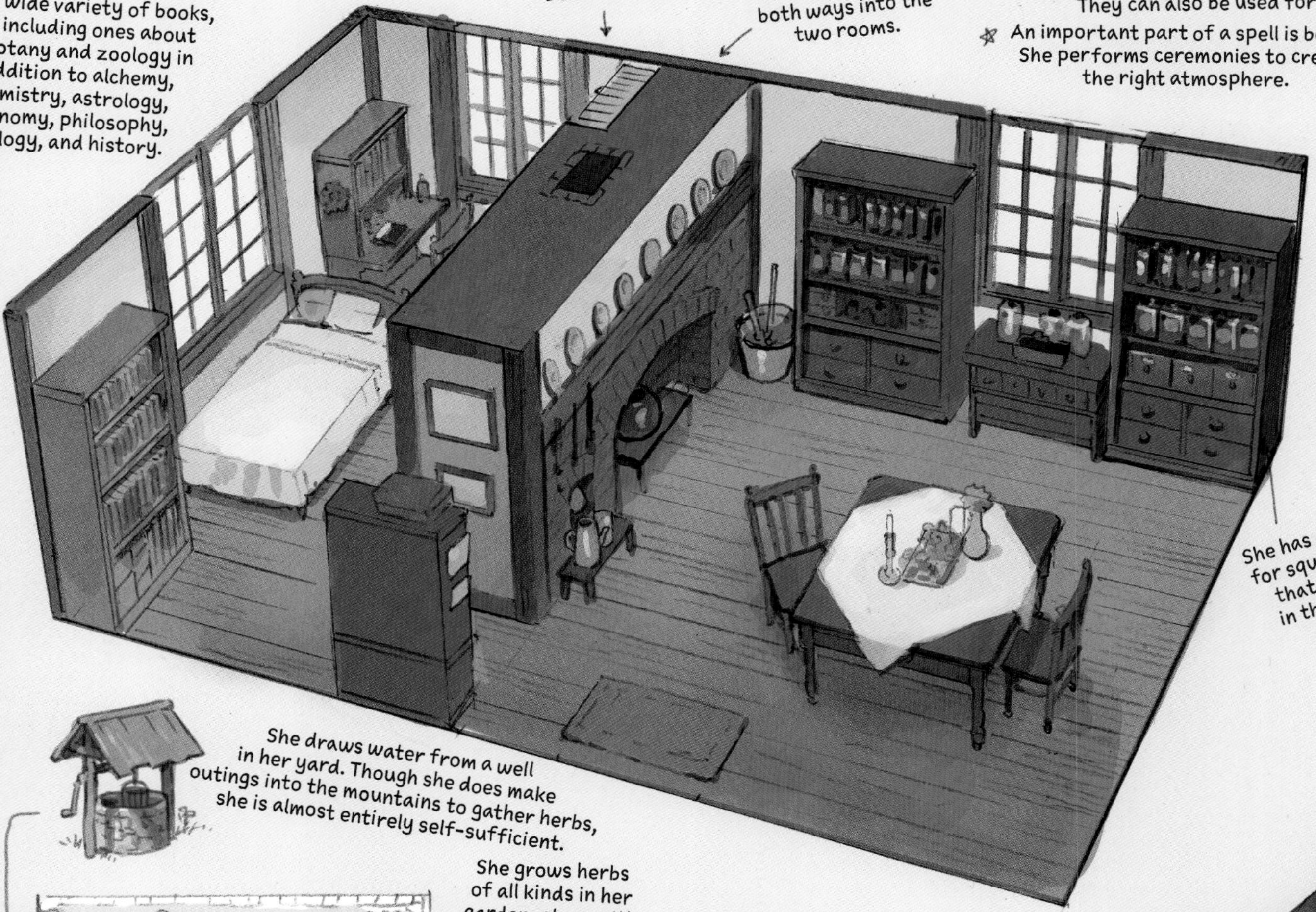
The witch has a wide variety of books, including ones about botany and zoology in addition to alchemy, chemistry, astrology, astronomy, philosophy, psychology, and history.
Bookshelves
The hearth opens both ways into the two rooms.
The witch's herbs are used medicinally for healing wounds, reducing fevers, deworming, and such. They can also be used for cooking.
An important part of a spell is belief. She performs ceremonies to create the right atmosphere.
She has a penchant for square bottles that fit snugly in the medicine cabinet.

She draws water from a well in her yard. Though she does make outings into the mountains to gather herbs, she is almost entirely self-sufficient.

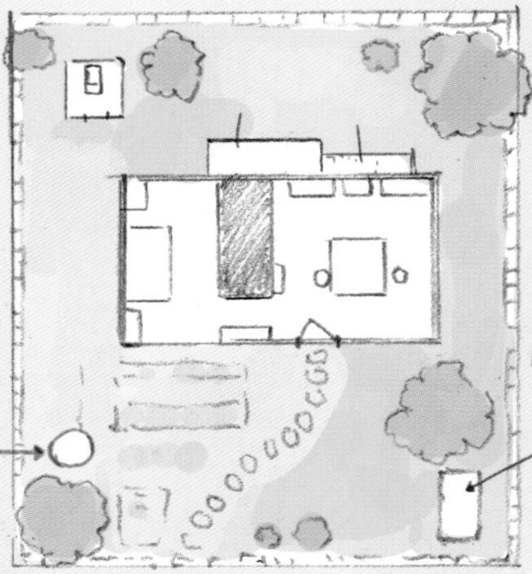
She grows herbs of all kinds in her garden, along with vegetables. She doesn't simply use her harvest in cooking but also dries the plants, stores them in oil, and uses all sorts of clever methods of her own devising to make them keep for long periods of time.
Henhouse: she uses chickens for eggs and meat, and they are indispensable for her ceremonies as well.

The mention of a witch might call up an image of a wild and flamboyantly dressed individual brewing a suspicious potion, but this young witch appears conservative and restrained. While at first conservatism and witchcraft seem quite at odds, being a witch was a useful discipline prior to the development of science, so perhaps this modern witch isn't such an odd concept.

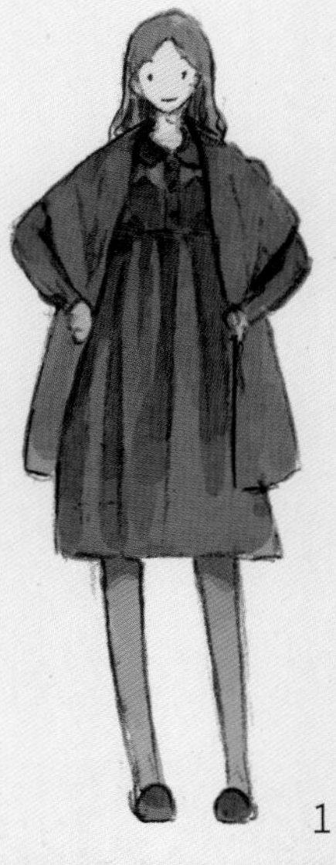

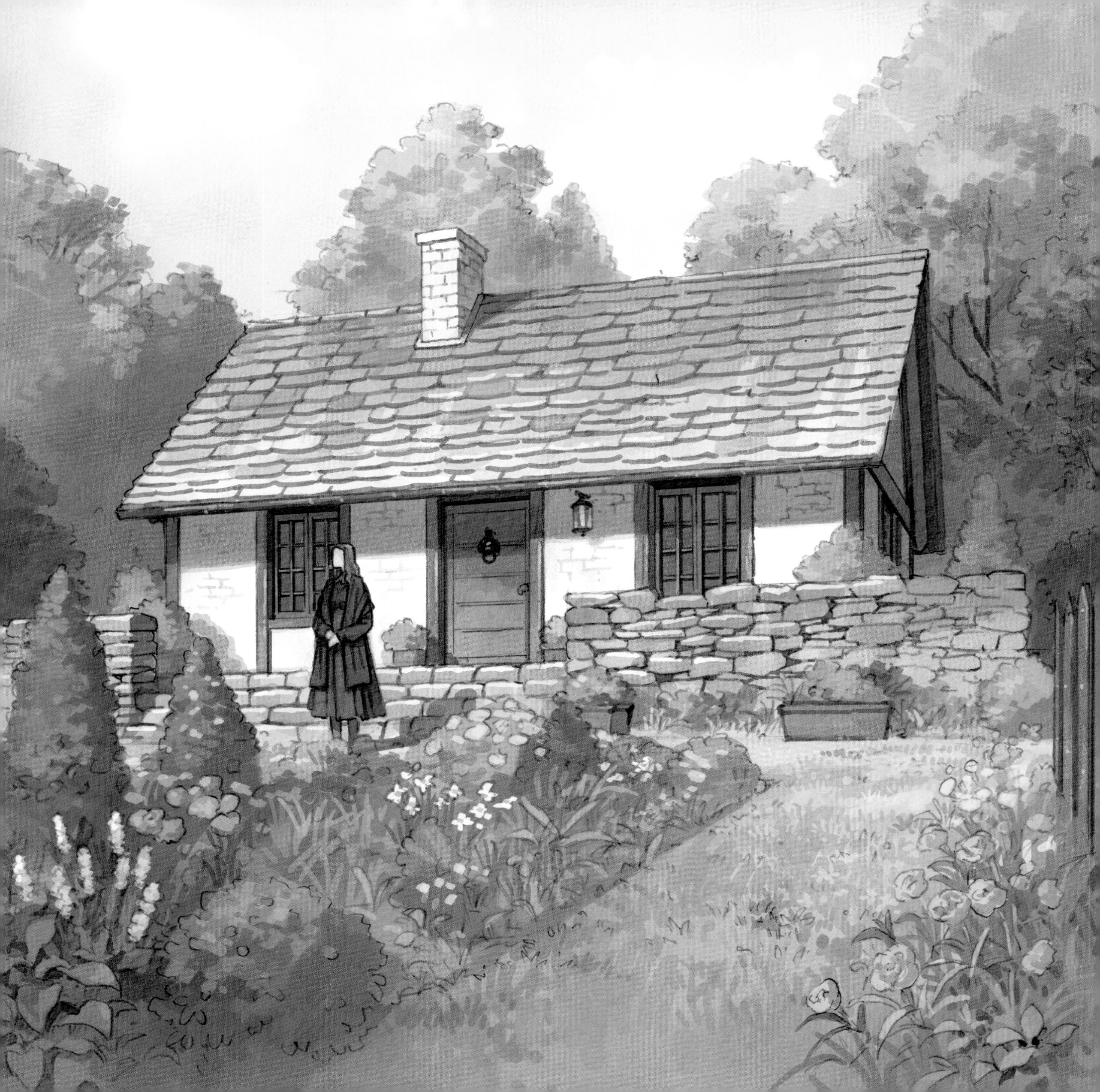

Methodical Witch's House

GARDEN

The witch's garden primarily features vegetables and herbs, but she grows all sorts of plants. Given the well, henhouse, and nature surrounding it, she appears to lead an idyllic life, but in actuality, her living space is quite typical for the time, and everything is set up for survival.

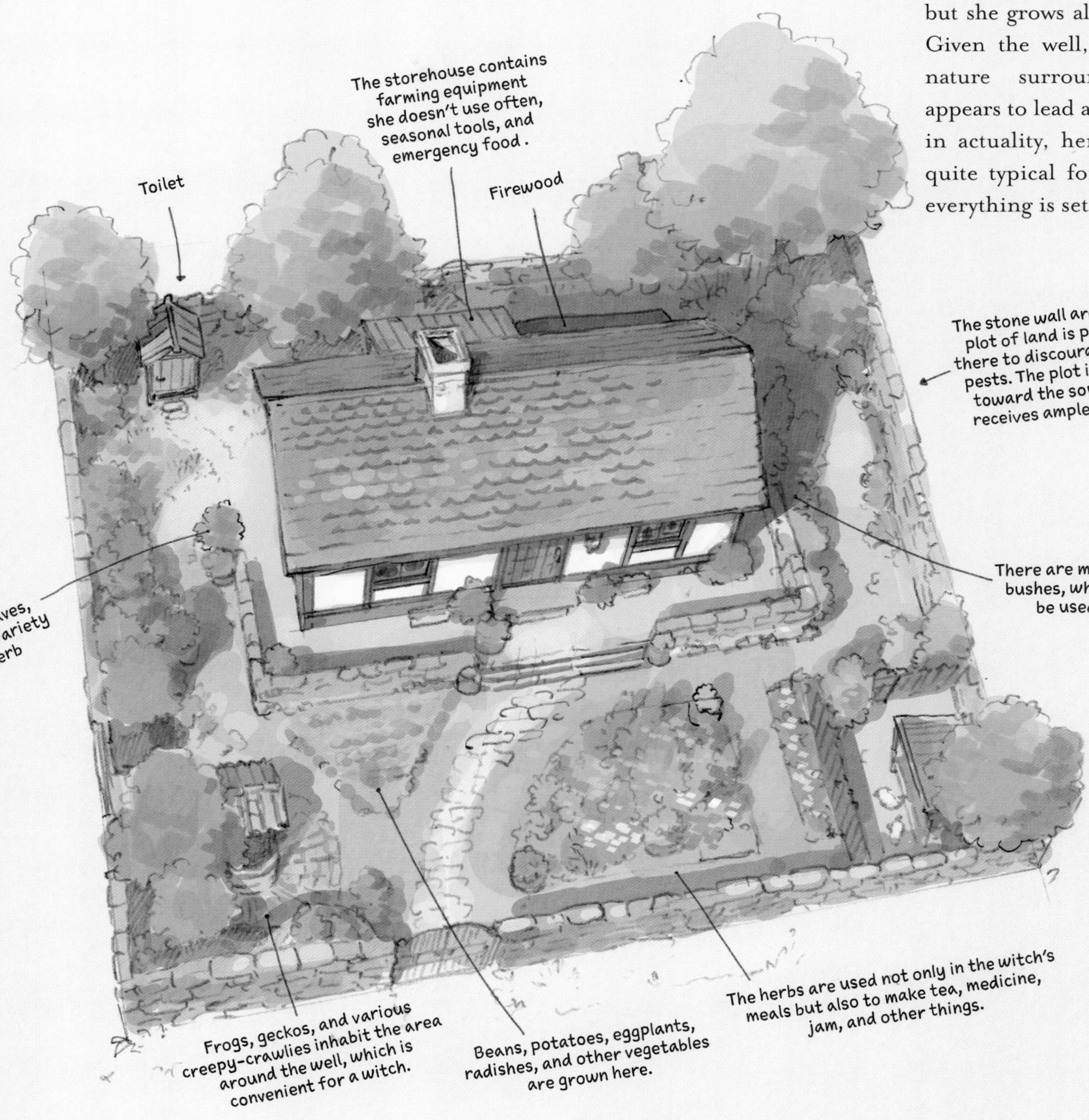

The storehouse contains farming equipment she doesn't use often, seasonal tools, and emergency food.
Toilet
Firewood
The stone wall around this plot of land is primarily there to discourage animal pests. The plot is inclined toward the south, so it receives ample sunlight.
There are many juneberry bushes, whose fruit can be used for jam.
Laurel leaves, a typical variety of herb
Frogs, geckos, and various creepy-crawlies inhabit the area around the well, which is convenient for a witch.
Beans, potatoes, eggplants, radishes, and other vegetables are grown here.
The herbs are used not only in the witch's meals but also to make tea, medicine, jam, and other things.

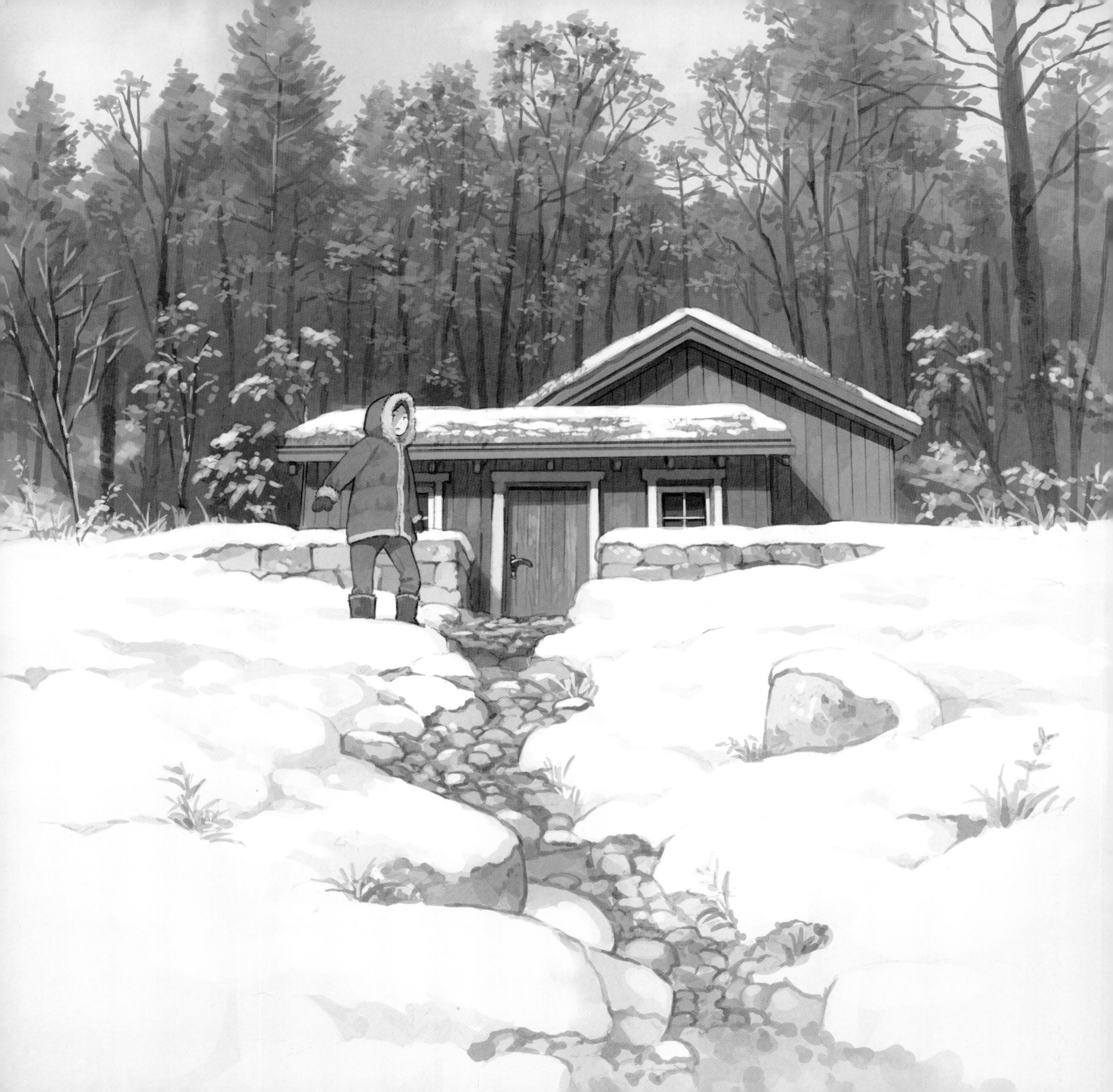

Grass-Roofed House in the Snowy Country

This home provides various methods of dealing with the harsh winter cold. The house is small in order to withstand the snow but is equipped with storage areas to compensate for its size. Grass has been planted on the roof to increase insulation. The house is filled with all sorts of clever tricks to make it possible to live alongside nature.

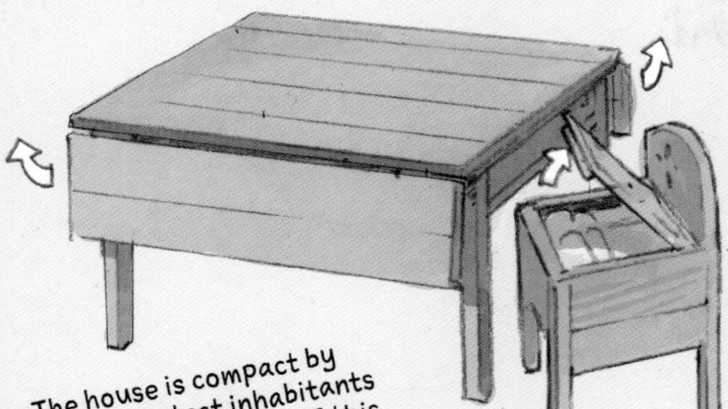
The house is compact by design to protect inhabitants from the cold. Because of this, the furniture often serves more than one function. The table can change size depending on the number of people using it, and the chairs also provide additional storage.

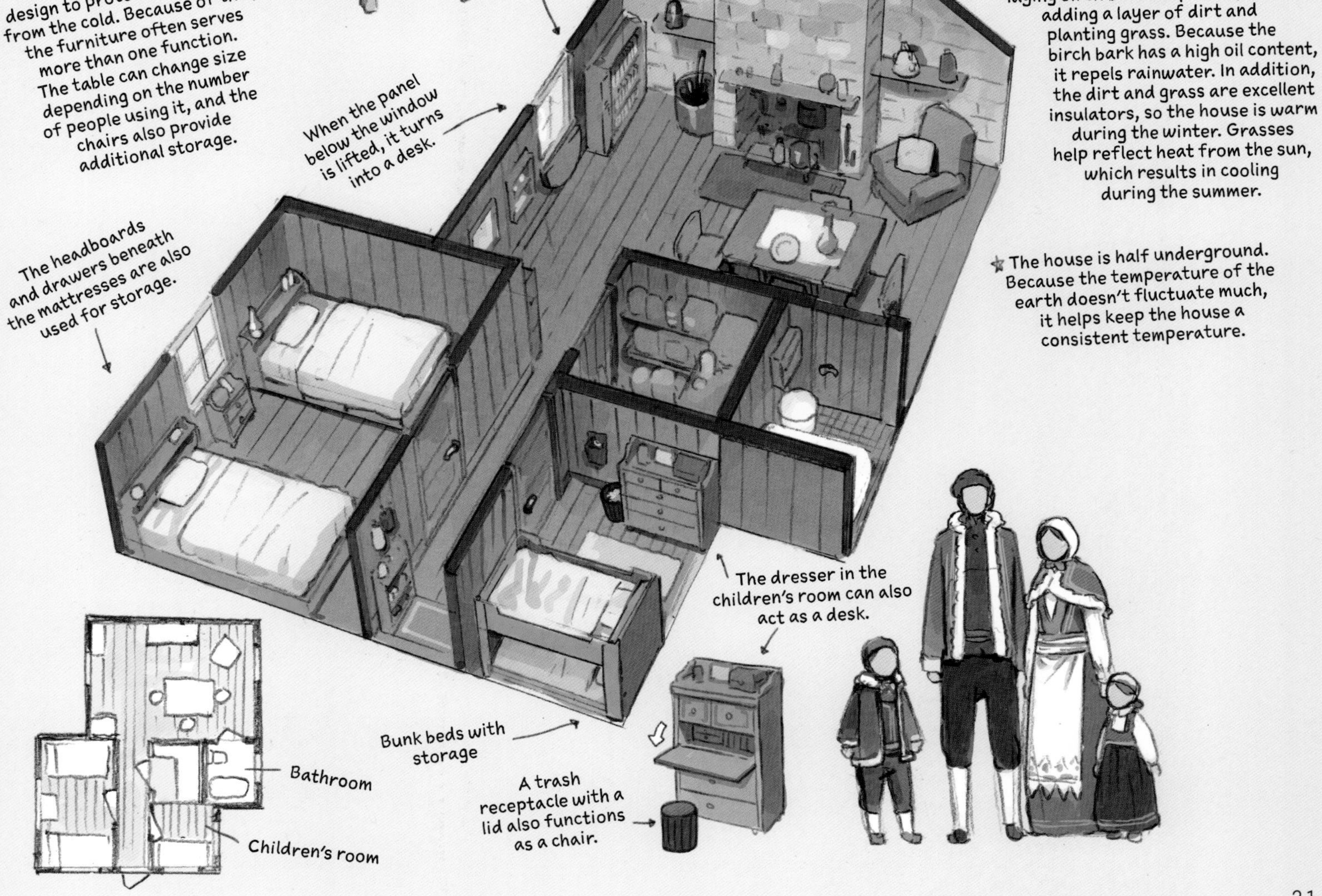
There is storage space behind the bookshelf too.
When the panel below the window is lifted, it turns into a desk.
★The grass roof was made by arranging white birch branches in rows and laying birch bark atop them, then adding a layer of dirt and planting grass. Because the birch bark has a high oil content, it repels rainwater. In addition, the dirt and grass are excellent insulators, so the house is warm during the winter. Grasses help reflect heat from the sun, which results in cooling during the summer.
★The house is half underground. Because the temperature of the earth doesn't fluctuate much, it helps keep the house a consistent temperature.
The headboards and drawers beneath the mattresses are also used for storage.
The dresser in the children's room can also act as a desk.
Bunk beds with storage
A trash receptacle with a lid also functions as a chair.
Bathroom
Children's room

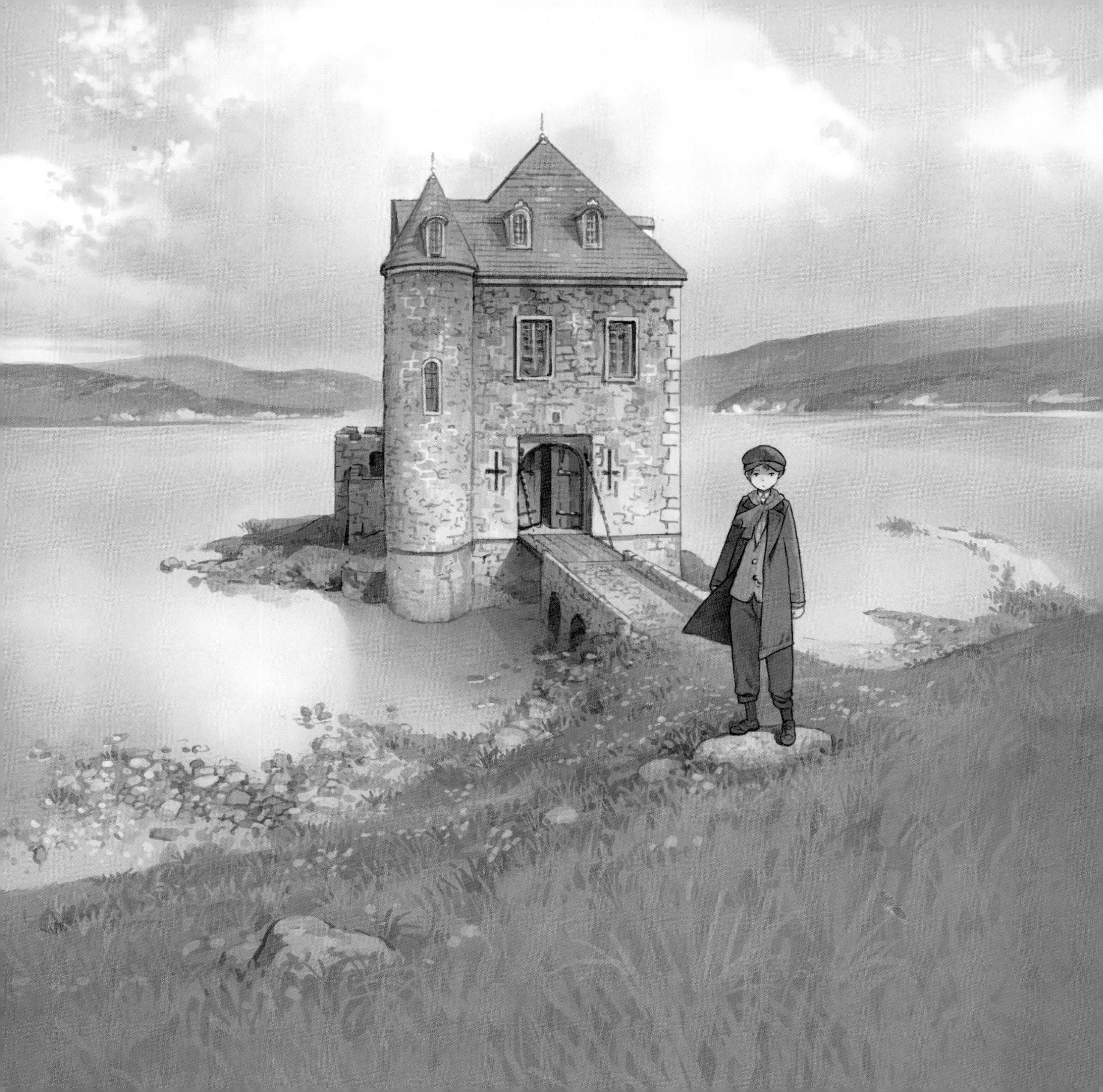

Forgotten Orphan's Castle

This old castle has watched over the land through several centuries. Following the loss of its original inhabitants, a lord and lady, the castle was left abandoned and became the target of robbers. Rumor has it an orphan has recently taken up residence there. The lord and lady of the castle had a young child who died, so it is also said that the orphan is actually a ghost.

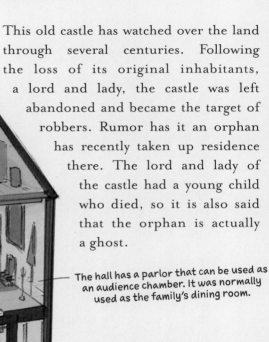

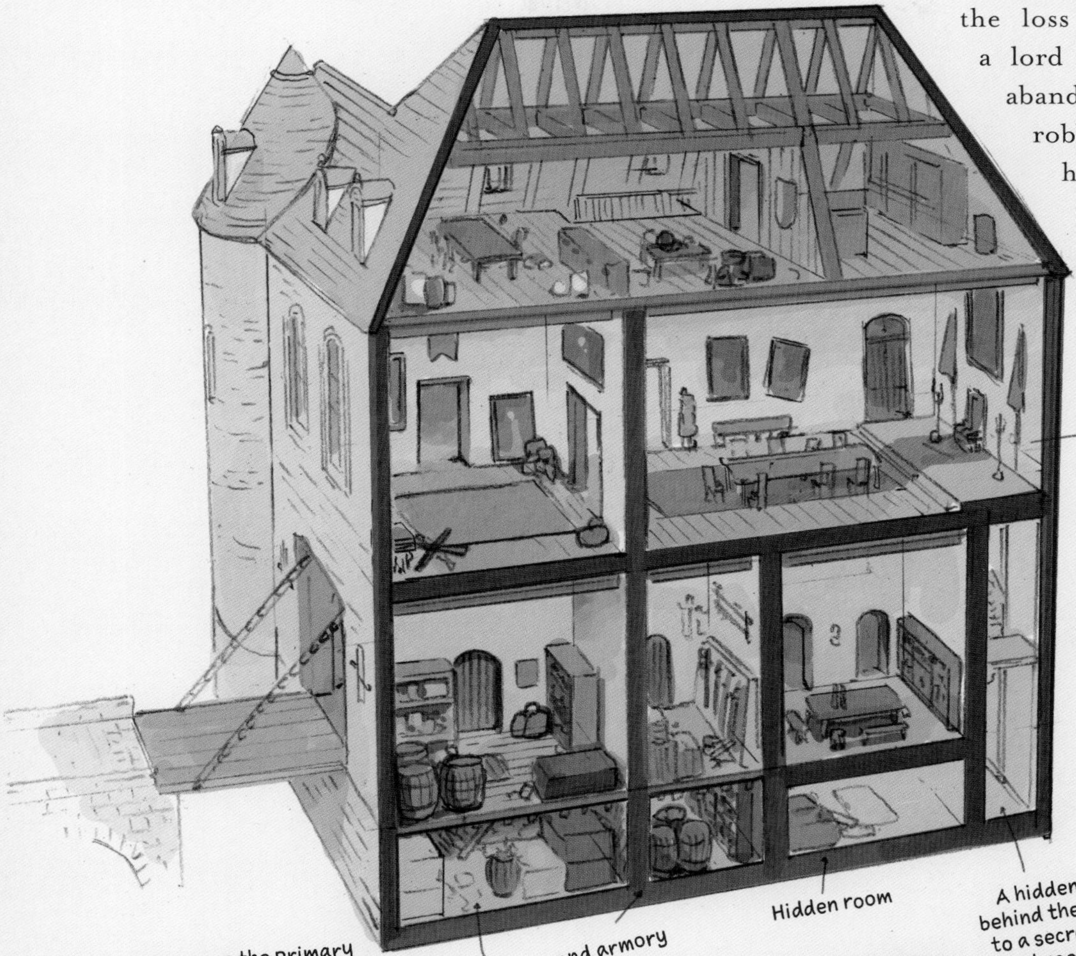
The hall has a parlor that can be used as an audience chamber. It was normally used as the family's dining room.
For a castle, it's very small, so only a few servants stayed overnight with the family. Its role was more that of a watchtower than a fortress.
Hidden room
Pantry and armory
A hidden passage behind the wall leads to a secret under-ground room. The room is furnished with food and blankets that would allow someone to live there for some time. It seems that not even the robbers have been able to find this room.
The attic was the primary living space used by the castle's family.

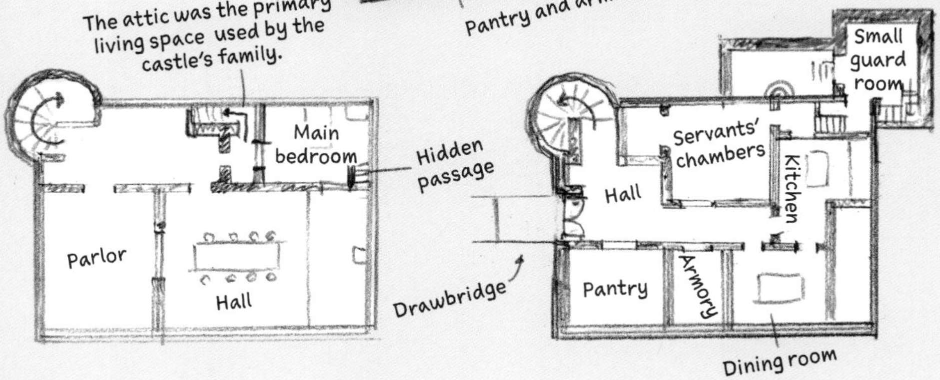
Main bedroom
Hidden passage
Parlor
Hall
Drawbridge
Small guard room
Servants' chambers
Kitchen
Hall
Pantry
Armory
Dining room

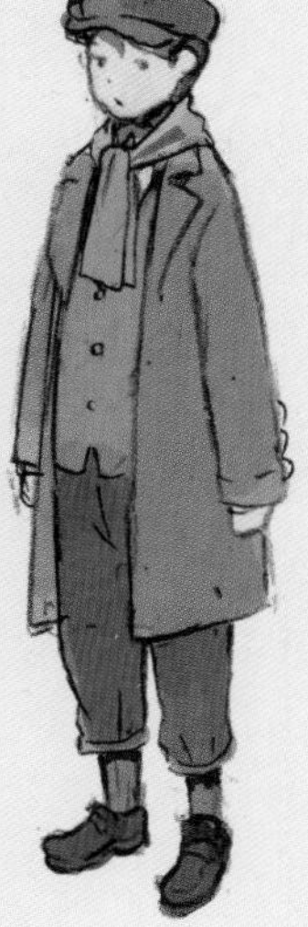

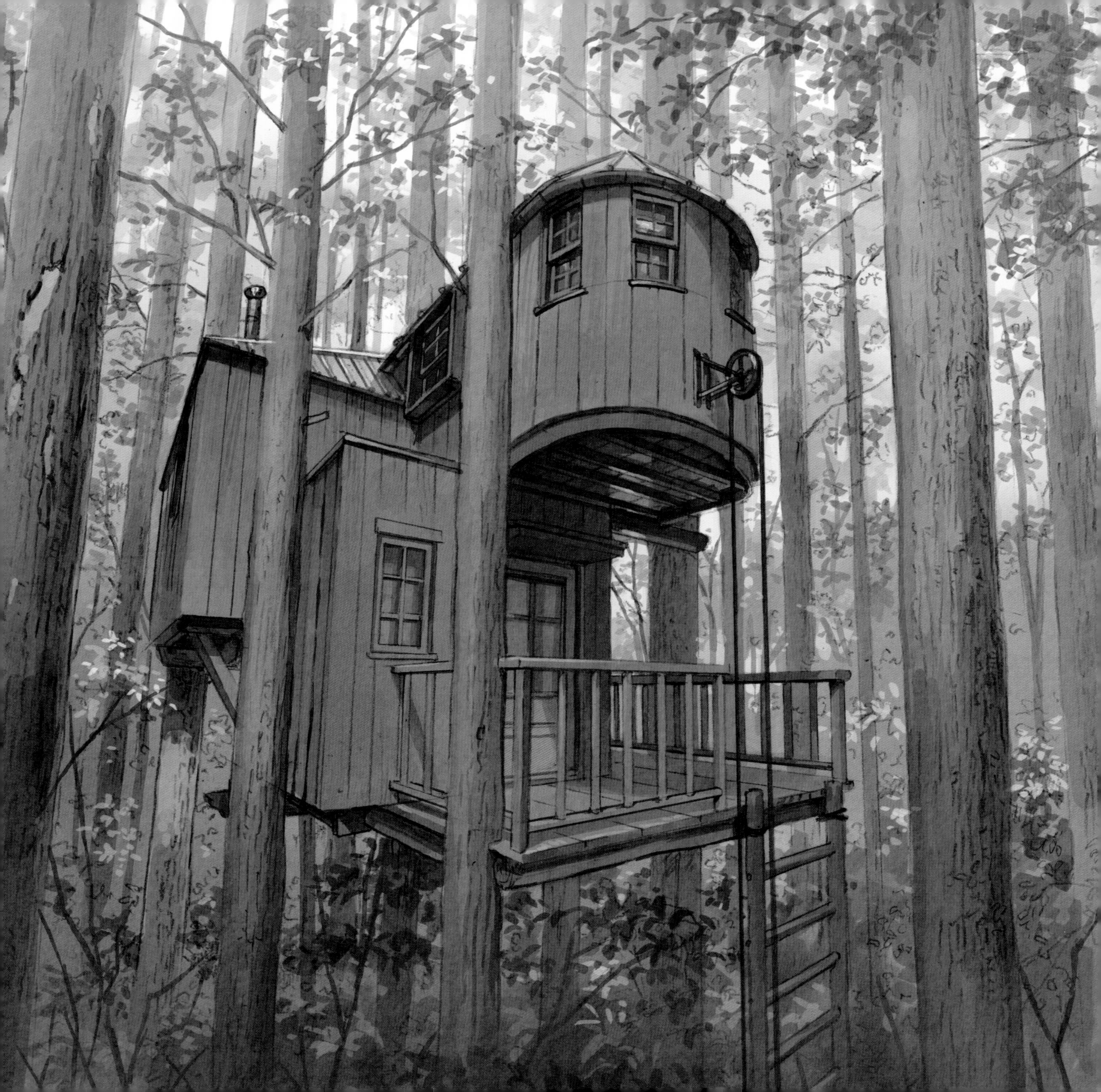

Dreamer's Tree House

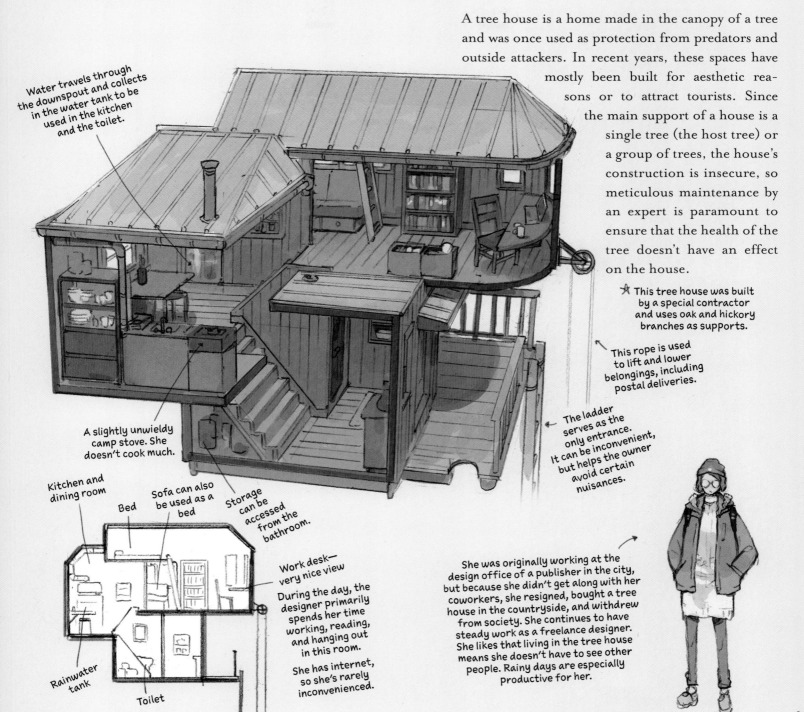

A tree house is a home made in the canopy of a tree and was once used as protection from predators and outside attackers. In recent years, these spaces have mostly been built for aesthetic reasons or to attract tourists. Since the main support of a house is a single tree (the host tree) or a group of trees, the house's construction is insecure, so meticulous maintenance by an expert is paramount to ensure that the health of the tree doesn't have an effect on the house.

Water travels through the downspout and collects in the water tank to be used in the kitchen and the toilet.
✭ This tree house was built by a special contractor and uses oak and hickory branches as supports.
This rope is used to lift and lower belongings, including postal deliveries.
The ladder serves as the only entrance. It can be inconvenient, but helps the owner avoid certain nuisances.
A slightly unwieldy camp stove. She doesn't cook much.
Storage can be accessed from the bathroom.

Kitchen and dining room
Bed
Sofa can also be used as a bed
Work desk—very nice view
During the day, the designer primarily spends her time working, reading, and hanging out in this room.
She has internet, so she's rarely inconvenienced.
Rainwater tank
Toilet

She was originally working at the design office of a publisher in the city, but because she didn't get along with her coworkers, she resigned, bought a tree house in the countryside, and withdrew from society. She continues to have steady work as a freelance designer. She likes that living in the tree house means she doesn't have to see other people. Rainy days are especially productive for her.

SIDEBAR Examples of Roofs

Roofs have an extensive range of styles. The many types of roofs all have different functions, but most importantly, they greatly influence the look of a building. Here are some types of roofs with particular focus on their shapes and materials.

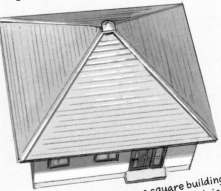

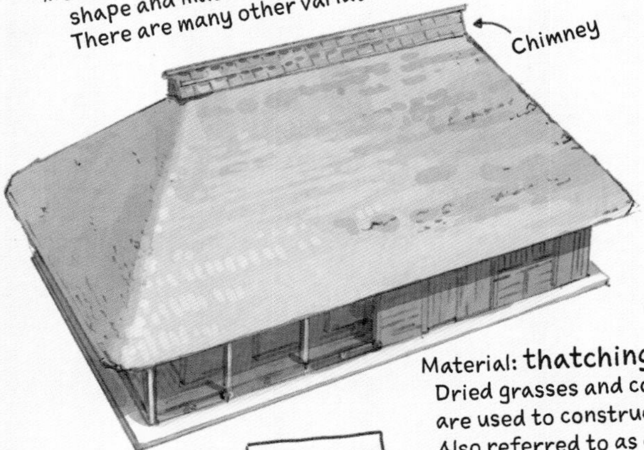

※Just one example of a possible roof shape and material combination. There are many other variations.
Chimney
Material: thatching
Dried grasses and common reeds are used to construct the roof. Also referred to as a thatched roof.
Hip roof
A simple shape common throughout the world—all sides slope downward to the walls. Bad for ventilation but great for warding off rain.

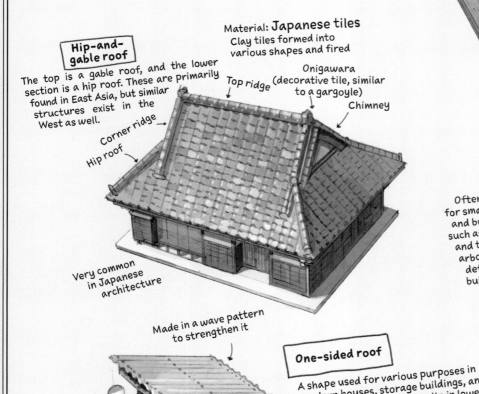

Hip-and-gable roof
The top is a gable roof, and the lower section is a hip roof. These are primarily found in East Asia, but similar structures exist in the West as well.
Material: Japanese tiles
Clay tiles formed into various shapes and fired
Top ridge
Onigawara (decorative tile, similar to a gargoyle)
Chimney
Corner ridge
Hip roof
Very common in Japanese architecture

Often used for small homes and buildings such as shrines and temples, arbors, and detached buildings.
Polygonal roof
A hip roof on a square building. Each side of the roof is a triangle. Can also be used on buildings that have six corners or eight corners. Sometimes called a pyramidal roof.
Material: Galvalume steel plates
Steel sheets that are coated with aluminum or zinc alloy. Because these materials are lightweight but still sturdy and cheap, recently constructed residences often use them.

Made in a wave pattern to strengthen it
One-sided roof
A shape used for various purposes in modern houses, storage buildings, and more. Its simplicity results in lower costs, but these roofs lack resistance to rain and other elements.
Material: galvanized sheet iron
Zinc-plated steel sheets. Easy to manufacture and resistant to corrosion.

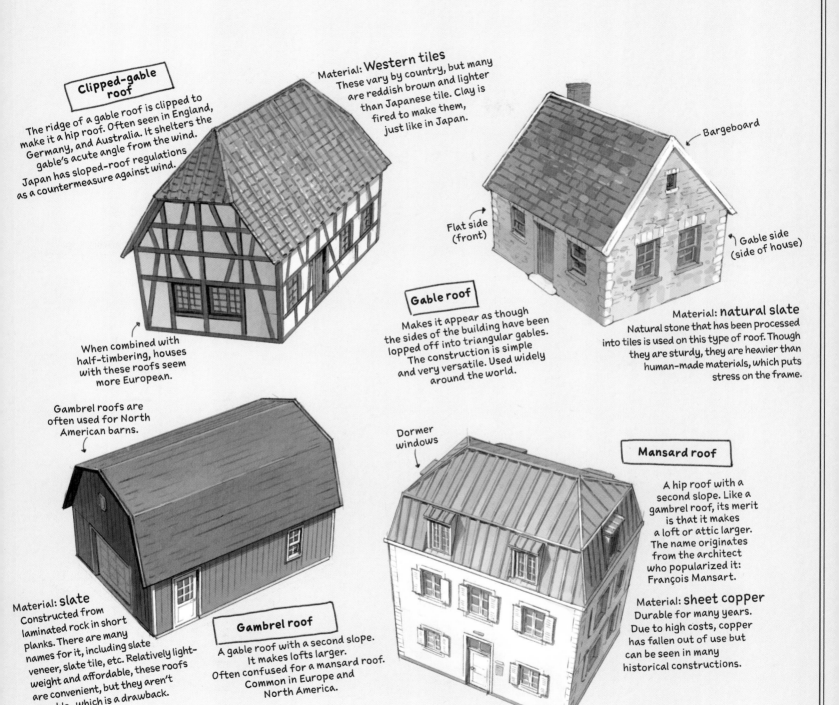

Clipped-gable roof

The ridge of a gable roof is clipped to make it a hip roof. Often seen in England, Germany, and Australia. It shelters the gable's acute angle from the wind. Japan has sloped-roof regulations as a countermeasure against wind.

Material: **Western tiles**
These vary by country, but many are reddish brown and lighter than Japanese tile. Clay is fired to make them, just like in Japan.

When combined with half-timbering, houses with these roofs seem more European.

Bargeboard
Flat side (front)
Gable side (side of house)

Gable roof

Makes it appear as though the sides of the building have been lopped off into triangular gables. The construction is simple and very versatile. Used widely around the world.

Material: **natural slate**
Natural stone that has been processed into tiles is used on this type of roof. Though they are sturdy, they are heavier than human-made materials, which puts stress on the frame.

Gambrel roofs are often used for North American barns.

Material: **slate**
Constructed from laminated rock in short planks. There are many names for it, including slate veneer, slate tile, etc. Relatively light-weight and affordable, these roofs are convenient, but they aren't durable, which is a drawback.

Gambrel roof

A gable roof with a second slope. It makes lofts larger. Often confused for a mansard roof. Common in Europe and North America.

Dormer windows

Mansard roof

A hip roof with a second slope. Like a gambrel roof, its merit is that it makes a loft or attic larger. The name originates from the architect who popularized it: François Mansart.

Material: **sheet copper**
Durable for many years. Due to high costs, copper has fallen out of use but can be seen in many historical constructions.

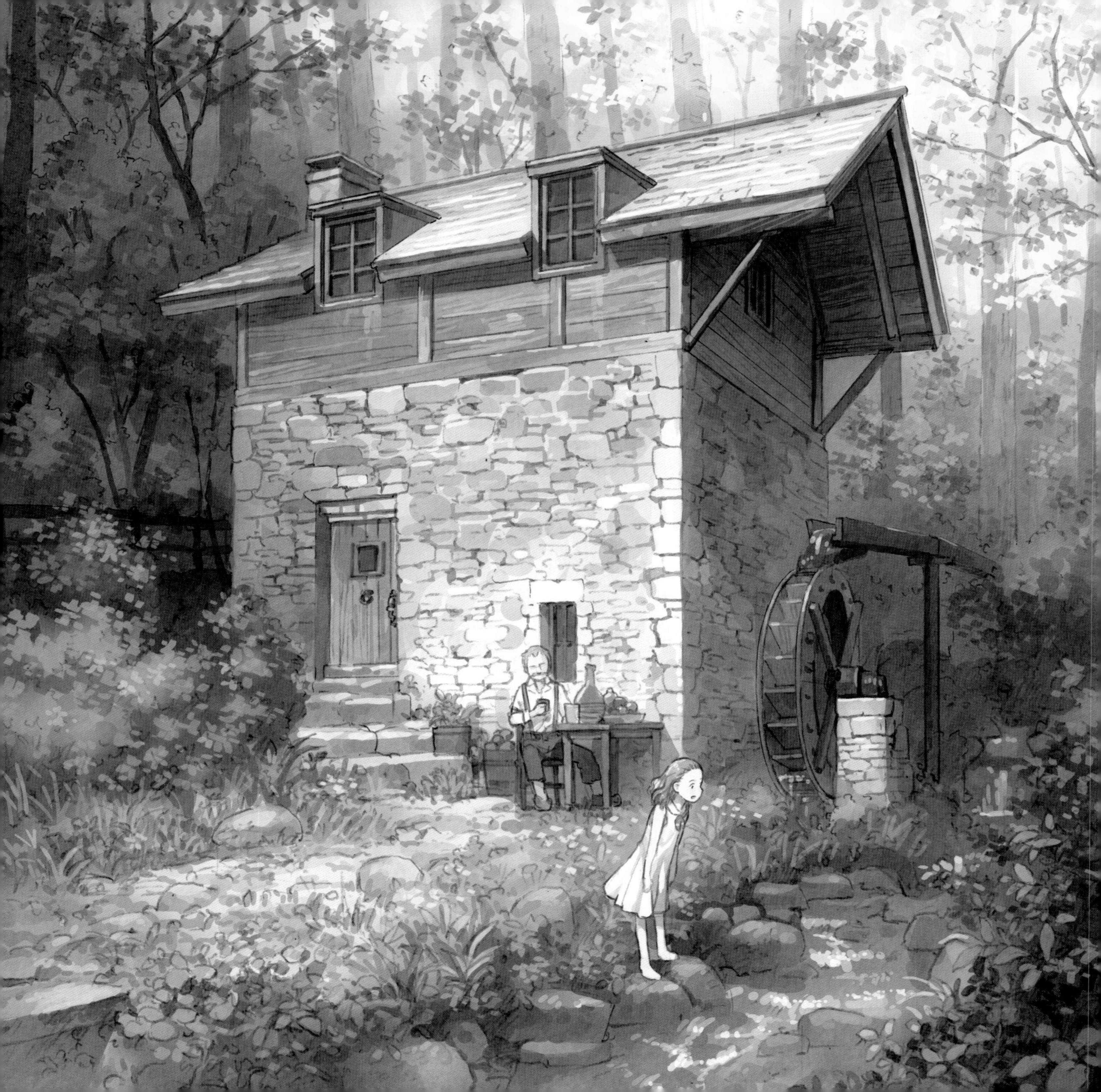

Apple Cider Water Mill

Apple cider is made by pressing ripe apples in a compressor to make juice, which is then collected in a tank. A water mill is used to run the compressor. This water mill in the middle of the woods is home to an elderly man who lives alone; however, his granddaughter often brings gifts from his daughter and her husband, which is one of the joys in his life.

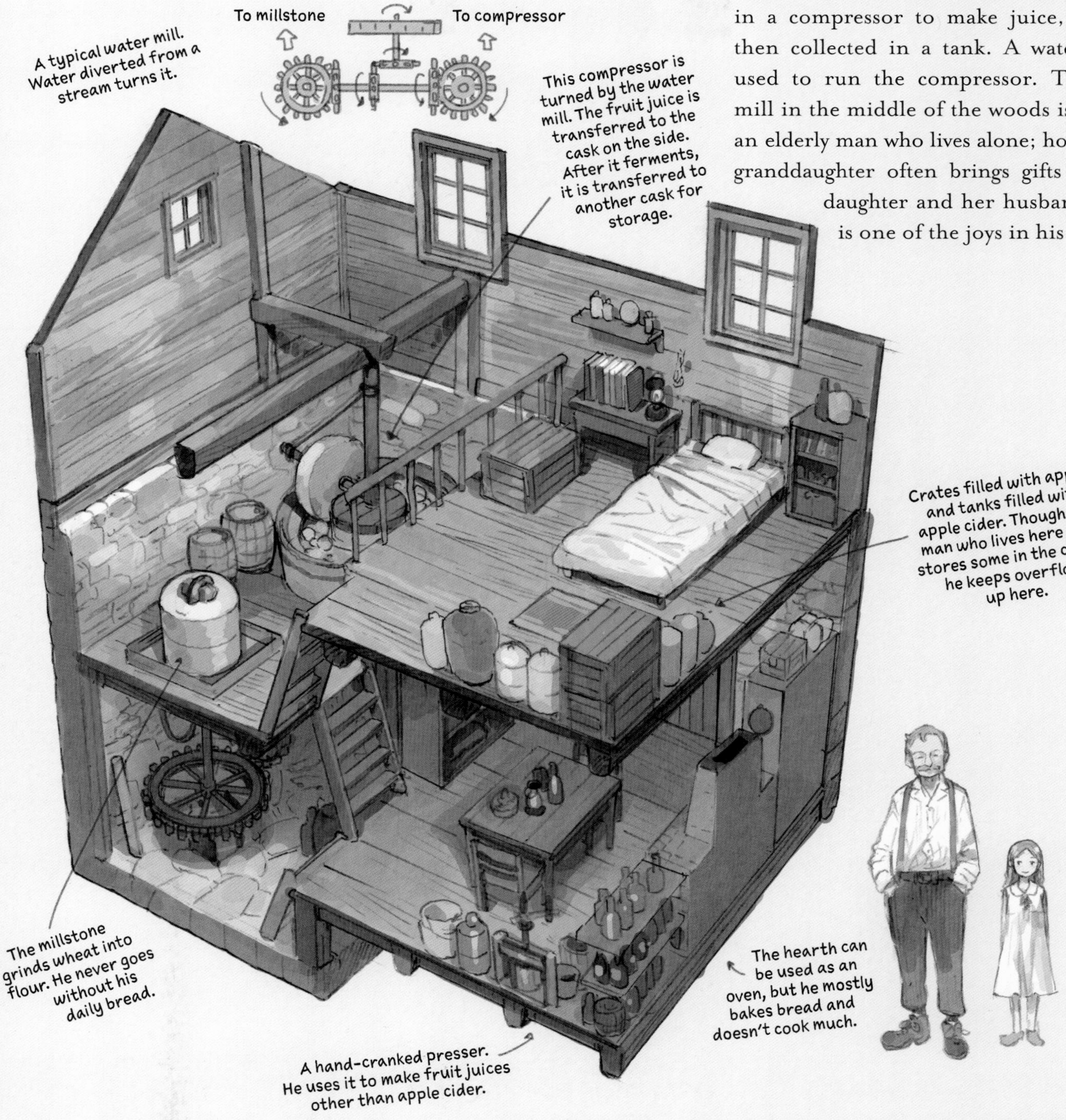

To millstone
To compressor
A typical water mill. Water diverted from a stream turns it.
This compressor is turned by the water mill. The fruit juice is transferred to the cask on the side. After it ferments, it is transferred to another cask for storage.
Crates filled with apples and tanks filled with apple cider. Though the man who lives here also stores some in the cellar, he keeps overflow up here.
The millstone grinds wheat into flour. He never goes without his daily bread.
The hearth can be used as an oven, but he mostly bakes bread and doesn't cook much.
A hand-cranked presser. He uses it to make fruit juices other than apple cider.

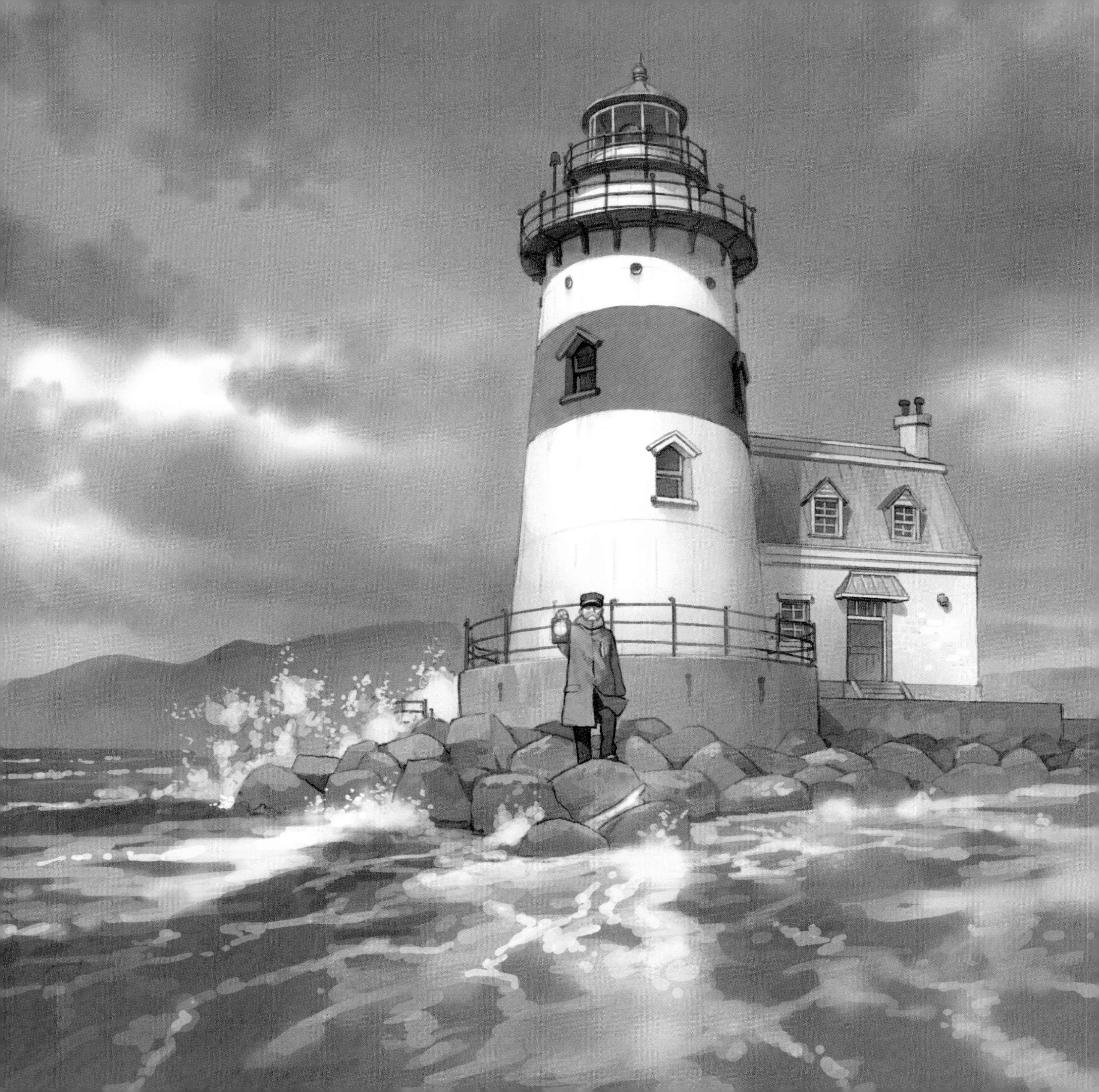

Melancholy Lighthouse Keeper

One day after a storm, the lighthouse keeper picks up a stick of driftwood. The flotsam is about as large as a human femur and glows with a pale light when a storm is approaching. The lighthouse keeper, drawn by curiosity, observes the branch during a storm. As though in response to the branch, a faint voice from the lighthouse's cellar stirs memories from two decades ago that the keeper had forgotten . . .

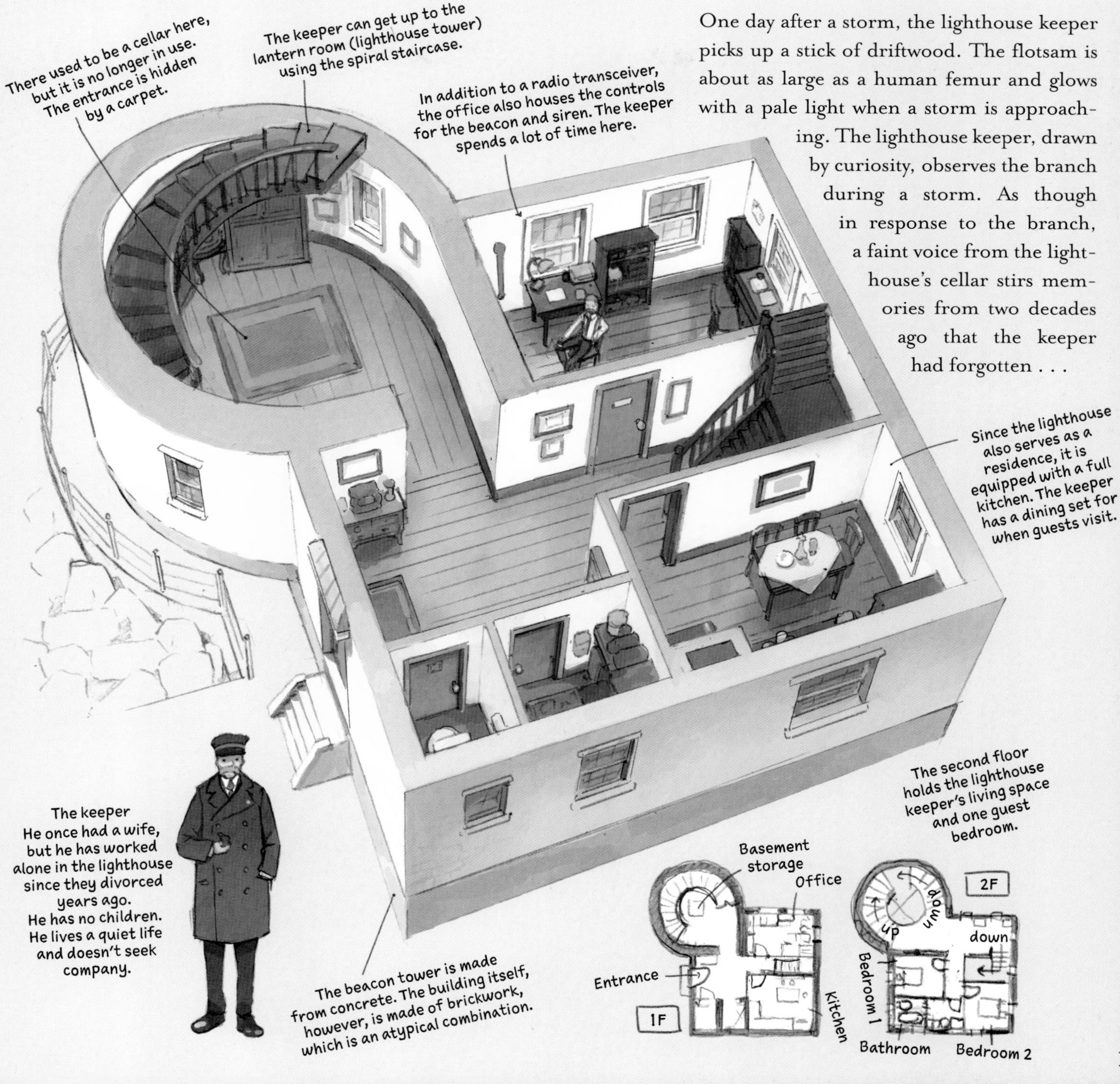

There used to be a cellar here, but it is no longer in use. The entrance is hidden by a carpet.
The keeper can get up to the lantern room (lighthouse tower) using the spiral staircase.
In addition to a radio transceiver, the office also houses the controls for the beacon and siren. The keeper spends a lot of time here.
Since the lighthouse also serves as a residence, it is equipped with a full kitchen. The keeper has a dining set for when guests visit.
The keeper
He once had a wife, but he has worked alone in the lighthouse since they divorced years ago.
He has no children.
He lives a quiet life and doesn't seek company.
The beacon tower is made from concrete. The building itself, however, is made of brickwork, which is an atypical combination.
The second floor holds the lighthouse keeper's living space and one guest bedroom.
Basement storage
Office
Entrance
Kitchen
1F
2F
up
down
down
Bedroom 1
Bathroom
Bedroom 2

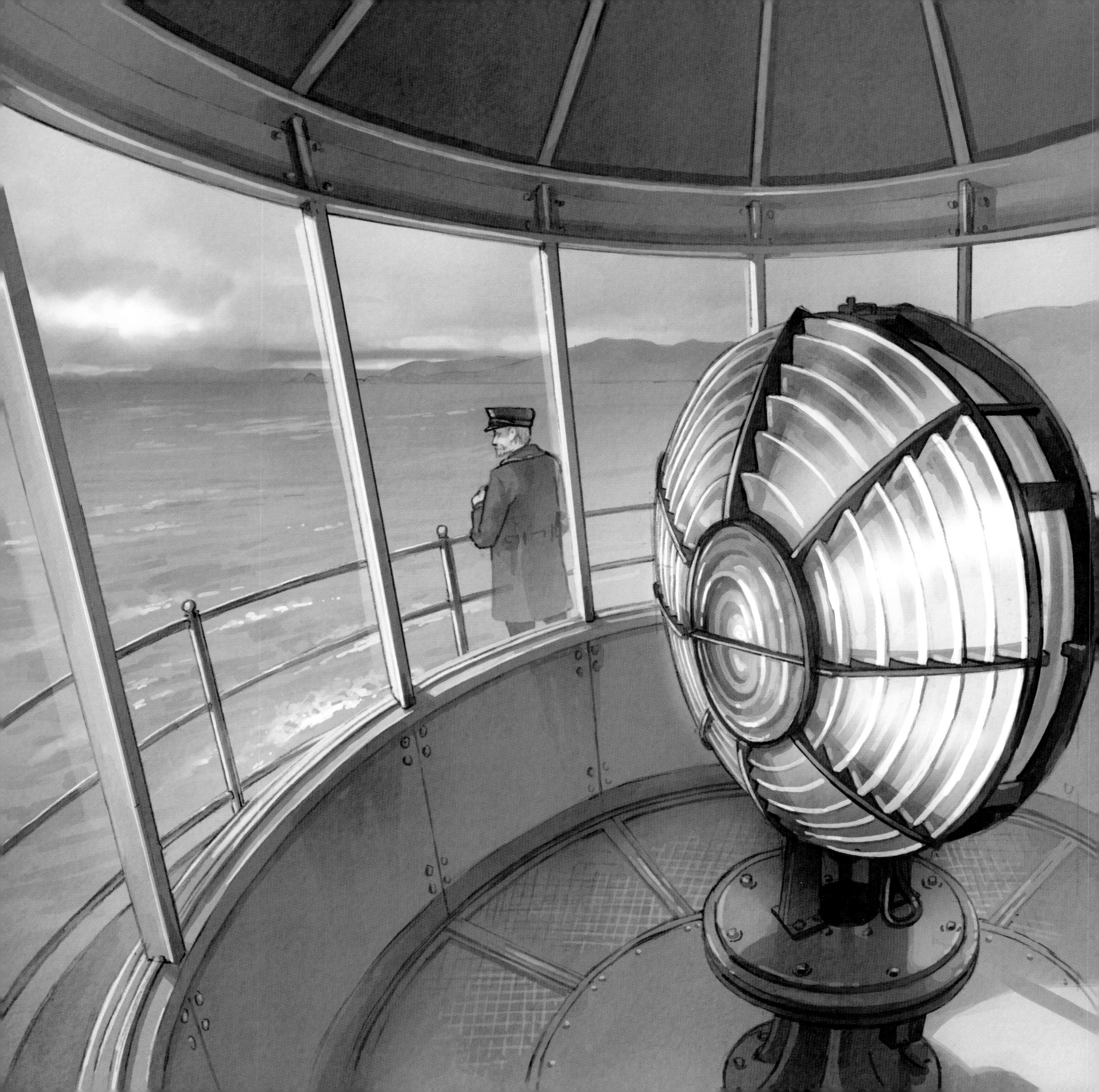

SIDE VIEW

A lighthouse acts as a landmark for vessels and aids navigation on water, especially at night and during storms, by shining a strong light that can be seen from far away. Some are placed at the ends of capes while others serve various roles, such as marking the entrance of a complicated harbor for approaching ships. Many large lighthouses make use of Fresnel lenses, which are comparatively lightweight.

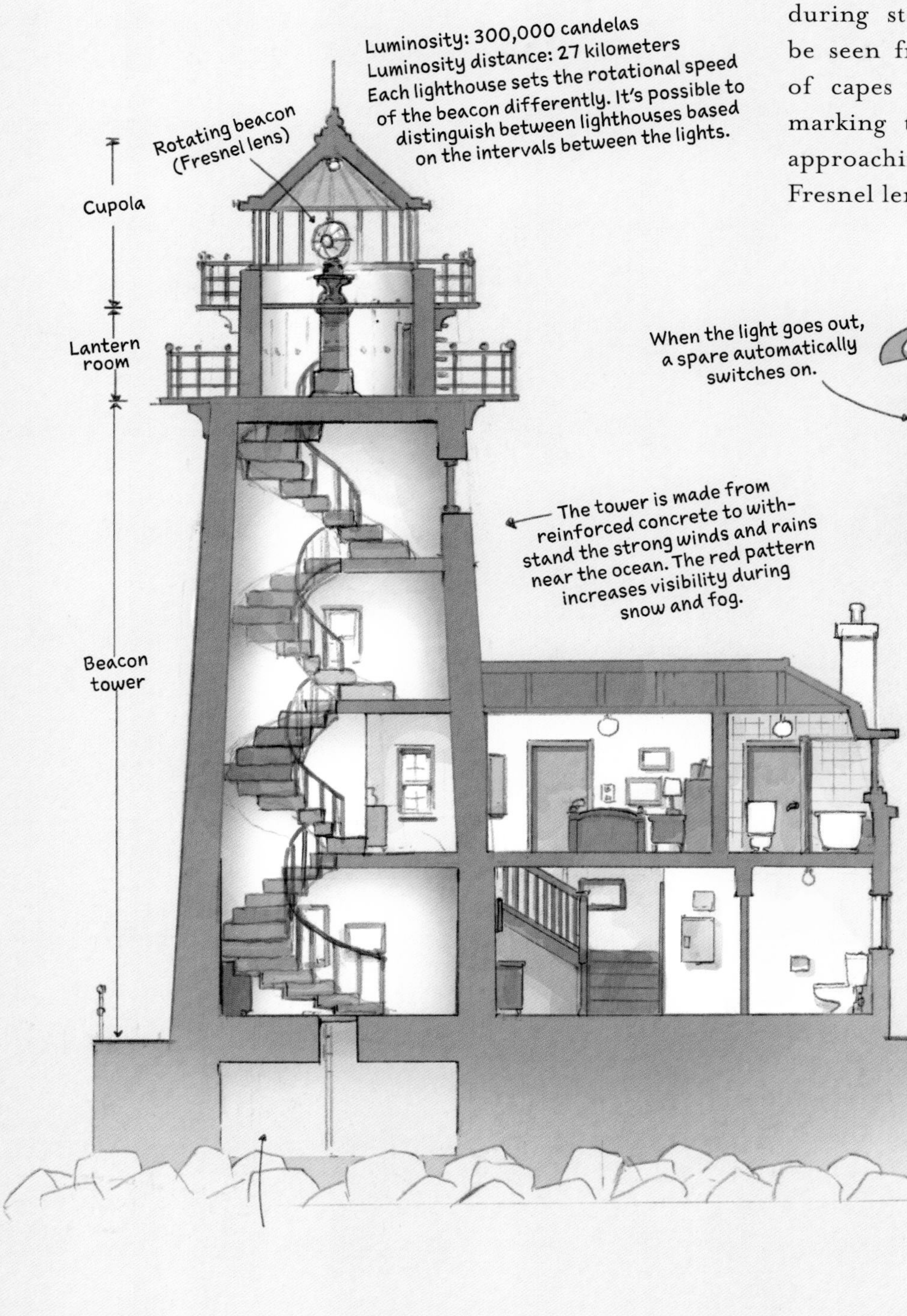
Luminosity: 300,000 candelas
Luminosity distance: 27 kilometers
Each lighthouse sets the rotational speed of the beacon differently. It's possible to distinguish between lighthouses based on the intervals between the lights.
Rotating beacon (Fresnel lens)
Cupola
Lantern room
Beacon tower
The tower is made from reinforced concrete to withstand the strong winds and rains near the ocean. The red pattern increases visibility during snow and fog.

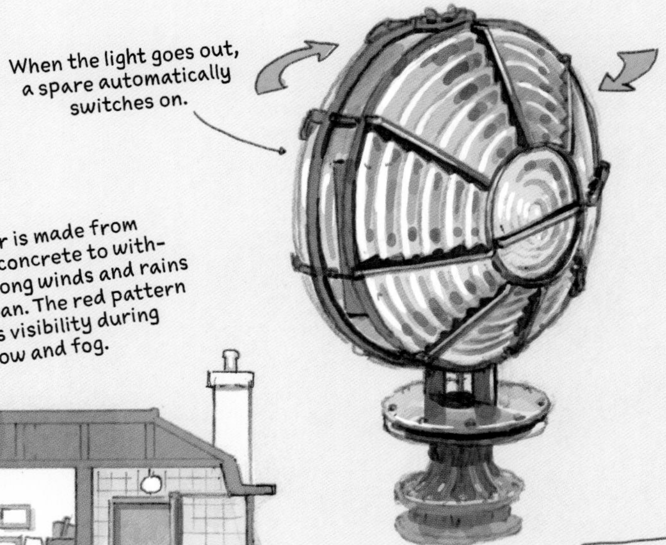
When the light goes out, a spare automatically switches on.

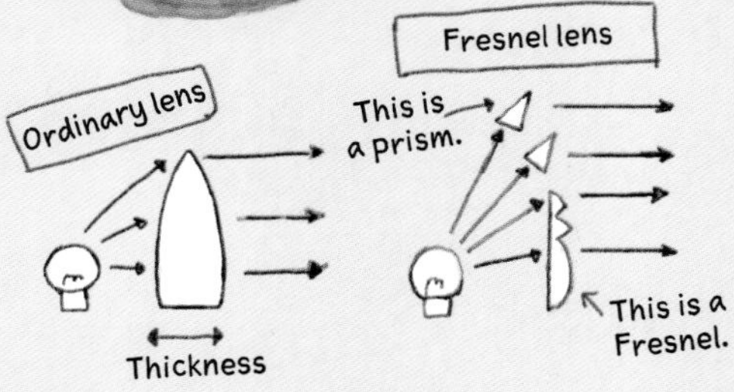
Ordinary lens
Thickness
Fresnel lens
This is a prism.
This is a Fresnel.

Though a large beacon requires a thick lens, when divided as in the diagram above, the lens becomes lighter and the manufacturing becomes easier. Many beacons make use of Fresnel lenses.

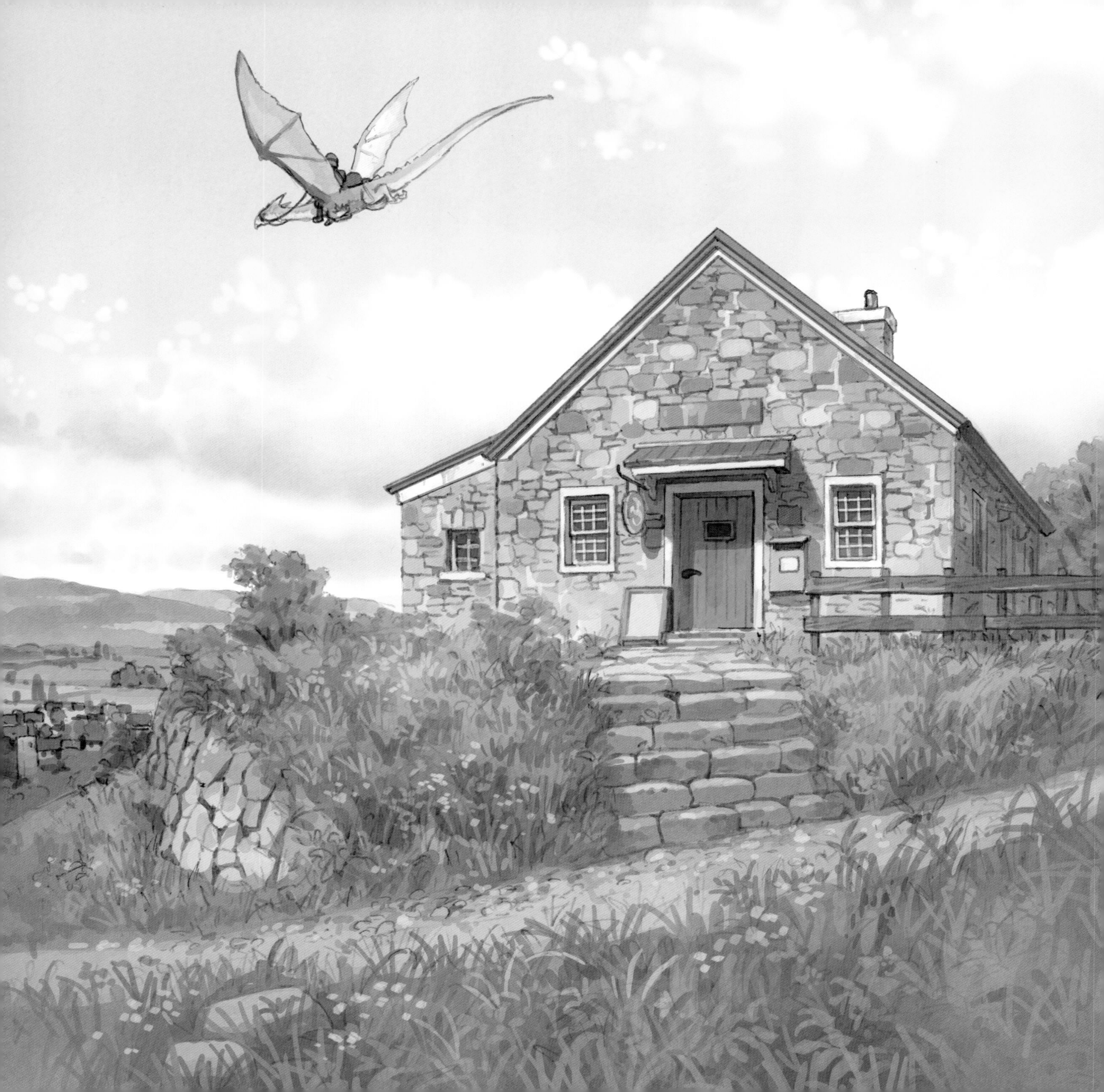

The Post Office of the Dragon Tamer

This dragon tamer primarily serves the highland region's postal service, which is normal for a dragon tamer in this world. Like a horse-drawn wagon, there is a limit on the size and weight of what can be delivered in one trip, but because of the quick delivery time, dragon posts are valued for urgent correspondence. Despite the great amount of practice it takes to tame a fickle dragon, mail carrier via dragon is a very popular occupation.

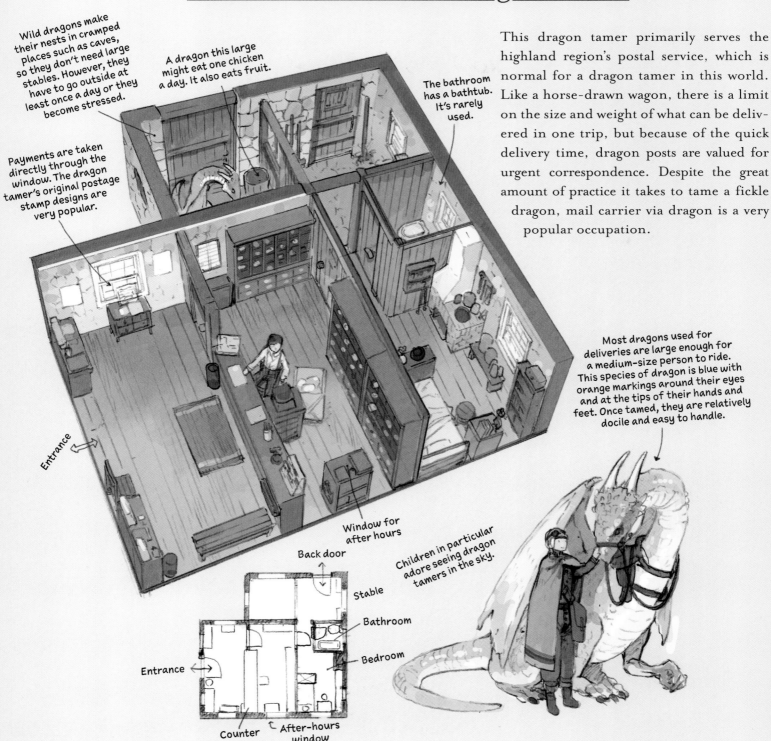

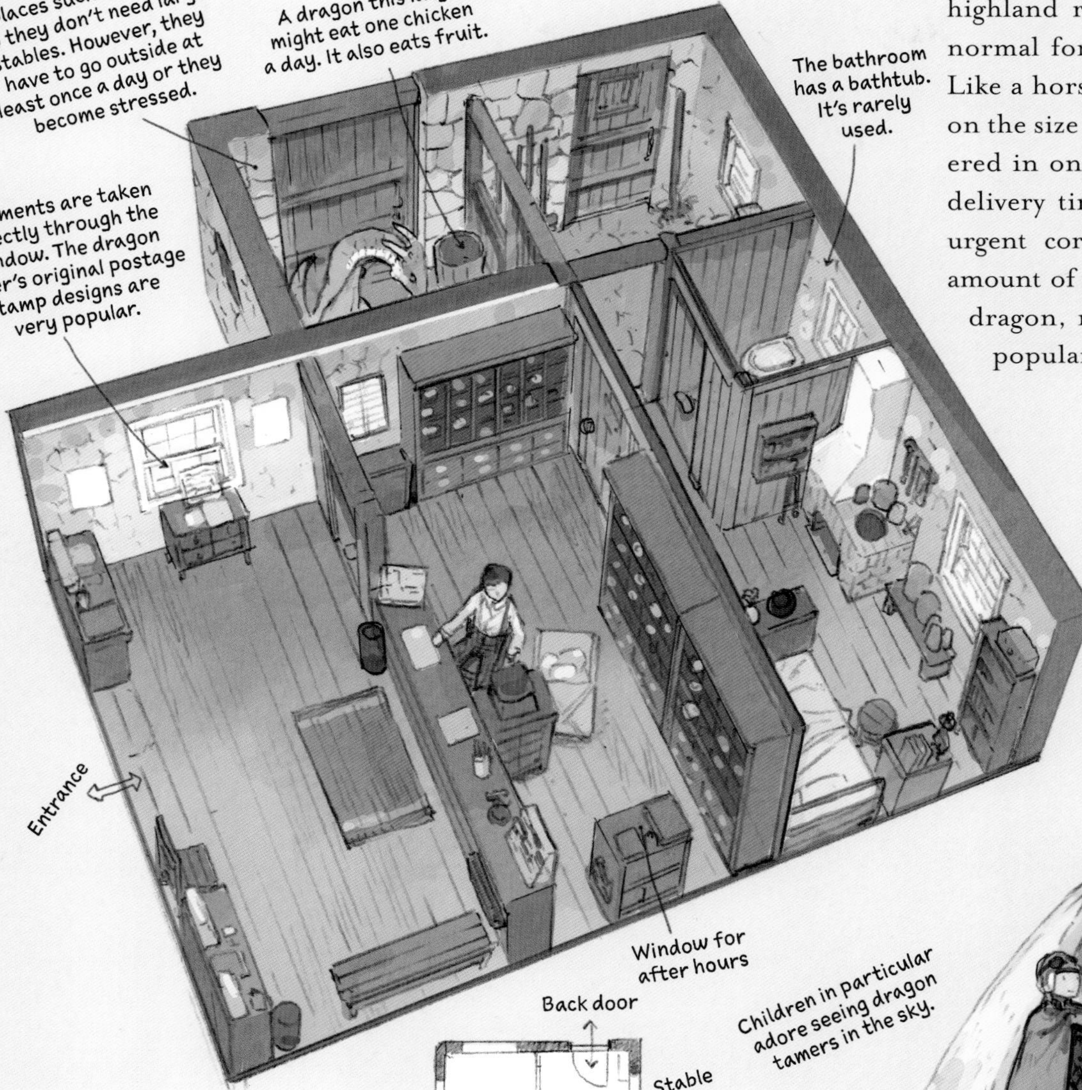
Wild dragons make their nests in cramped places such as caves, so they don't need large stables. However, they have to go outside at least once a day or they become stressed.
A dragon this large might eat one chicken a day. It also eats fruit.
The bathroom has a bathtub. It's rarely used.
Payments are taken directly through the window. The dragon tamer's original postage stamp designs are very popular.
Entrance
Window for after hours

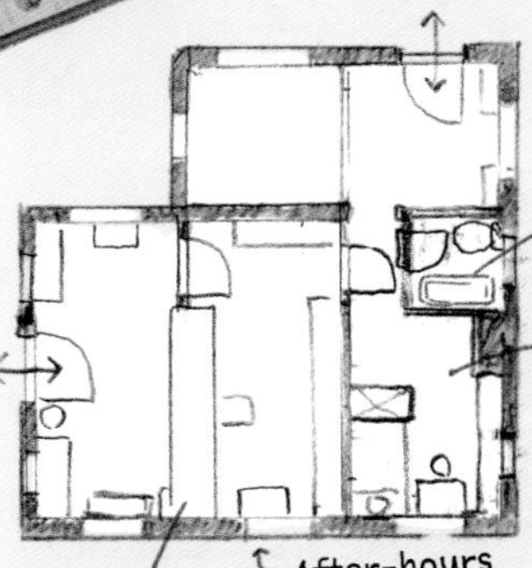
Back door
Stable
Bathroom
Bedroom
Entrance
Counter
After-hours window

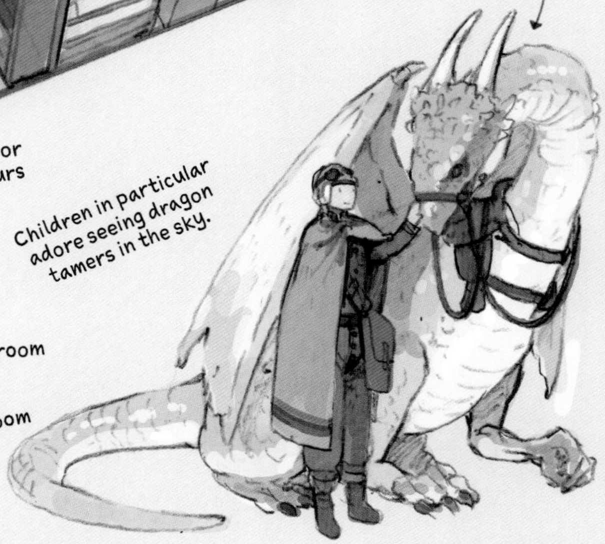
Most dragons used for deliveries are large enough for a medium-size person to ride. This species of dragon is blue with orange markings around their eyes and at the tips of their hands and feet. Once tamed, they are relatively docile and easy to handle.
Children in particular adore seeing dragon tamers in the sky.

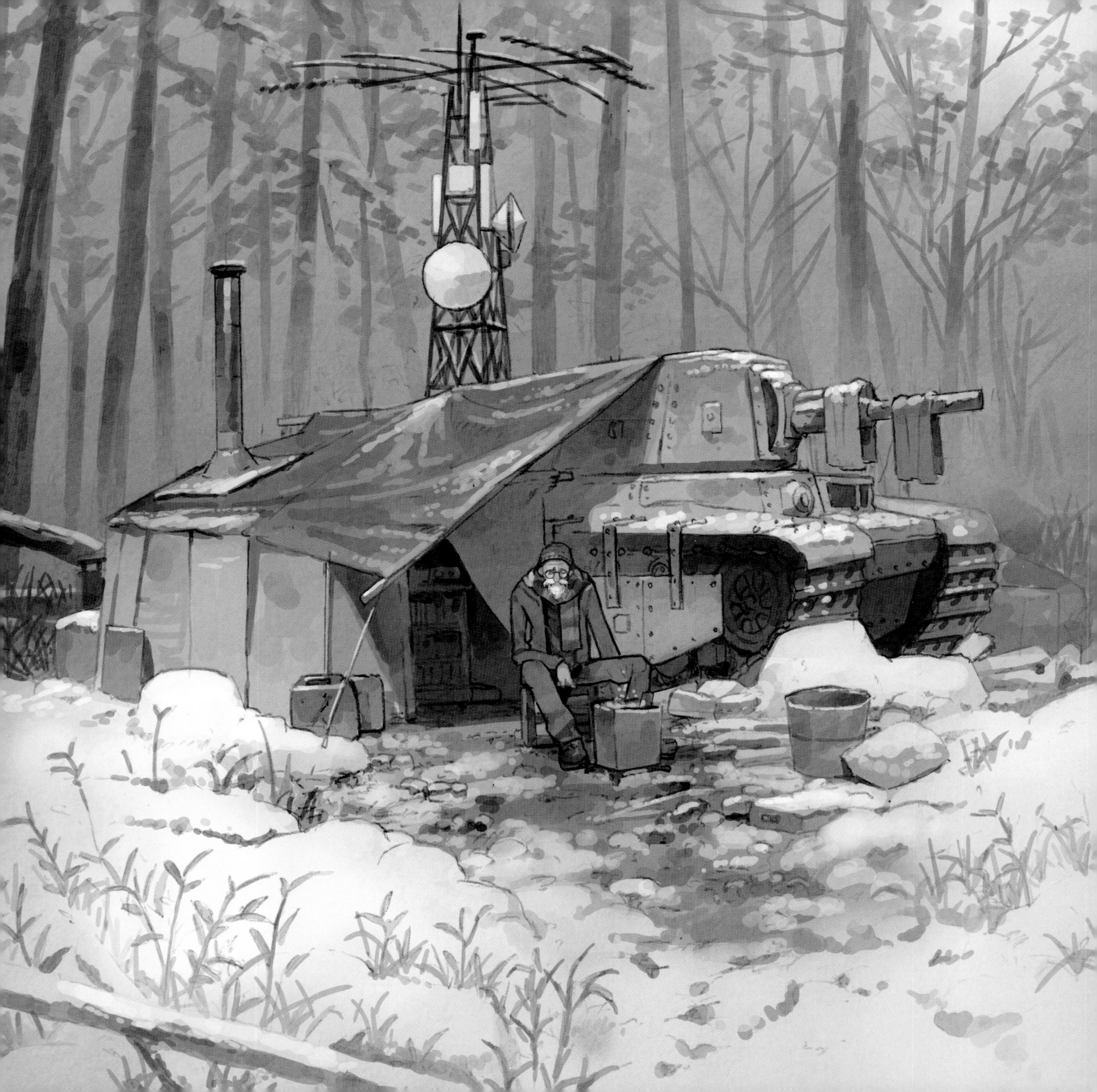

Secluded Information Broker

Though he was once an active information broker who fought against multiple government agencies, he has now withdrawn from the front lines to live as a recluse. He lives in a tentlike house made from a military vehicle abandoned after a large war. He no longer receives visitors.

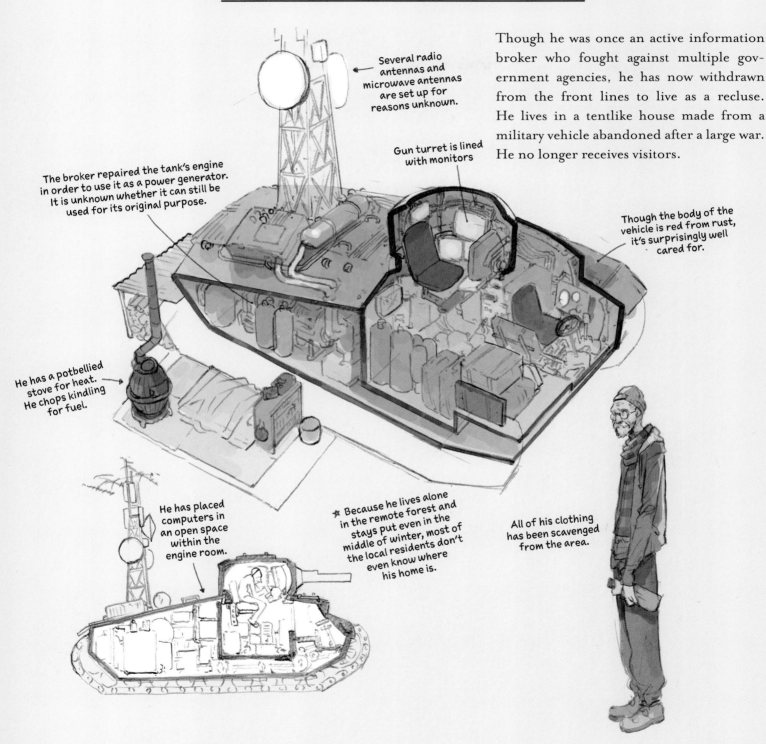

Several radio antennas and microwave antennas are set up for reasons unknown.
Gun turret is lined with monitors
The broker repaired the tank's engine in order to use it as a power generator. It is unknown whether it can still be used for its original purpose.
Though the body of the vehicle is red from rust, it's surprisingly well cared for.
He has a potbellied stove for heat. He chops kindling for fuel.

He has placed computers in an open space within the engine room.
★ Because he lives alone in the remote forest and stays put even in the middle of winter, most of the local residents don't even know where his home is.

All of his clothing has been scavenged from the area.

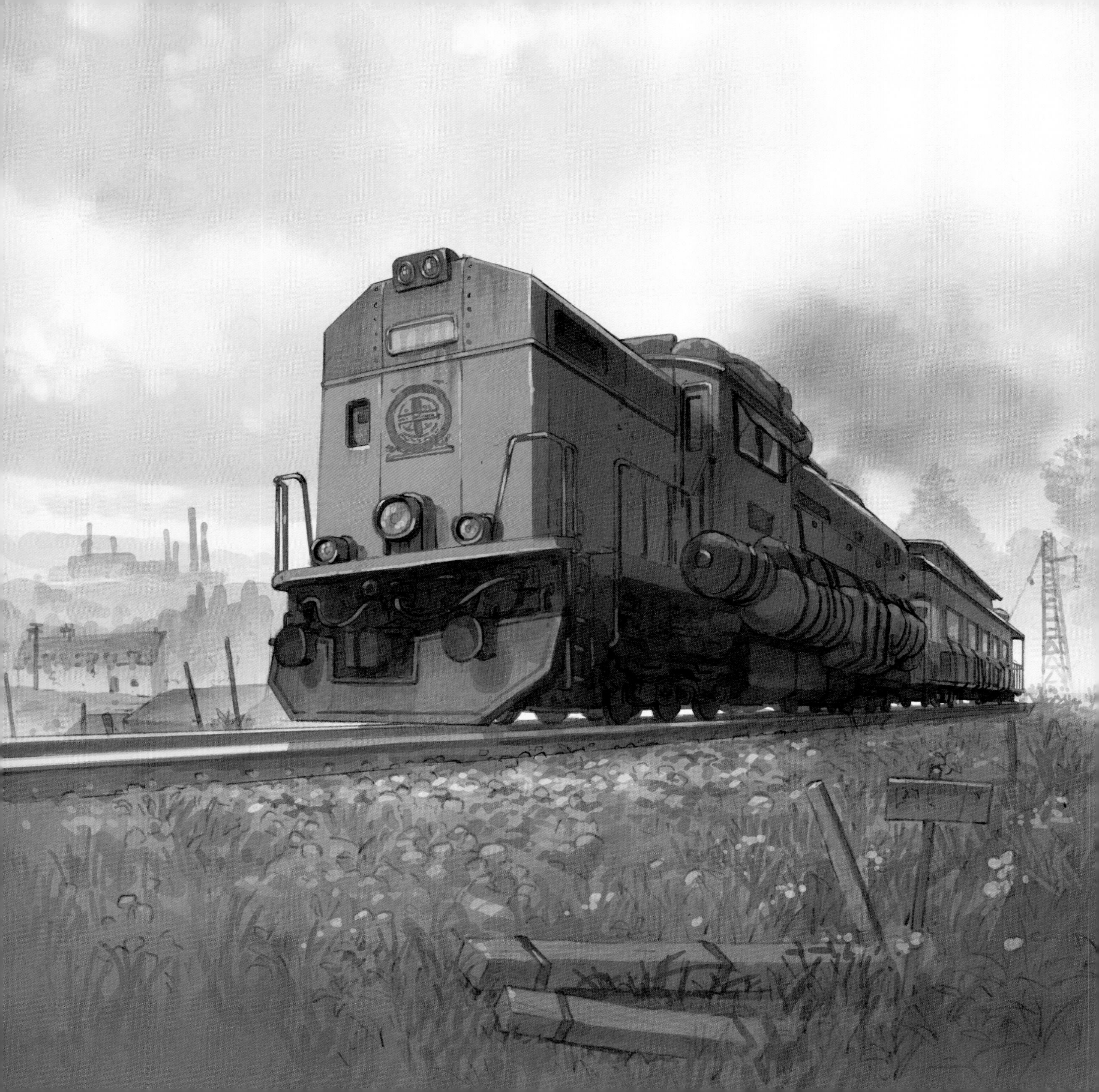

Diesel Sisters

A pair of sisters travels across the continent in this diesel vehicle. The passenger car is full of their luggage, and it is furnished with a comfortable living space. They buy and sell valuables at their destinations and also deal in expensive artwork. Where they source the art is a secret only the sisters know.

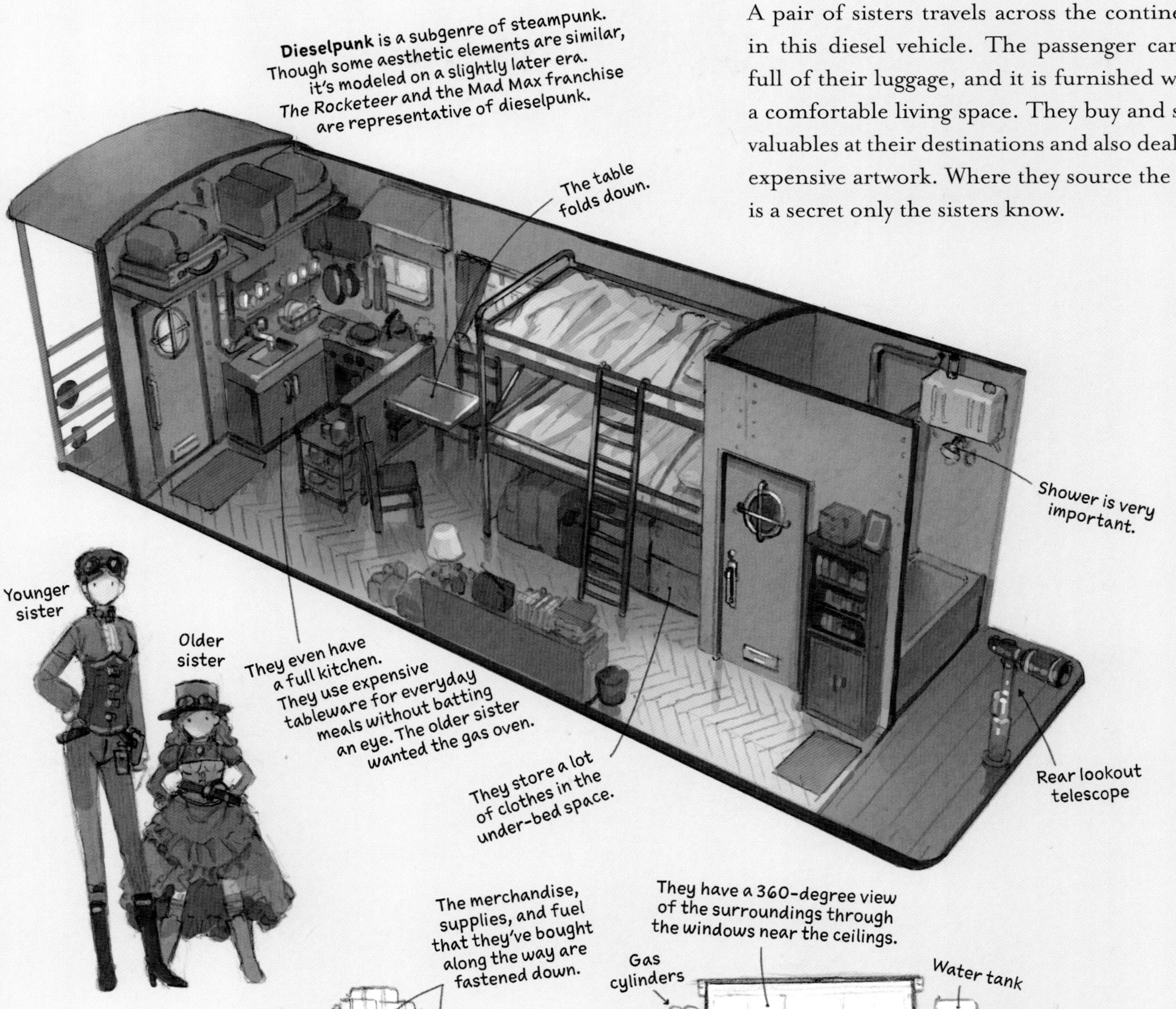

Dieselpunk is a subgenre of steampunk. Though some aesthetic elements are similar, it's modeled on a slightly later era. *The Rocketeer* and the *Mad Max* franchise are representative of dieselpunk.
The table folds down.
Shower is very important.
Younger sister
Older sister
They even have a full kitchen. They use expensive tableware for everyday meals without batting an eye. The older sister wanted the gas oven.
They store a lot of clothes in the under-bed space.
Rear lookout telescope

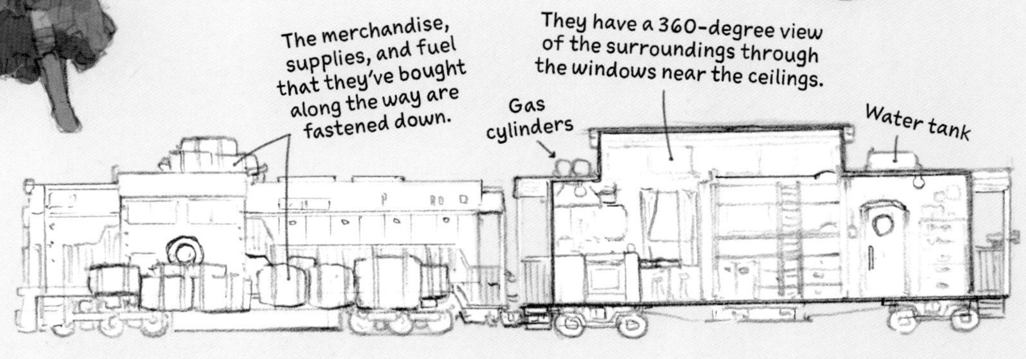

The merchandise, supplies, and fuel that they've bought along the way are fastened down.
They have a 360-degree view of the surroundings through the windows near the ceilings.
Gas cylinders
Water tank

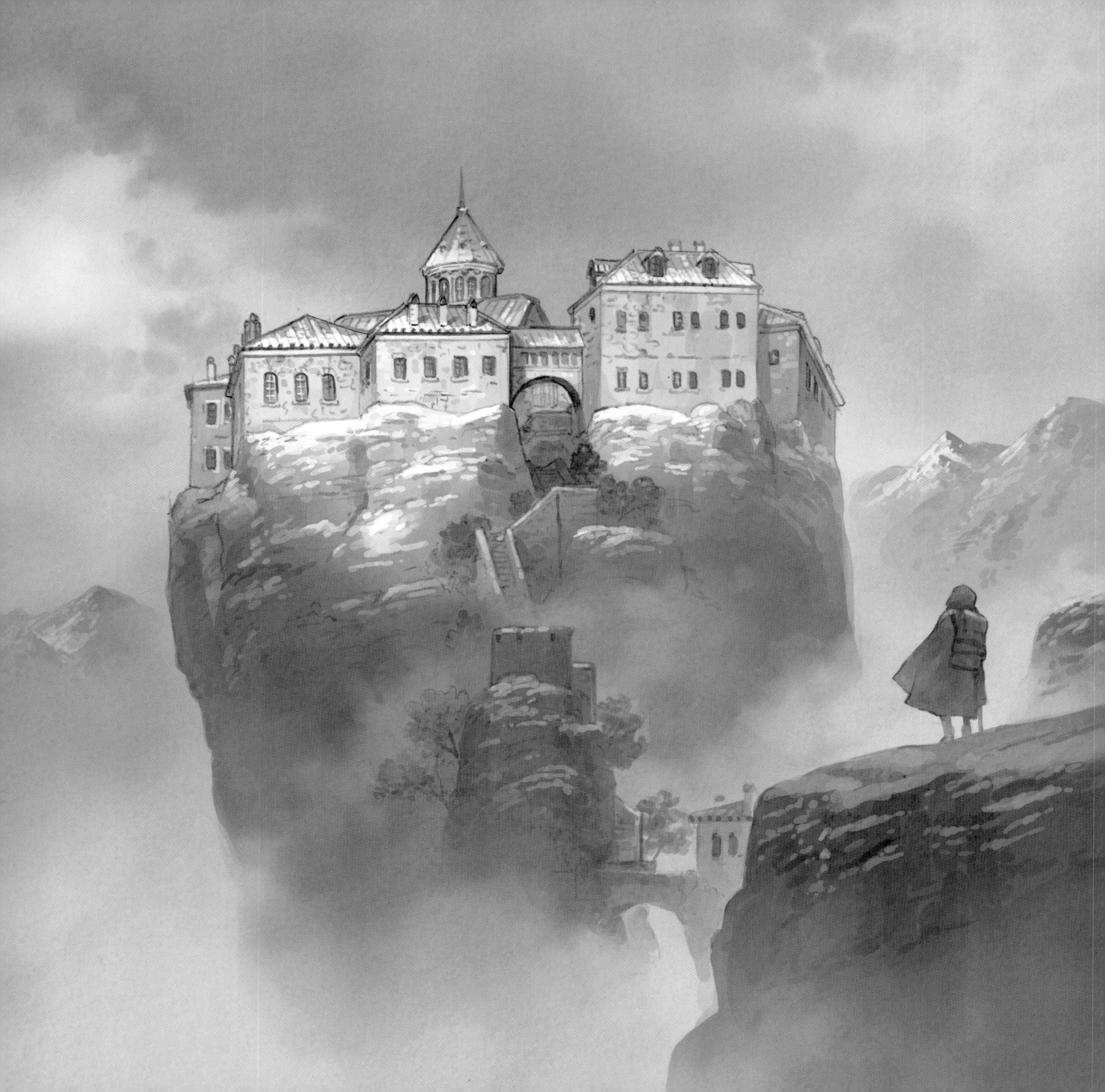

The Library of Lost Books

This is a library where all the books that have been entirely lost to this world have been gathered. Because it exists in one of the most unexplored reaches of the planet, the library normally has no visitors. But it is rumored to exist, and some truly believe it is a real place. Supposedly, one who is willing to wager their life to read one of the library's tomes sometimes reach the location, but rarely.

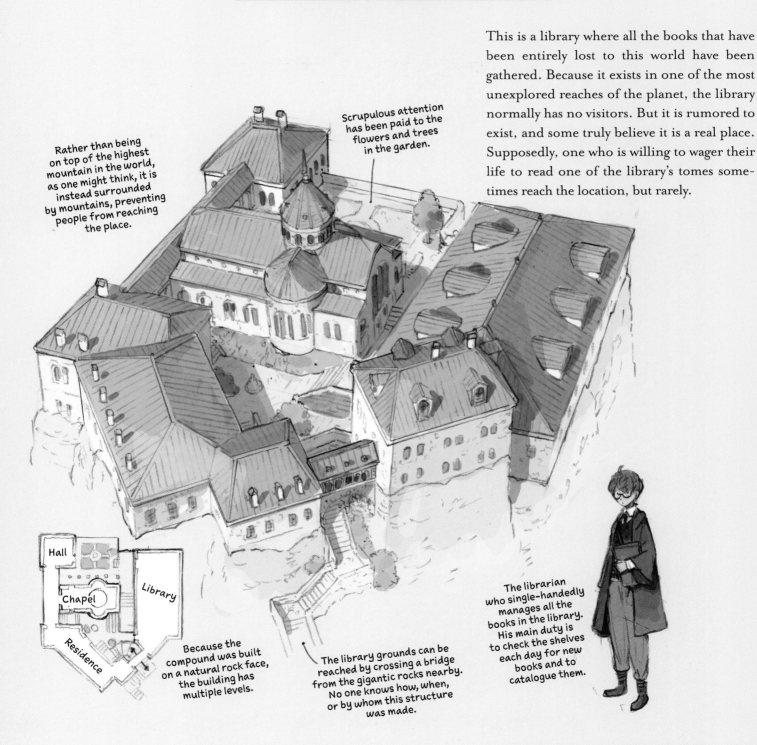

Rather than being on top of the highest mountain in the world, as one might think, it is instead surrounded by mountains, preventing people from reaching the place.

Scrupulous attention has been paid to the flowers and trees in the garden.

Because the compound was built on a natural rock face, the building has multiple levels.

The library grounds can be reached by crossing a bridge from the gigantic rocks nearby. No one knows how, when, or by whom this structure was made.

The librarian who single-handedly manages all the books in the library. His main duty is to check the shelves each day for new books and to catalogue them.

Hall

Chapel

Library

Residence

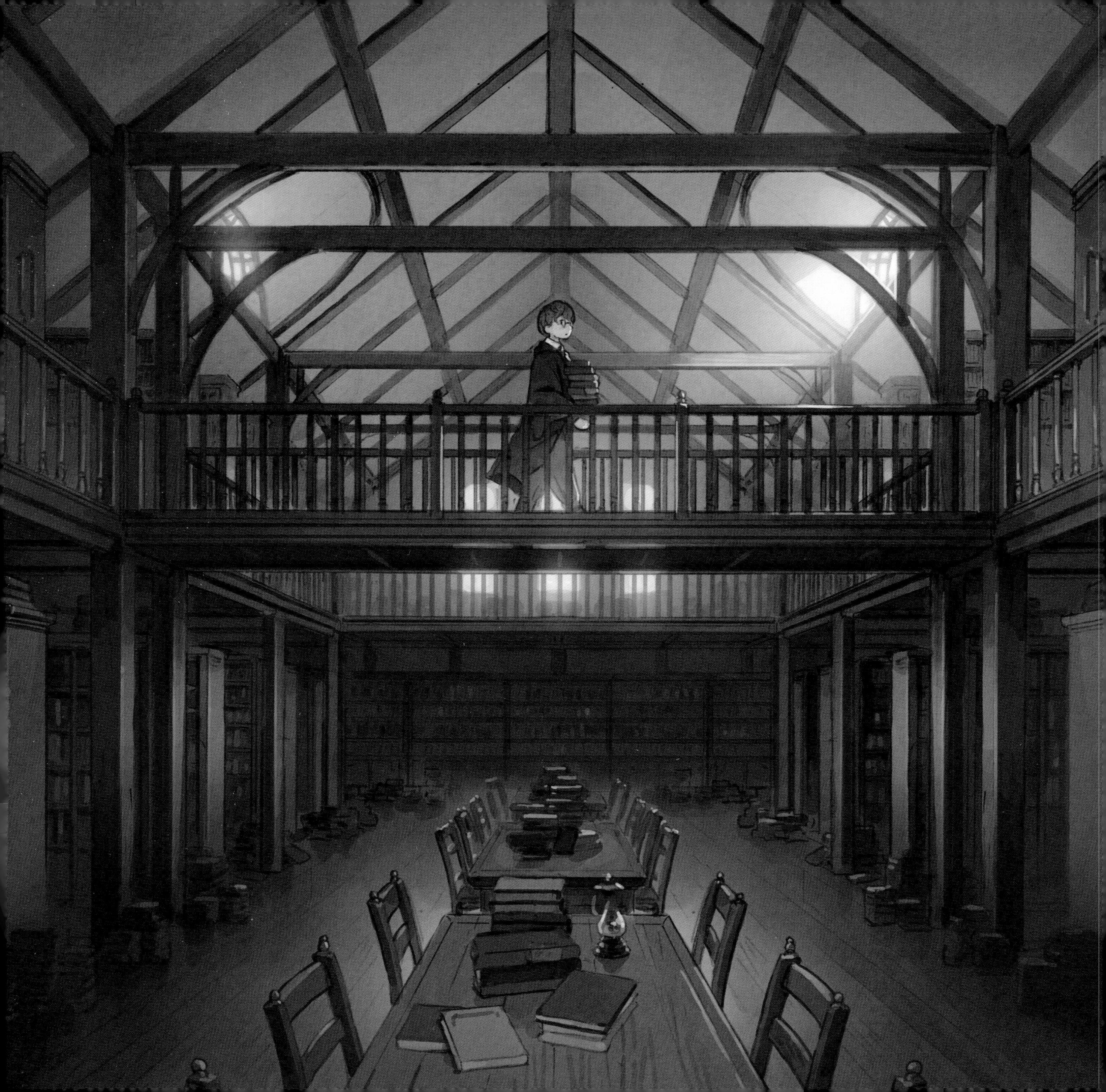

The Library of Lost Books

INTERIOR

Although the library is a two-story hall, because of the sheer number of books, it is remarkably cramped and full of piled tomes that cannot be shelved. The atrium stairway next to the entrance on the south side leads to an office, which is occupied by an elderly man who is known only as "the manager." The manager never leaves the room. No one knows who he is, but rumor has it that the office is connected to another world, where the manager is from.

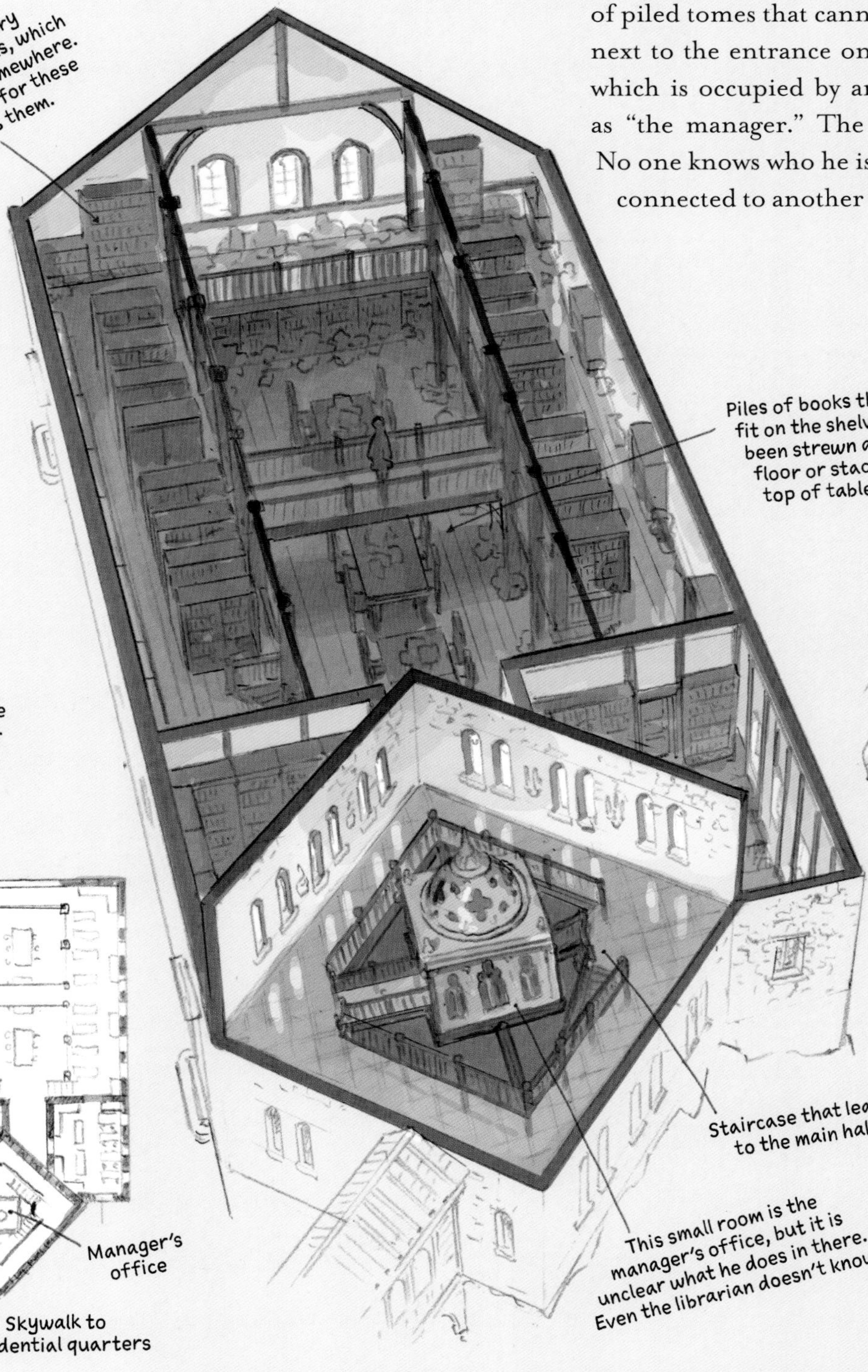
Each day, the library grows by several books, which appear on shelves somewhere. The librarian looks for these and organizes them.
Piles of books that won't fit on the shelves have been strewn about the floor or stacked on top of tables.
Staircase that leads to the main hall
This small room is the manager's office, but it is unclear what he does in there. Even the librarian doesn't know.

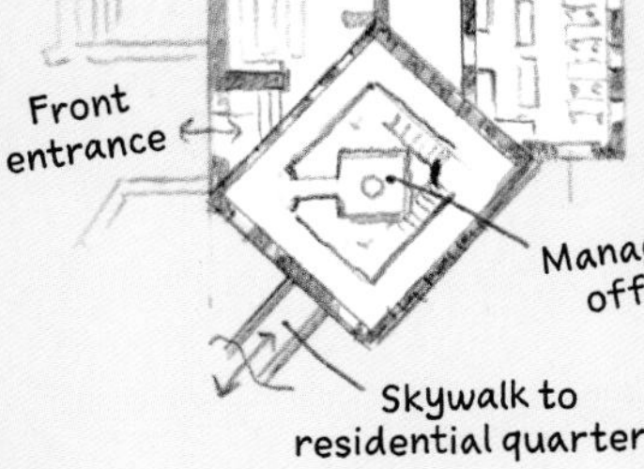
Second-floor entrance You can directly enter and leave the second floor from here.
Front entrance
Manager's office
Skywalk to residential quarters

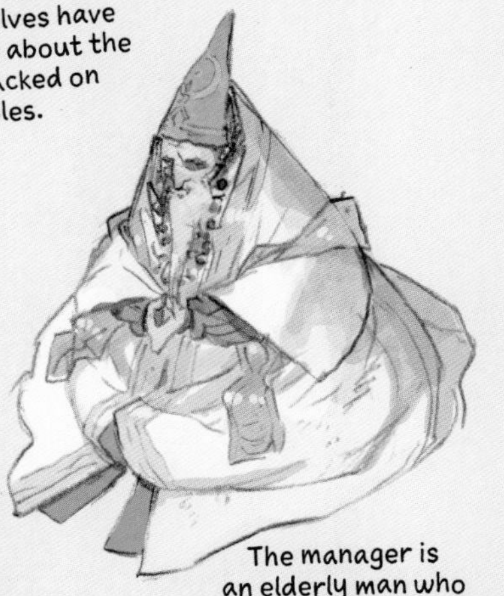
The manager is an elderly man who is always in the office. No one knows why he's there or what he does. It seems he must bring the books to the library somehow, but he has never told anyone about the magic he uses, if it even is magic.

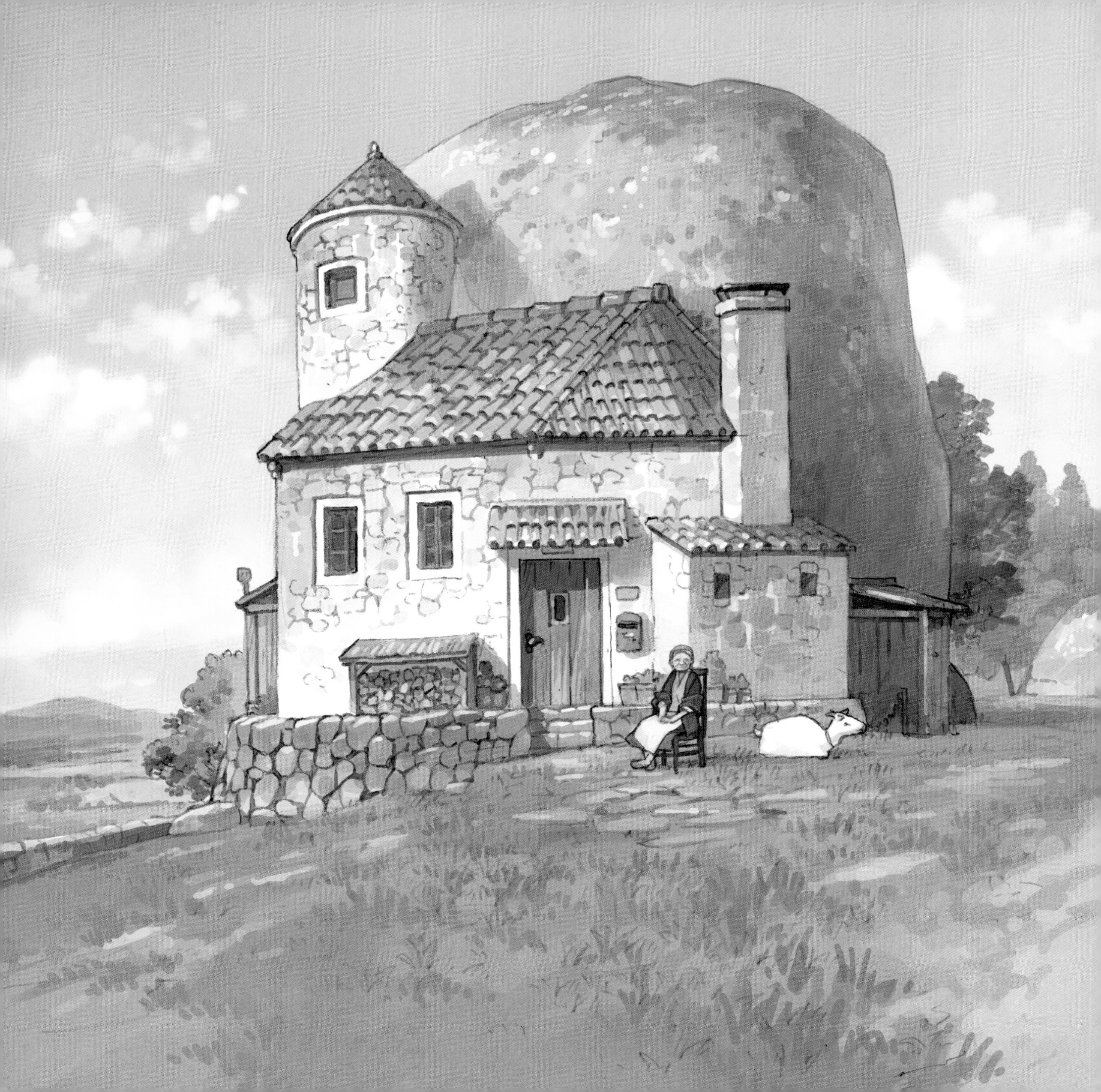

The Megalithic House

This homeowner lives in a house built up against an enormous rock. As part of this village's beliefs, a resident will incorporate a boulder as one wall of their home, which they touch daily to strengthen their faith. Though simple, this elderly woman's house is notable in that it has been integrated into a boulder, which enhances the megalith's constant presence.

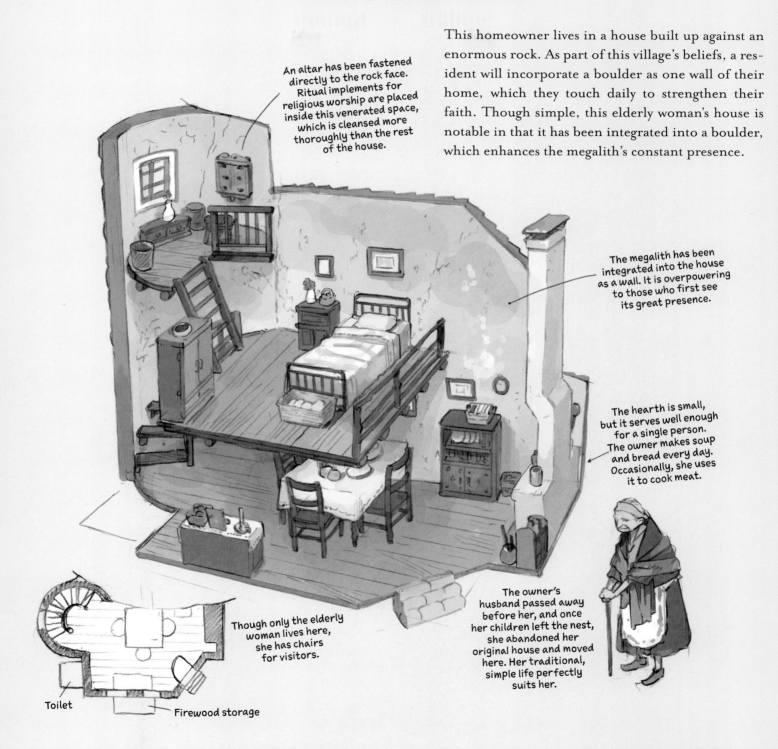

An altar has been fastened directly to the rock face. Ritual implements for religious worship are placed inside this venerated space, which is cleansed more thoroughly than the rest of the house.

The megalith has been integrated into the house as a wall. It is overpowering to those who first see its great presence.

The hearth is small, but it serves well enough for a single person. The owner makes soup and bread every day. Occasionally, she uses it to cook meat.

Though only the elderly woman lives here, she has chairs for visitors.

The owner's husband passed away before her, and once her children left the nest, she abandoned her original house and moved here. Her traditional, simple life perfectly suits her.

Toilet

Firewood storage

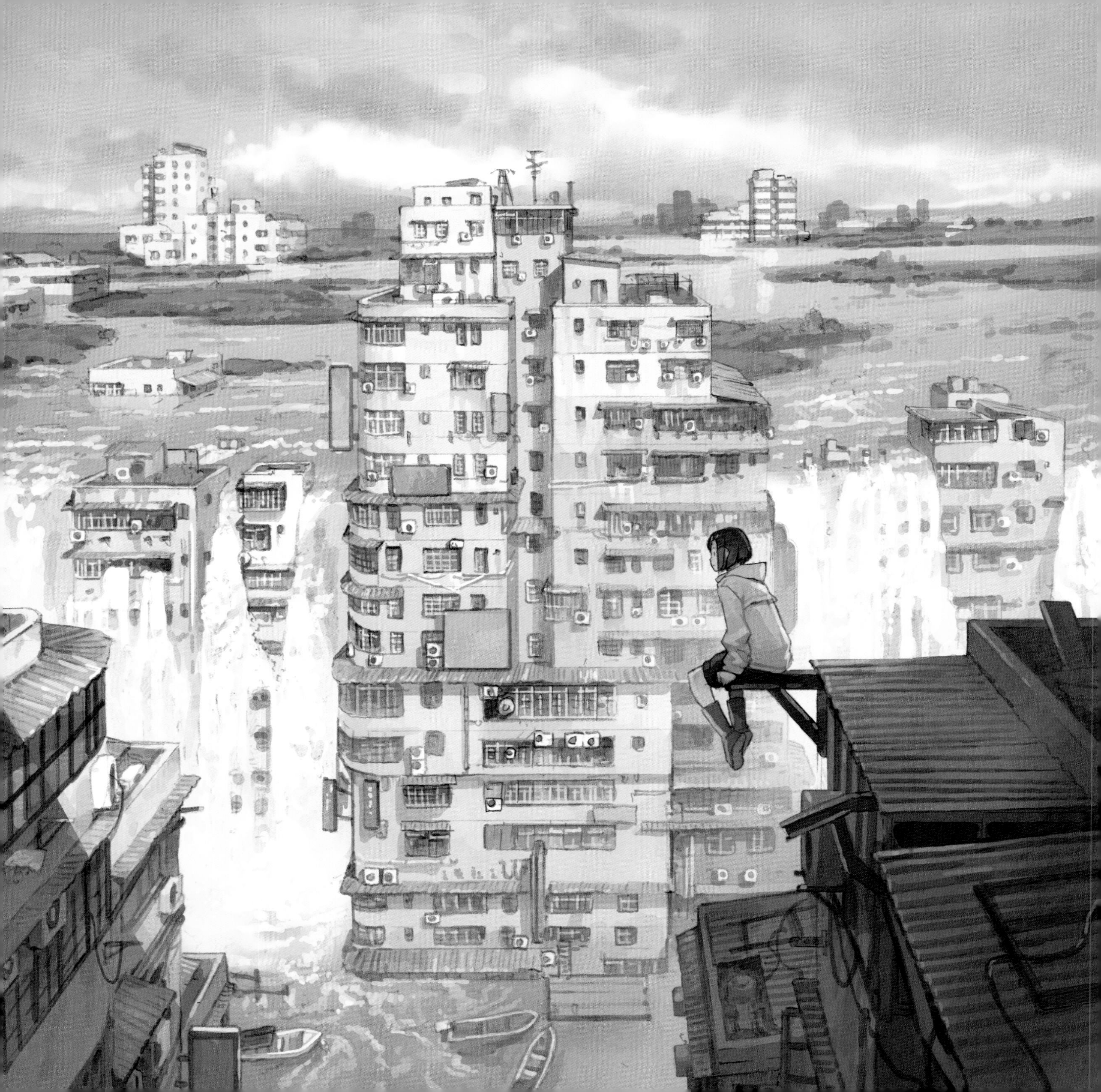

A Girl in the Submerged City

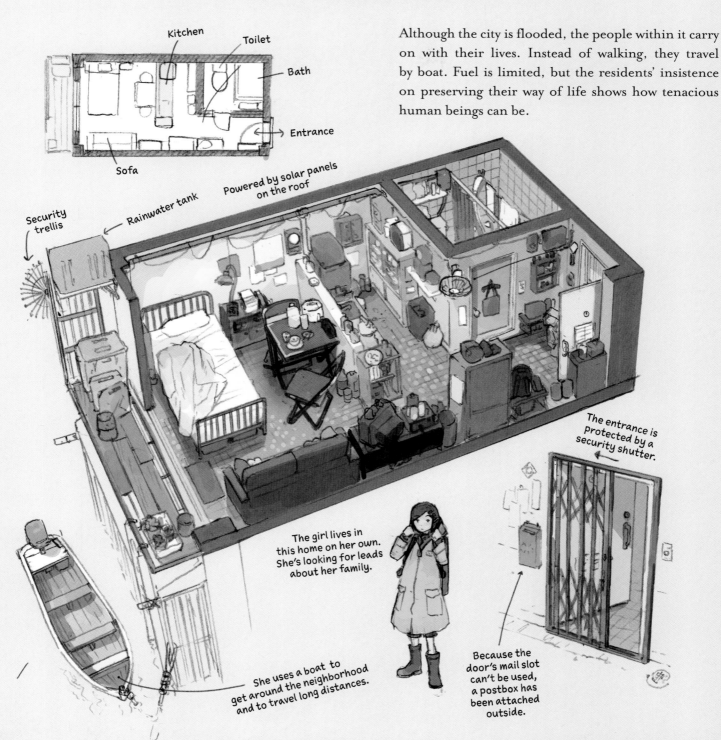

Kitchen

Toilet

Bath

Entrance

Sofa

Although the city is flooded, the people within it carry on with their lives. Instead of walking, they travel by boat. Fuel is limited, but the residents' insistence on preserving their way of life shows how tenacious human beings can be.

Security trellis

Rainwater tank

Powered by solar panels on the roof

The entrance is protected by a security shutter.

The girl lives in this home on her own. She's looking for leads about her family.

She uses a boat to get around the neighborhood and to travel long distances.

Because the door's mail slot can't be used, a postbox has been attached outside.

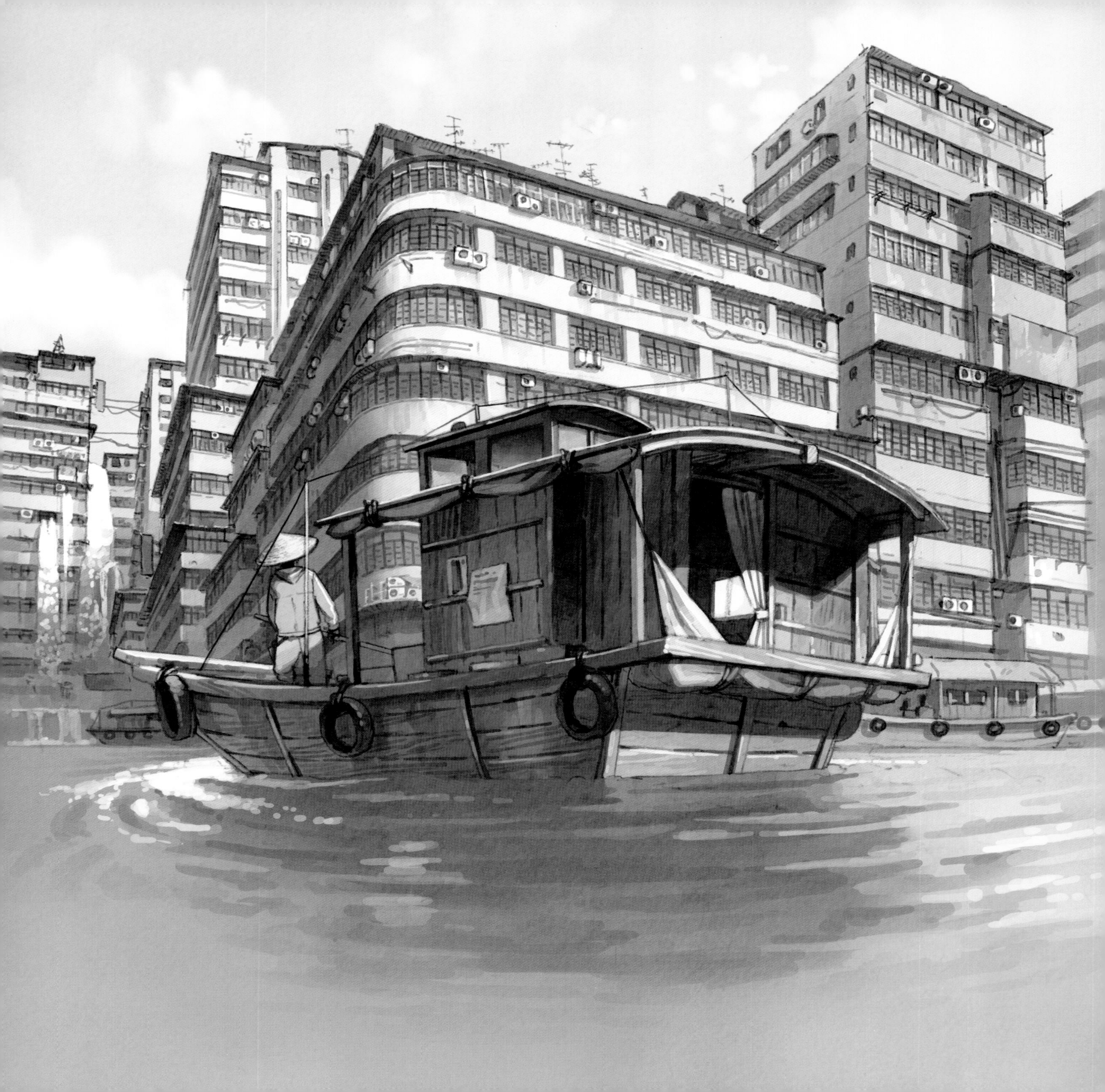

HOUSEBOAT

This is a houseboat owned by one of the people living on the water. It's very convenient for living in a submerged city. Some serve food or put on shows on their decks; however, many work as traders and make a living peddling their wares all across the city.

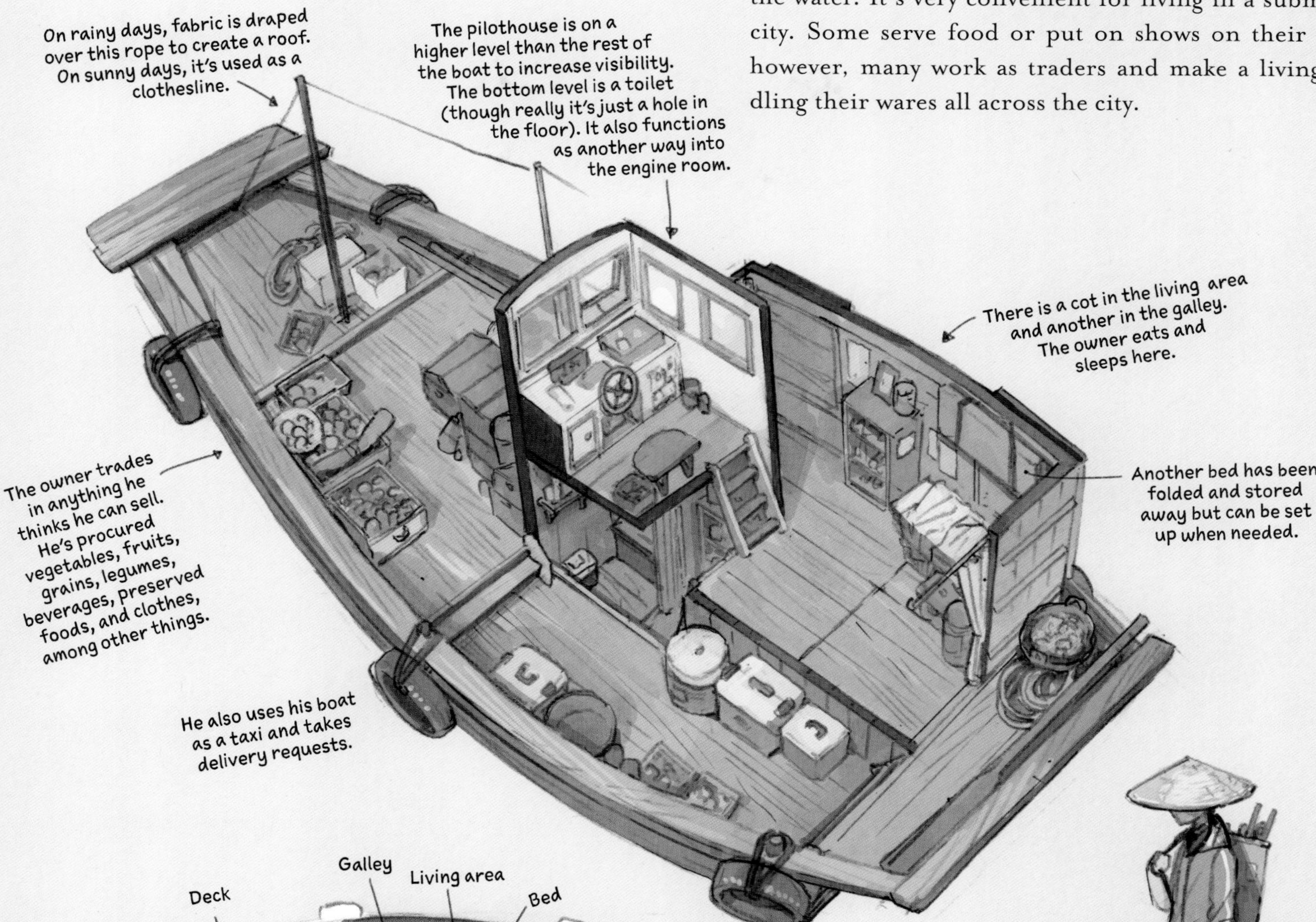
On rainy days, fabric is draped over this rope to create a roof. On sunny days, it's used as a clothesline.
The pilothouse is on a higher level than the rest of the boat to increase visibility. The bottom level is a toilet (though really it's just a hole in the floor). It also functions as another way into the engine room.
There is a cot in the living area and another in the galley. The owner eats and sleeps here.
The owner trades in anything he thinks he can sell. He's procured vegetables, fruits, grains, legumes, beverages, preserved foods, and clothes, among other things.
Another bed has been folded and stored away but can be set up when needed.
He also uses his boat as a taxi and takes delivery requests.

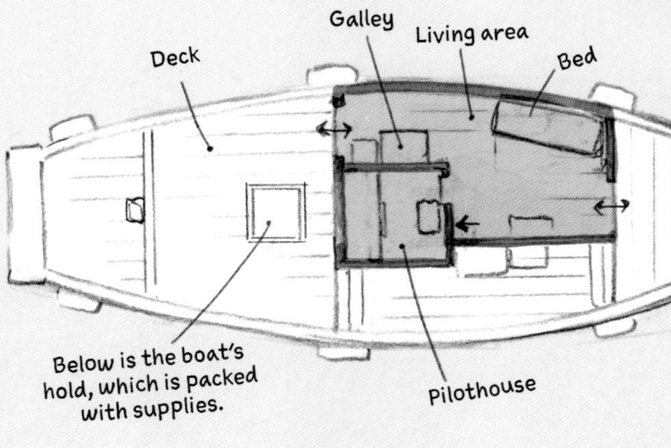
Galley
Living area
Deck
Bed
Below is the boat's hold, which is packed with supplies.
Pilothouse

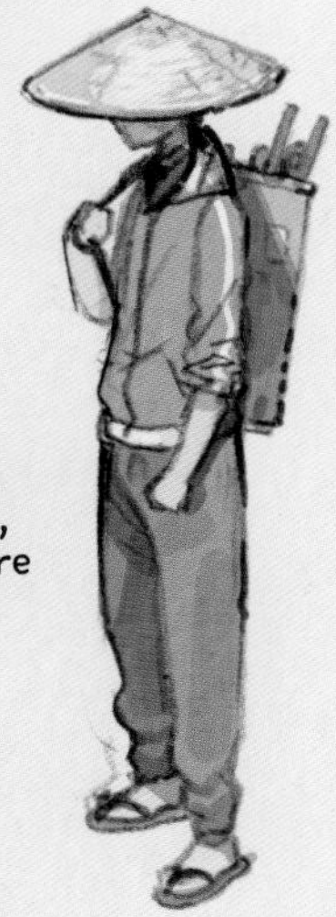
The wooden boat is old-fashioned, but the owner has added facilities as needed. Though he deals in commerce, it's really more like bartering, and there are no standard market prices.

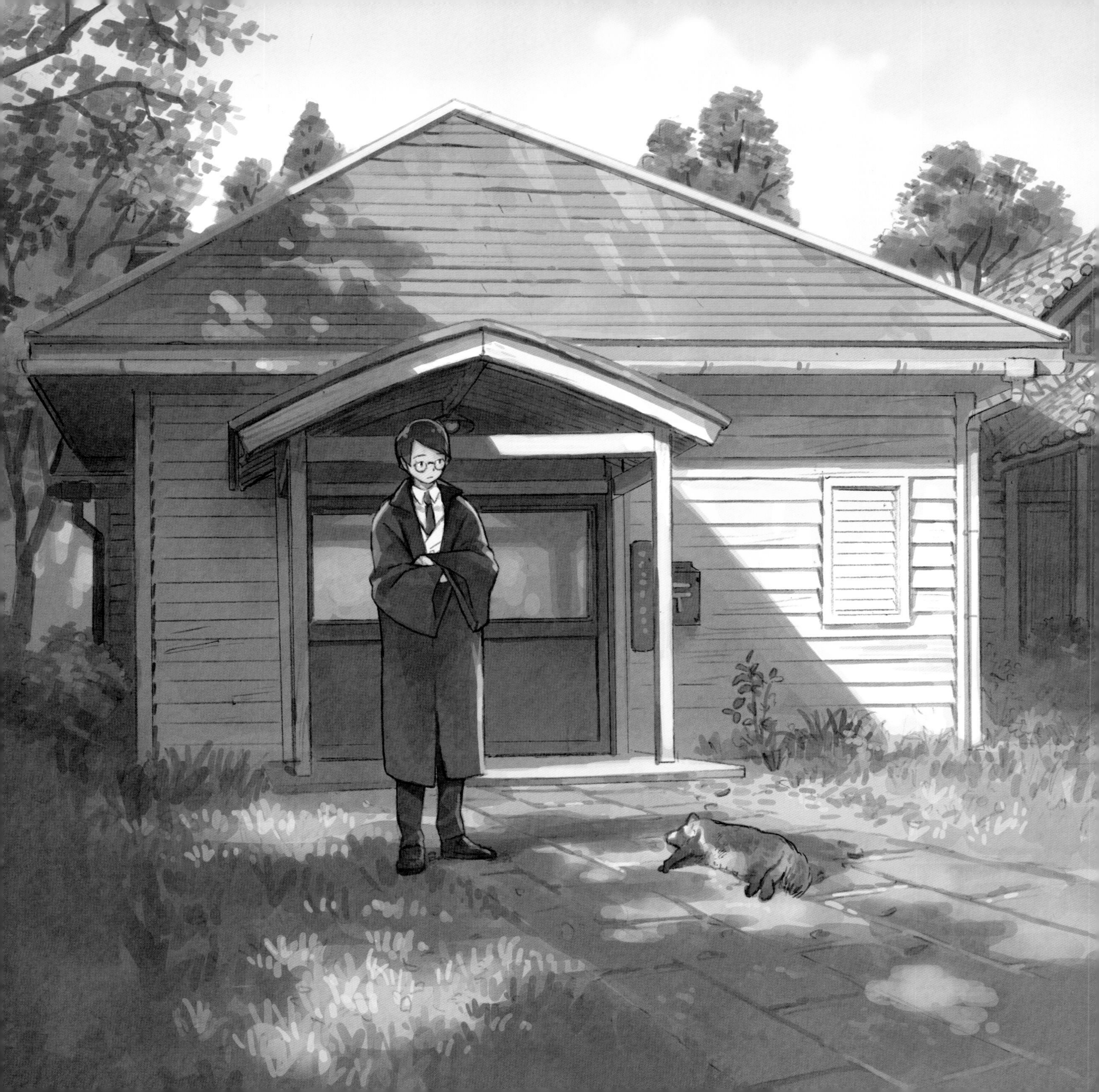

Clinic in the Woods

This is a clinic in a small village within a forest. Few come to visit, so the young doctor manages it on his own. Some days he doesn't have a single patient. On one such day, he helps an injured raccoon dog on a whim, and quite unusual clients soon begin to call upon the doctor . . .

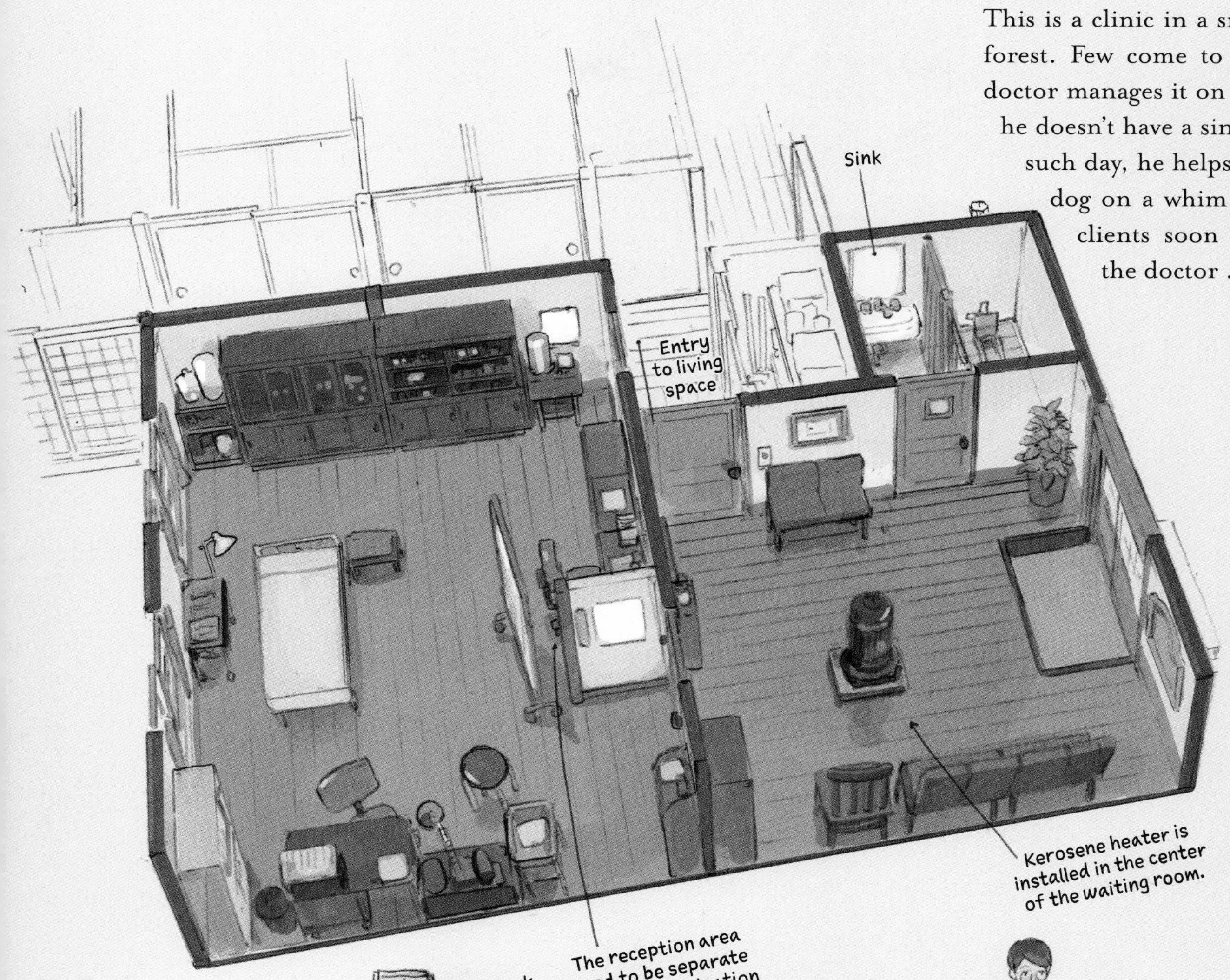

Sink
Entry to living space
Kerosene heater is installed in the center of the waiting room.
The reception area used to be separate from the examination room, but because the physician is the only worker and the walls were in the way, he removed them.

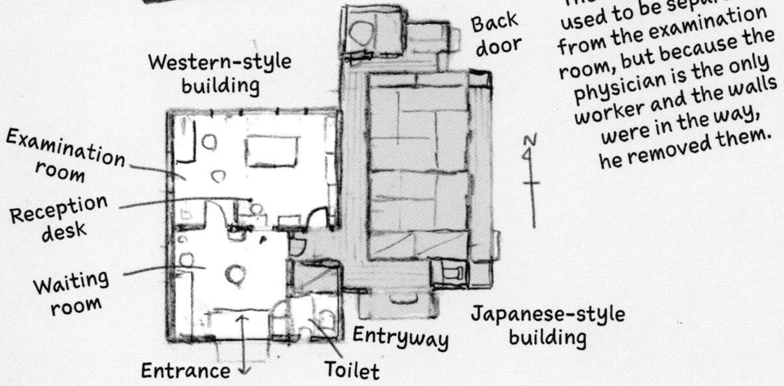

Western-style building
Back door
Examination room
Reception desk
Waiting room
Japanese-style building
Entryway
Entrance
Toilet
N

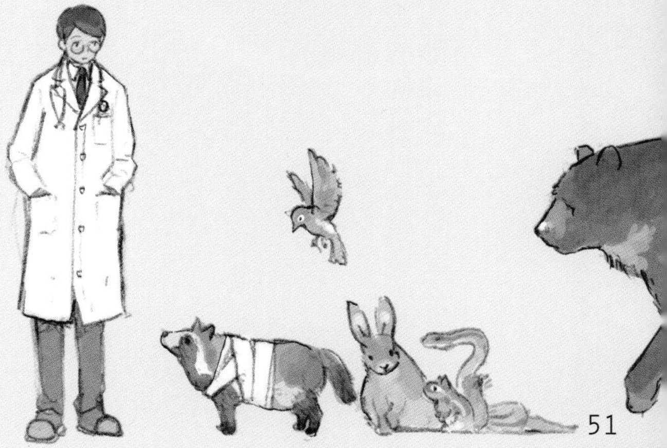

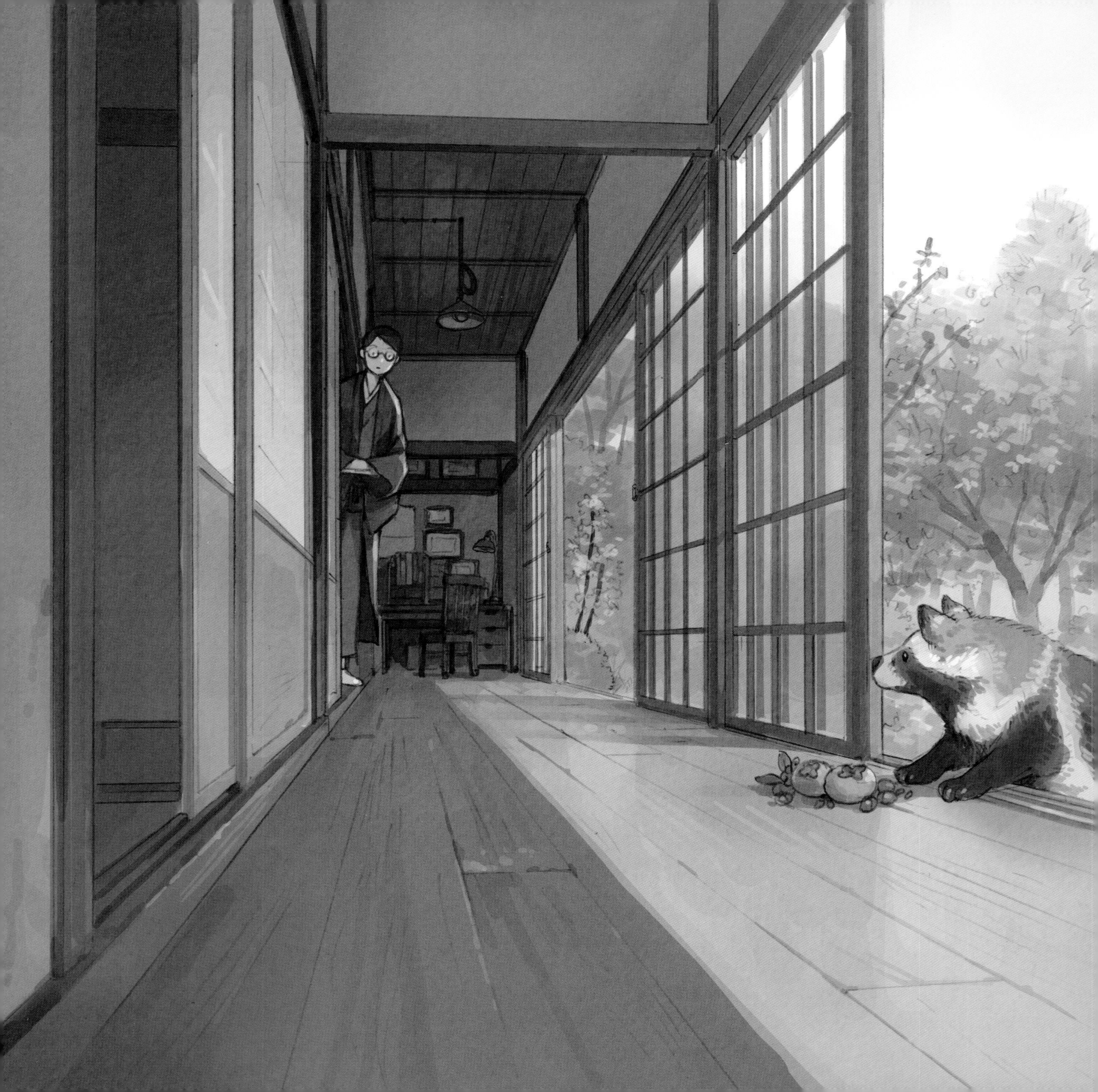

Clinic in the Woods

INTERIOR

The clinic, constructed in the early Showa era (1926–1989 CE), is an example of Japanese-Western eclectic architecture. Though the medical facilities are built in the Western style, the living areas are decidedly Japanese. These types of constructions were made for Japanese people who were not used to living in Western facilities. In the living area, there's a Japanese-style veranda hall, alcove, and cauldron-style bath, just as in any other traditional home.

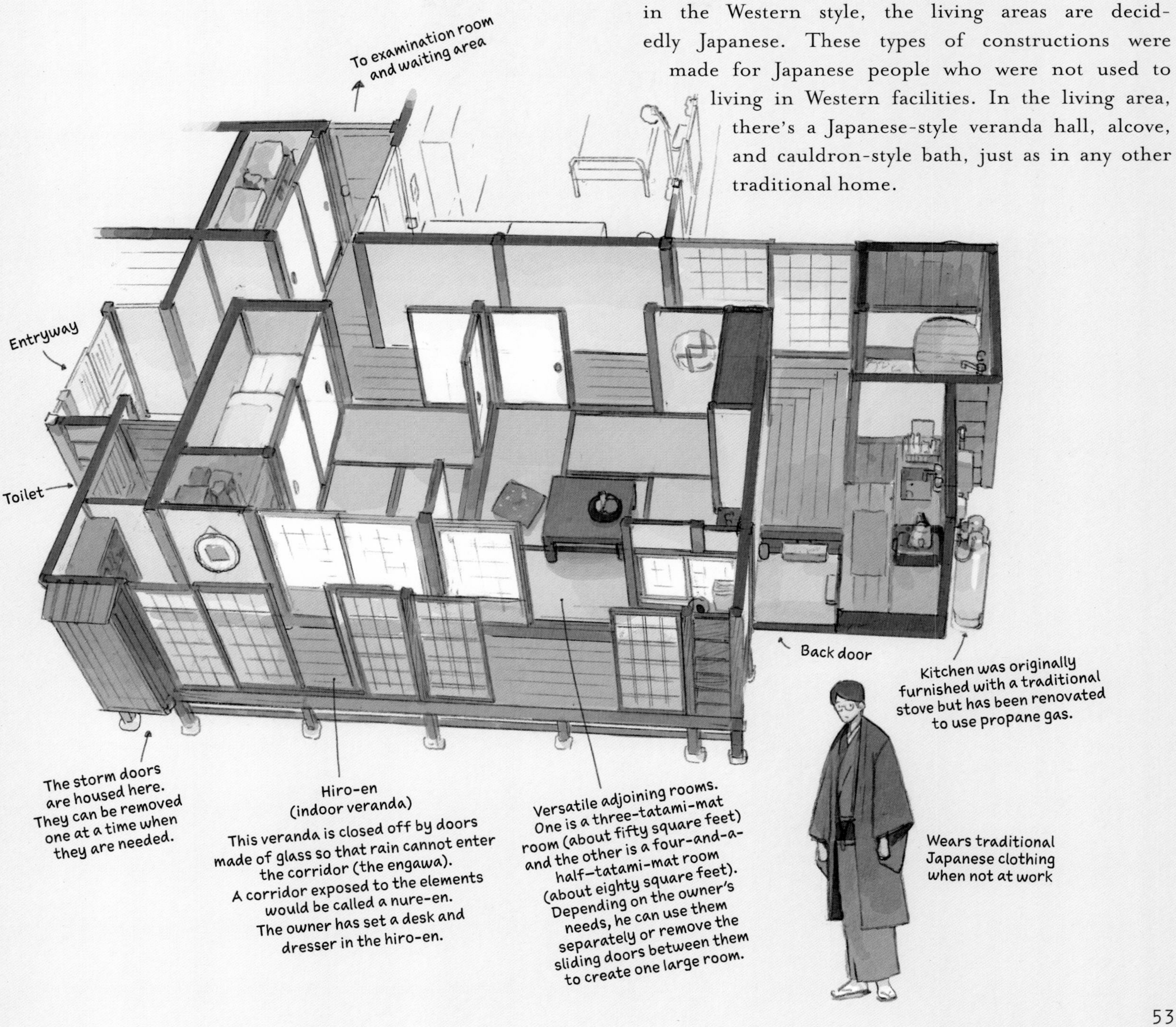

To examination room and waiting area
Entryway
Toilet
Back door
Kitchen was originally furnished with a traditional stove but has been renovated to use propane gas.
The storm doors are housed here. They can be removed one at a time when they are needed.
Hiro-en (indoor veranda)
This veranda is closed off by doors made of glass so that rain cannot enter the corridor (the engawa). A corridor exposed to the elements would be called a nure-en. The owner has set a desk and dresser in the hiro-en.
Versatile adjoining rooms. One is a three-tatami-mat room (about fifty square feet) and the other is a four-and-a-half–tatami-mat room (about eighty square feet). Depending on the owner's needs, he can use them separately or remove the sliding doors between them to create one large room.
Wears traditional Japanese clothing when not at work

SIDEBAR A Word on Toilets

A toilet can easily be overlooked when drawing buildings. The form a toilet takes can vary greatly depending not only on the era but also on the region, so drawing a hygienic modern toilet could look rather jarring. Though one could argue that fixating on reality more than necessary isn't strictly required, it helps to be aware of the toilets used in the past.

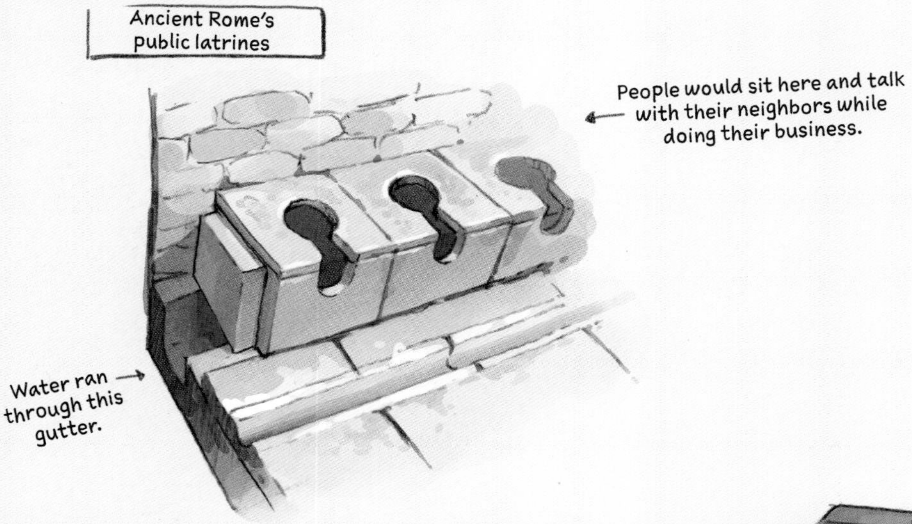

Ancient Rome's public latrines
People would sit here and talk with their neighbors while doing their business.
Water ran through this gutter.

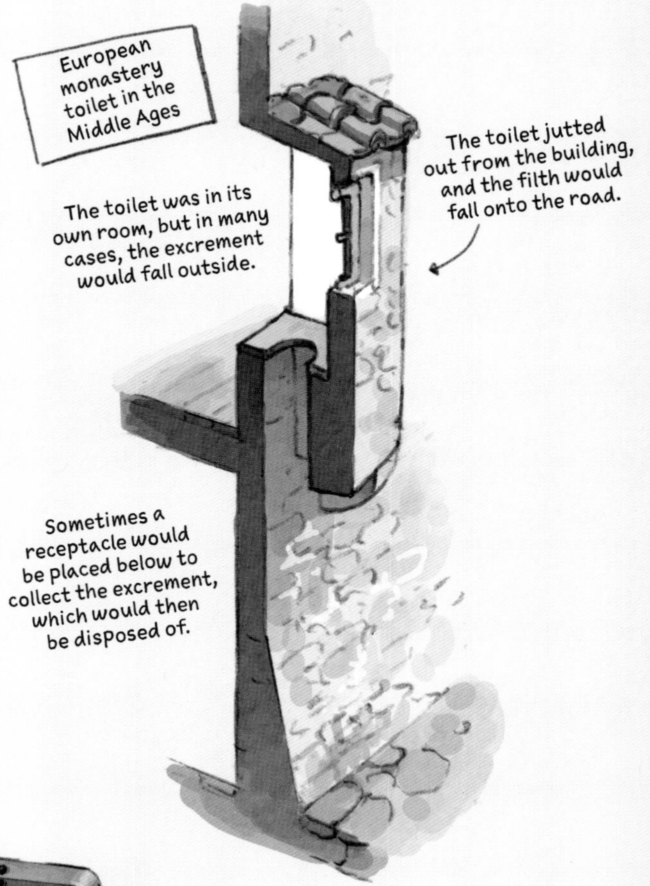

European monastery toilet in the Middle Ages
The toilet jutted out from the building, and the filth would fall onto the road.
The toilet was in its own room, but in many cases, the excrement would fall outside.
Sometimes a receptacle would be placed below to collect the excrement, which would then be disposed of.

The history of toilets runs deep. Water-flush toilets with sewage systems supposedly existed in 4,000 BCE; of those, ancient Roman toilets are particularly famed. In 600 BCE, Romans had serviced sewage systems, and people even socialized in public latrines.

However, Europe in the Middle Ages did not keep up the same cultured practices, and waste was instead thrown directly onto the streets. This state of affairs continued unabated until the early nineteenth century, when the unsanitary conditions were determined to be a major contributor to the prevalence of cholera, the Black Plague, and other contagious diseases. It was then that water and sewage systems were established and people began to use modern-day toilets

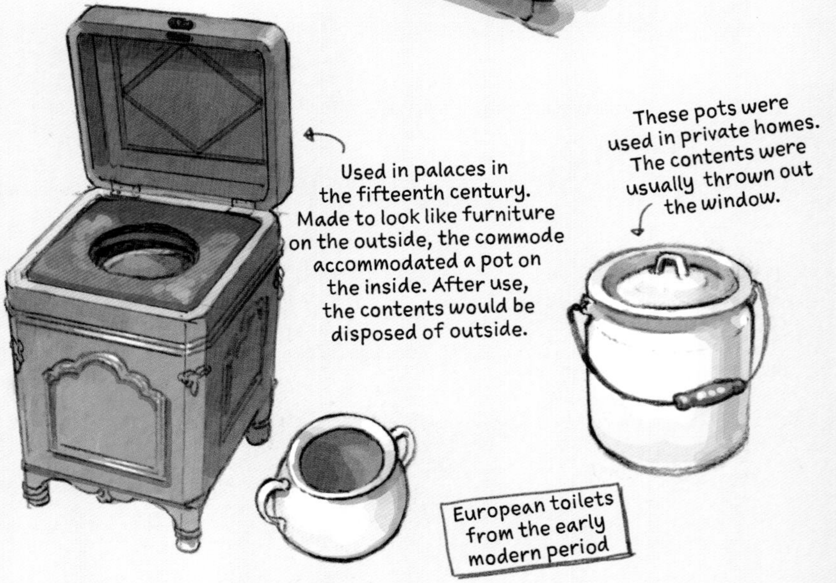

Used in palaces in the fifteenth century. Made to look like furniture on the outside, the commode accommodated a pot on the inside. After use, the contents would be disposed of outside.
These pots were used in private homes. The contents were usually thrown out the window.
European toilets from the early modern period

Japan's culture of toilets was very different from that of Europe. Japan had few areas of level land but abundant rivers, which aided in setting up water and sewage systems. Supposedly, toilets were flushed with water even in the Asuka period (approximately 538–710 CE). In addition, Japan has a long history of using human excrement as fertilizer, and because specialists who bought and sold human waste appeared during the Edo period (1603–1867 CE), sanitary conditions were maintained even in areas of high population density, such as in the Edo capital. Human manure usage in agriculture steadily decreased through the Taisho period (1912–1926 CE), and during the mid-Showa era (1926–1989 CE), flush toilets spread.

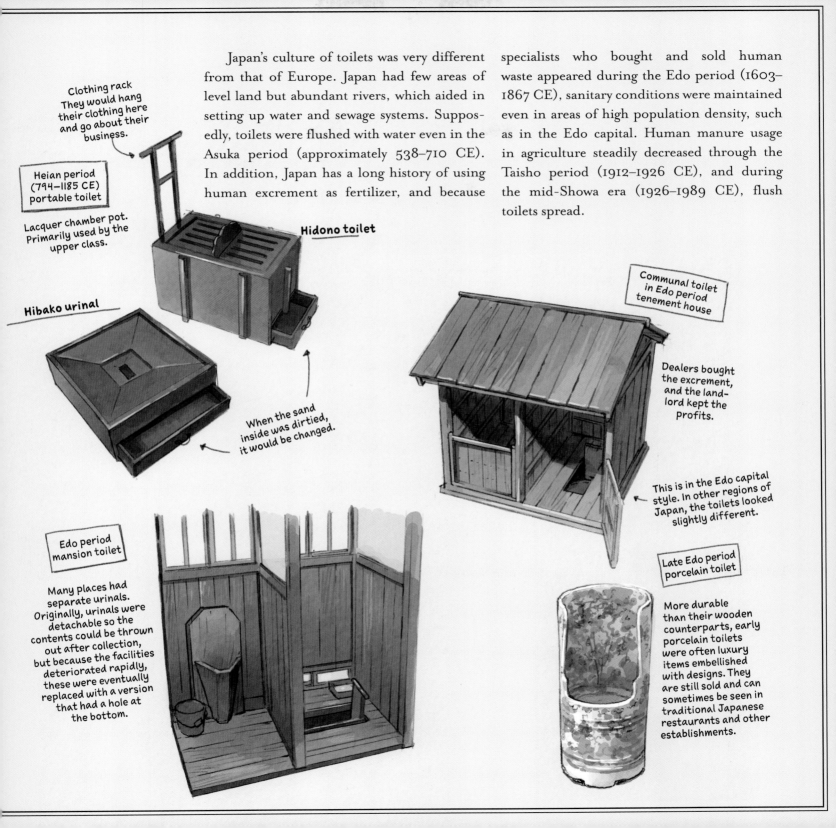

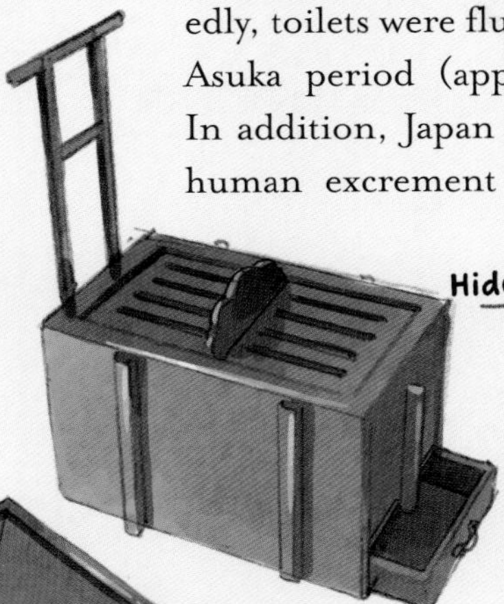
Clothing rack
They would hang their clothing here and go about their business.
Heian period (794–1185 CE) portable toilet
Lacquer chamber pot. Primarily used by the upper class.
Hidono toilet

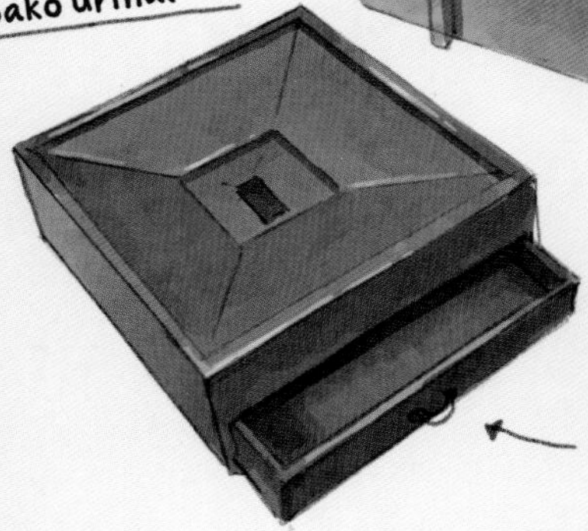
Hibako urinal
When the sand inside was dirtied, it would be changed.

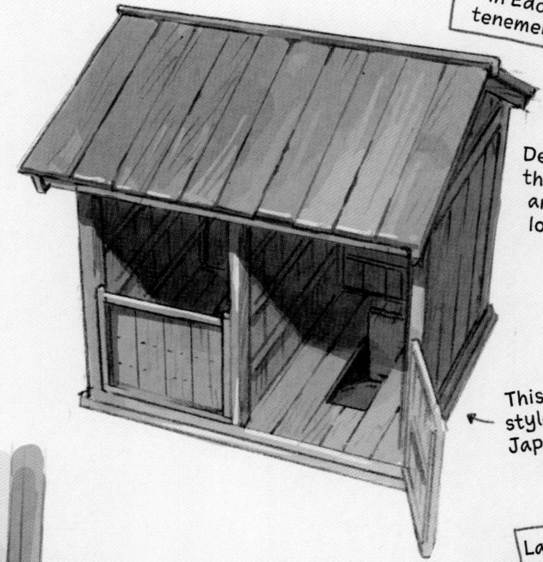
Communal toilet in Edo period tenement house
Dealers bought the excrement, and the landlord kept the profits.
This is in the Edo capital style. In other regions of Japan, the toilets looked slightly different.

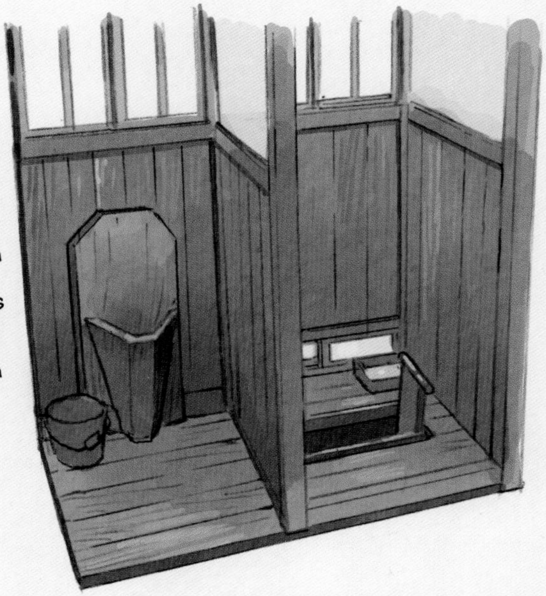
Edo period mansion toilet
Many places had separate urinals. Originally, urinals were detachable so the contents could be thrown out after collection, but because the facilities deteriorated rapidly, these were eventually replaced with a version that had a hole at the bottom.

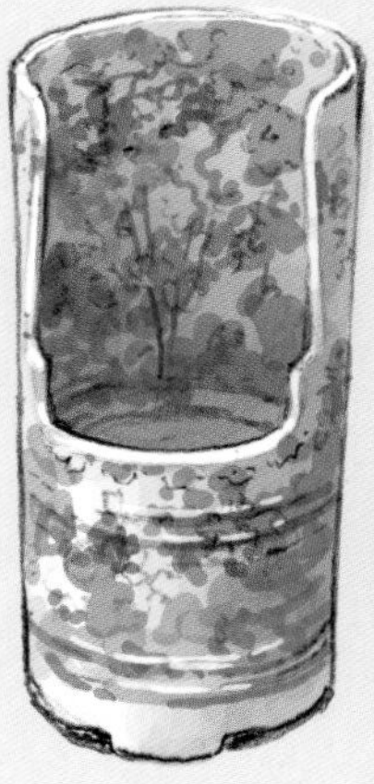
Late Edo period porcelain toilet
More durable than their wooden counterparts, early porcelain toilets were often luxury items embellished with designs. They are still sold and can sometimes be seen in traditional Japanese restaurants and other establishments.

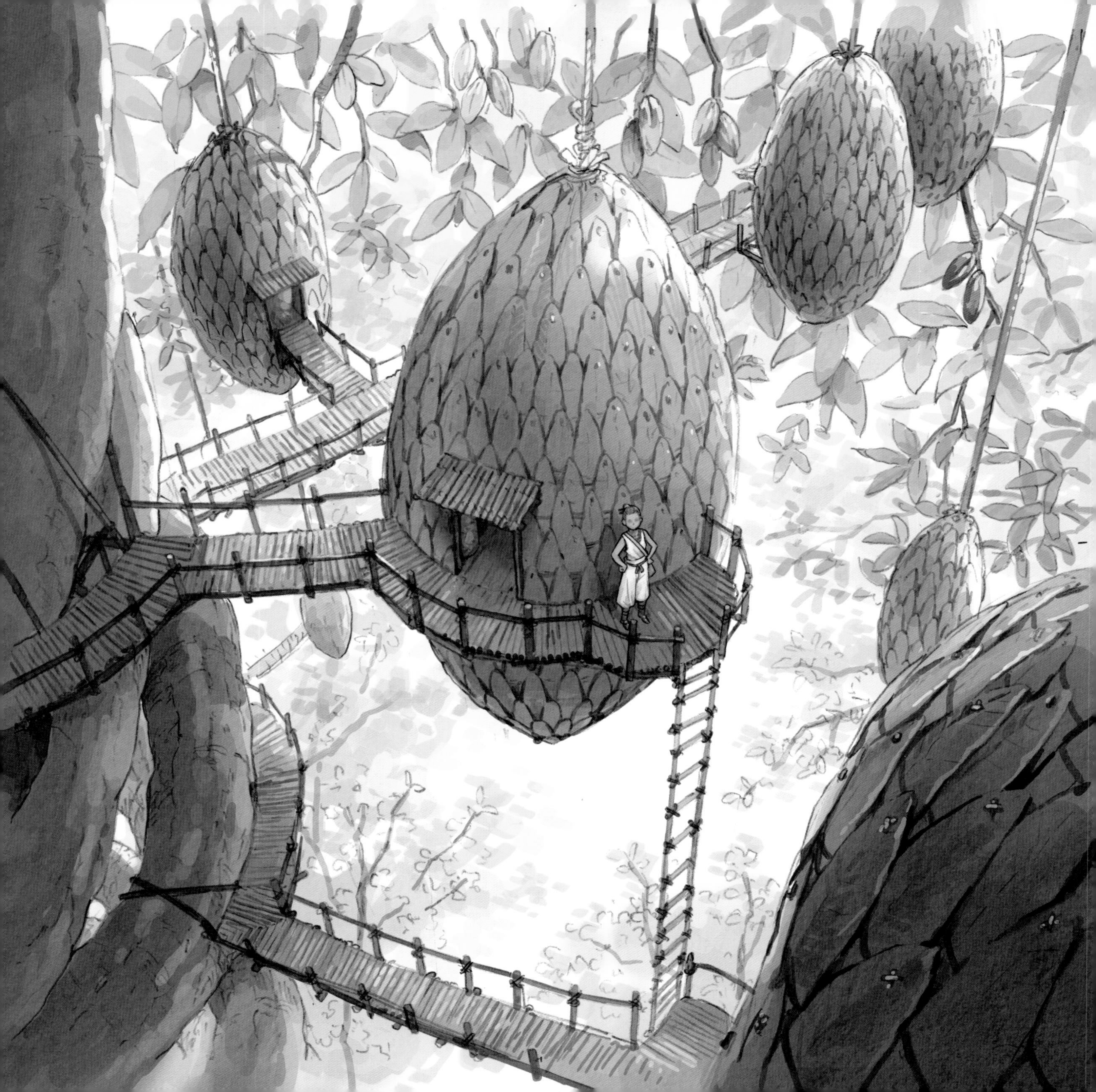

Cacao Tree Houses

Tiny people live in this cacao tree. They use the cocoa pods not only as a source of food but also in all other aspects of their daily lives. The tree's active ingredients are used for medicine, the cocoa butter as a salve, the branches and leaves as building materials, and the fibers for cloth. The people live in dwellings that hang from the tree. They are born in the cacao tree and spend most of their lives there.

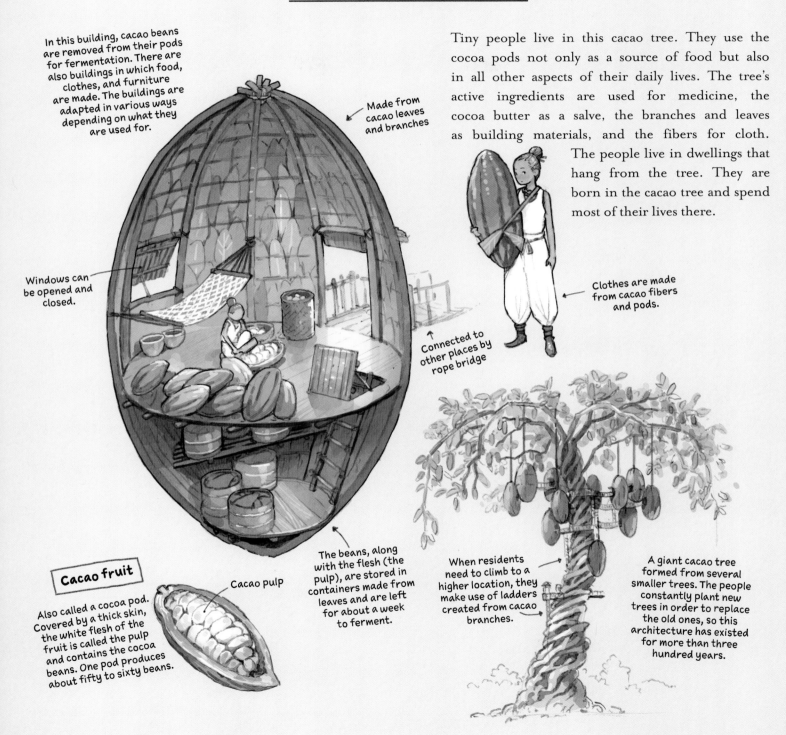

In this building, cacao beans are removed from their pods for fermentation. There are also buildings in which food, clothes, and furniture are made. The buildings are adapted in various ways depending on what they are used for.
Made from cacao leaves and branches
Windows can be opened and closed.
Connected to other places by rope bridge
The beans, along with the flesh (the pulp), are stored in containers made from leaves and are left for about a week to ferment.

Clothes are made from cacao fibers and pods.

When residents need to climb to a higher location, they make use of ladders created from cacao branches.
A giant cacao tree formed from several smaller trees. The people constantly plant new trees in order to replace the old ones, so this architecture has existed for more than three hundred years.

Cacao fruit

Cacao pulp

Also called a cocoa pod. Covered by a thick skin, the white flesh of the fruit is called the pulp and contains the cocoa beans. One pod produces about fifty to sixty beans.

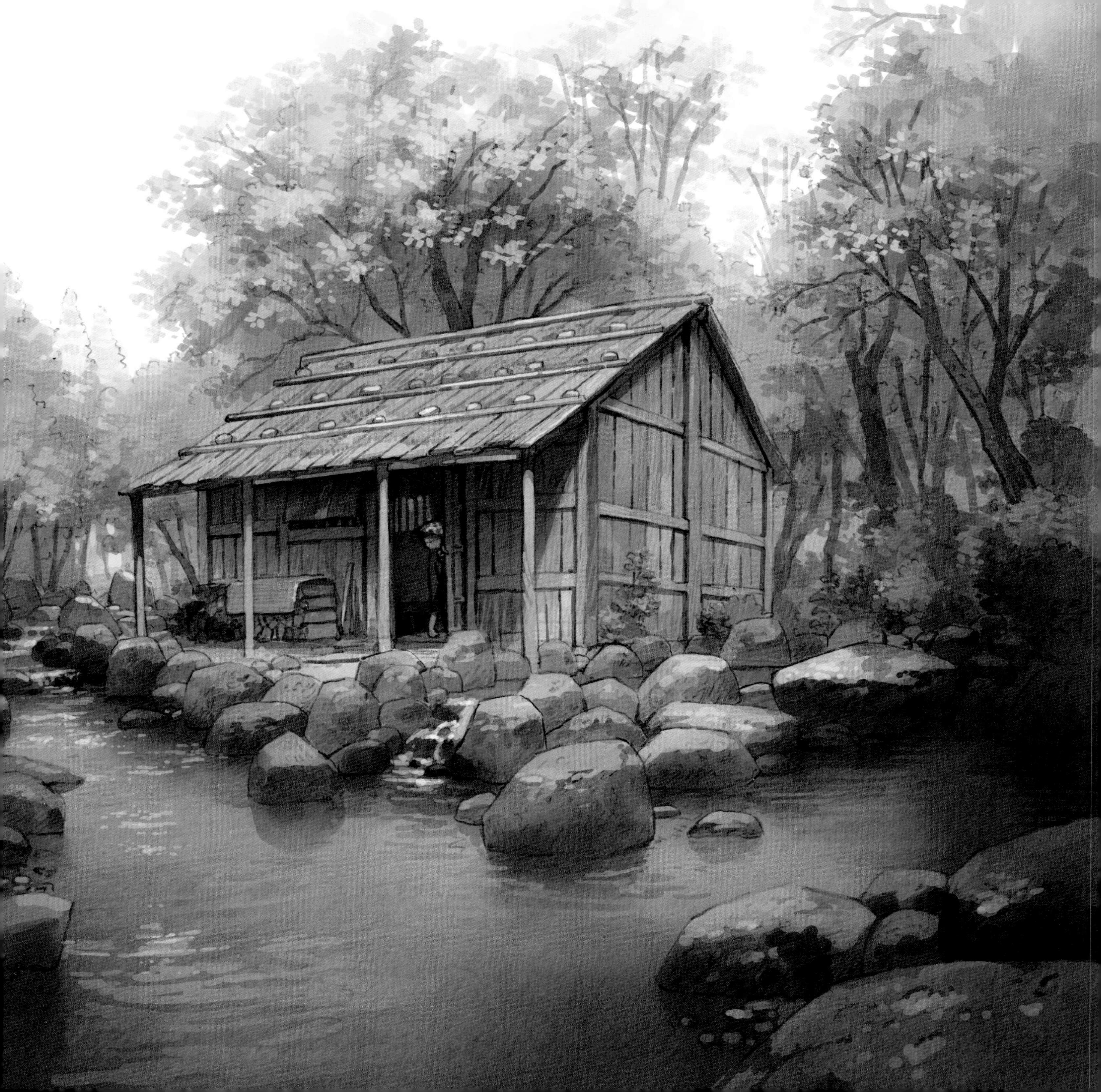

A Timid Ogre's Hideout

An ogre appeared and set up a home deep in the mountains. Though this ogre is very strong, he is very timid, and his greatest fear is being seen by humans. He would never dream of rampaging through a human village because of this. He scavenges tools from abandoned houses in the mountains and makes clever use of them to survive. He has a hot spring by the house he built, so he lives in relative comfort.

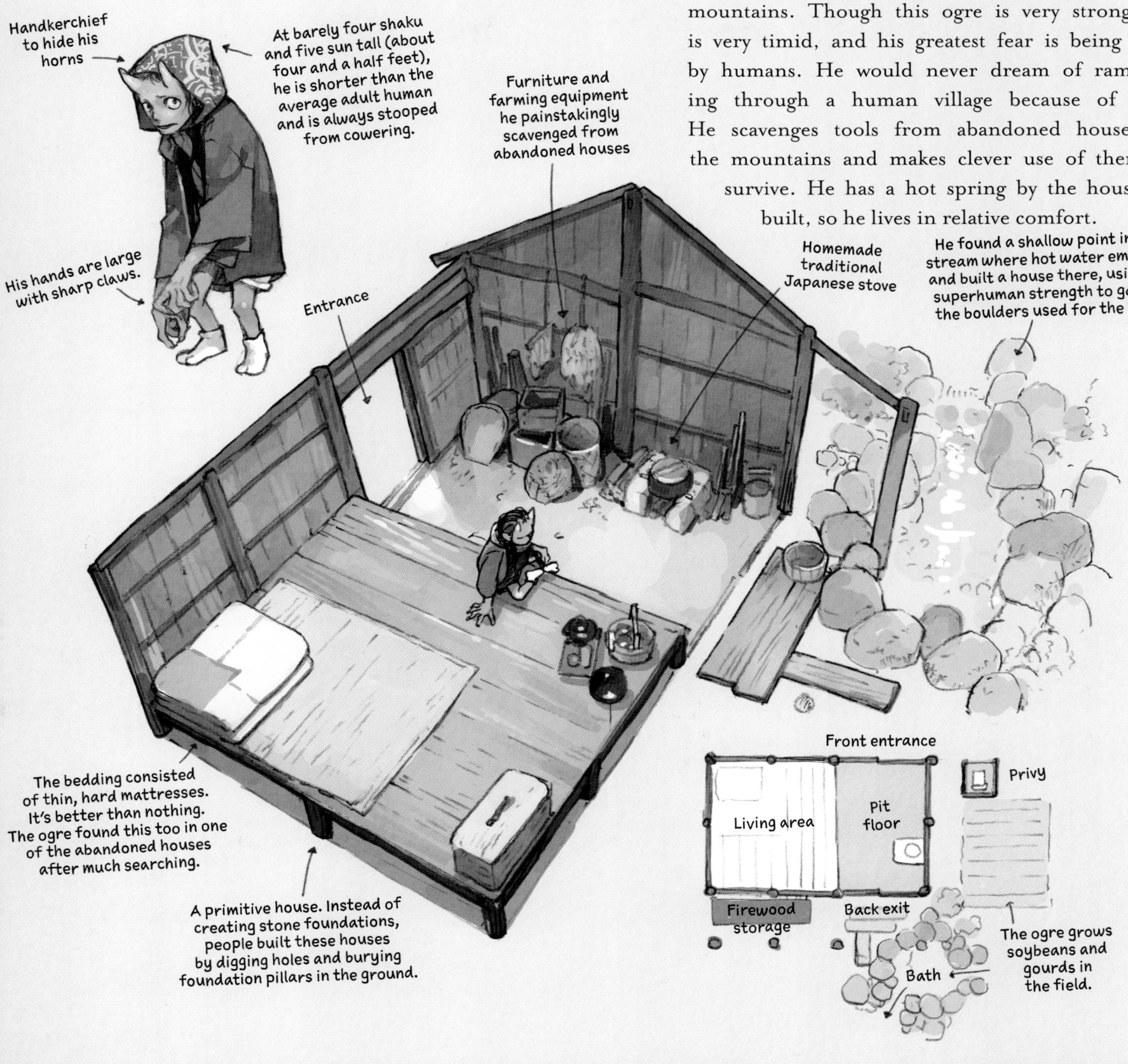

Handkerchief to hide his horns
At barely four shaku and five sun tall (about four and a half feet), he is shorter than the average adult human and is always stooped from cowering.
His hands are large with sharp claws.
Furniture and farming equipment he painstakingly scavenged from abandoned houses
Homemade traditional Japanese stove
He found a shallow point in the stream where hot water emerged and built a house there, using his superhuman strength to gather the boulders used for the bath.
Entrance
The bedding consisted of thin, hard mattresses. It's better than nothing. The ogre found this too in one of the abandoned houses after much searching.
A primitive house. Instead of creating stone foundations, people built these houses by digging holes and burying foundation pillars in the ground.
Front entrance
Privy
Living area
Pit floor
Firewood storage
Back exit
Bath
The ogre grows soybeans and gourds in the field.

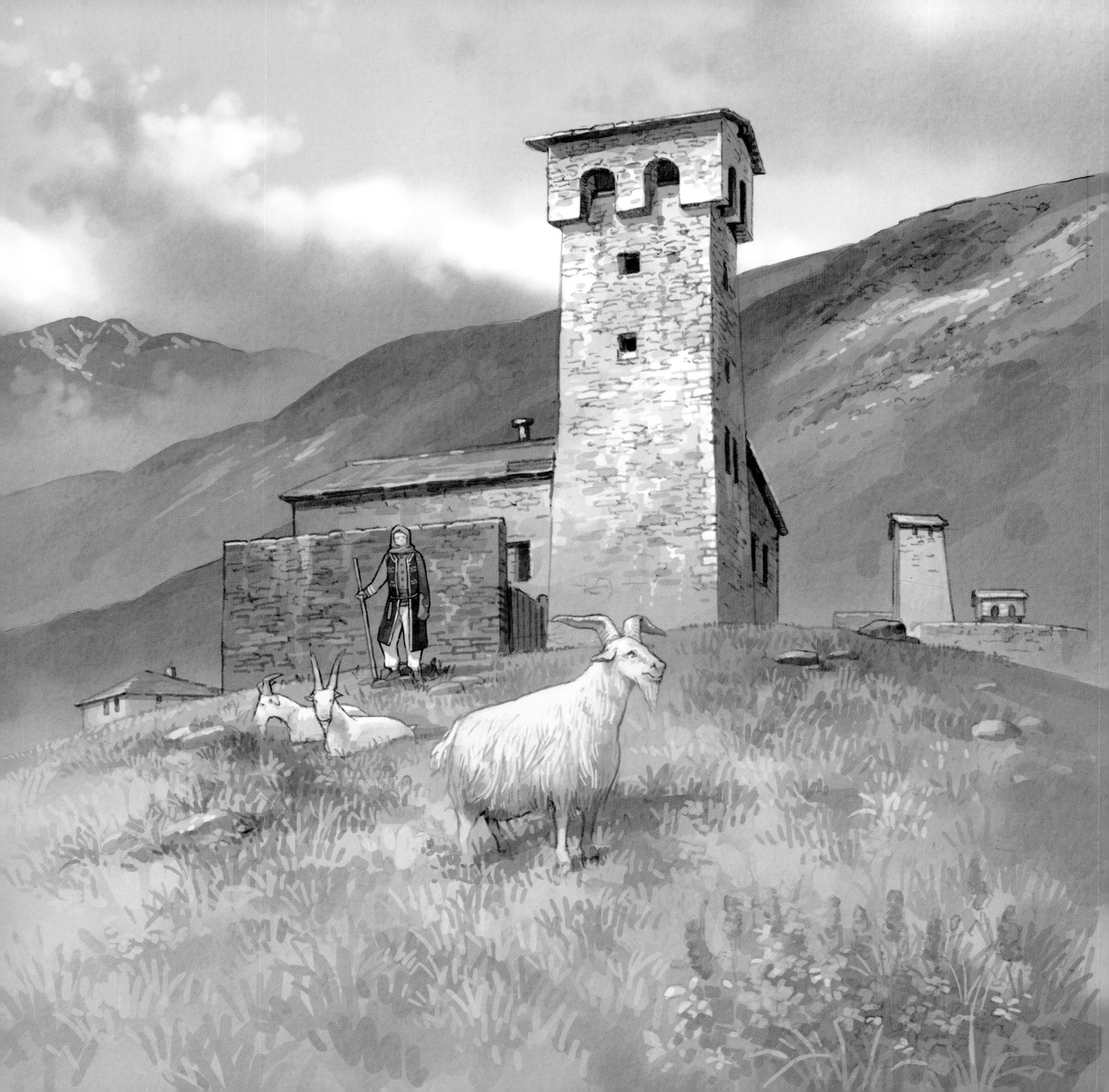

A Tower House Near the Border

This town, which lies very close to a border, has been subjected to war countless times. Because of that, the townspeople have erected tall tower houses so residents can live in confinement for long periods of time. In these sturdy towers, they store emergency food supplies, daily necessities, and even livestock so they can subsist inside for more than half a year at a time.

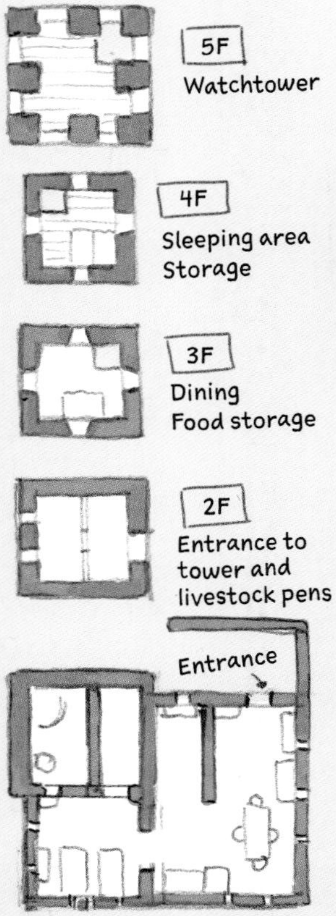

5F
Watchtower
4F
Sleeping area
Storage
3F
Dining
Food storage
2F
Entrance to tower and livestock pens
Entrance
1F
The living space during peaceful times. Normally the owners live here.

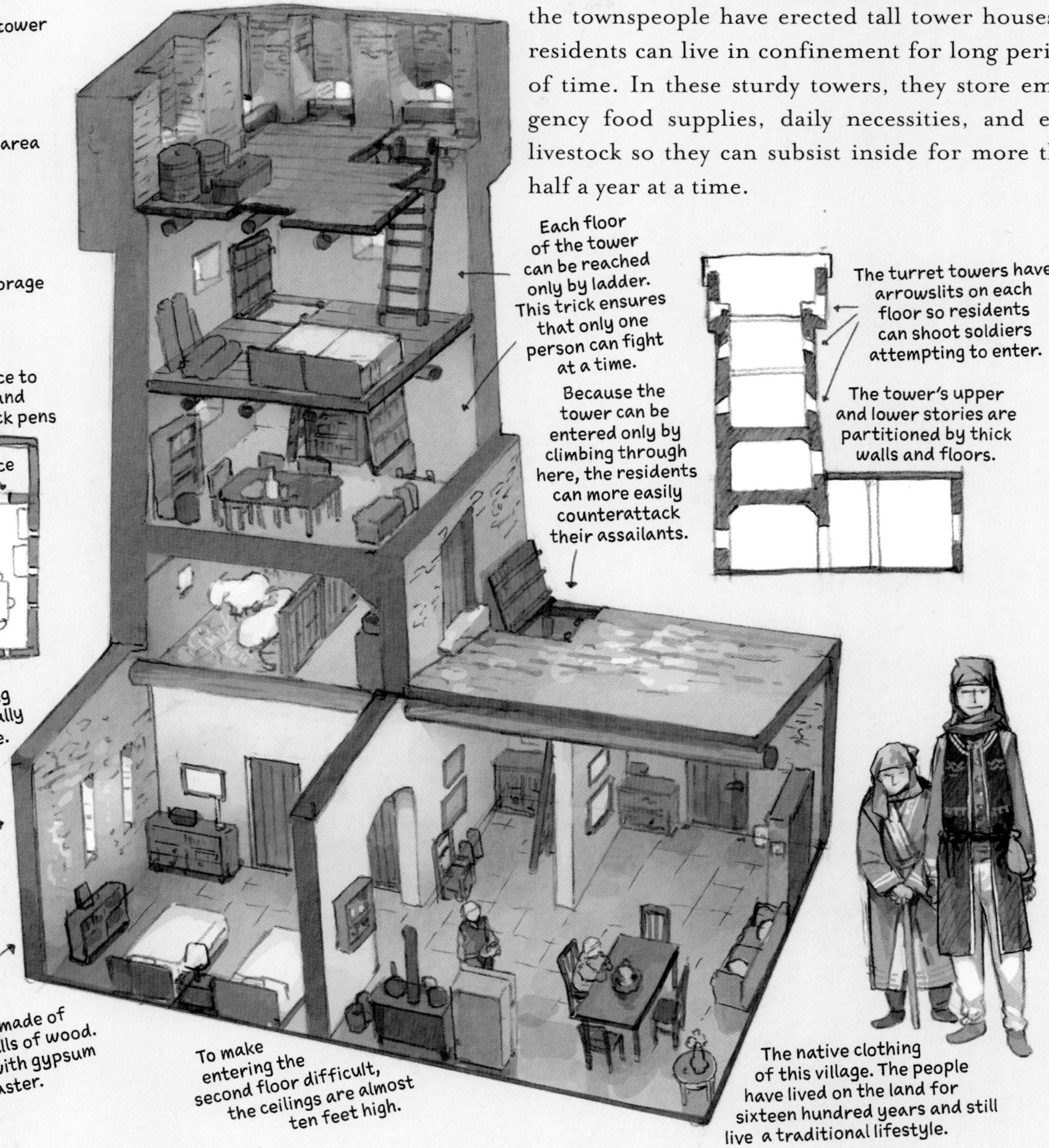

Each floor of the tower can be reached only by ladder. This trick ensures that only one person can fight at a time.
Because the tower can be entered only by climbing through here, the residents can more easily counterattack their assailants.
To protect against forced entry, the first-floor windows are slits.
The outer walls are made of stone and the inner walls of wood. Both are reinforced with gypsum mortar and plaster.
To make entering the second floor difficult, the ceilings are almost ten feet high.
The turret towers have arrowslits on each floor so residents can shoot soldiers attempting to enter.
The tower's upper and lower stories are partitioned by thick walls and floors.
The native clothing of this village. The people have lived on the land for sixteen hundred years and still live a traditional lifestyle.

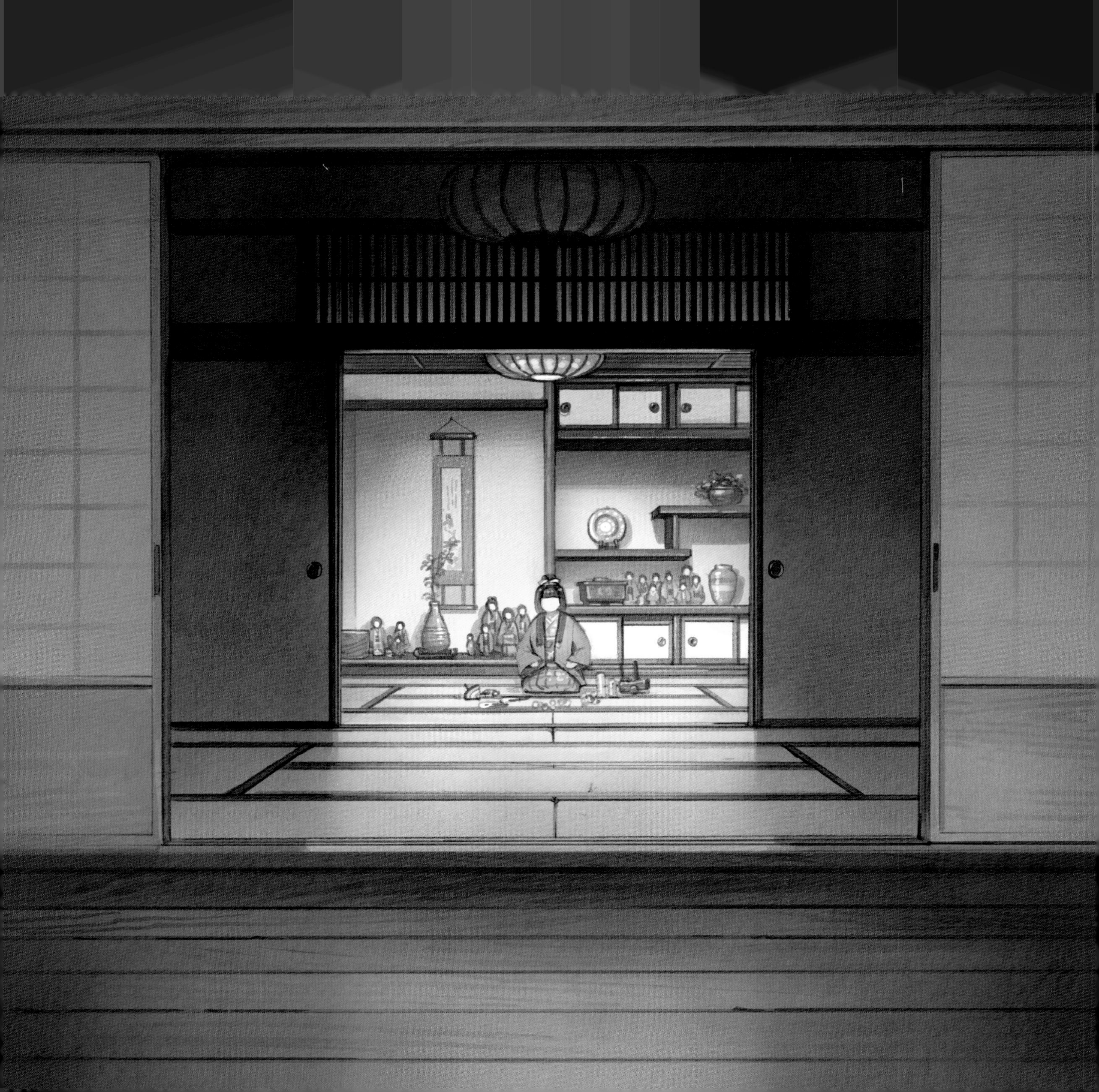

An Outbuilding Inhabited by a Poltergeist

The legends of zashiki-warashi, Japanese poltergeists, have been passed down throughout the Tohoku region. They are called zashiki-bokko, zashiki-kozo, or karako-warashi depending on the region. Most take a child's form and appear in the back rooms of old residences that feature zashiki (Japanese-style parlors) or in warehouses. They make noises or leave behind footprints, supposedly pulling harmless pranks. Houses that have resident zashiki-warashi tend to flourish, and when the ghosts leave, the households go into decline. Some regions still hold ceremonies to summon zashiki-warashi.

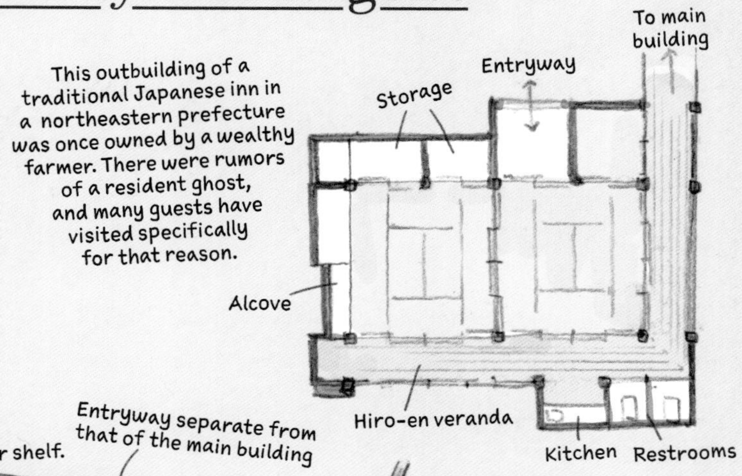
This outbuilding of a traditional Japanese inn in a northeastern prefecture was once owned by a wealthy farmer. There were rumors of a resident ghost, and many guests have visited specifically for that reason.
To main building
Entryway
Storage
Alcove
Hiro-en veranda
Kitchen
Restrooms

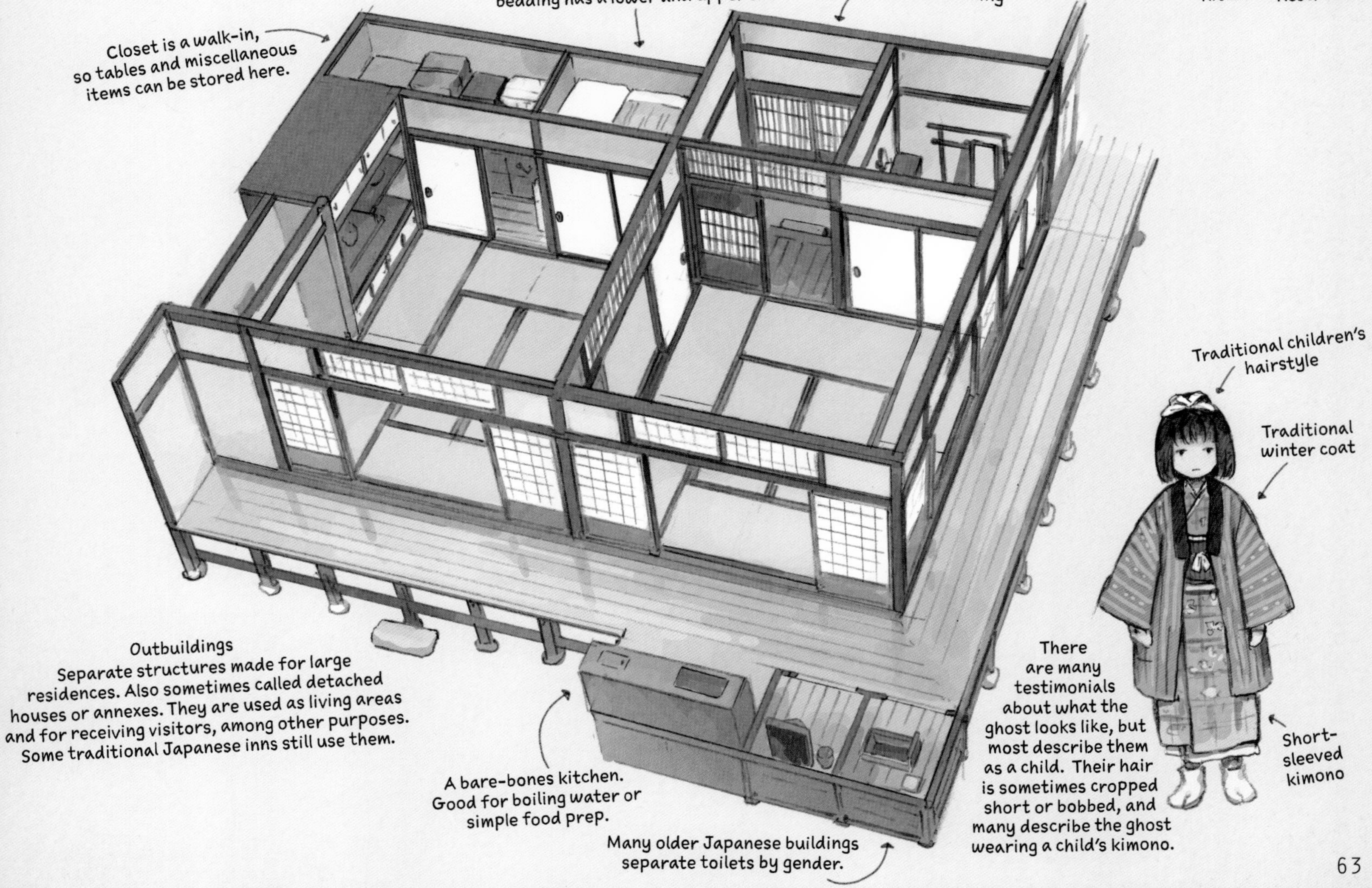
Storage built for bedding has a lower and upper shelf.
Entryway separate from that of the main building
Closet is a walk-in, so tables and miscellaneous items can be stored here.
Traditional children's hairstyle
Traditional winter coat
Outbuildings
Separate structures made for large residences. Also sometimes called detached houses or annexes. They are used as living areas and for receiving visitors, among other purposes. Some traditional Japanese inns still use them.
There are many testimonials about what the ghost looks like, but most describe them as a child. Their hair is sometimes cropped short or bobbed, and many describe the ghost wearing a child's kimono.
Short-sleeved kimono
A bare-bones kitchen. Good for boiling water or simple food prep.
Many older Japanese buildings separate toilets by gender.

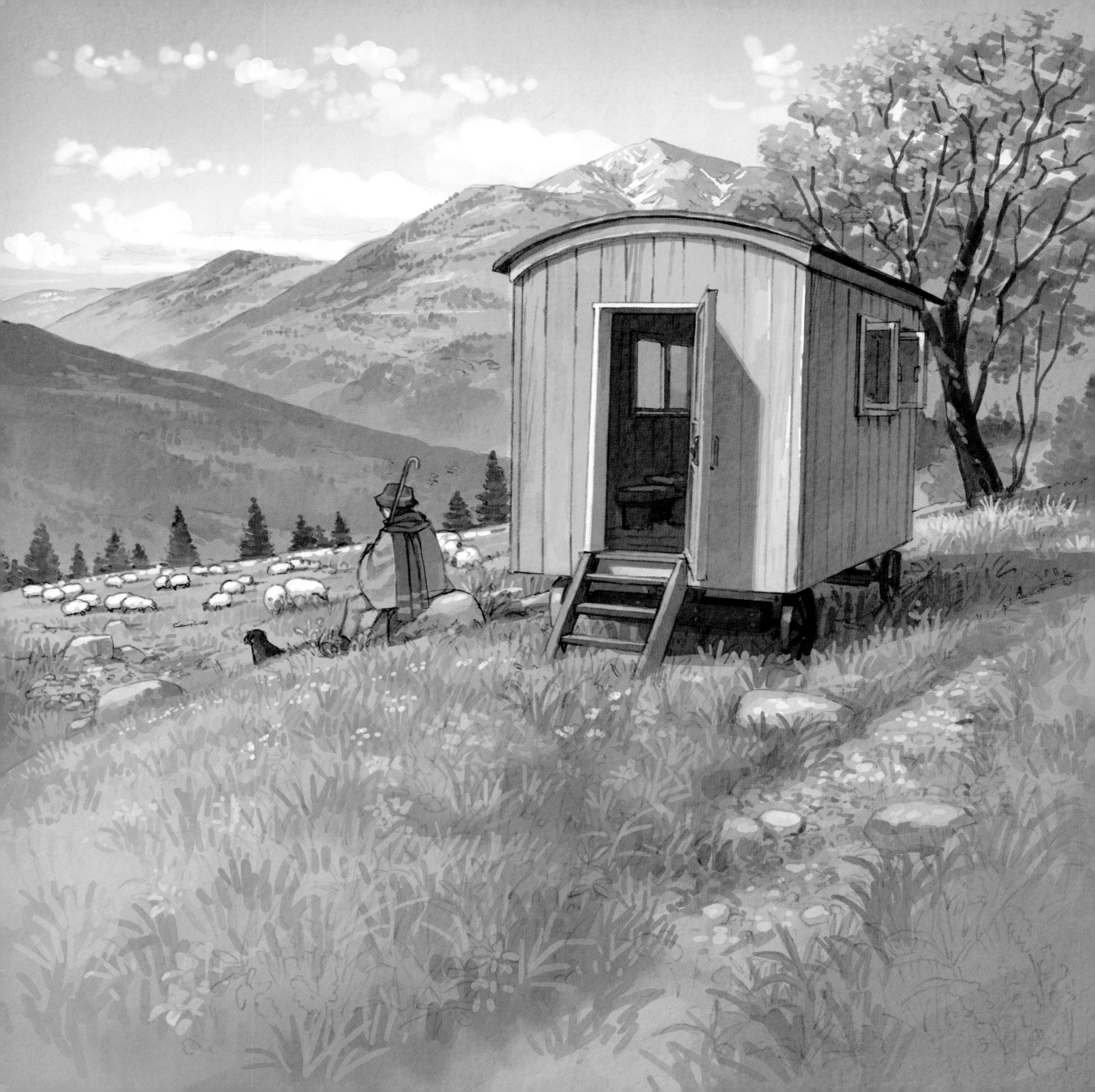

A Shepherd's Hut

Shepherding was one of the earliest occupations in history. Because it was difficult to make a living in mountainous regions where the flatland necessary for farming was scarce, many naturally gravitated toward herding. Shepherds often lived in groups, but some lived in small, portable huts and traveled with their flocks.

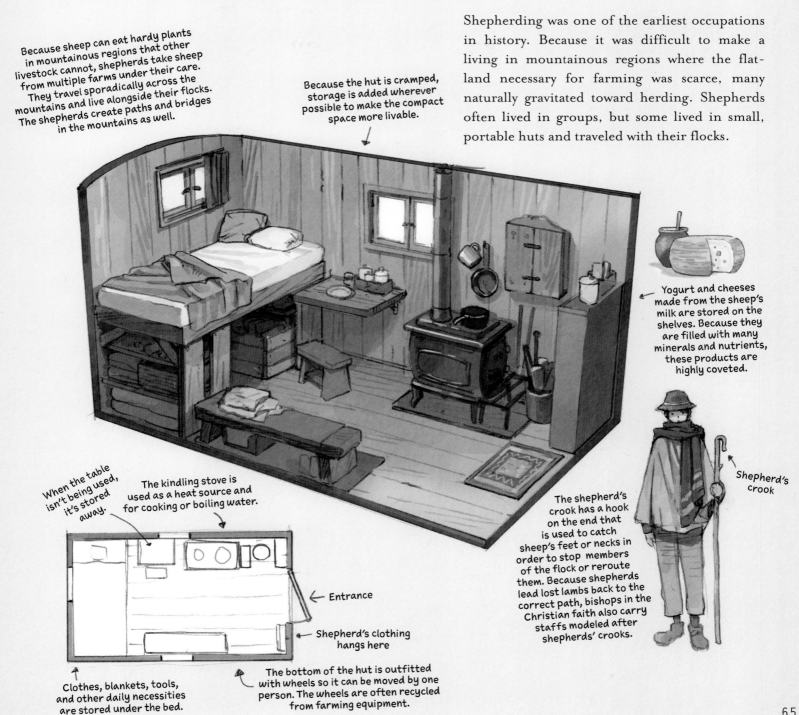

Because sheep can eat hardy plants in mountainous regions that other livestock cannot, shepherds take sheep from multiple farms under their care. They travel sporadically across the mountains and live alongside their flocks. The shepherds create paths and bridges in the mountains as well.

Because the hut is cramped, storage is added wherever possible to make the compact space more livable.

Yogurt and cheeses made from the sheep's milk are stored on the shelves. Because they are filled with many minerals and nutrients, these products are highly coveted.

When the table isn't being used, it's stored away.

The kindling stove is used as a heat source and for cooking or boiling water.

← Entrance

← Shepherd's clothing hangs here

Clothes, blankets, tools, and other daily necessities are stored under the bed.

The bottom of the hut is outfitted with wheels so it can be moved by one person. The wheels are often recycled from farming equipment.

The shepherd's crook has a hook on the end that is used to catch sheep's feet or necks in order to stop members of the flock or reroute them. Because shepherds lead lost lambs back to the correct path, bishops in the Christian faith also carry staffs modeled after shepherds' crooks.

Shepherd's crook

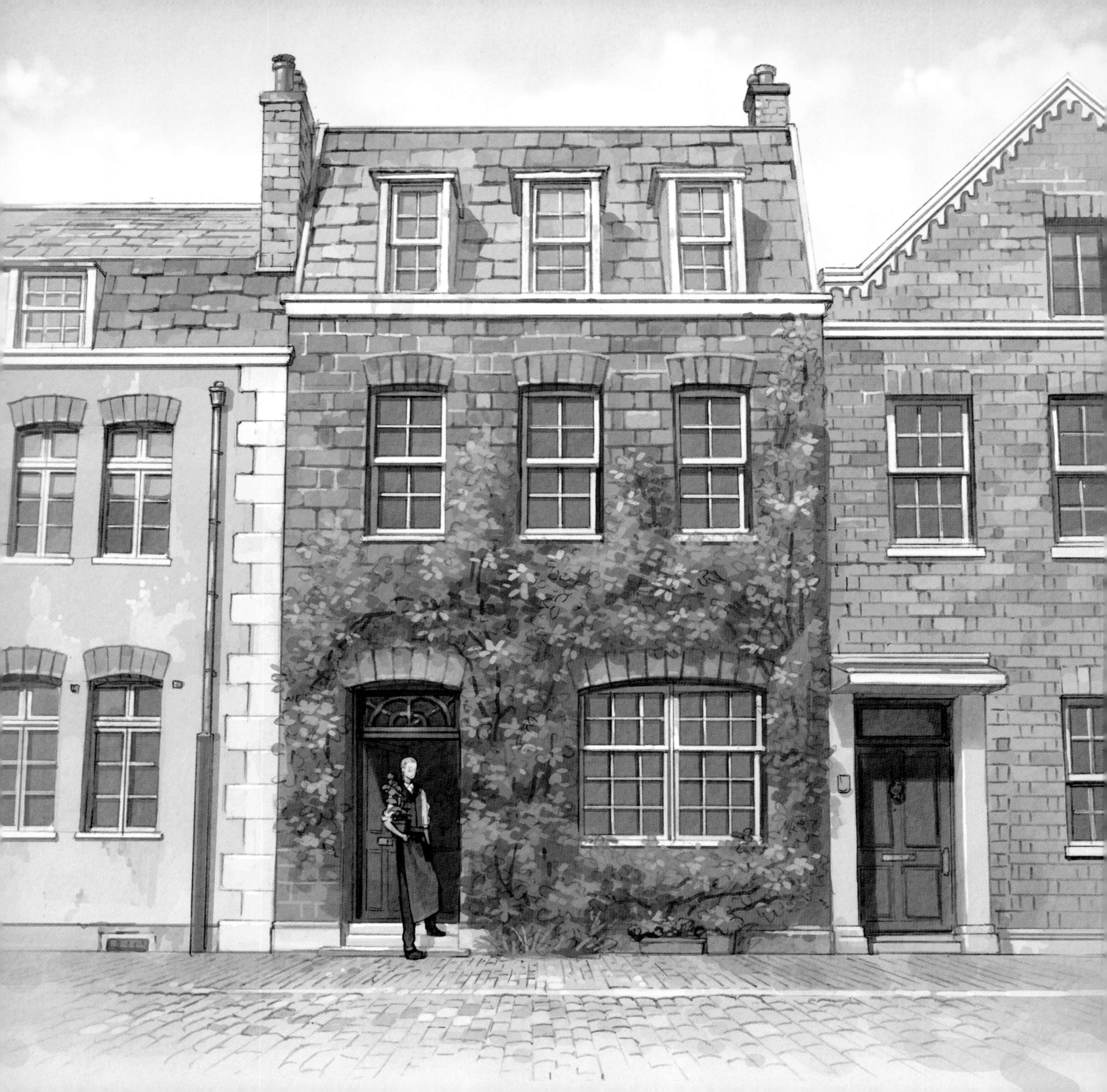

An Eccentric Botanist's Laboratory

Though many grow plants simply because they are soothing, this botanist is enamored with them out of scientific interest. His lab has been taken over by plants, and he has reconstructed the whole facility to serve their needs. He strives to create a comfortable environment for the plants like no other. In fact, this may be the epitome of a human cohabitating with vegetation.

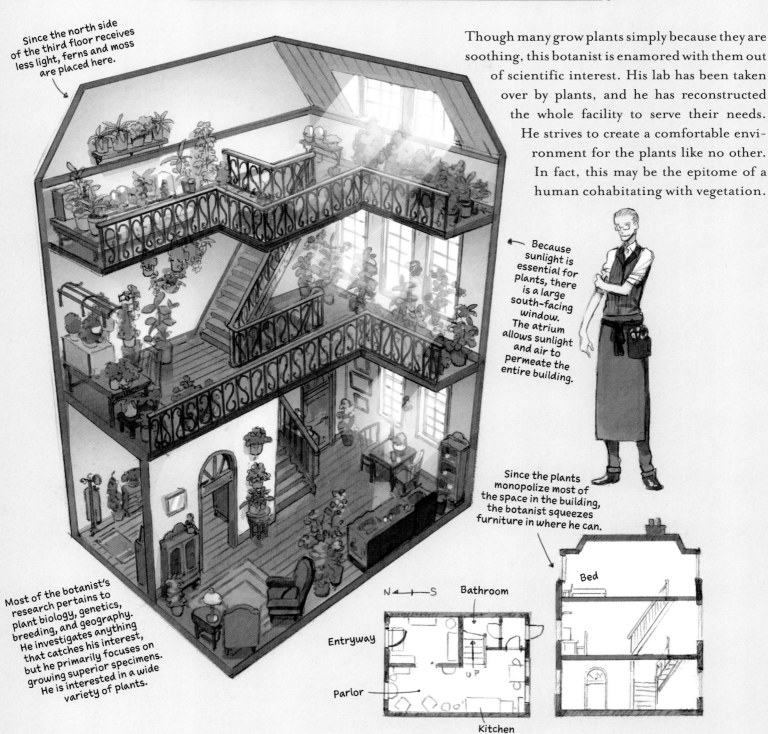

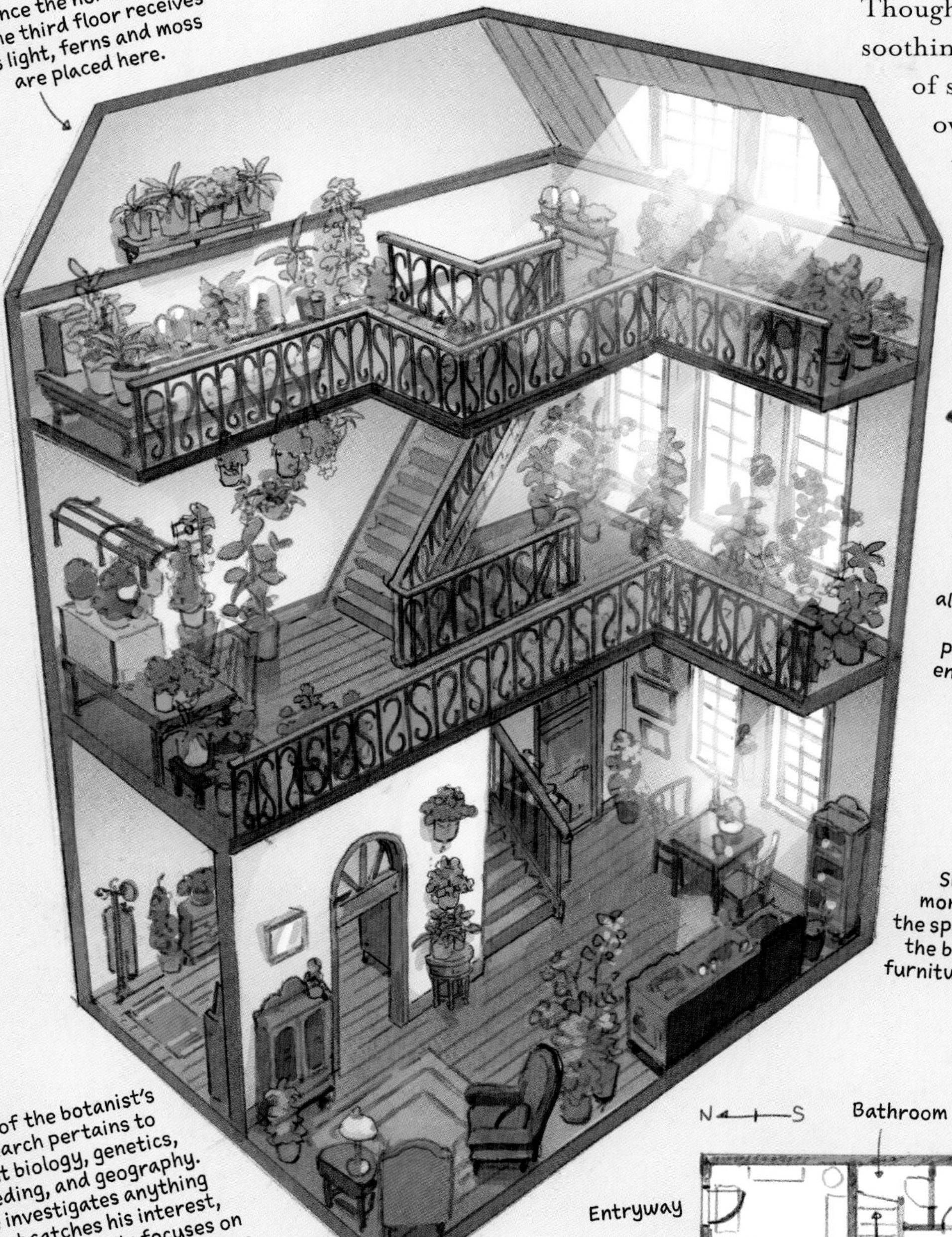
Since the north side of the third floor receives less light, ferns and moss are placed here.
Because sunlight is essential for plants, there is a large south-facing window. The atrium allows sunlight and air to permeate the entire building.
Most of the botanist's research pertains to plant biology, genetics, breeding, and geography. He investigates anything that catches his interest, but he primarily focuses on growing superior specimens. He is interested in a wide variety of plants.

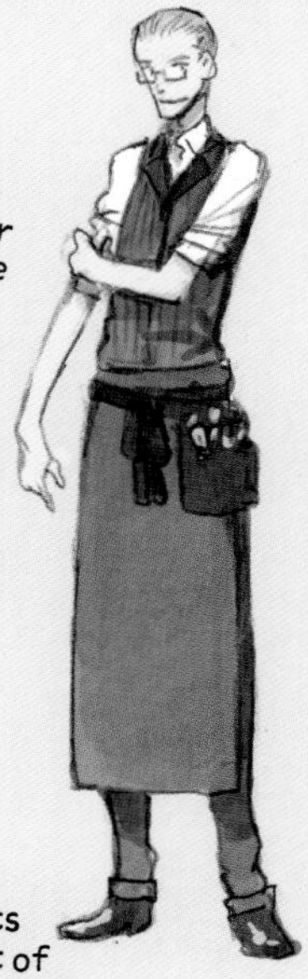

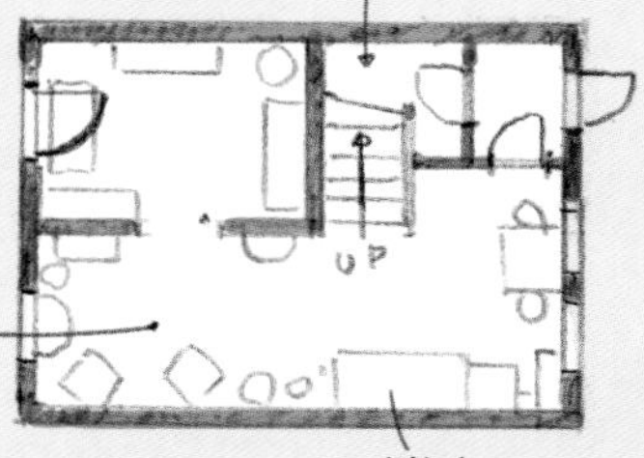
N S
Bathroom
Entryway
UP
Parlor
Kitchen

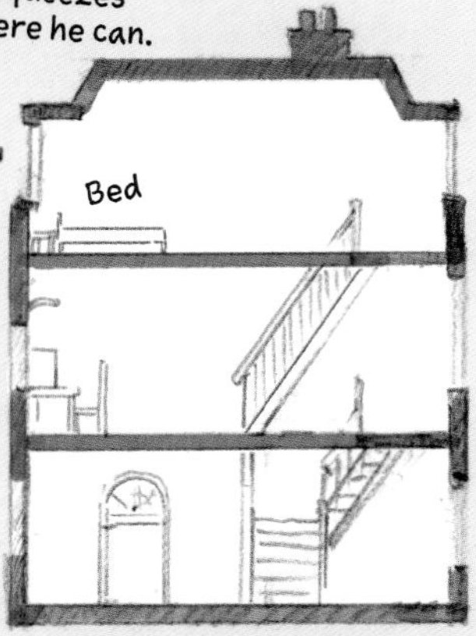
Since the plants monopolize most of the space in the building, the botanist squeezes furniture in where he can.
Bed

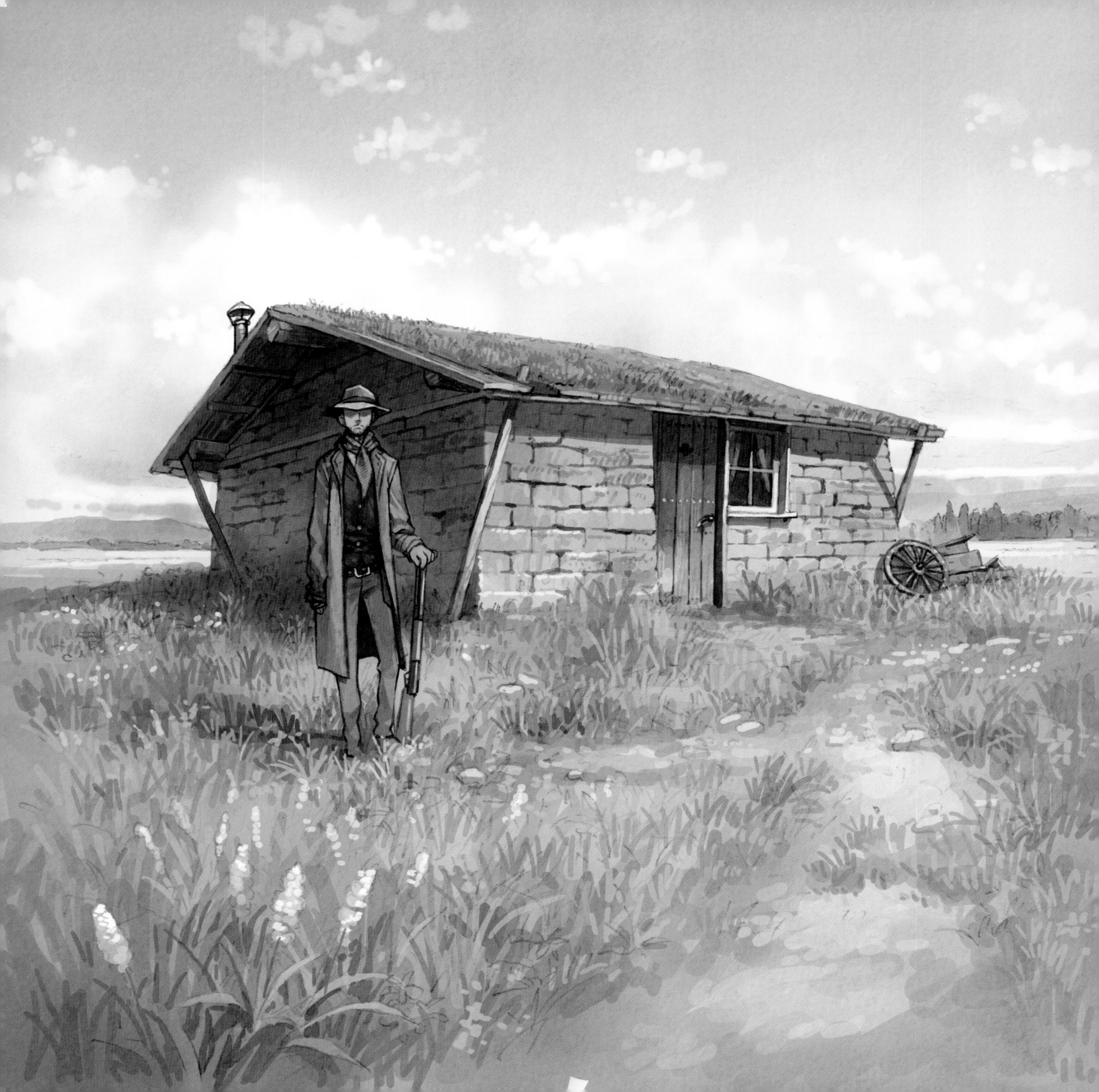

A Wanted Man's Sod House

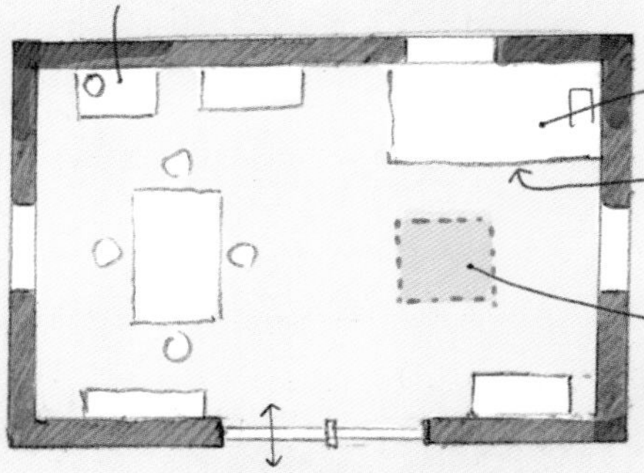

Stove
Bed
Under the bed is a tin filled with decoy money.
The man has dug a hole in the floor to act as a makeshift safe. The boards and dirt placed on top camouflage his loot.
Entrance

The Great Plains has limited wood and rock, which are typically used as construction materials, so instead, readily available sod was cut and stacked to form the walls of this sod house. Though these dwellings deteriorated easily and required regular maintenance, their attraction was that they were cheap to build and adaptable. This rather cramped house is inhabited by a wanted man. Based on the way he carefully hides his money, which was likely acquired through a stagecoach robbery or a similar theft, it is unclear whether he betrayed his companions and took the spoils for himself or was simply the only survivor.

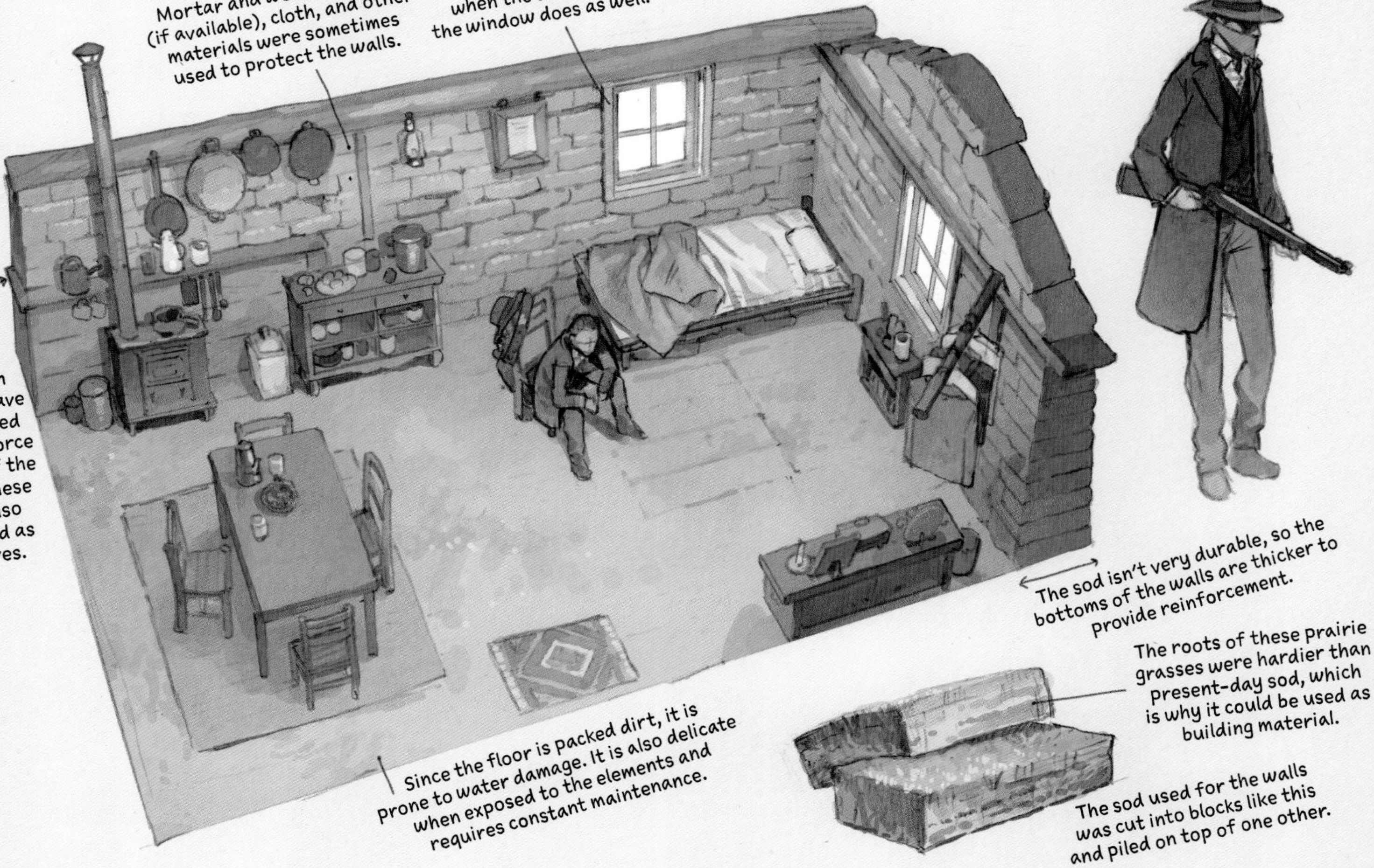

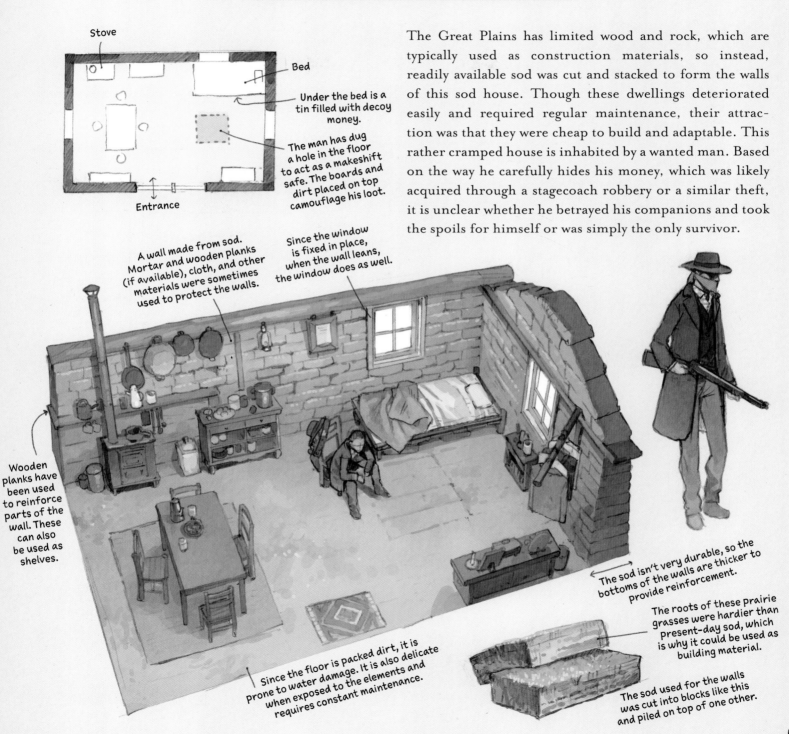

A wall made from sod. Mortar and wooden planks (if available), cloth, and other materials were sometimes used to protect the walls.
Since the window is fixed in place, when the wall leans, the window does as well.
Wooden planks have been used to reinforce parts of the wall. These can also be used as shelves.
The sod isn't very durable, so the bottoms of the walls are thicker to provide reinforcement.
The roots of these prairie grasses were hardier than present-day sod, which is why it could be used as building material.
Since the floor is packed dirt, it is prone to water damage. It is also delicate when exposed to the elements and requires constant maintenance.
The sod used for the walls was cut into blocks like this and piled on top of one other.

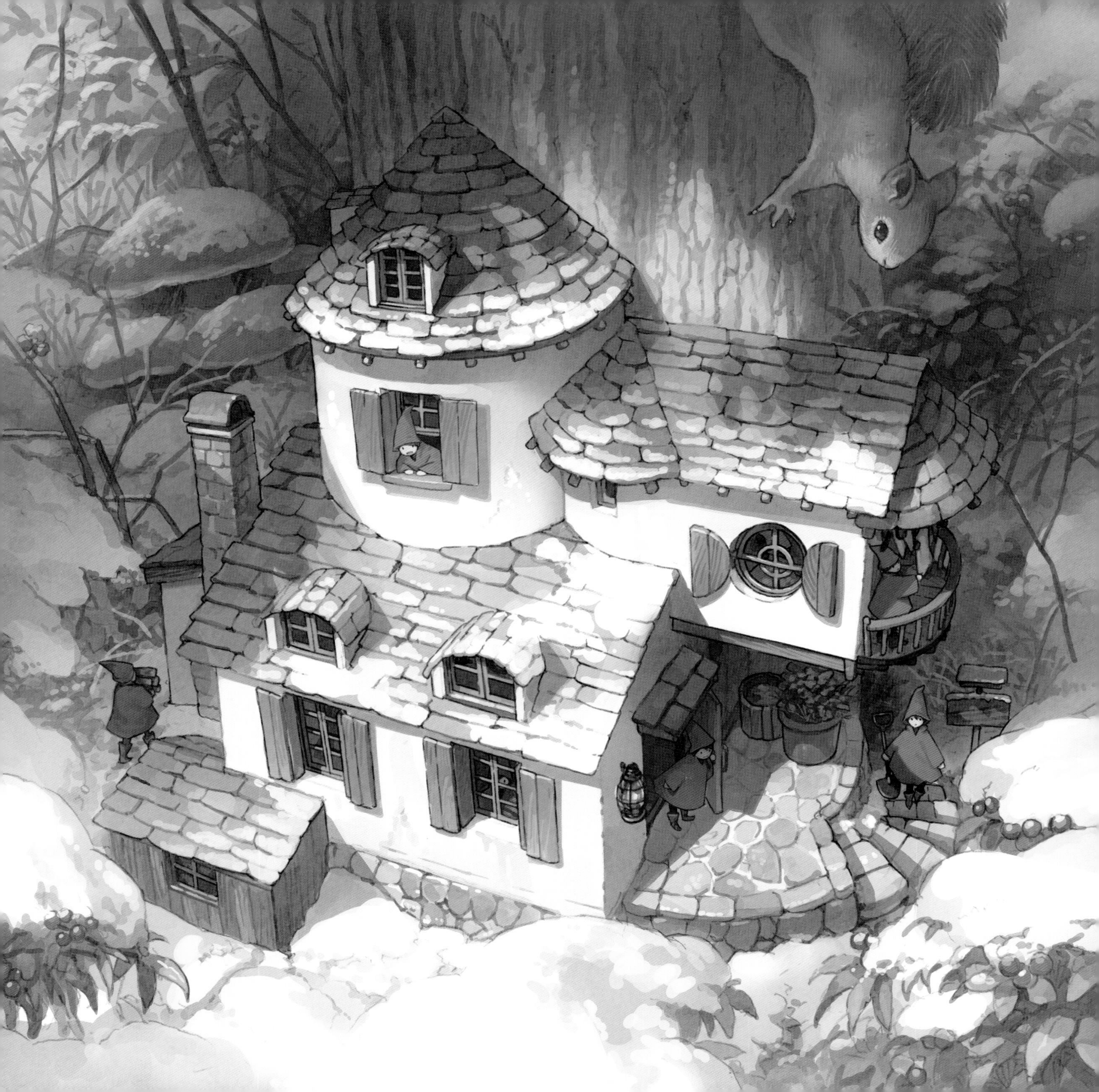

The Seven Dwarfs' House

This is a house for the seven dwarves who appear in Grimms' tale about Snow White. Dwarves have a brawny workman-like image nowadays, but they were originally more like sprites—the merry type that live deep in the woods or dwell in holes and are disposed toward mischief. They live a communal lifestyle and stay in the house during the winter, so a roof that mimics their charming triangular hats seemed fitting.

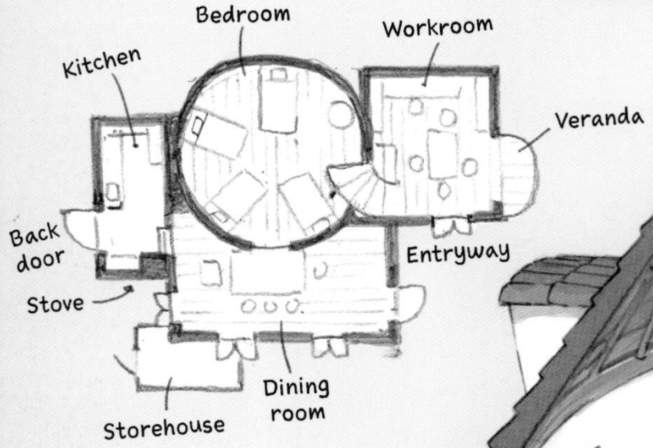
Bedroom
Workroom
Kitchen
Veranda
Back door
Entryway
Stove
Dining room
Storehouse

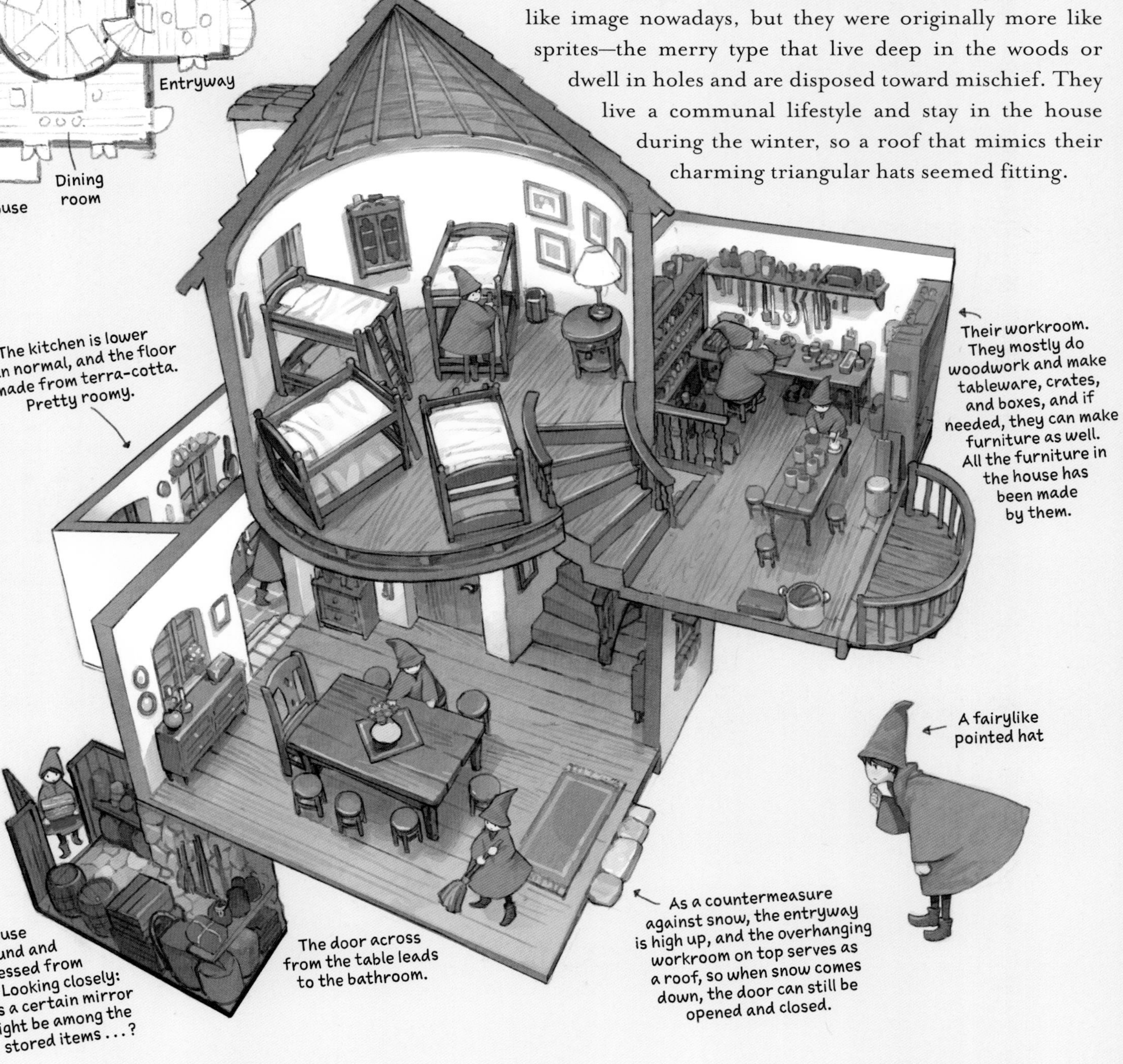
The kitchen is lower than normal, and the floor is made from terra-cotta. Pretty roomy.
Their workroom. They mostly do woodwork and make tableware, crates, and boxes, and if needed, they can make furniture as well. All the furniture in the house has been made by them.
A fairylike pointed hat
The storehouse is underground and can be accessed from outdoors. Looking closely: it seems a certain mirror might be among the stored items . . . ?
The door across from the table leads to the bathroom.
As a countermeasure against snow, the entryway is high up, and the overhanging workroom on top serves as a roof, so when snow comes down, the door can still be opened and closed.

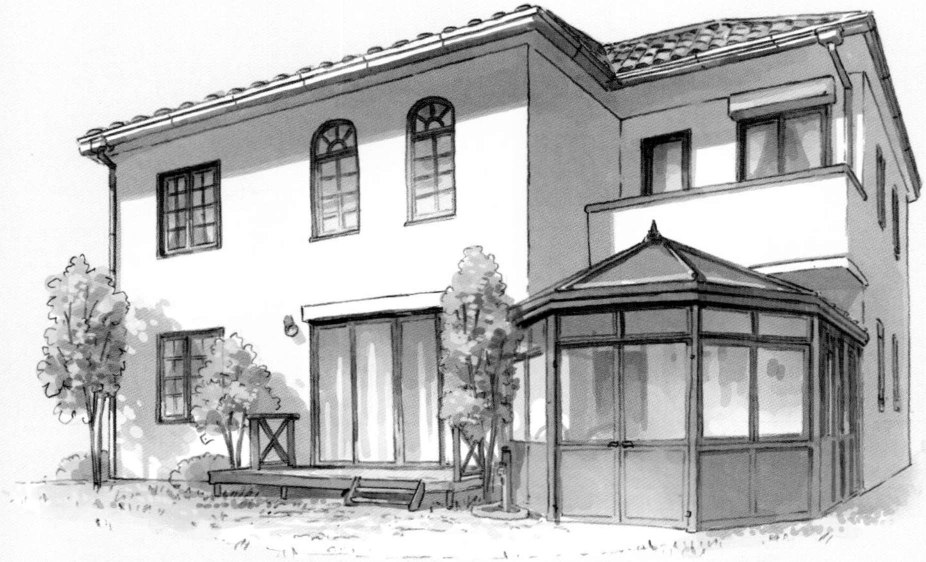

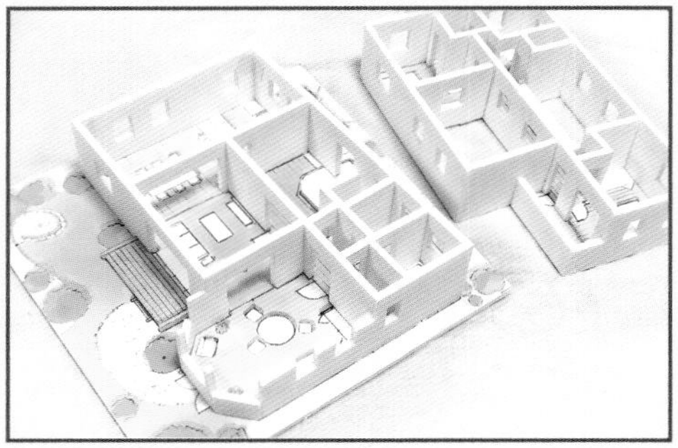

I've created a simple architectural model of the House with a Dragon for display. These are relatively easy for anyone to make by cutting out a floor plan and gluing store-bought foam board to the paper. Models can make a home seem more lifelike than blueprints. Another merit is that the flow of the plan is more plainly visible, so I recommend trying it out if you enjoy handicrafts.

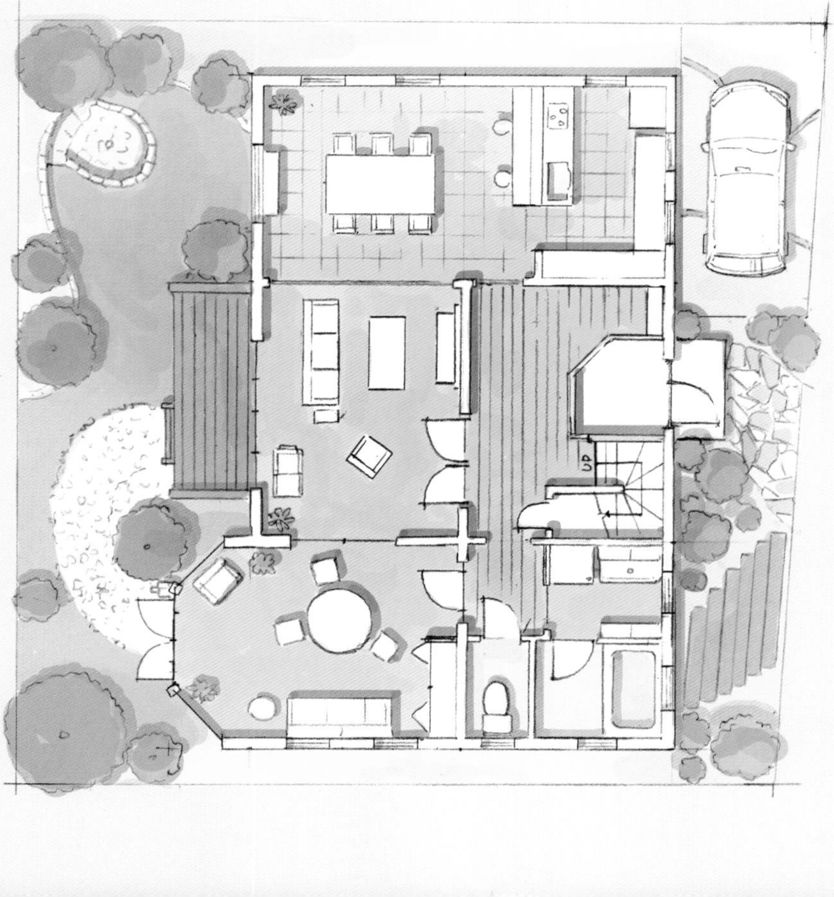
UP

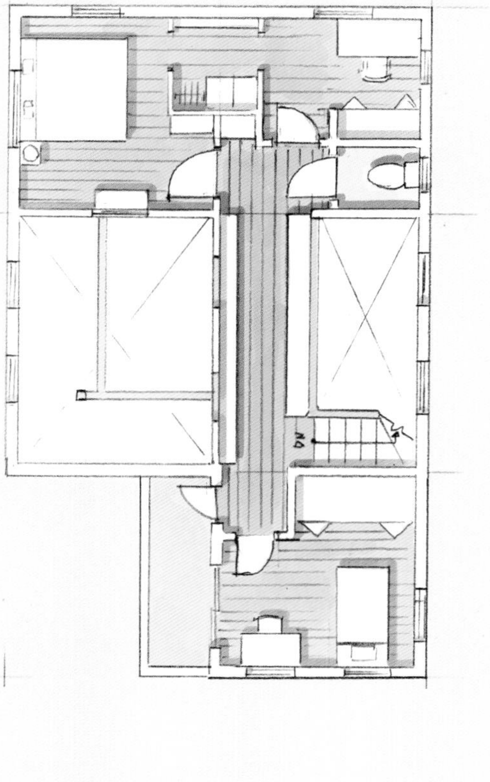
DN

House with a Dragon

This is a house designed for living with a pet dragon. The living room has a beam the dragon can walk along. There are two large atria as well as many other clever features that make living with a dragon feasible.

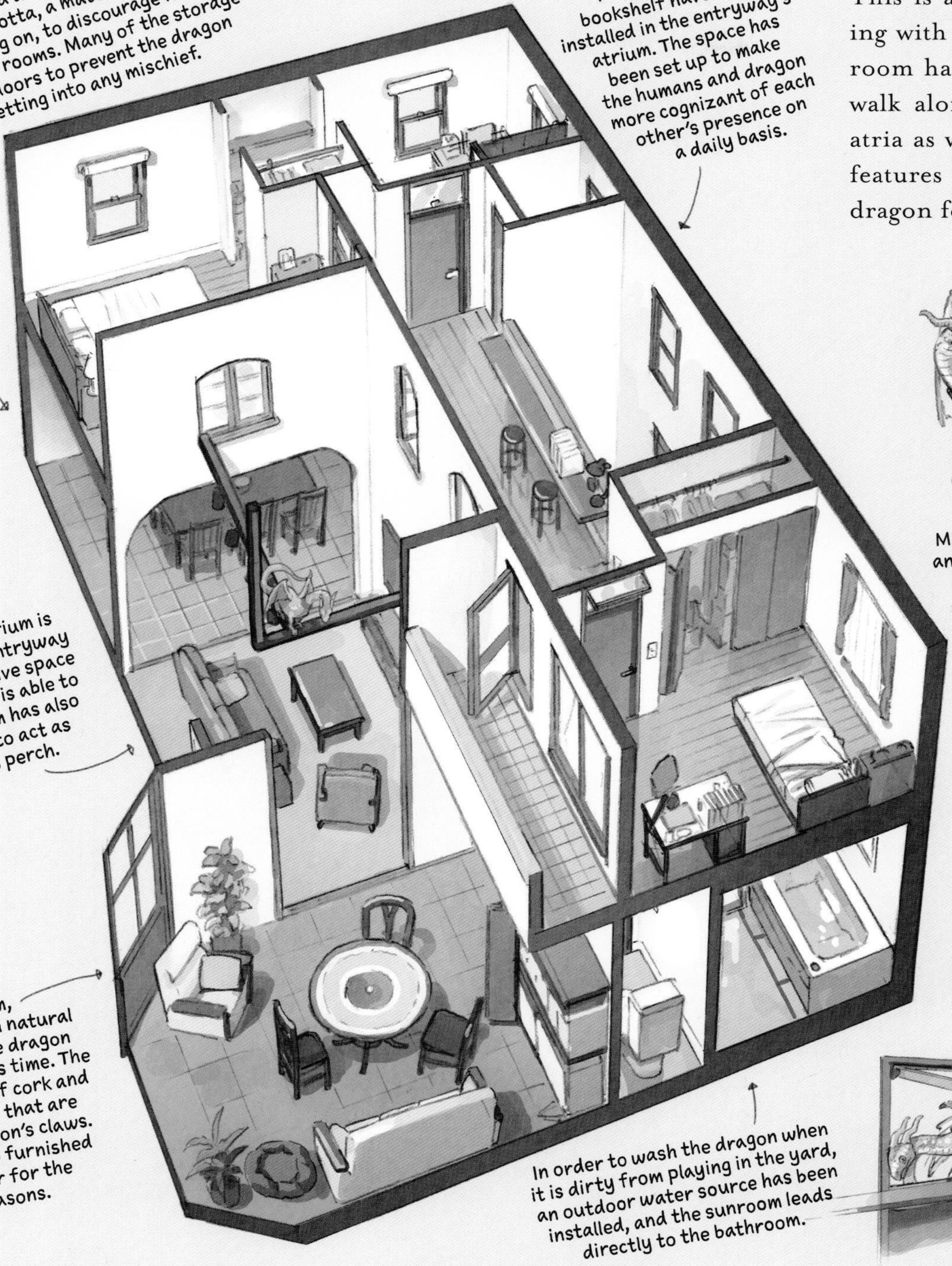

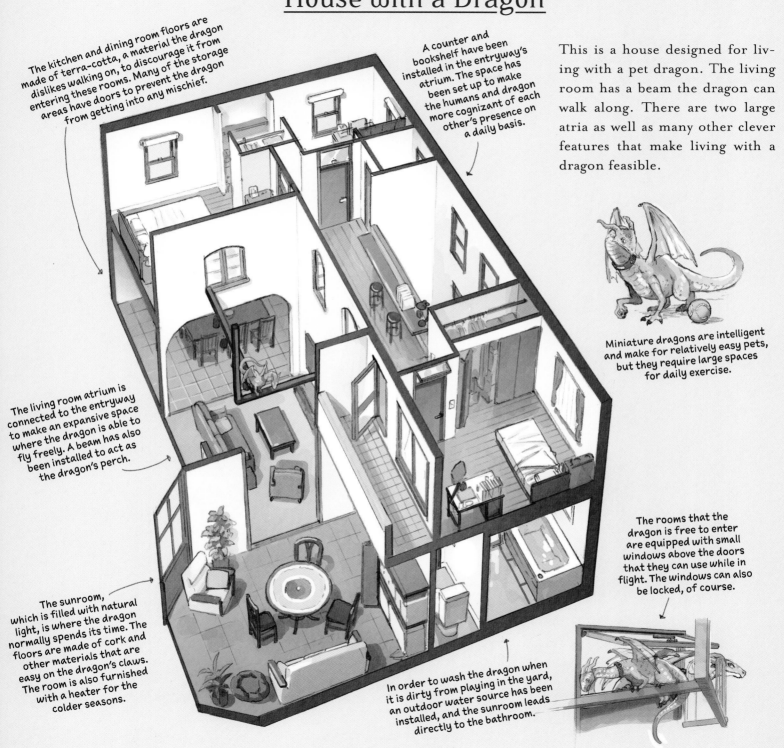

The kitchen and dining room floors are made of terra-cotta, a material the dragon dislikes walking on, to discourage it from entering these rooms. Many of the storage areas have doors to prevent the dragon from getting into any mischief.
A counter and bookshelf have been installed in the entryway's atrium. The space has been set up to make the humans and dragon more cognizant of each other's presence on a daily basis.
The living room atrium is connected to the entryway to make an expansive space where the dragon is able to fly freely. A beam has also been installed to act as the dragon's perch.
The sunroom, which is filled with natural light, is where the dragon normally spends its time. The floors are made of cork and other materials that are easy on the dragon's claws. The room is also furnished with a heater for the colder seasons.
In order to wash the dragon when it is dirty from playing in the yard, an outdoor water source has been installed, and the sunroom leads directly to the bathroom.

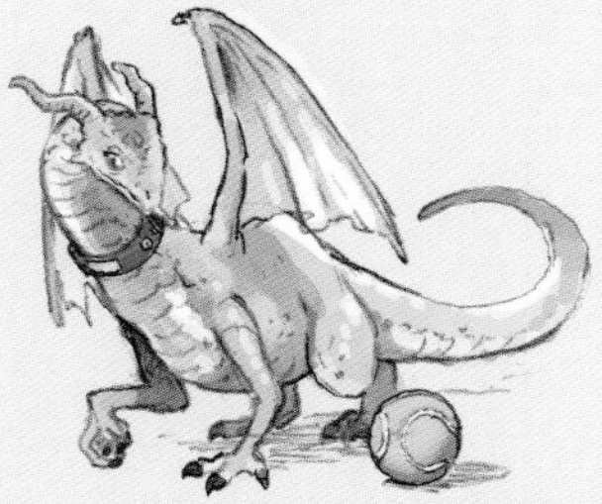

Miniature dragons are intelligent and make for relatively easy pets, but they require large spaces for daily exercise.

The rooms that the dragon is free to enter are equipped with small windows above the doors that they can use while in flight. The windows can also be locked, of course.

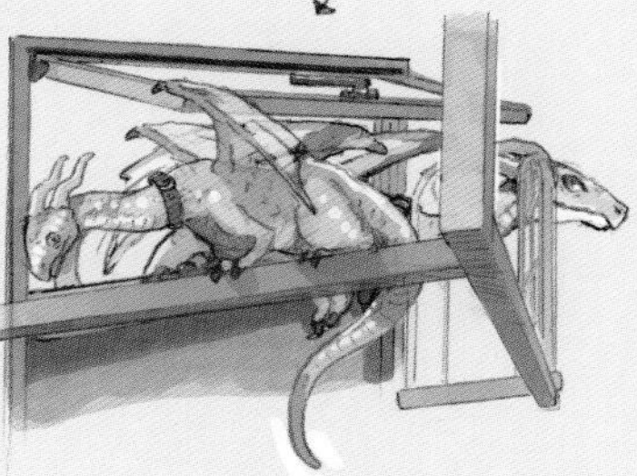

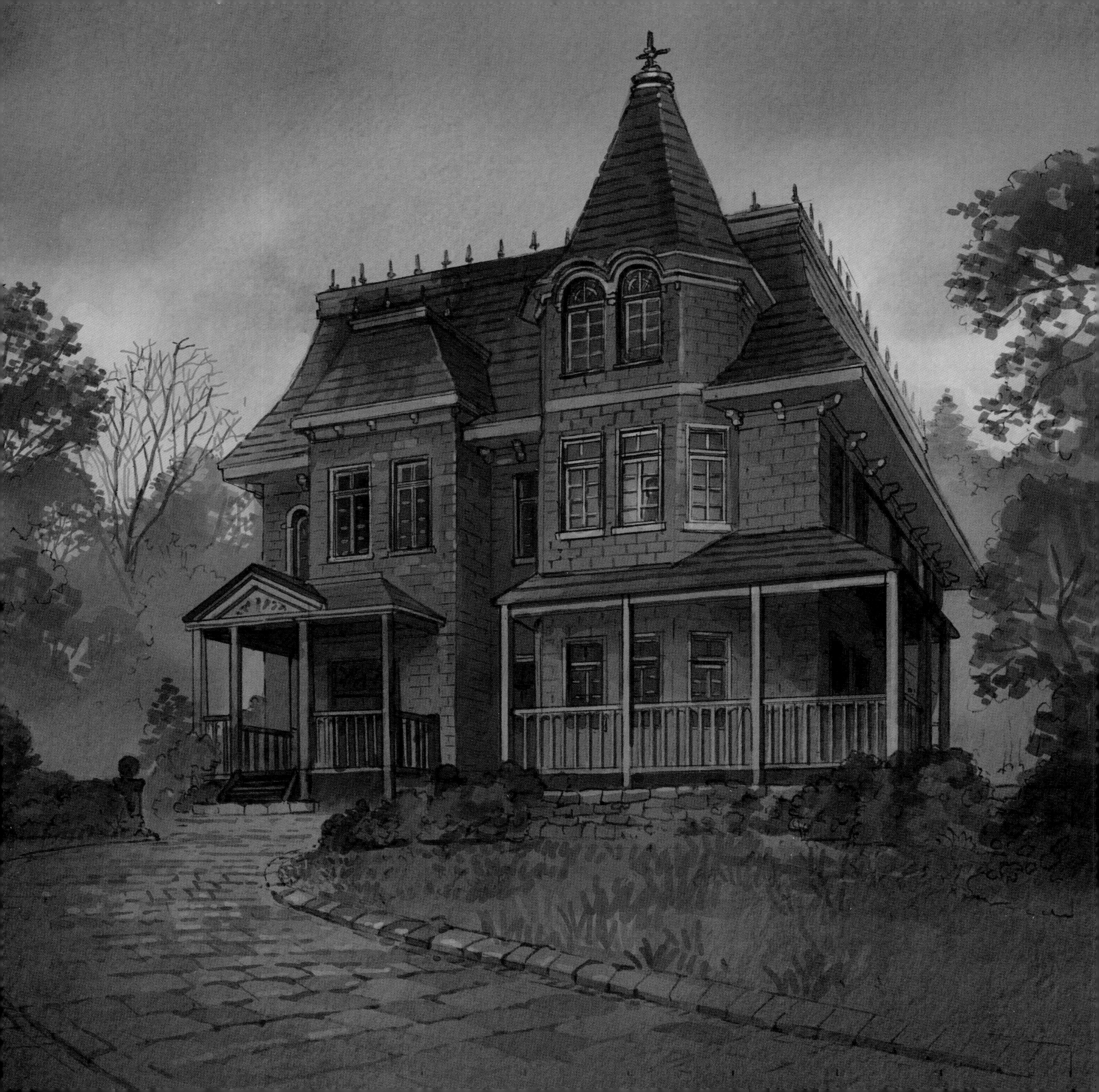

A Lonely Ghost's Mansion

Though somewhat dated, this mansion is of sturdy construction. At present, it is empty, and no buyers have come forward because a ghost is rumored to live here. A family that once lived in the house had a small girl who supposedly died young. It's said that the ghost is that very girl. Kids who have heard the rumors sometimes dare each other to go into the house.

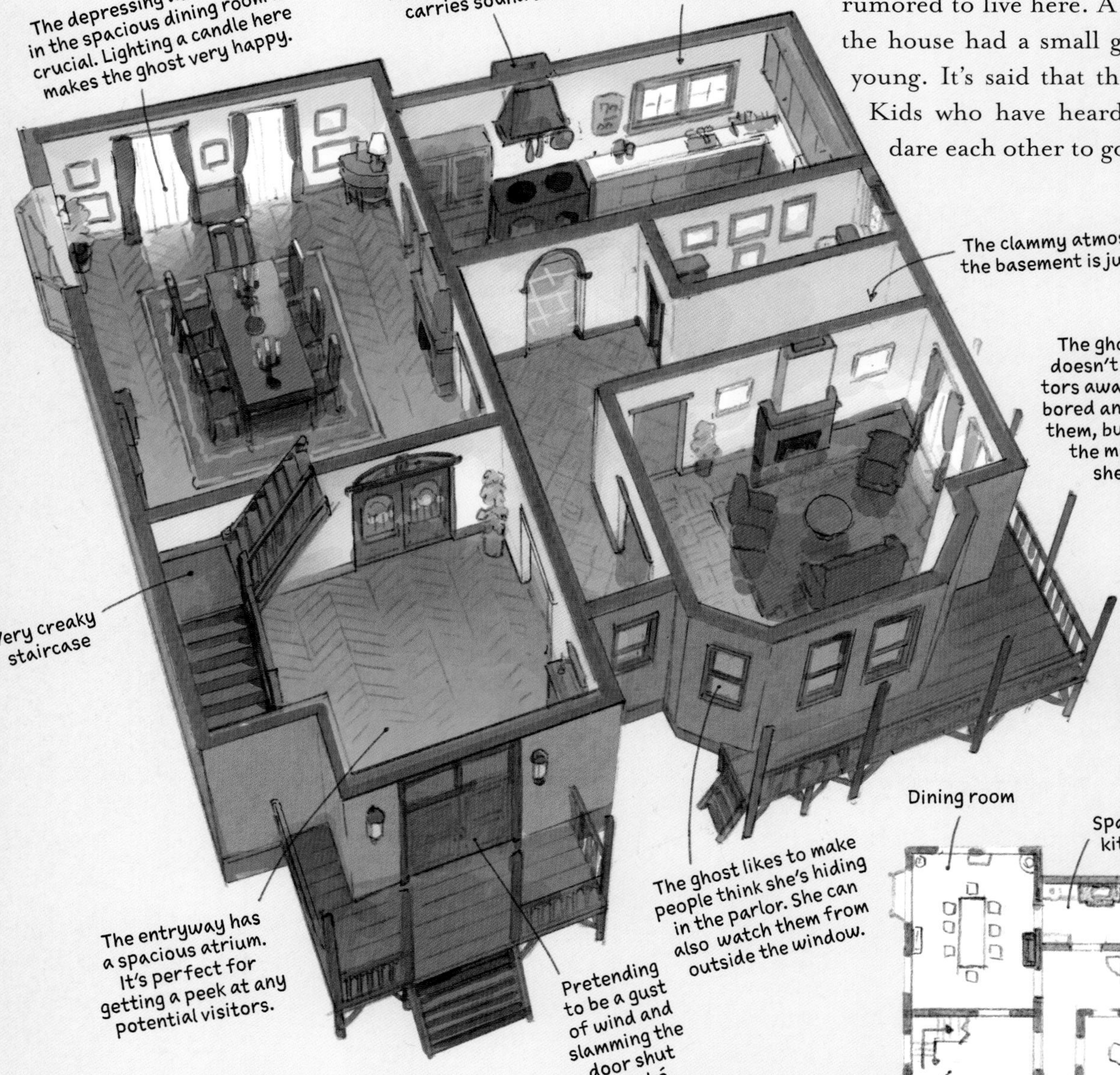
The depressing atmosphere in the spacious dining room is crucial. Lighting a candle here makes the ghost very happy.
Handy stovepipe that carries sound well
Many objects in the kitchen for rattling about
The clammy atmosphere in the basement is just divine!
Very creaky staircase
The entryway has a spacious atrium. It's perfect for getting a peek at any potential visitors.
Pretending to be a gust of wind and slamming the door shut is cliché, yet effective.
The ghost likes to make people think she's hiding in the parlor. She can also watch them from outside the window.

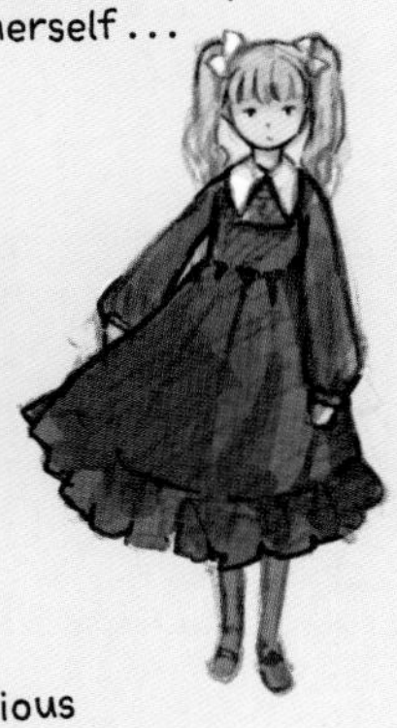
The ghost of the little girl doesn't mean to chase visitors away. She's actually just bored and wants to play with them, but when they come in the middle of the night, she just can't help herself . . .

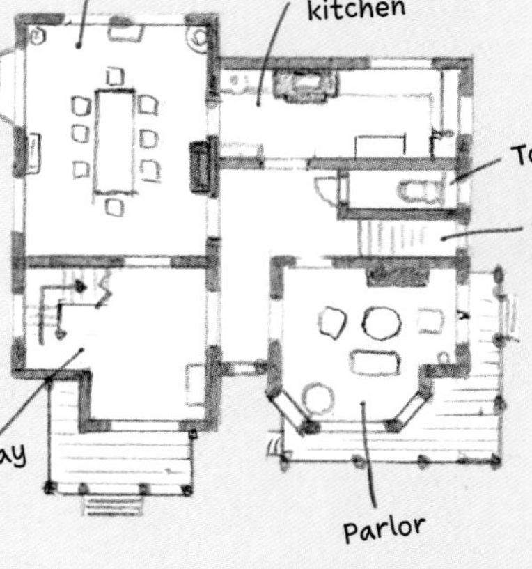
Dining room
Spacious kitchen
Toilet
Stairs to underground cellar
Entryway hall
Parlor

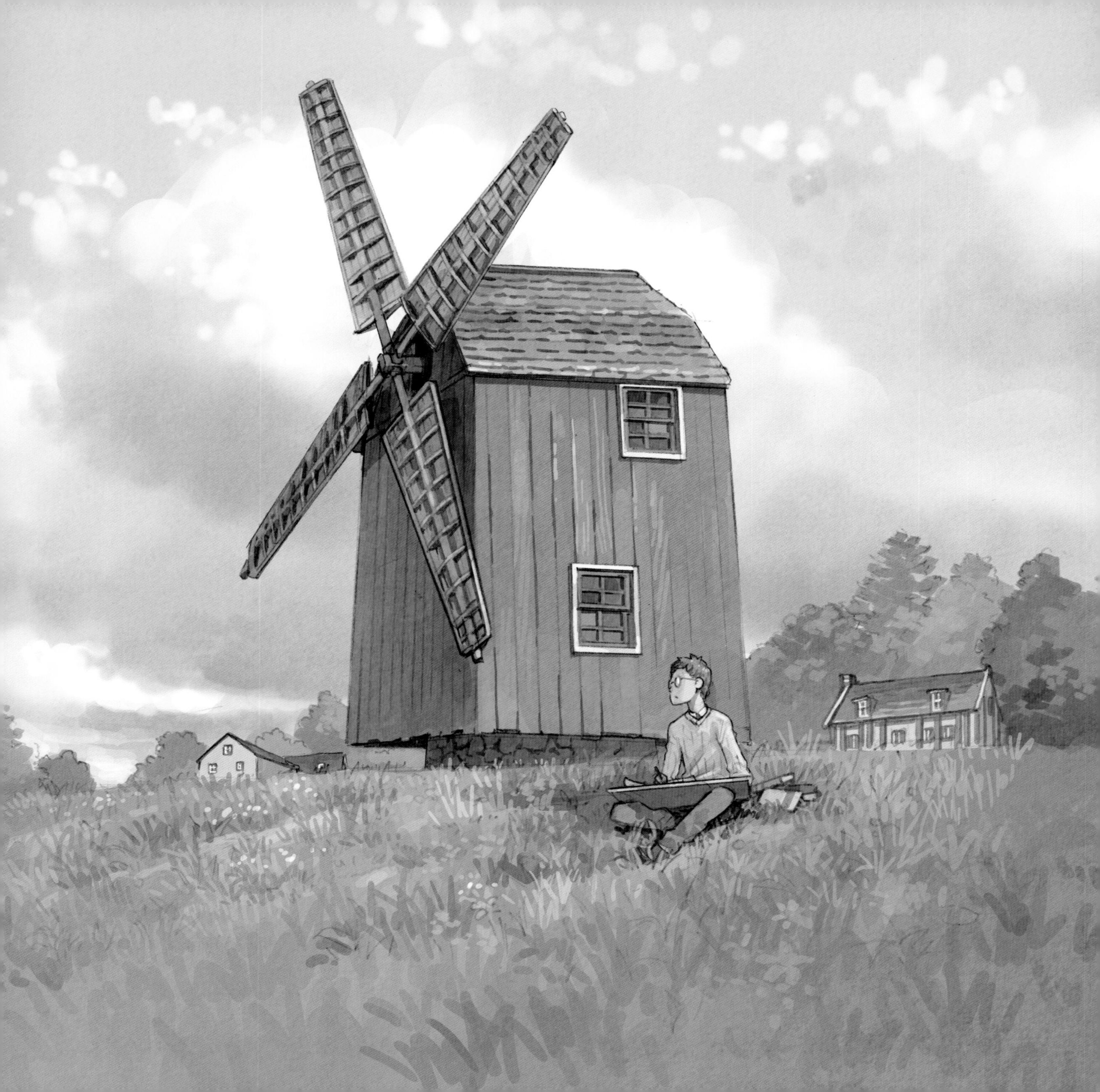

A Young Inventor's Windmill

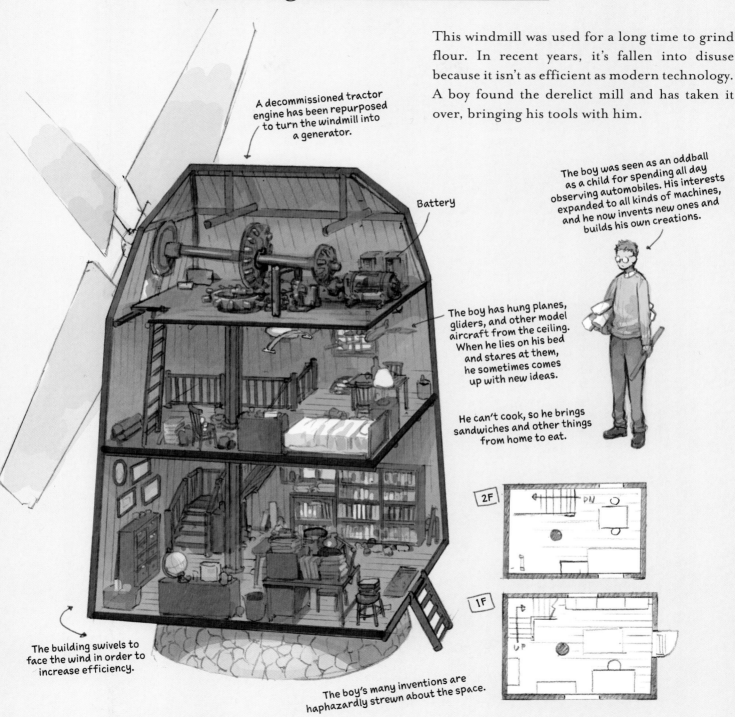

This windmill was used for a long time to grind flour. In recent years, it's fallen into disuse because it isn't as efficient as modern technology. A boy found the derelict mill and has taken it over, bringing his tools with him.

A decommissioned tractor engine has been repurposed to turn the windmill into a generator.

Battery

The boy was seen as an oddball as a child for spending all day observing automobiles. His interests expanded to all kinds of machines, and he now invents new ones and builds his own creations.

The boy has hung planes, gliders, and other model aircraft from the ceiling. When he lies on his bed and stares at them, he sometimes comes up with new ideas.

He can't cook, so he brings sandwiches and other things from home to eat.

The building swivels to face the wind in order to increase efficiency.

The boy's many inventions are haphazardly strewn about the space.

2F

1F

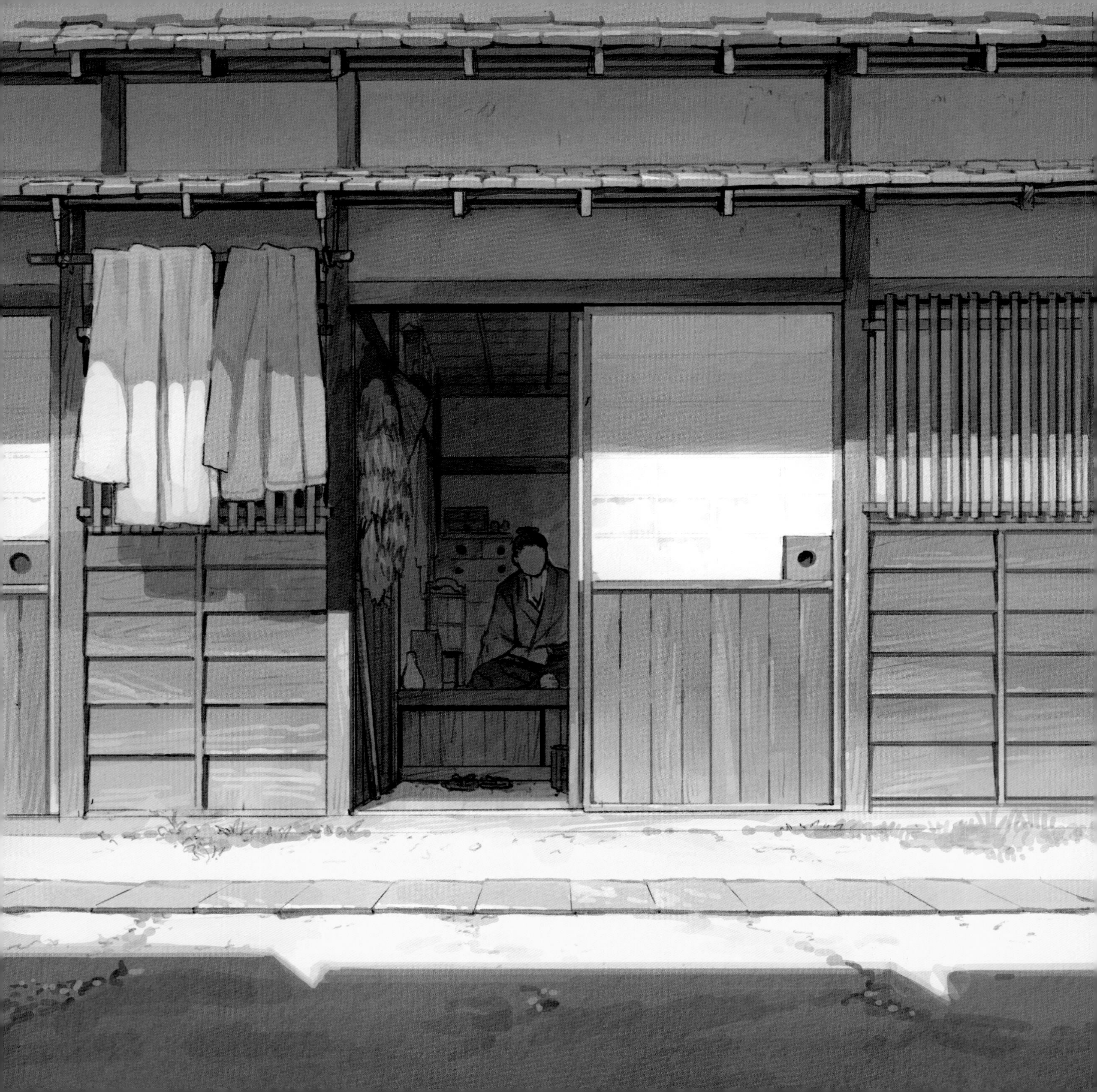

A Ronin's Tenement House

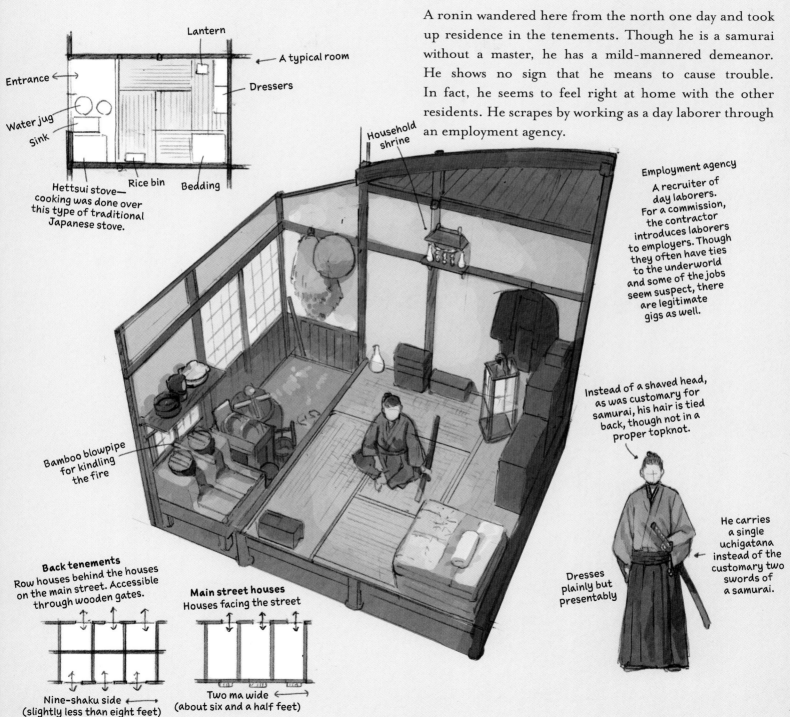

A ronin wandered here from the north one day and took up residence in the tenements. Though he is a samurai without a master, he has a mild-mannered demeanor. He shows no sign that he means to cause trouble. In fact, he seems to feel right at home with the other residents. He scrapes by working as a day laborer through an employment agency.

Lantern
A typical room
Entrance
Dressers
Water jug
Sink
Hettsui stove—cooking was done over this type of traditional Japanese stove.
Rice bin
Bedding

Household shrine
Employment agency
A recruiter of day laborers. For a commission, the contractor introduces laborers to employers. Though they often have ties to the underworld and some of the jobs seem suspect, there are legitimate gigs as well.
Bamboo blowpipe for kindling the fire

Instead of a shaved head, as was customary for samurai, his hair is tied back, though not in a proper topknot.
He carries a single uchigatana instead of the customary two swords of a samurai.
Dresses plainly but presentably

Back tenements
Row houses behind the houses on the main street. Accessible through wooden gates.
Nine-shaku side
(slightly less than eight feet)

Main street houses
Houses facing the street
Two ma wide
(about six and a half feet)

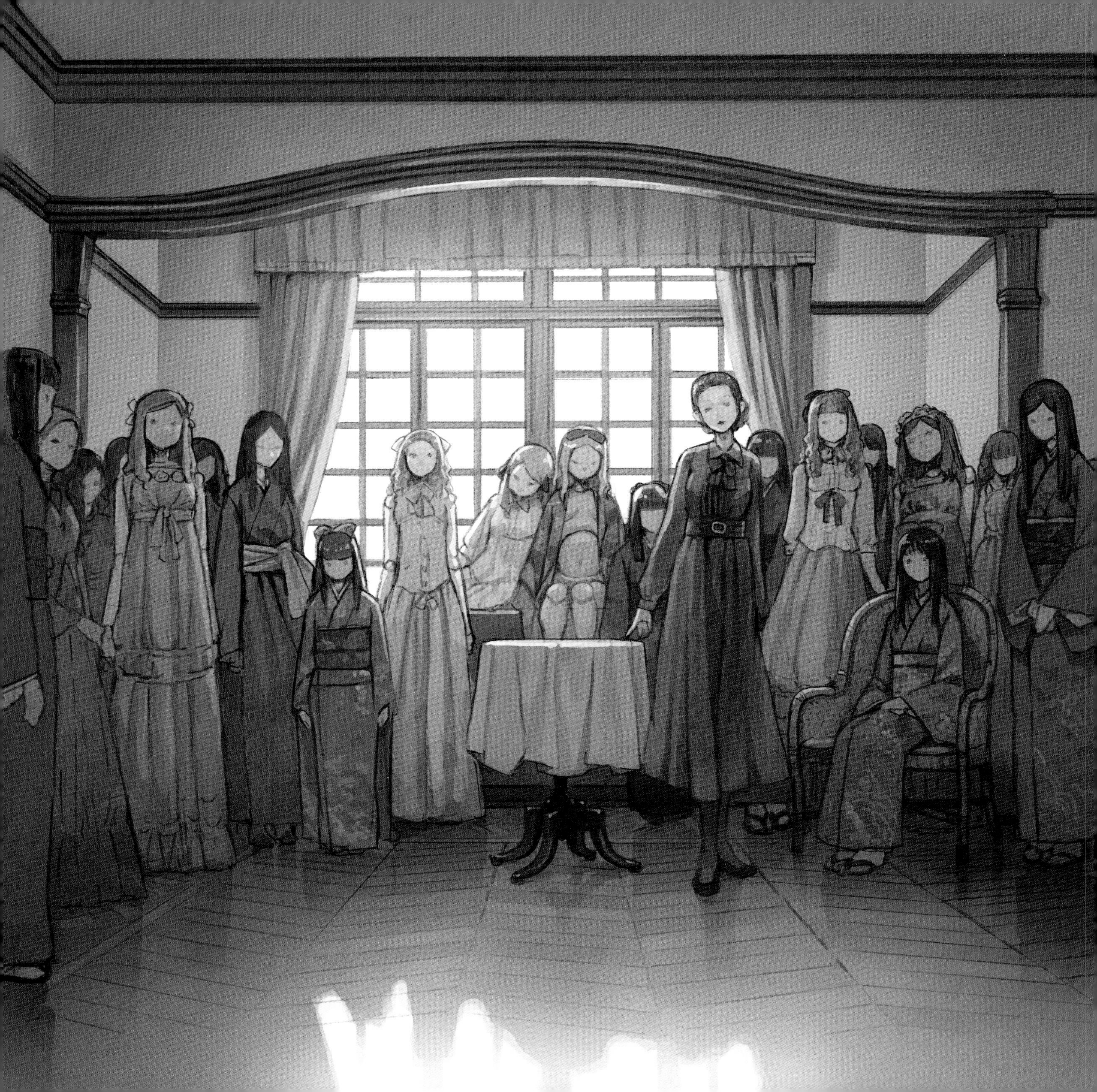

The House of a Woman Fascinated by Dolls

A woman lives alone in a modern house. She was once an aristocrat, but she began to devote herself to dolls after a childhood trauma, and she now lives in a house littered with them. The neighbors call it "the dollhouse" and do not seem to appreciate it.

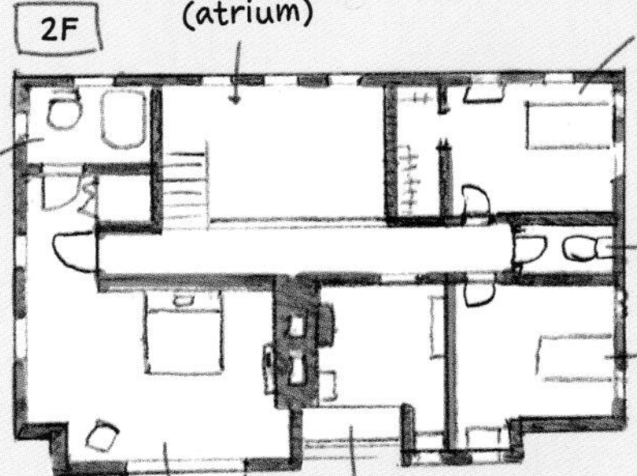
2F
Entryway hall (atrium)
Bedroom
Bathroom
Toilet
Guest room
Main bedroom
Study

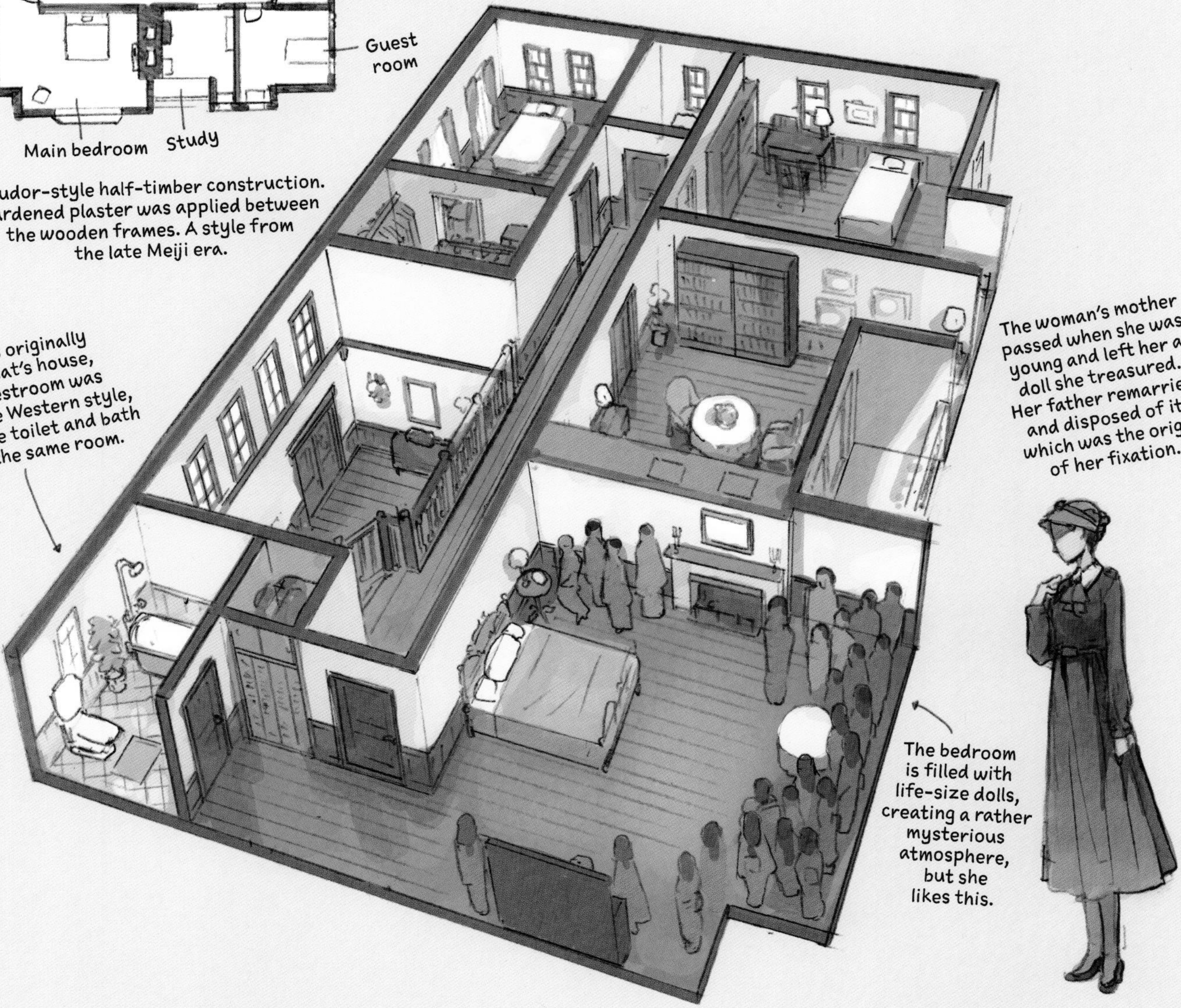
A Tudor-style half-timber construction. Hardened plaster was applied between the wooden frames. A style from the late Meiji era.
This was originally a diplomat's house, so the restroom was made in the Western style, in which the toilet and bath occupy the same room.
The woman's mother passed when she was young and left her a doll she treasured. Her father remarried and disposed of it, which was the origin of her fixation.
The bedroom is filled with life-size dolls, creating a rather mysterious atmosphere, but she likes this.

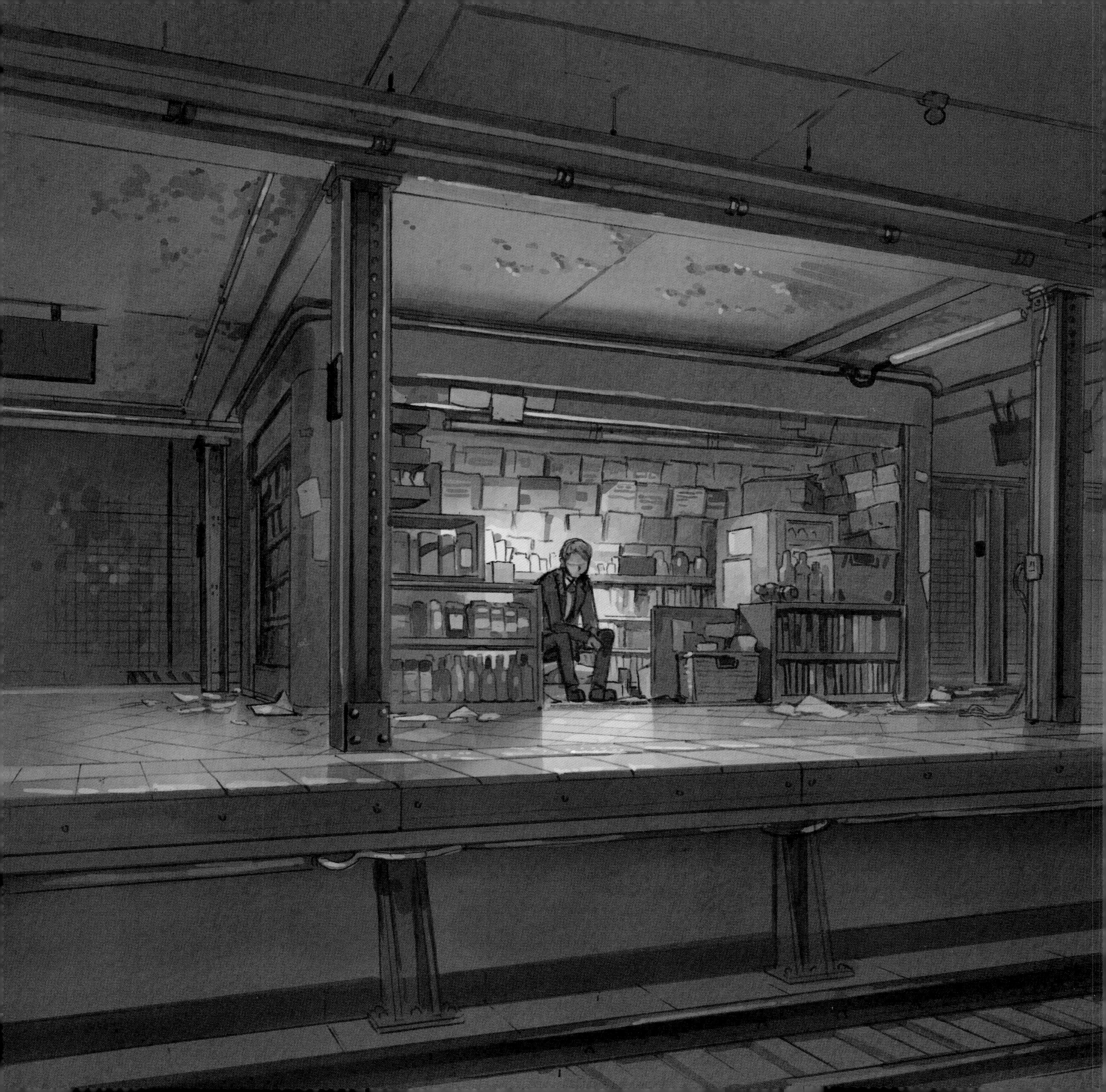

A Man in an Abandoned Subway Station

This man has taken up residence in an unused subway station. He uses a kiosk as his bed and goes out every day. He doesn't seem to be in hiding or on the run. It's as though he's waiting for someone or searching for something.

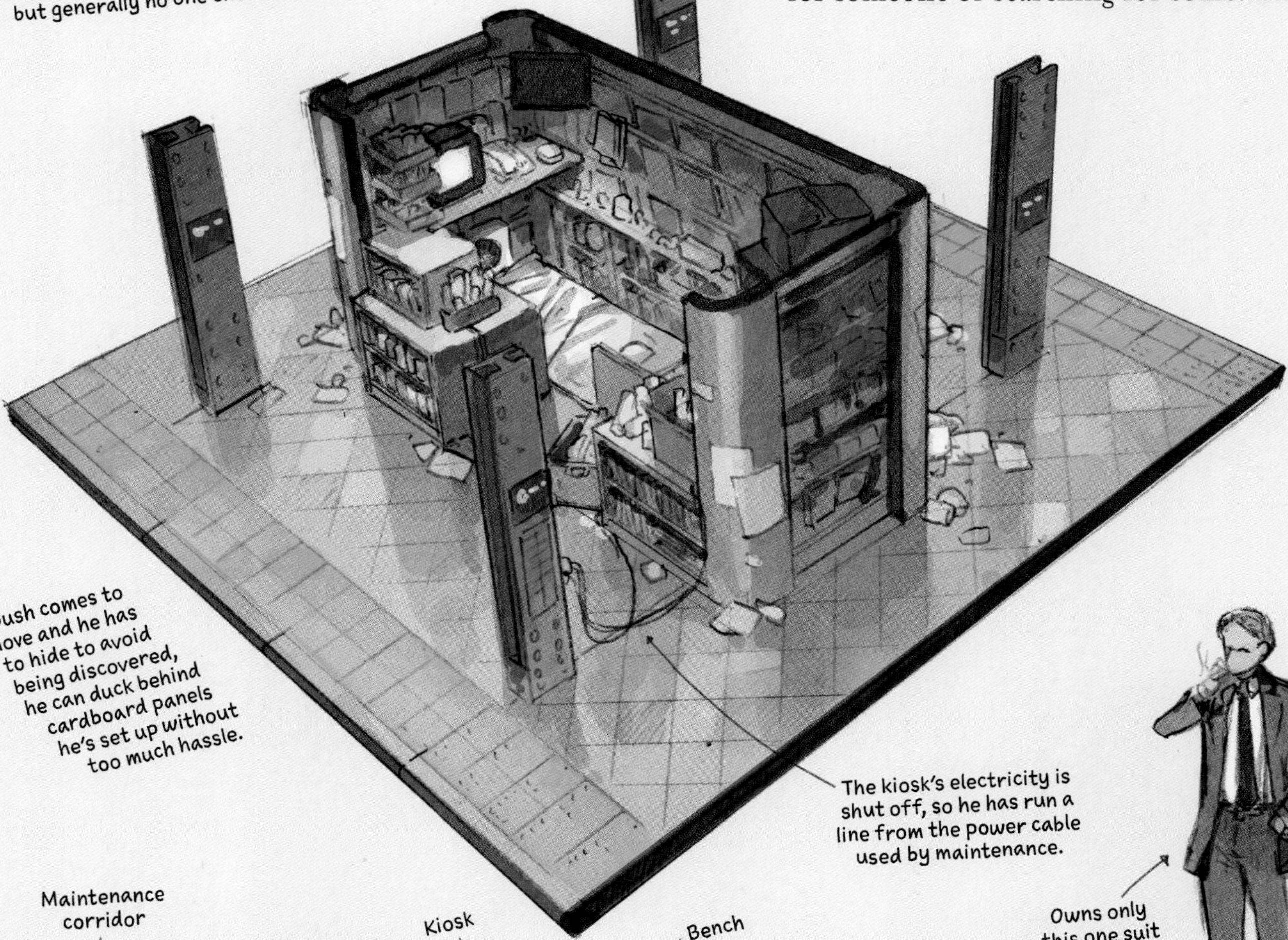

A fire started when the subway was already facing financial hardship, so the station was essentially left as it was. Inspectors sometimes visit, but generally no one enters.
The subway still operates at a limited capacity.
If push comes to shove and he has to hide to avoid being discovered, he can duck behind cardboard panels he's set up without too much hassle.
The kiosk's electricity is shut off, so he has run a line from the power cable used by maintenance.

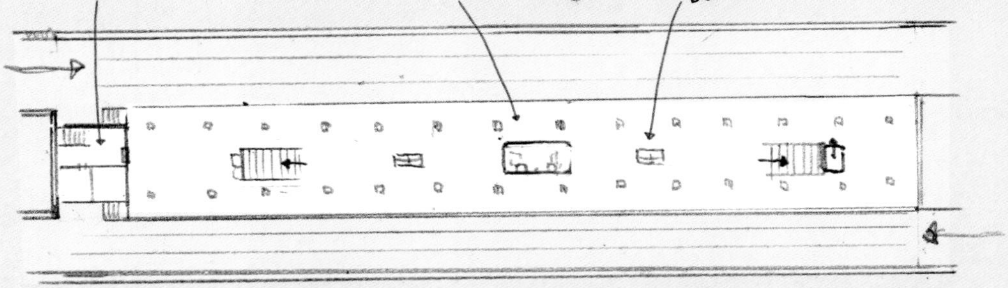

Maintenance corridor
Kiosk
Bench

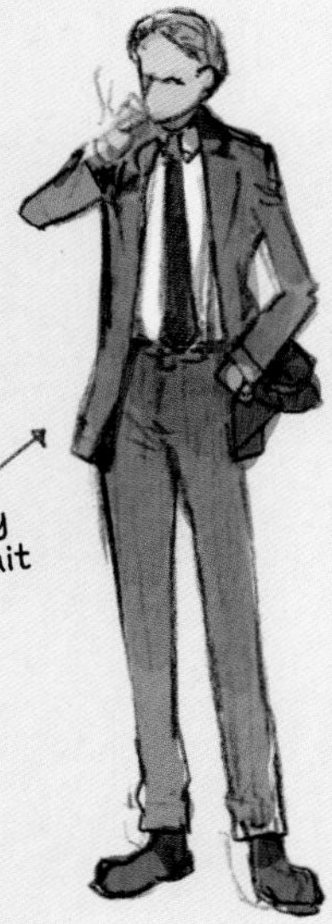

Owns only this one suit

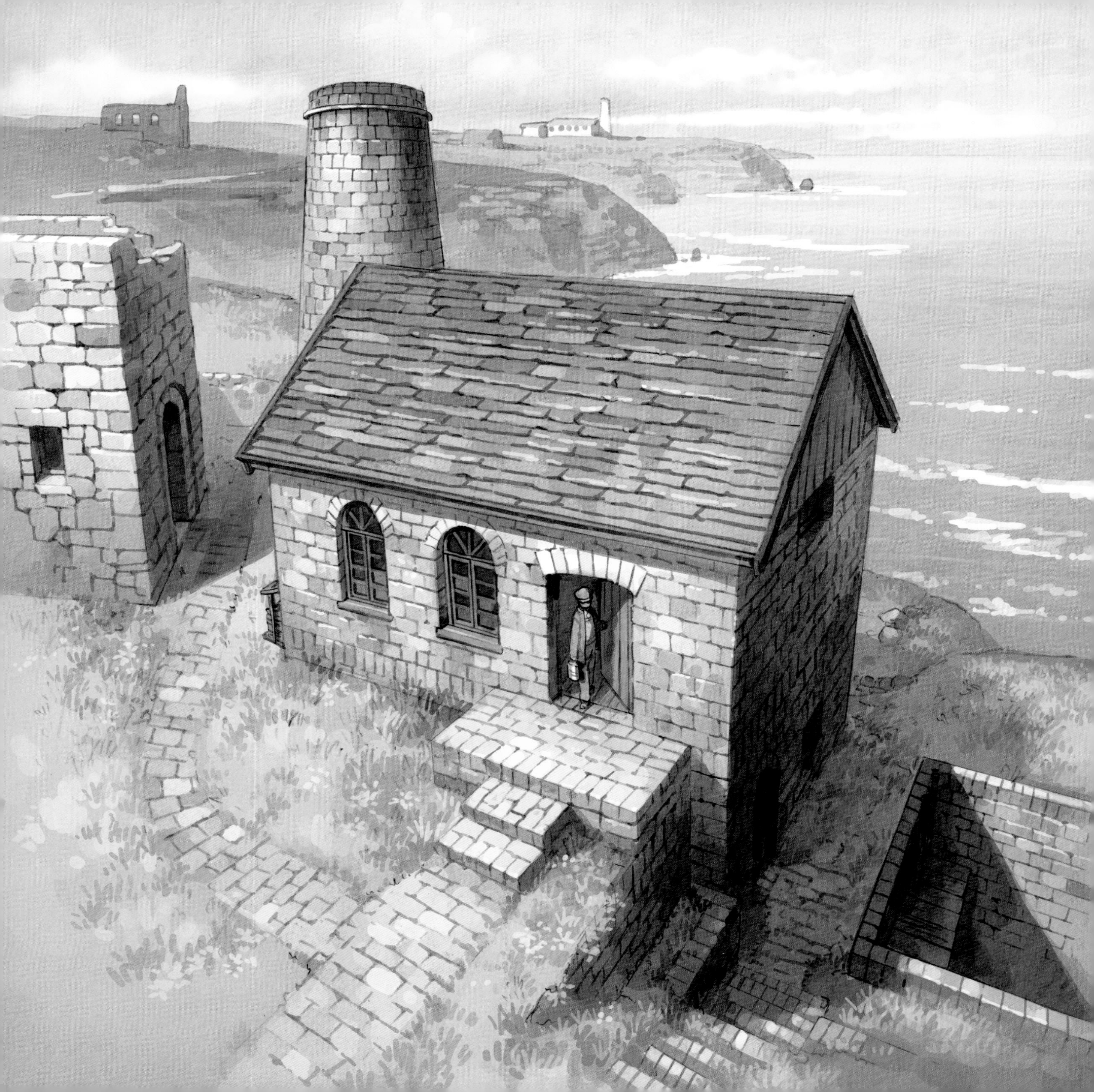

A Miner's Engine House

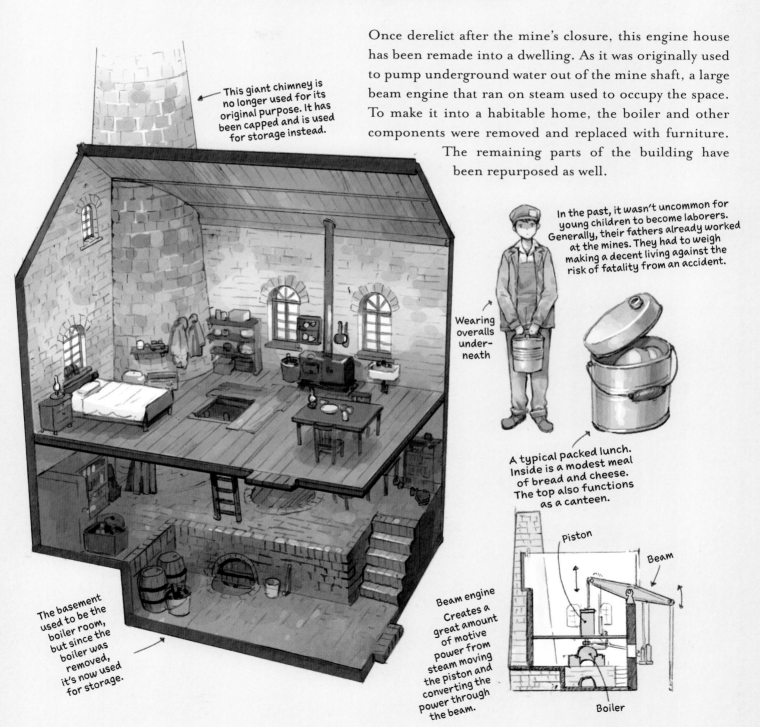

Once derelict after the mine's closure, this engine house has been remade into a dwelling. As it was originally used to pump underground water out of the mine shaft, a large beam engine that ran on steam used to occupy the space. To make it into a habitable home, the boiler and other components were removed and replaced with furniture. The remaining parts of the building have been repurposed as well.

This giant chimney is no longer used for its original purpose. It has been capped and is used for storage instead.
The basement used to be the boiler room, but since the boiler was removed, it's now used for storage.

In the past, it wasn't uncommon for young children to become laborers. Generally, their fathers already worked at the mines. They had to weigh making a decent living against the risk of fatality from an accident.
Wearing overalls underneath

A typical packed lunch. Inside is a modest meal of bread and cheese. The top also functions as a canteen.

Beam engine
Creates a great amount of motive power from steam moving the piston and converting the power through the beam.
Piston
Beam
Boiler

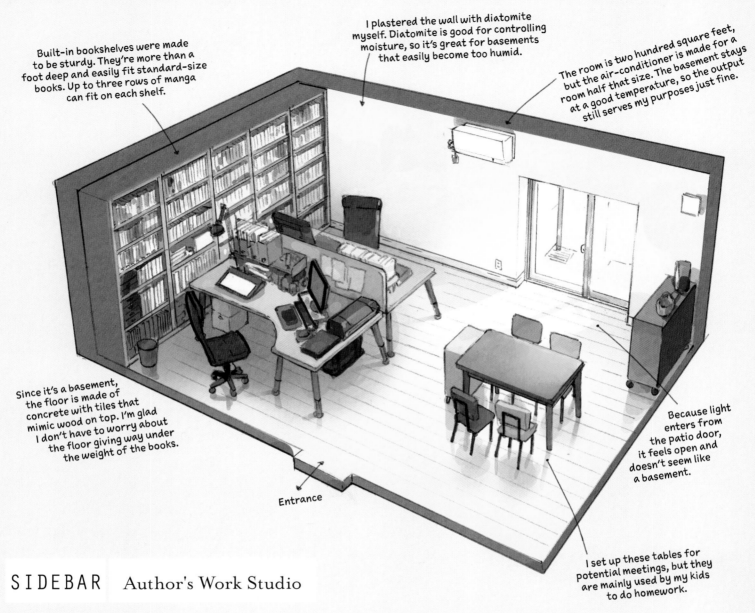

Built-in bookshelves were made to be sturdy. They're more than a foot deep and easily fit standard-size books. Up to three rows of manga can fit on each shelf.

I plastered the wall with diatomite myself. Diatomite is good for controlling moisture, so it's great for basements that easily become too humid.

The room is two hundred square feet, but the air-conditioner is made for a room half that size. The basement stays at a good temperature, so the output still serves my purposes just fine.

Since it's a basement, the floor is made of concrete with tiles that mimic wood on top. I'm glad I don't have to worry about the floor giving way under the weight of the books.

Because light enters from the patio door, it feels open and doesn't seem like a basement.

Entrance

I set up these tables for potential meetings, but they are mainly used by my kids to do homework.

SIDEBAR Author's Work Studio

My home was constructed in 2012 and has a work studio in the basement. As a freelancer, I primarily work from home, so I wanted a separate room to differentiate between work and home life. I prefer a quiet environment to work in, so I committed to building this workroom. I feel the room has more than paid for itself.

I used my experience as a background artist to pay special attention to various details of the house. The experience of building the house was also surprisingly informative; the knowledge I gleaned ranged from each construction material's characteristics to building regulations, such as the Building Standards Act and the Fire Service Act.

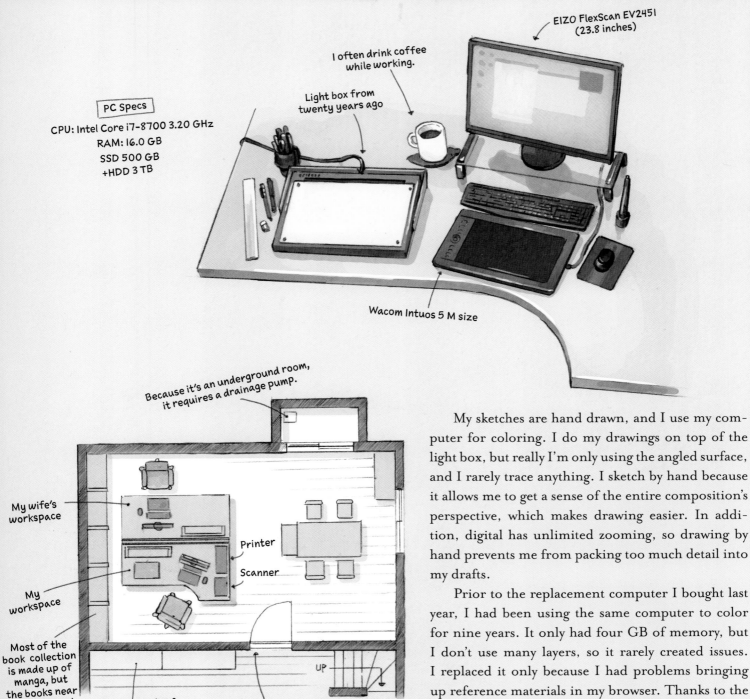

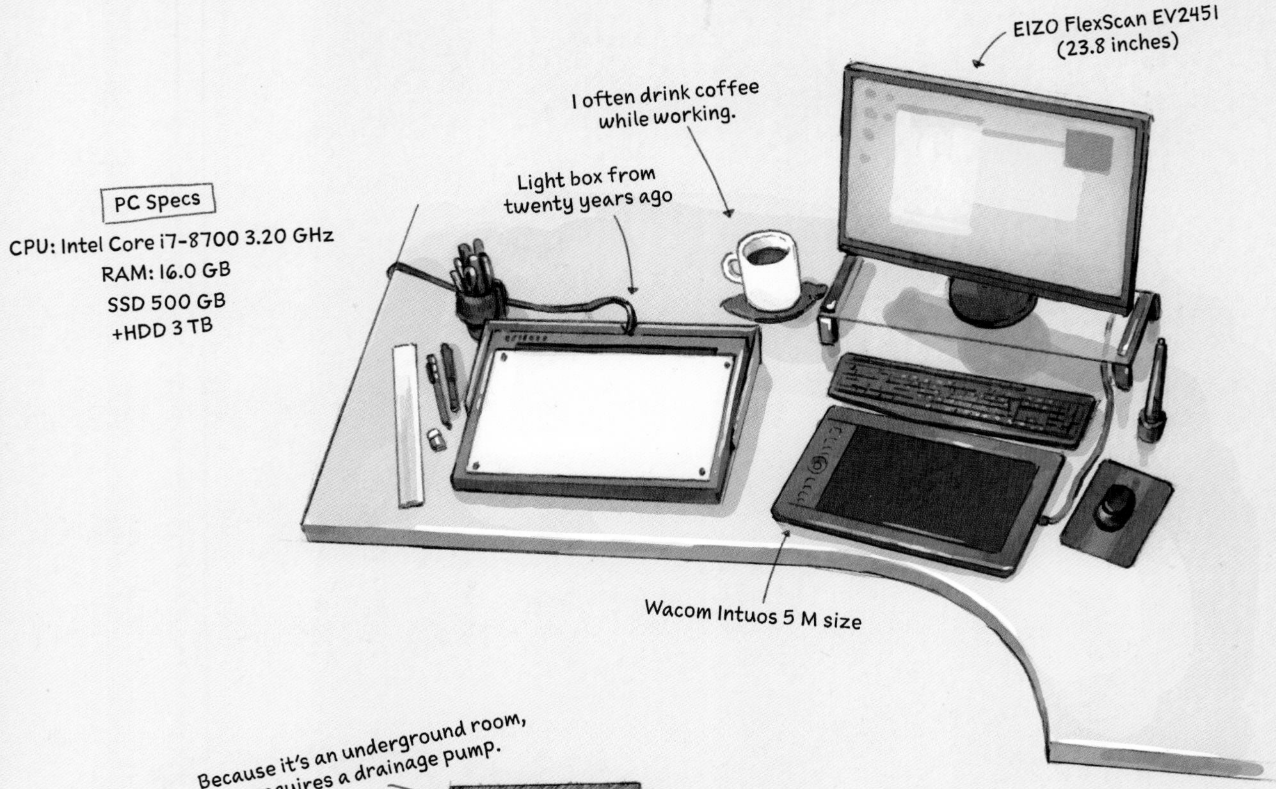
EIZO FlexScan EV2451
(23.8 inches)
I often drink coffee
while working.
Light box from
twenty years ago
PC Specs
CPU: Intel Core i7-8700 3.20 GHz
RAM: 16.0 GB
SSD 500 GB
+HDD 3 TB
Wacom Intuos 5 M size

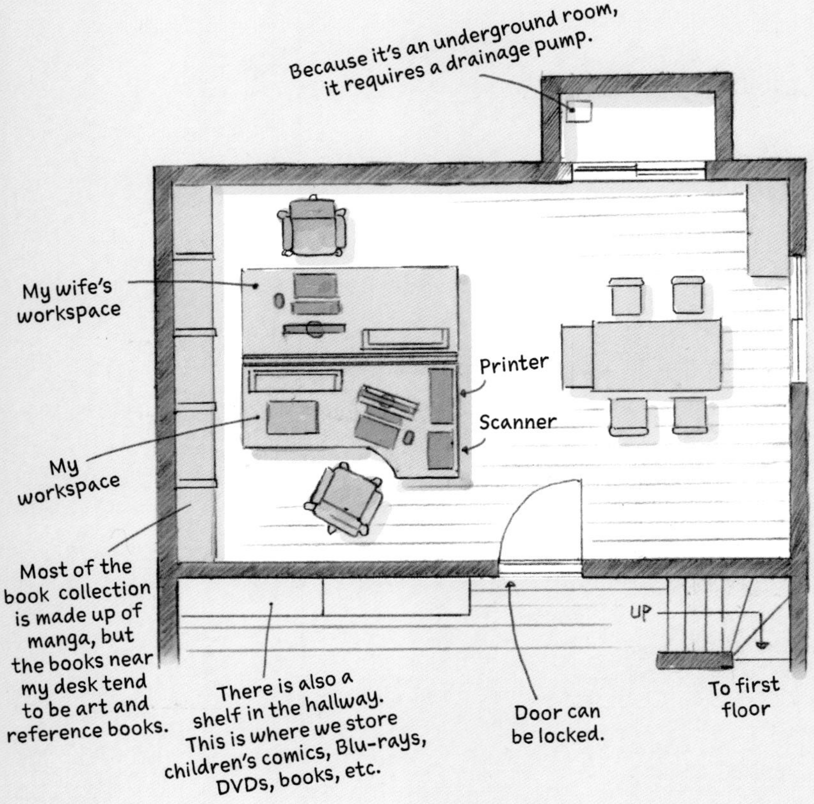
Because it's an underground room,
it requires a drainage pump.
My wife's
workspace
Printer
Scanner
My
workspace
Most of the
book collection
is made up of
manga, but
the books near
my desk tend
to be art and
reference books.
There is also a
shelf in the hallway.
This is where we store
children's comics, Blu-rays,
DVDs, books, etc.
Door can
be locked.
UP
To first
floor

My sketches are hand drawn, and I use my computer for coloring. I do my drawings on top of the light box, but really I'm only using the angled surface, and I rarely trace anything. I sketch by hand because it allows me to get a sense of the entire composition's perspective, which makes drawing easier. In addition, digital has unlimited zooming, so drawing by hand prevents me from packing too much detail into my drafts.

Prior to the replacement computer I bought last year, I had been using the same computer to color for nine years. It only had four GB of memory, but I don't use many layers, so it rarely created issues. I replaced it only because I had problems bringing up reference materials in my browser. Thanks to the new computer, things are much easier, and I'm now able to edit videos and do other memory-intensive things, which has been a great help.

RESERVED MECHANIC'S COTTAGE

Panel Story

Reserved Mechanic's Cottage

THE END OF A DAY

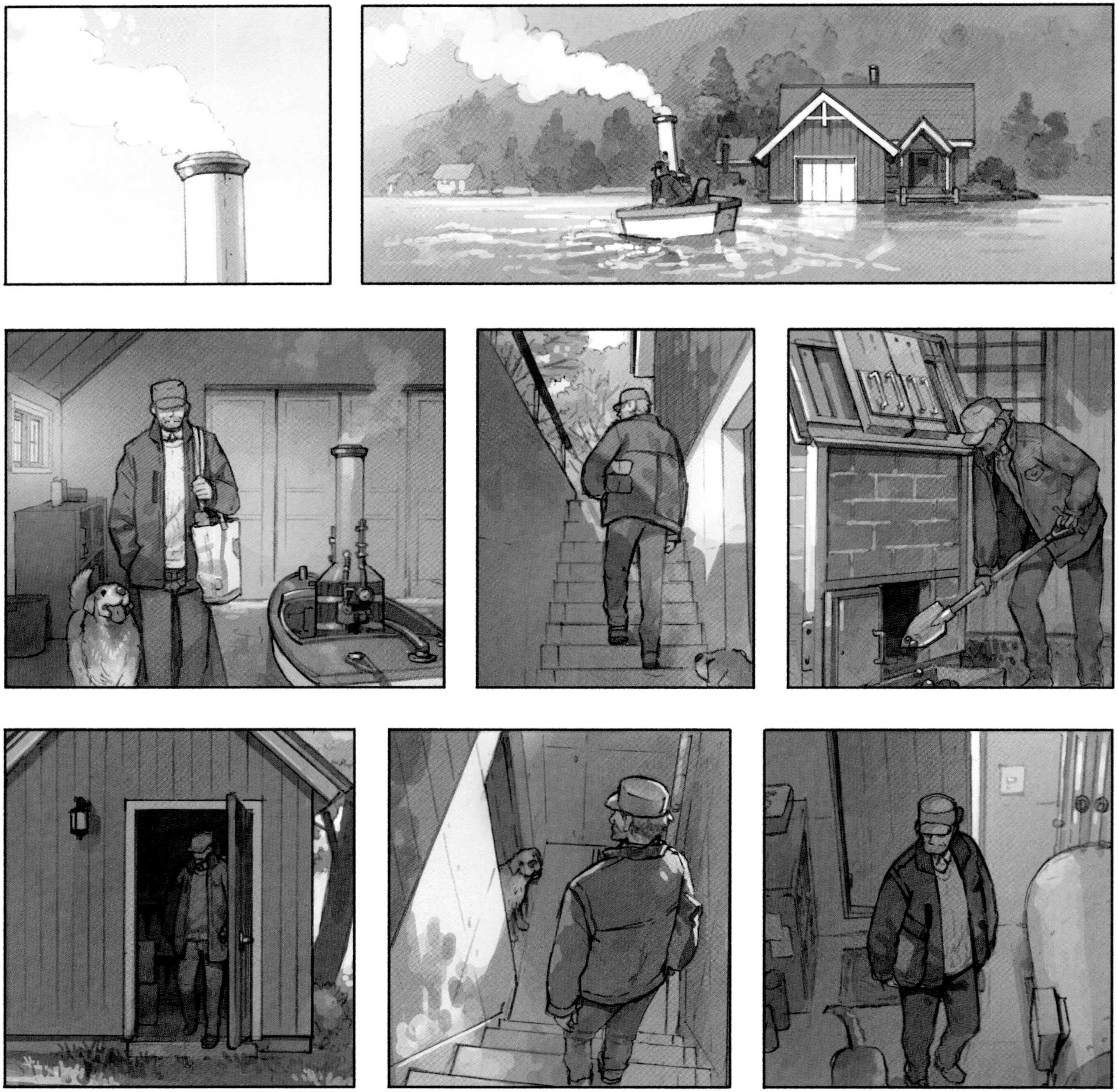

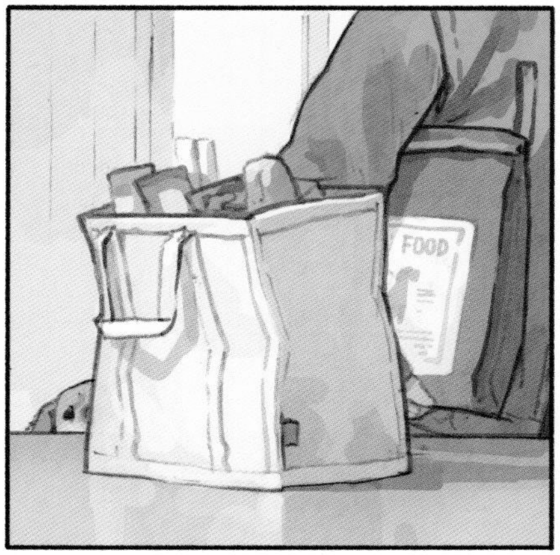
FOOD
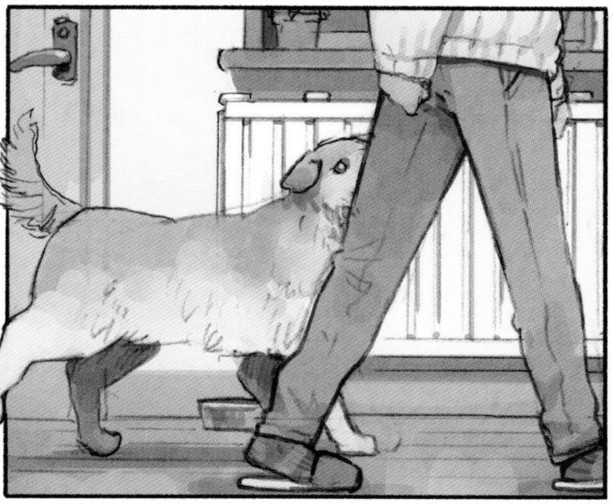
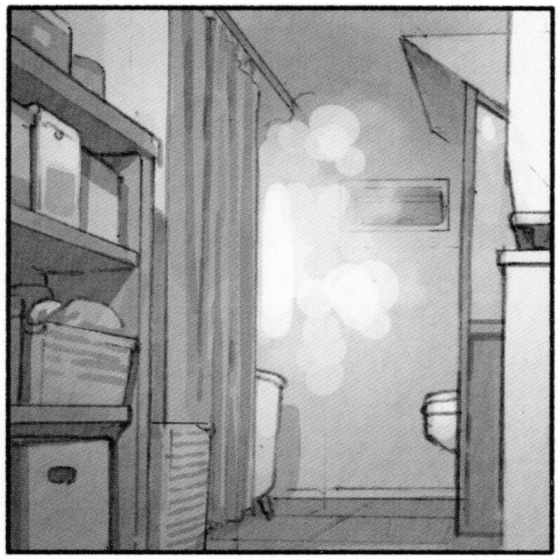
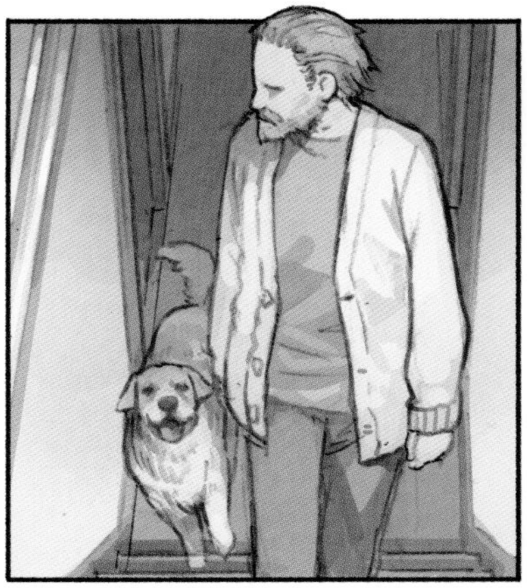
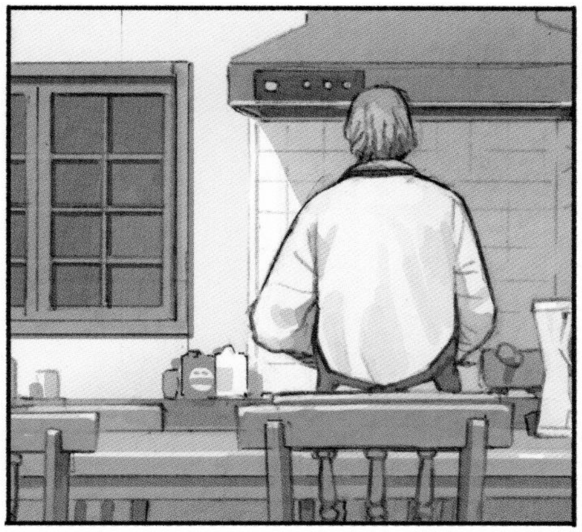
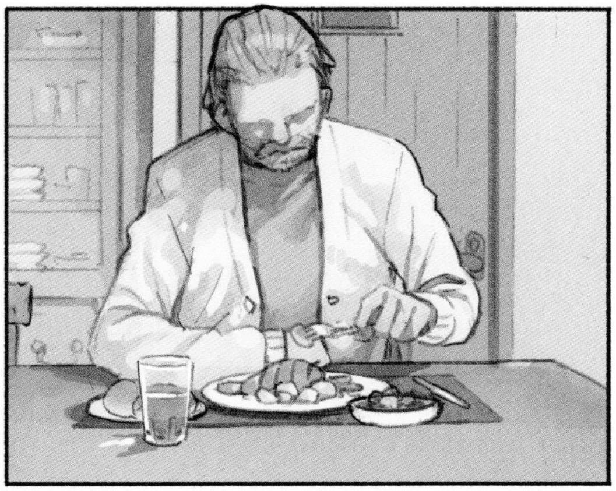
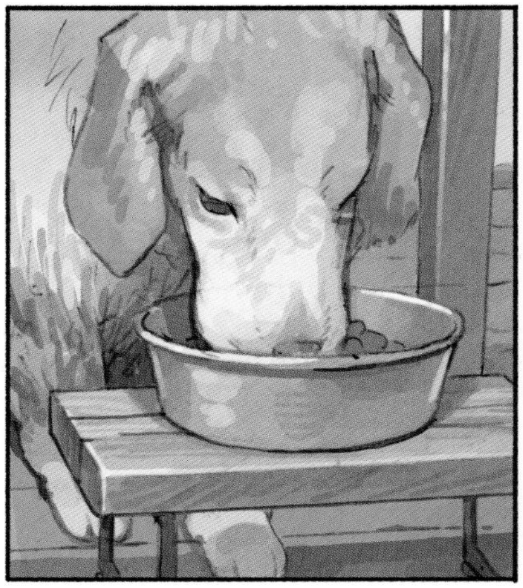
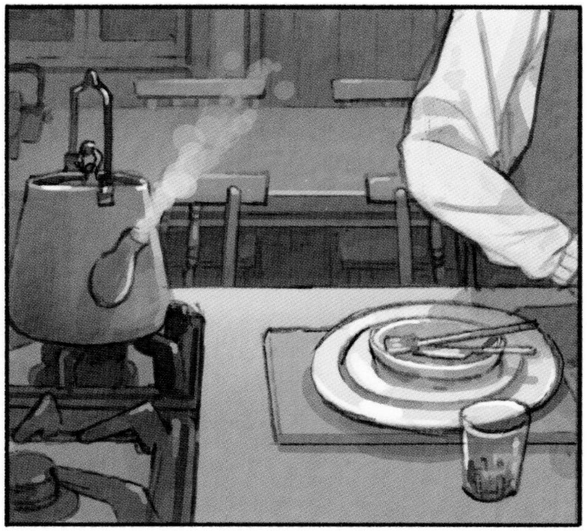
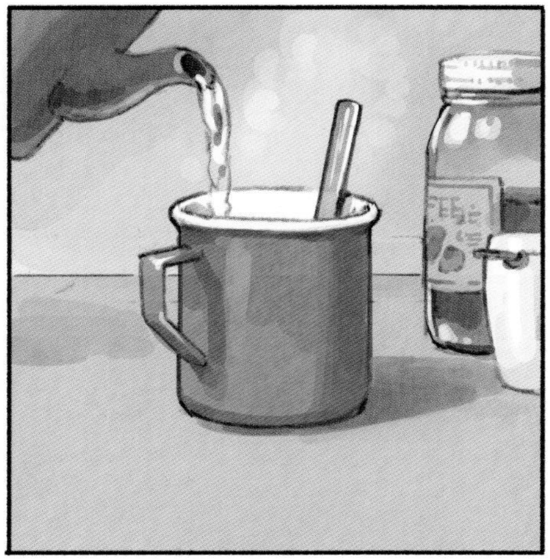

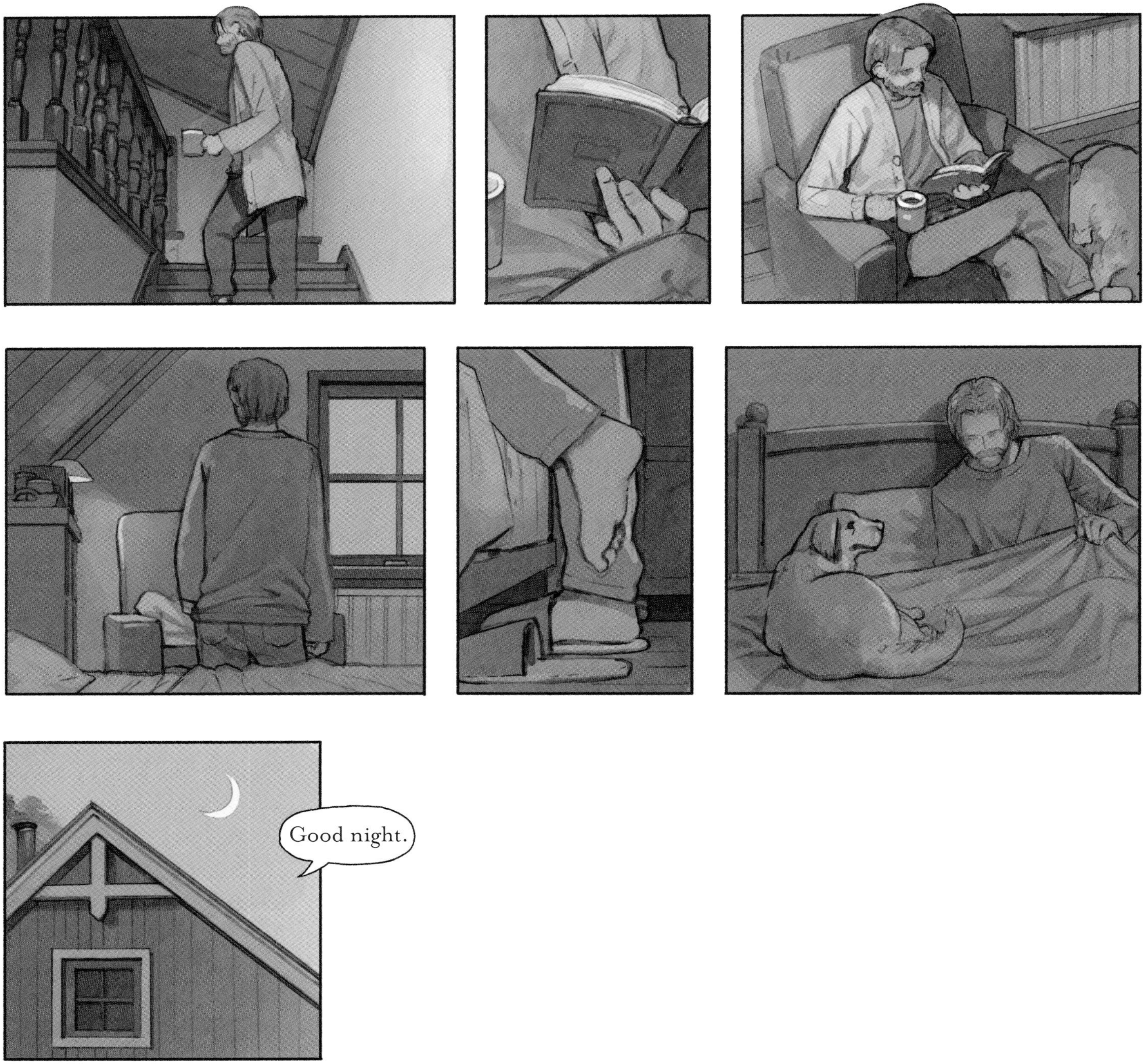
Good night.

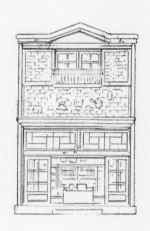

CONCEPTS AND COMMENTARY

Line Drawings

Mischievous Bridge Tower Keeper

Country: England
Time period: circa thirteenth century
Set slightly after the Crusades during the Middle Ages. The design of the knightlike character is based on the Arthurian romances from the Crusades and after.

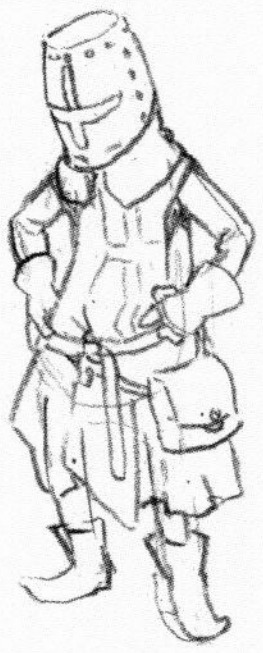

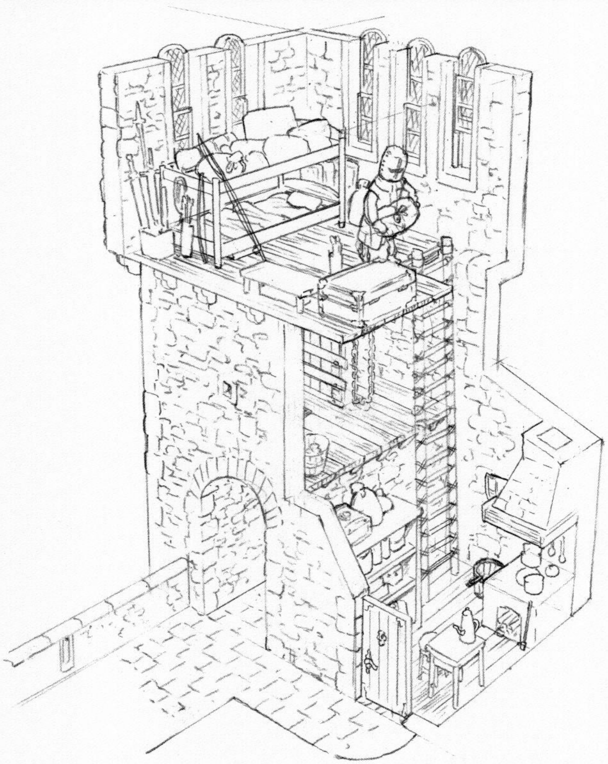

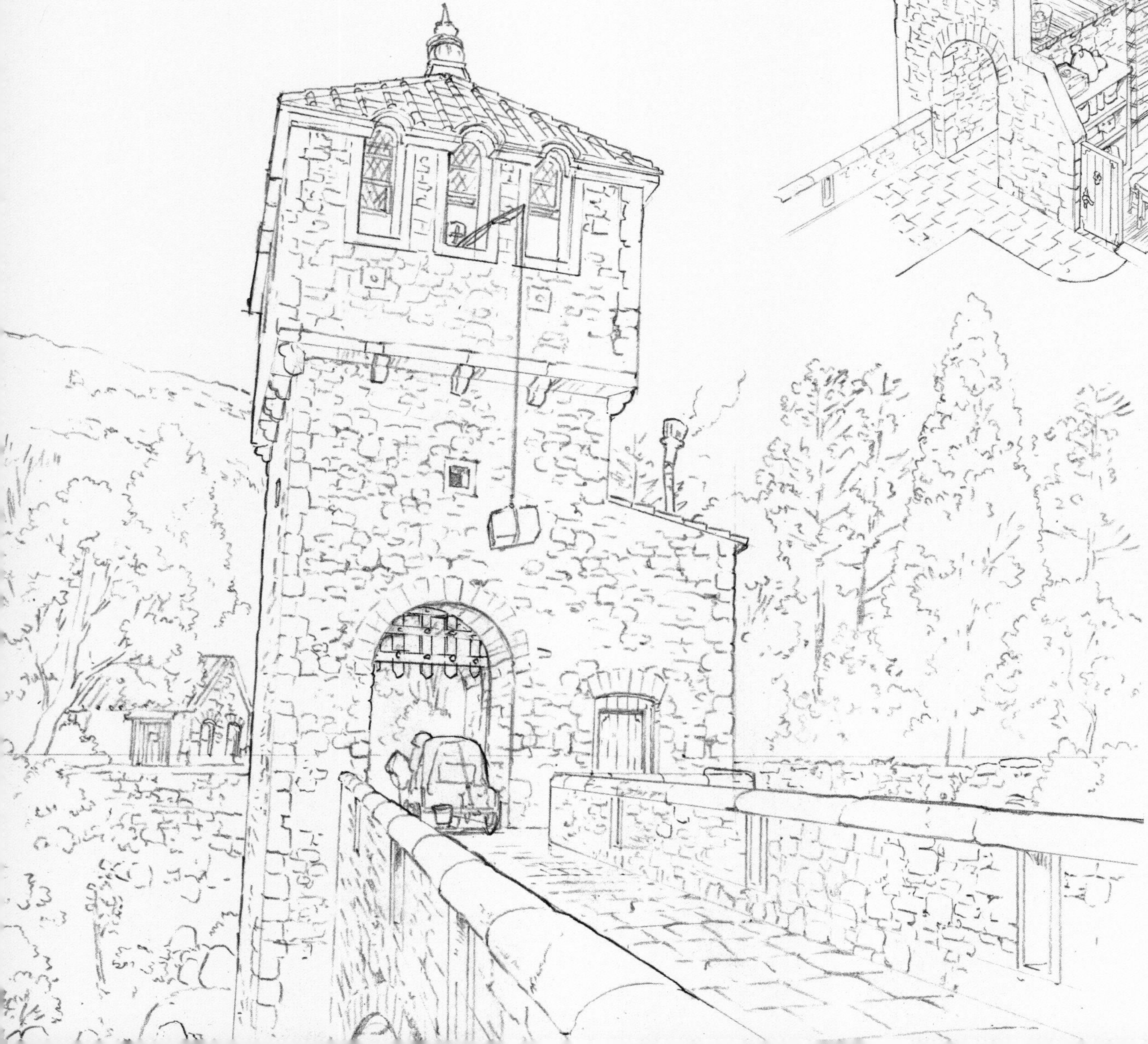

Kaidan-Do Bookstore

Country: Japan
Time period: 2000s
Japan from the past, but this building is appropriate for modern day as well. The shopkeeper is actually a fox and once occupied the shrine on the land where this bookshop now stands.

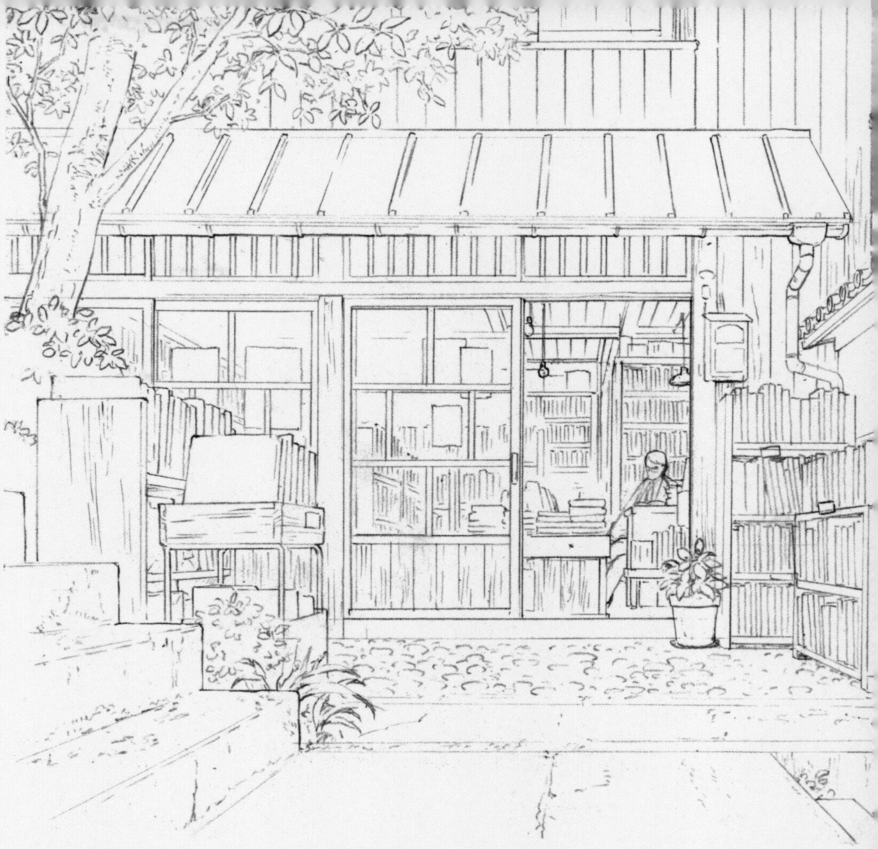

World-Weary Astronomer's Residence

Country: Spain
Time period: circa fifteenth century
Right before the Renaissance, before astronomy became an academic pursuit and was still called astrology. The astronomer doesn't live here by choice but by necessity because he was forced out of the community for his dissident claims.

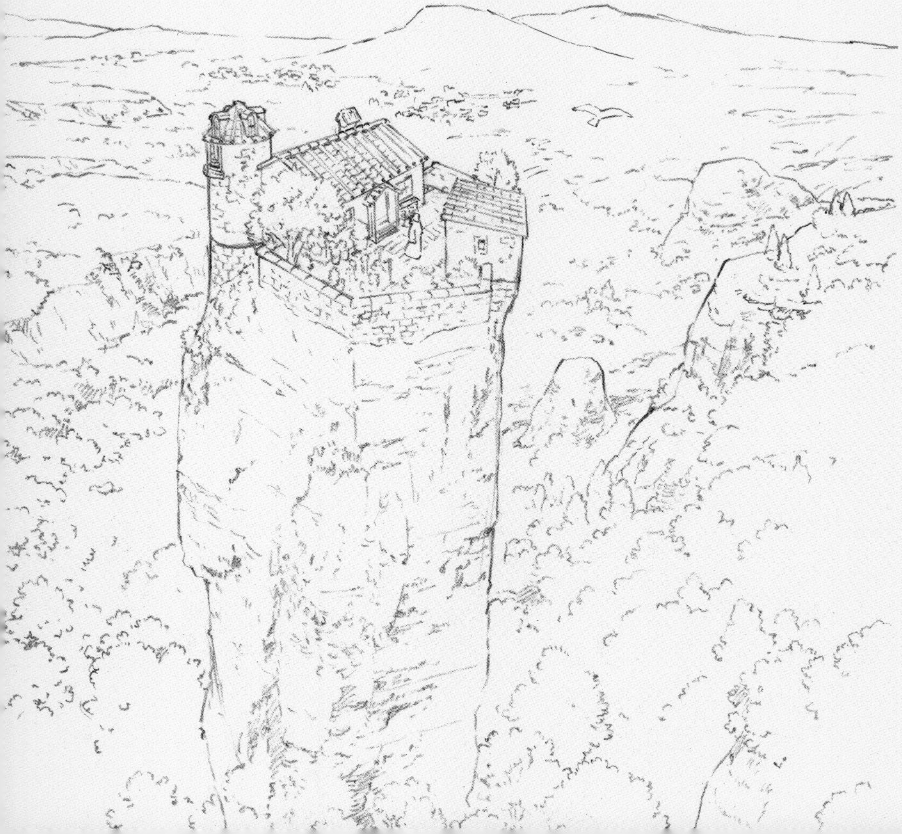

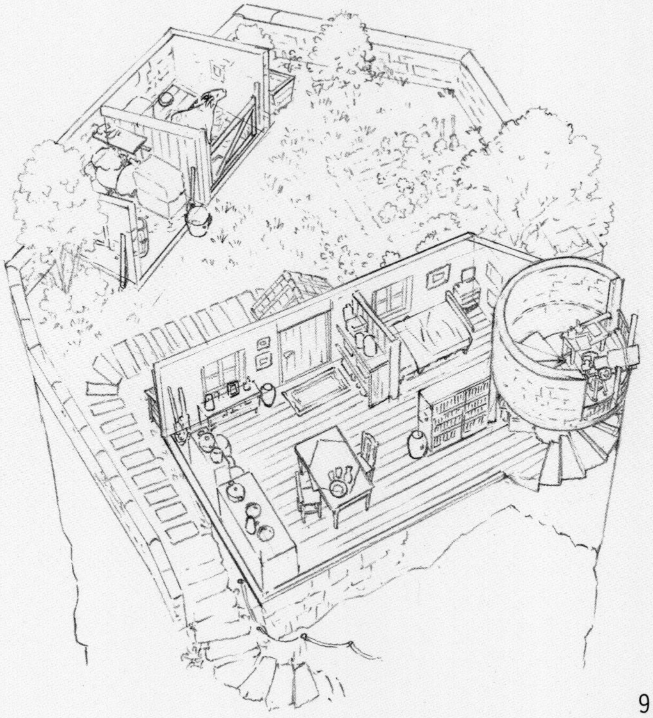

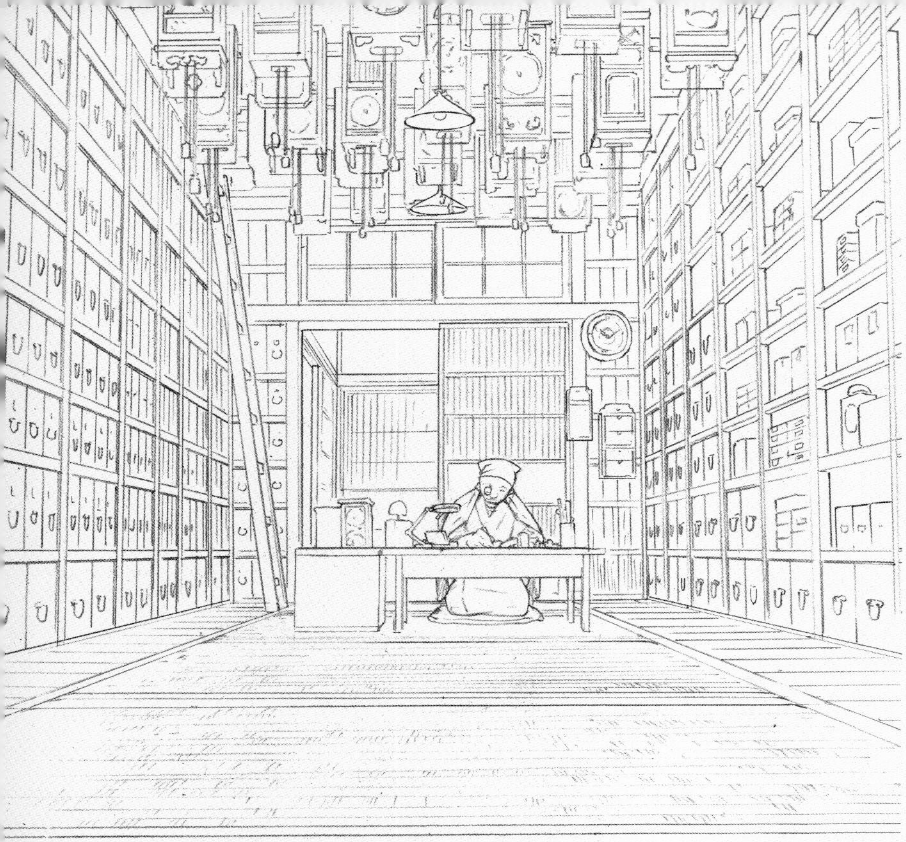

Meticulous Clockmaker

Country: Japan
Time period: early nineteenth century
Japanese clocks were mass-produced and used widely during the Meiji era (1868–1912 CE). The interior is based on a stationery store called Takei Sanshodo at the Edo-Tokyo Open Air Architectural Museum.

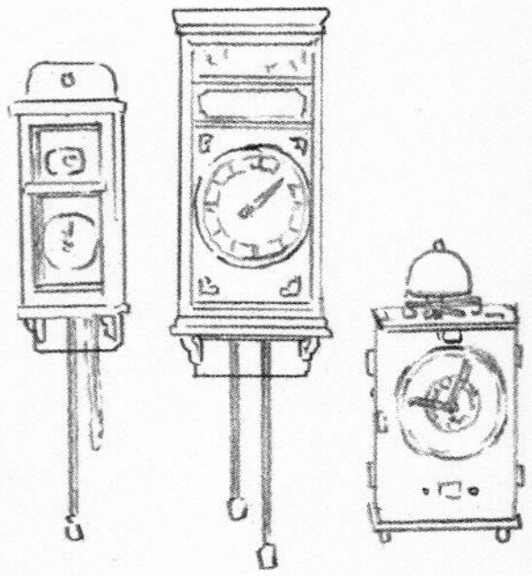

Reserved Mechanic's Cottage

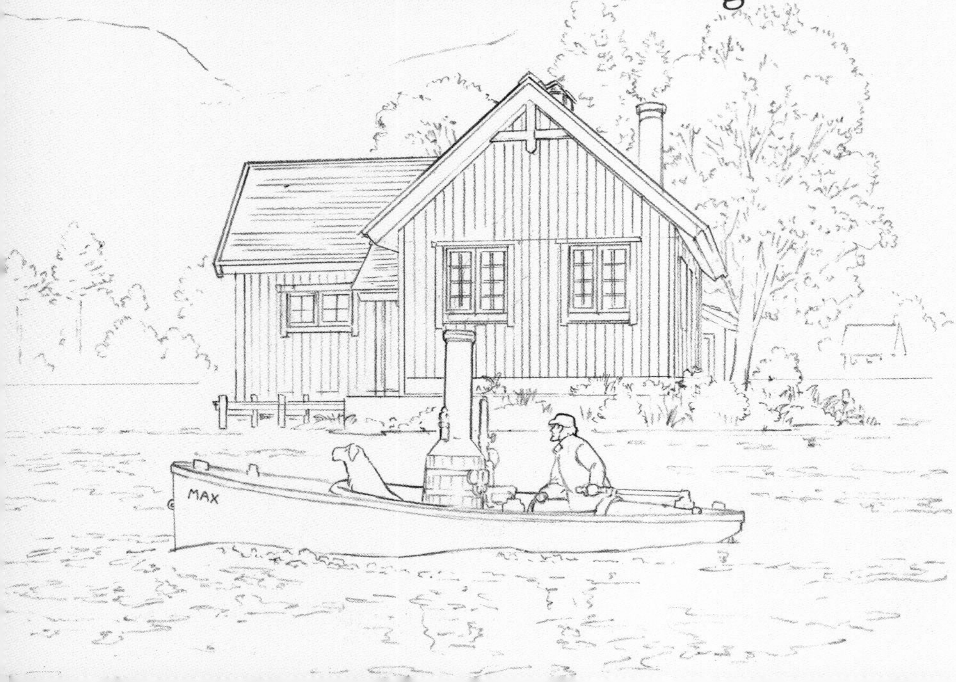
MAX

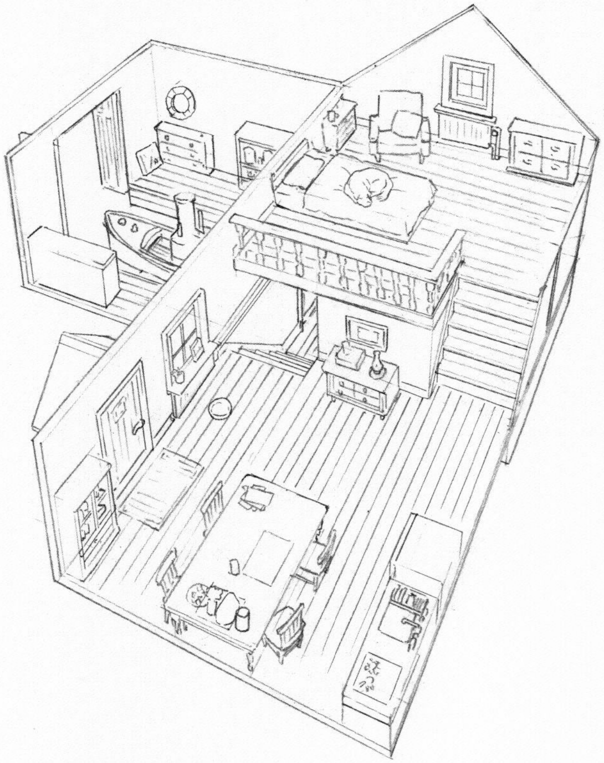

Country: United States (Montana)
Time period: modern day
A summer retreat with natural vistas by a lake at the foot of the Rocky Mountains in Montana. The state is famous for its beautiful national parks, such as Glacier National Park. It is a popular area to drive through and has been used as a filming location for many movies.

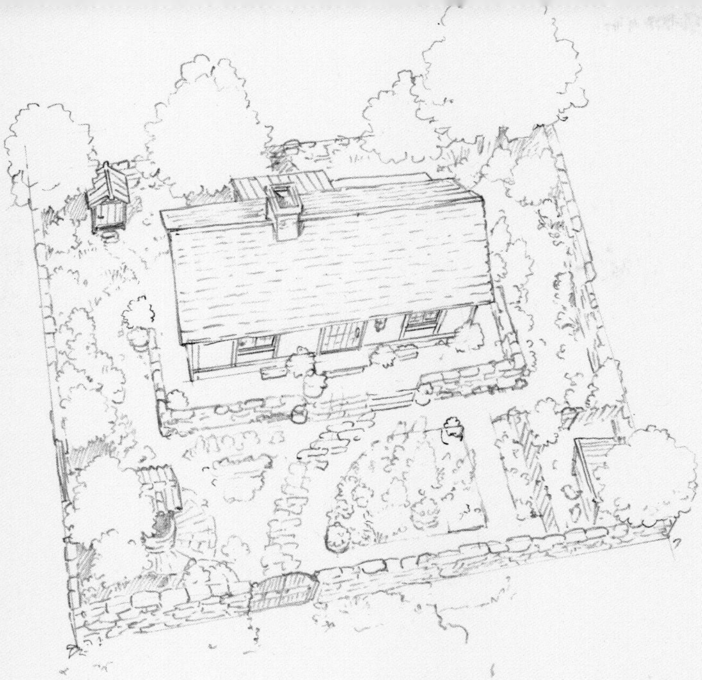

Methodical Witch's House

Country: Scotland
Time period: mid-nineteenth century
This witch survived past the time of witch hunts. She lives a self-sufficient lifestyle. Imagine a time period slightly before the movie *Kiki's Delivery Service*. Though witch culture has recently made a resurgence, there was a time following the hunts when it lost its verve. This witch is lying low around that time.

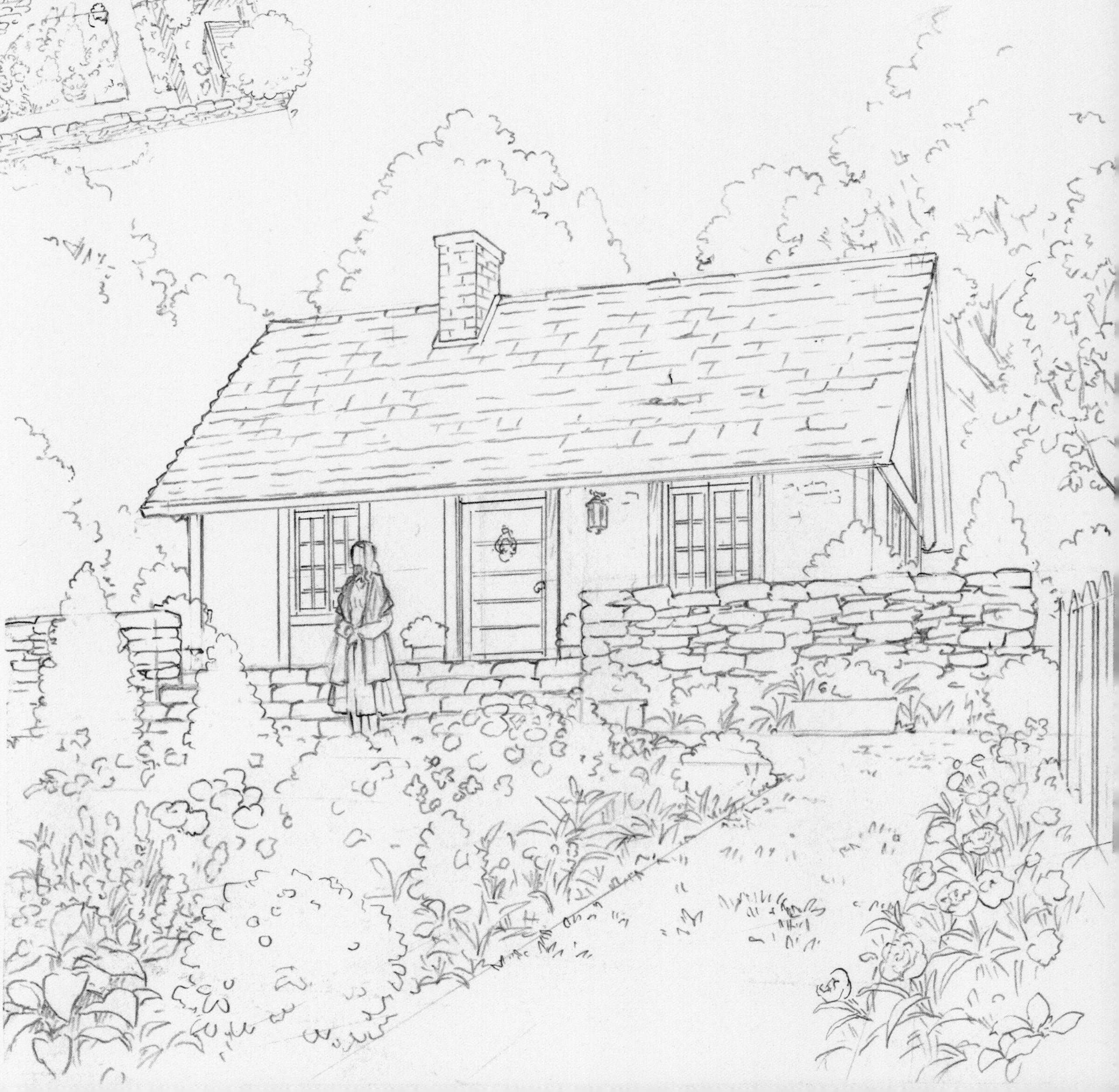

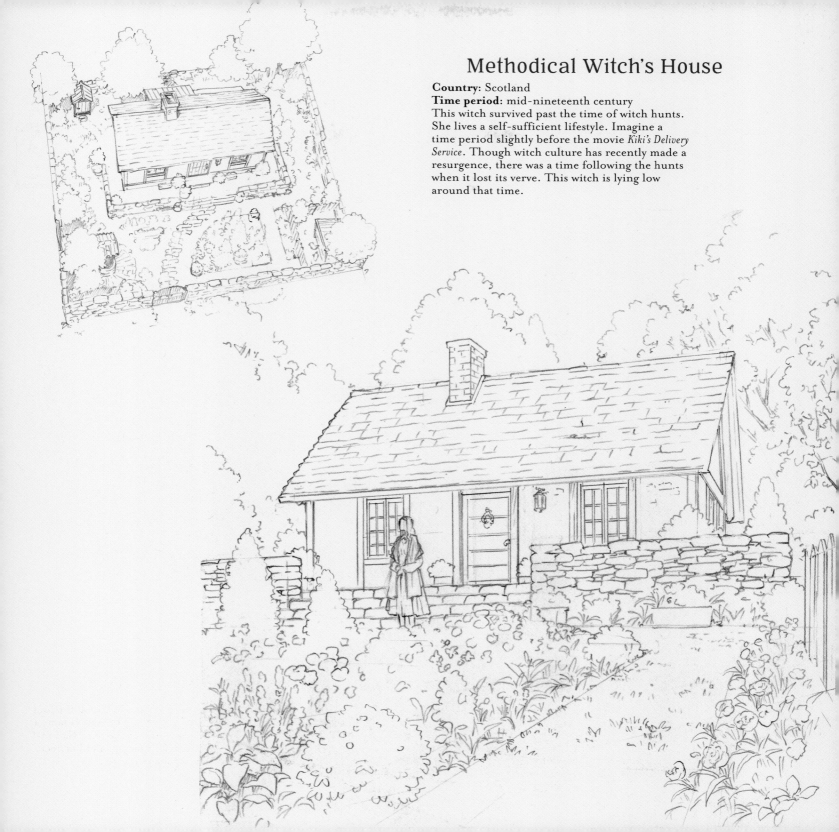

Methodical Witch's House

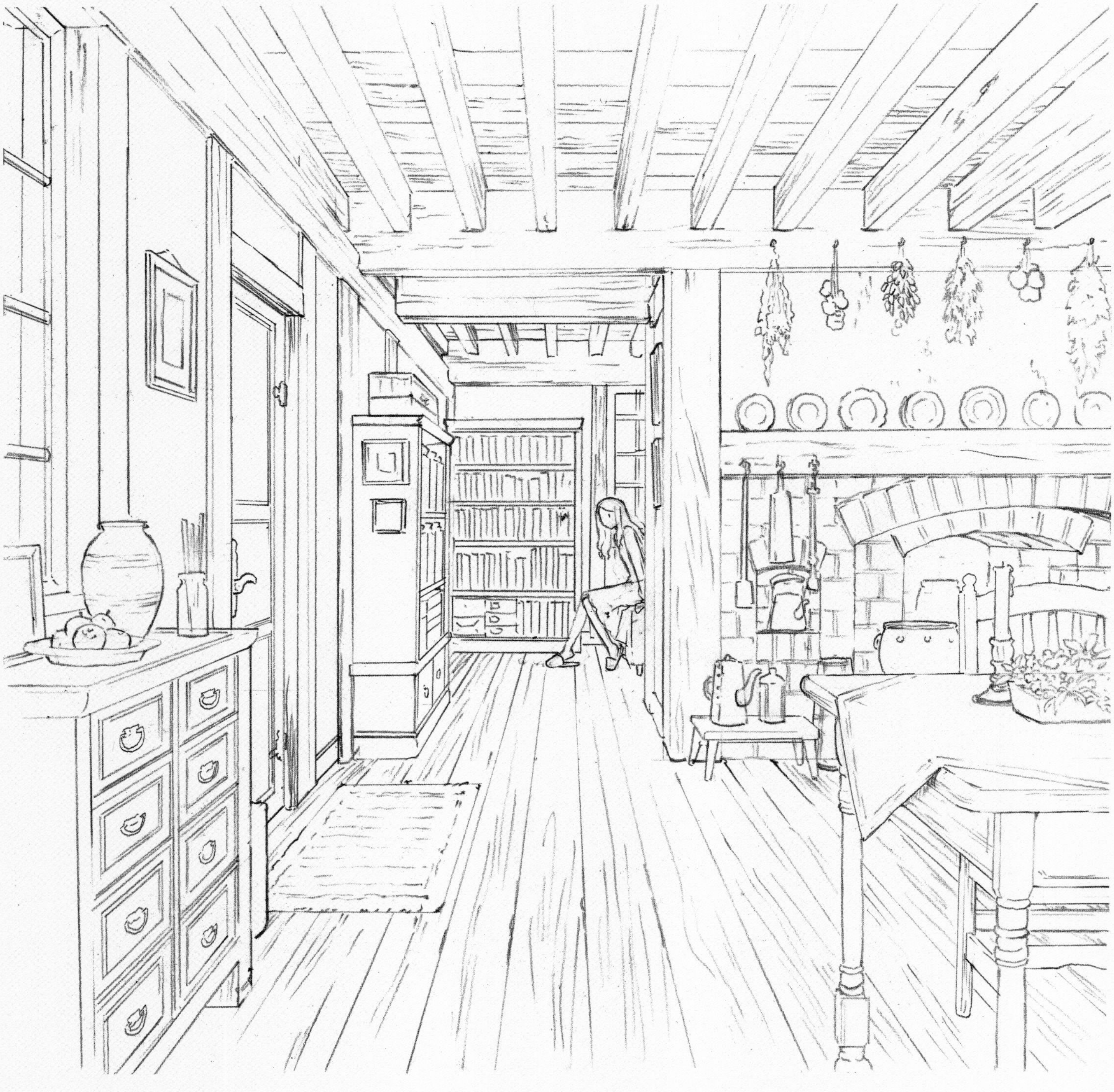

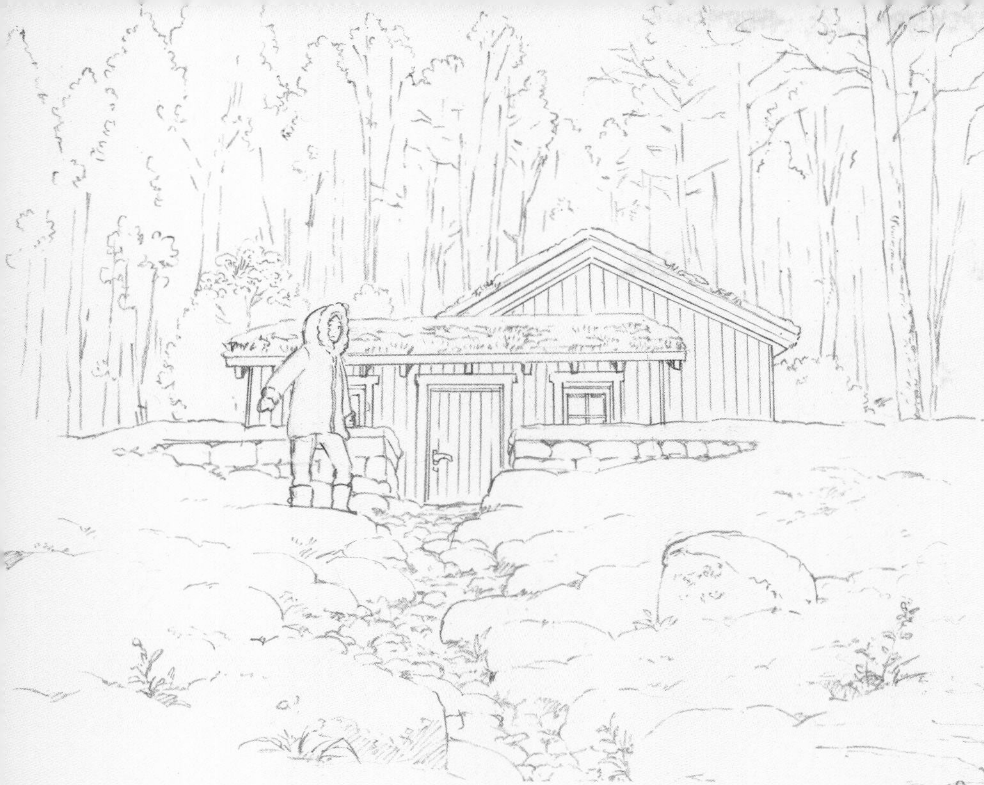

Grass-Roofed House in the Snowy Country

Country: Norway
Time period: early twentieth century
A very normal family that has lived on this land a long time. They preserve the traditional lifestyle. To efficiently use the scarce resources in the Nordic countries, they have found clever ways to make and incorporate their furniture in small spaces. The designs were also beautiful, so I enjoyed collecting reference material for this.

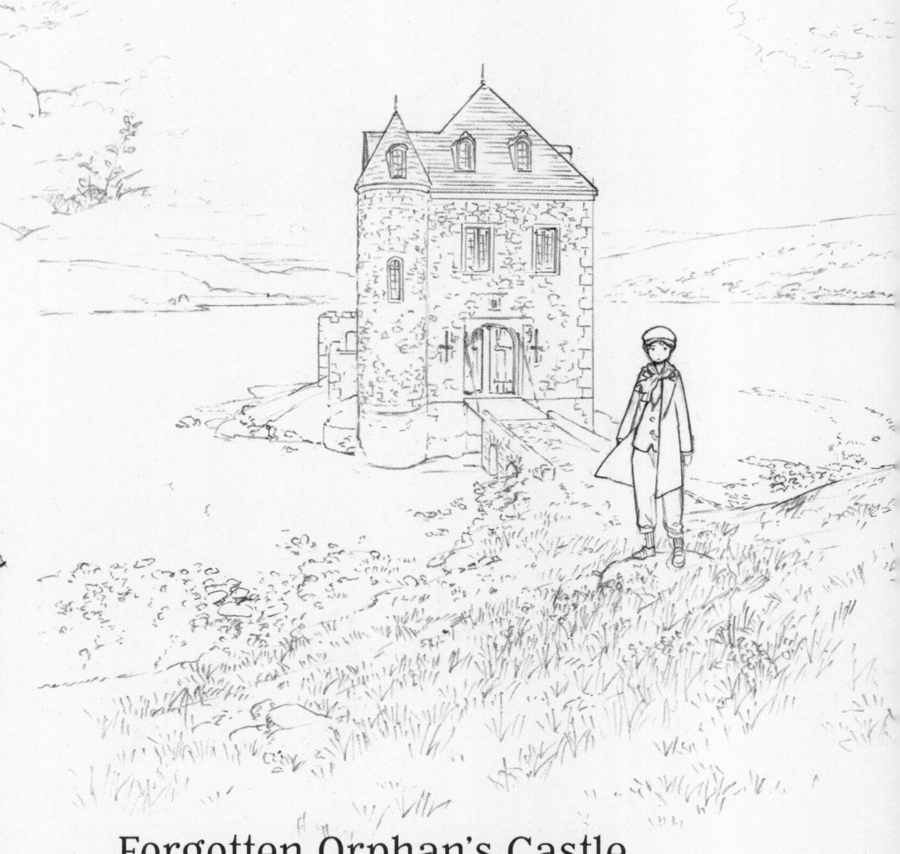

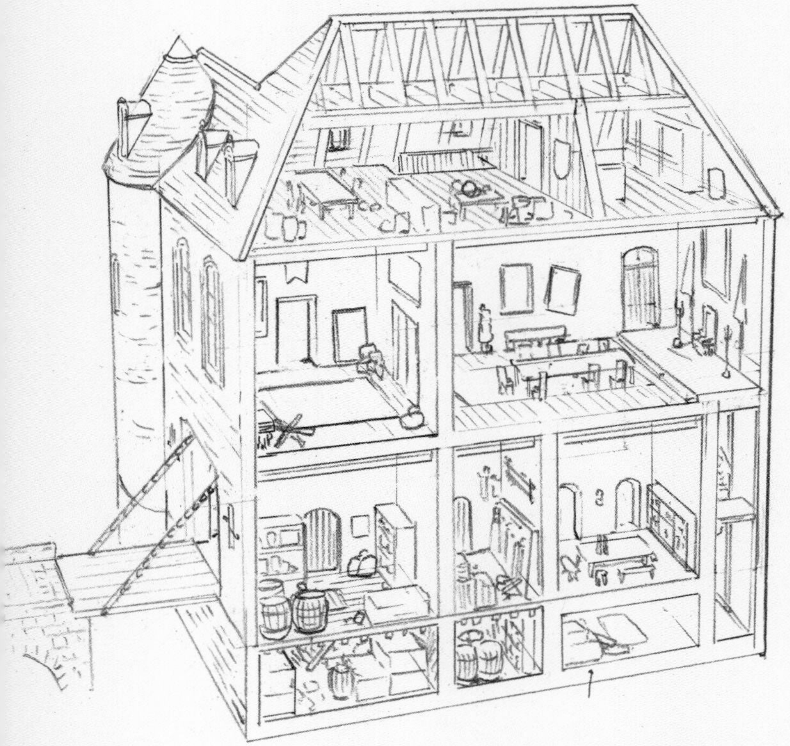

Forgotten Orphan's Castle

Country: Wales
Time period: nineteenth century
The original aristocrats reigning over this land were killed by robbers, so the castle was abandoned. Wales has many old castles that are now tourist attractions.

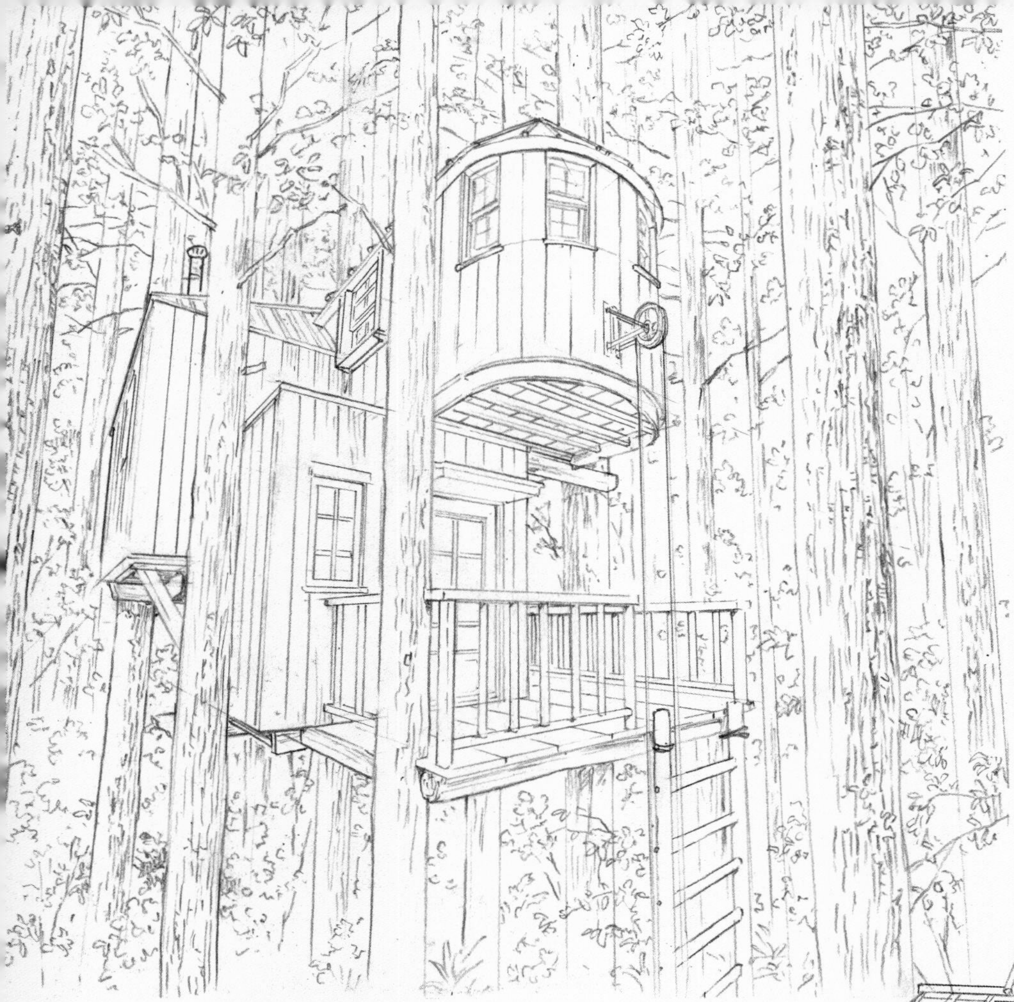

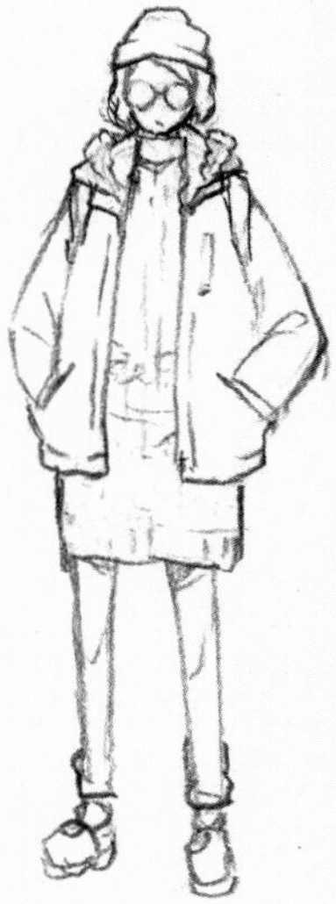

Dreamer's Tree House

Country: United States (Connecticut)
Time period: modern day
On a mountain northeast of New York City, where the owner of this house originally worked. Tree houses as residences are popular novelties in America, and there are even builders who specialize in them.

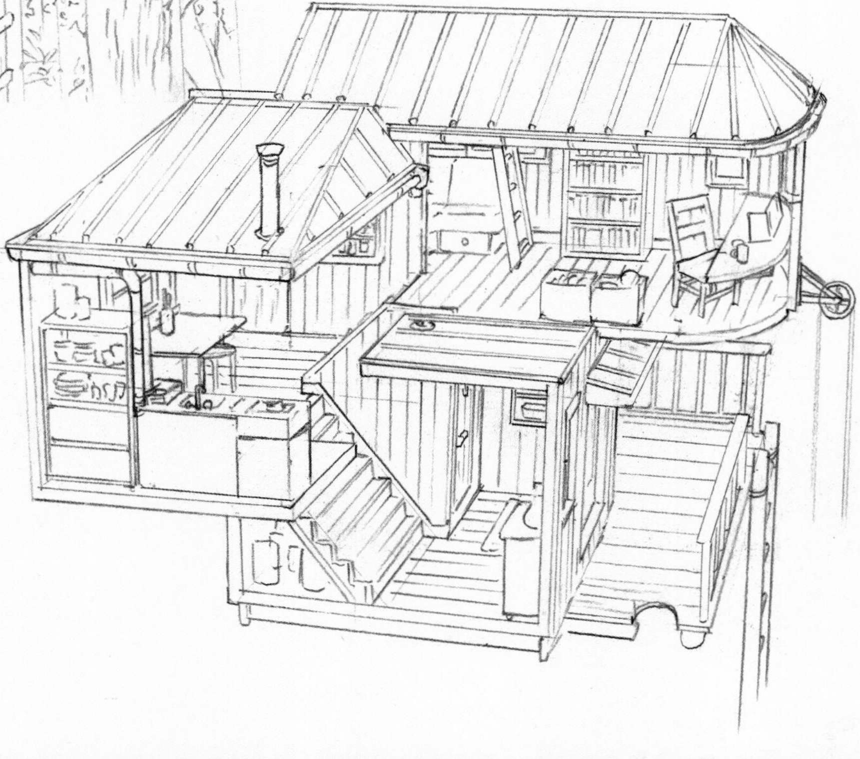

Apple Cider Water Mill

Country: France
Time period: eighteenth century
In this era, unboiled water was not safe to drink, so instead many people drank “hard” cider, which was slightly alcoholic. The alcohol killed germs. This supposes a setting on the border of Germany where there are many forests, similar to that of a Grimms' fairy tale.

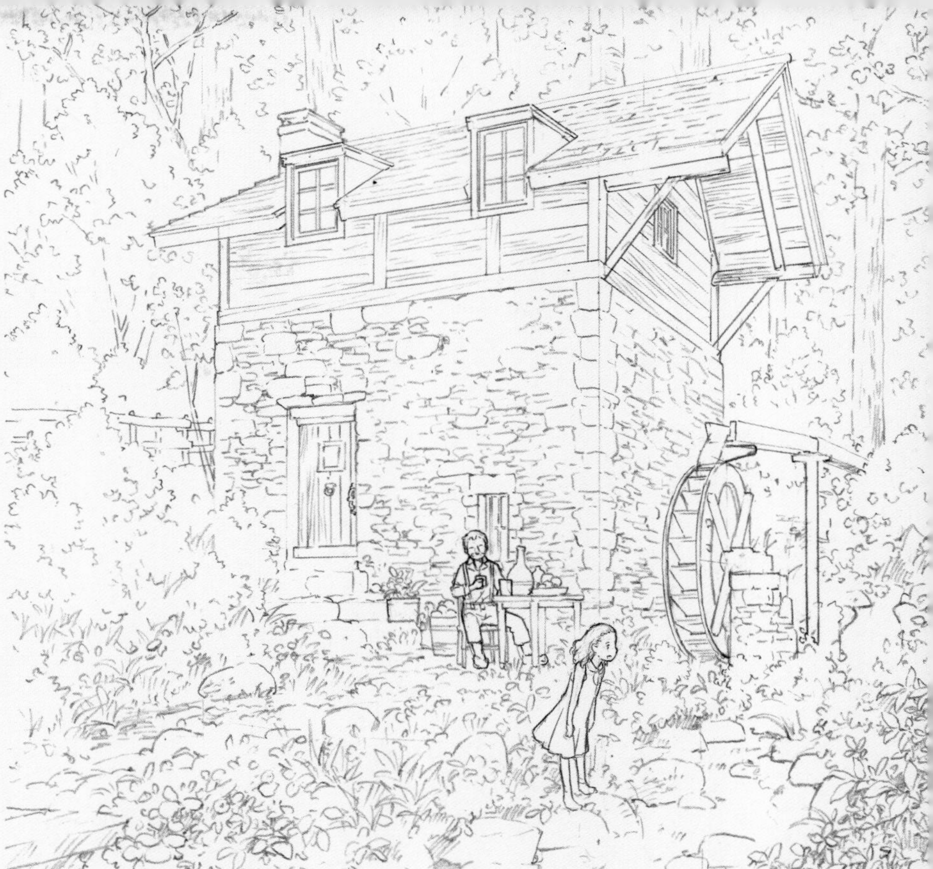

Melancholy Lighthouse Keeper

Country: United States (Rhode Island)
Time period: early twentieth century
Rhode Island was the birthplace of Howard Phillips Lovecraft, father of the Cthulhu Mythos. Beyond the complex shorelines and port towns is the Atlantic Ocean, across which many ships traveled to and from Europe. I created this building with the idea that the features of the land might have been connected to the peculiar aspects of the Cthulhu Mythos and worldbuilding.

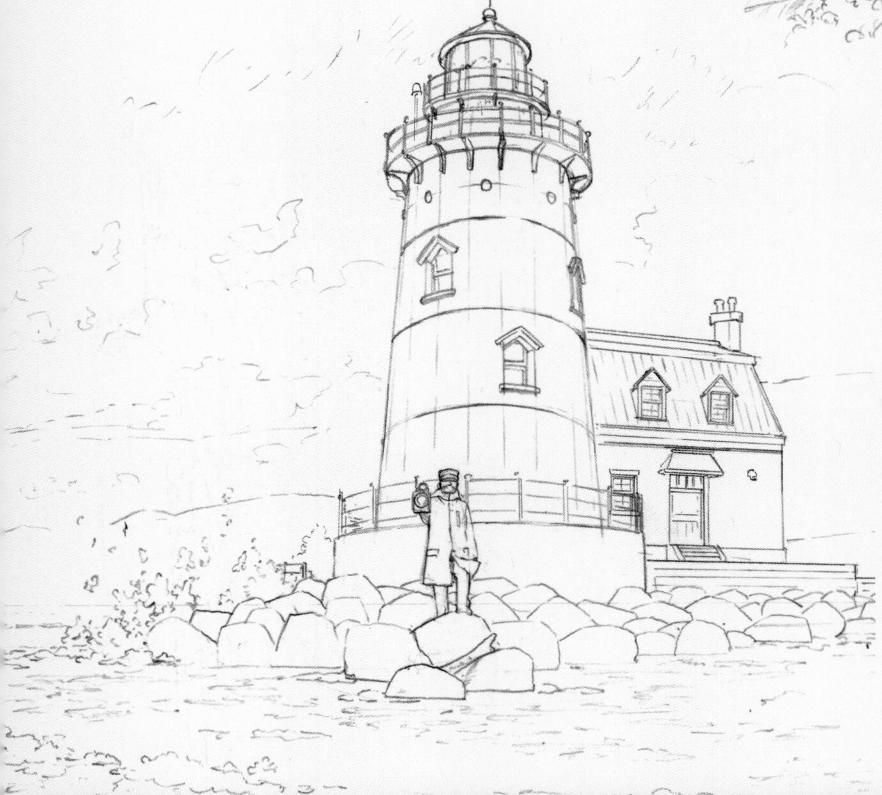

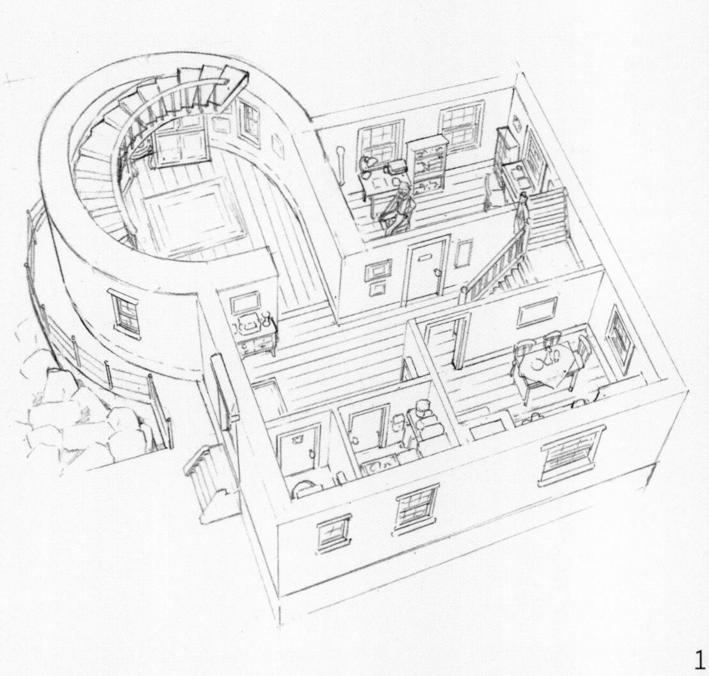

The Post Office of the Dragon Tamer

Country: Scotland
Time period: fictional nineteenth century
Scotland is renowned for its majestic natural landscape. This is especially true of the Highland region, which would be a perfect setting for a fantasy novel. I imagined seeing a dragon against that scenery.

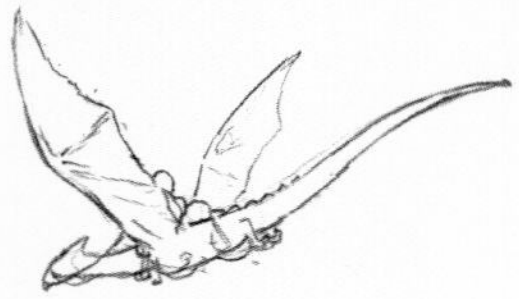

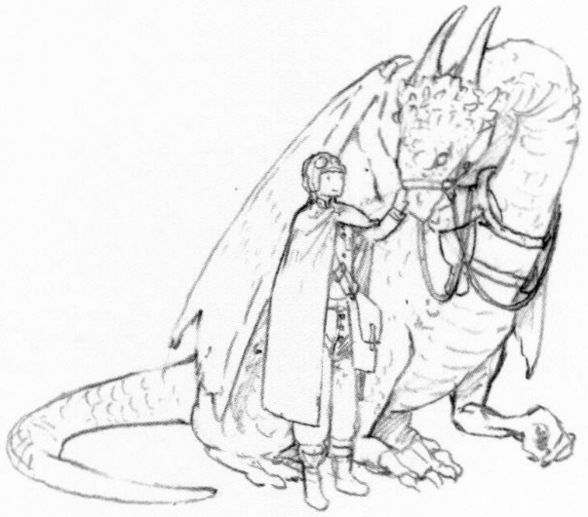

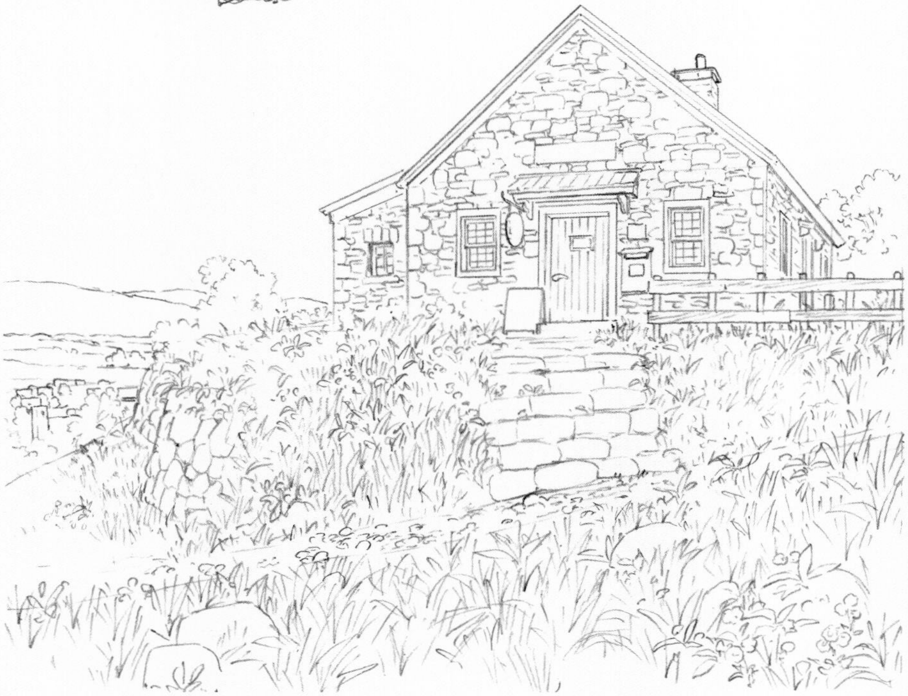

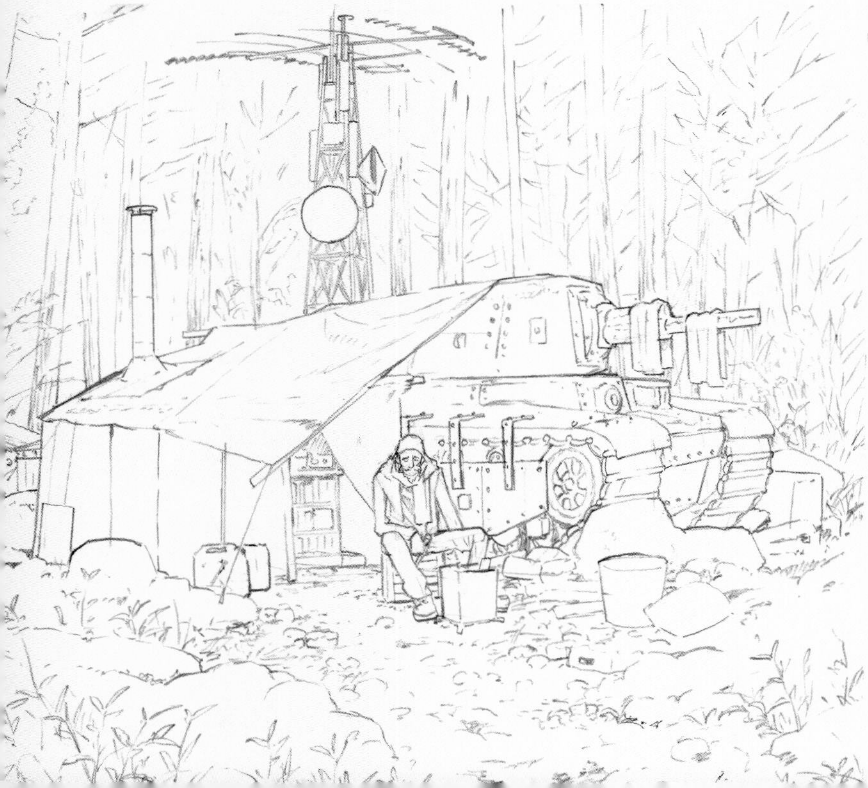

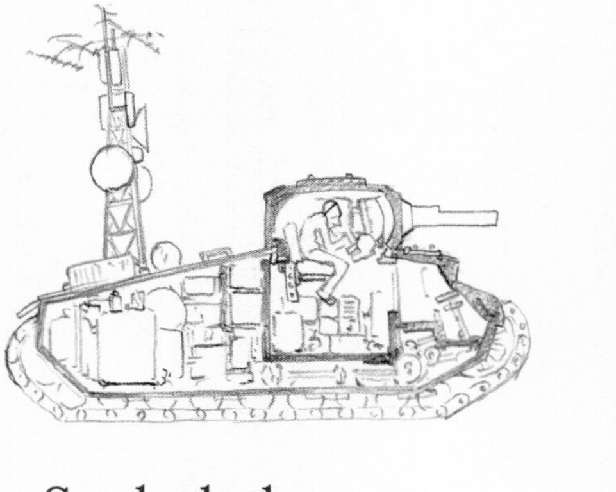

Secluded Information Broker

Country: Russia
Time period: present day
I imagine the broker as a character in a spy movie. I've heard that unused tanks have been left all around Russia, so the idea grew from there. Though this tank looks like it's out of commission, I think it would be very exciting if it started to move in a pivotal scene during the movie's climax.

Diesel Sisters

Country: fictional England
Time period: early twentieth century
This takes place in a dieselpunk world slightly after the steampunk era. Steampunk's worldbuilding is based on steam engines, which makes it slightly antique looking, but in dieselpunk, oil is the main element. Here, only the clothing appears to be steampunk.

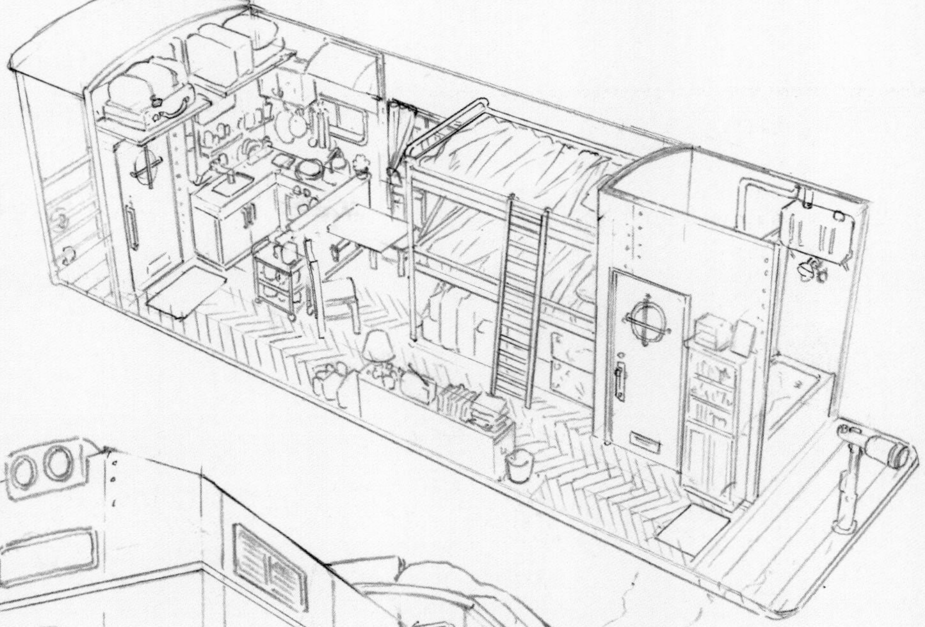

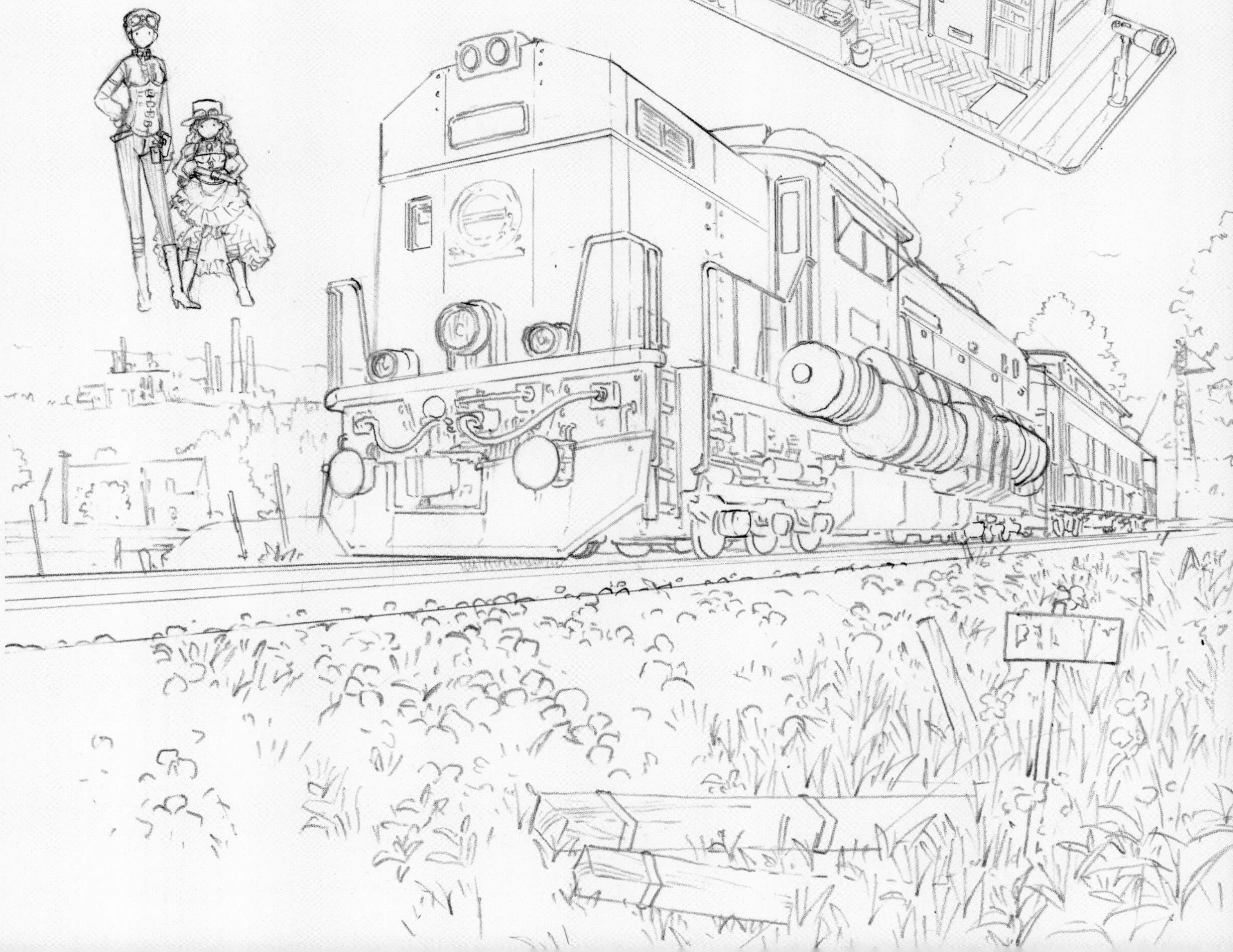

The Library of Lost Books

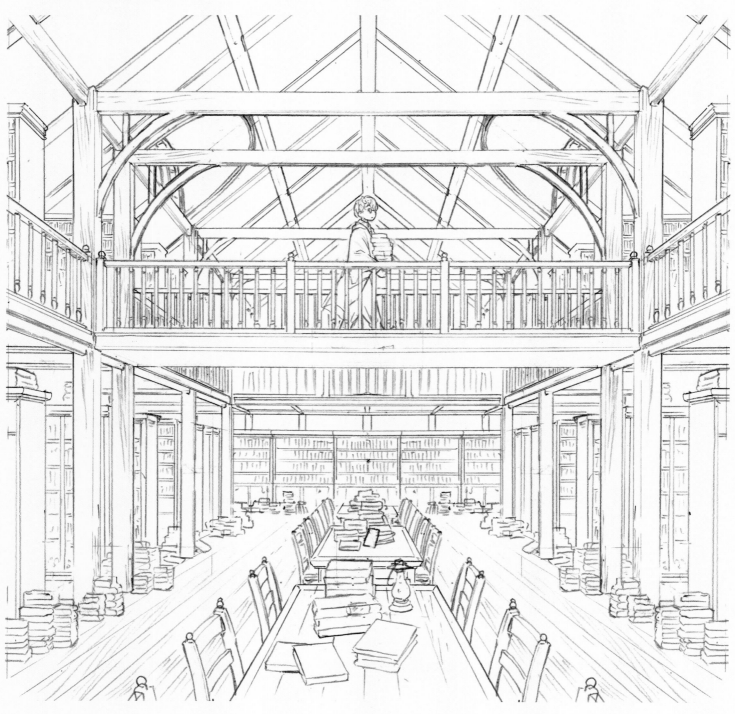

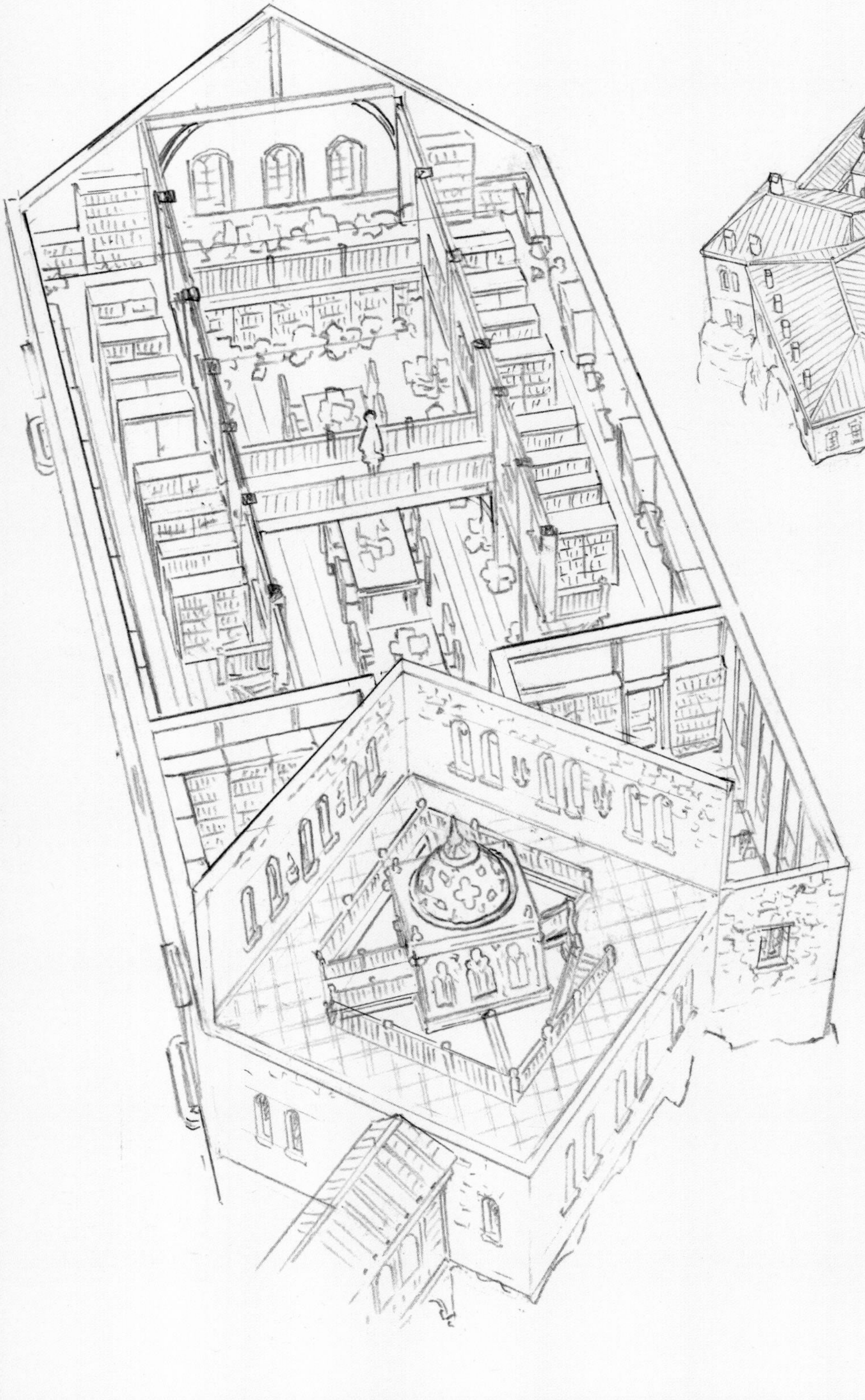

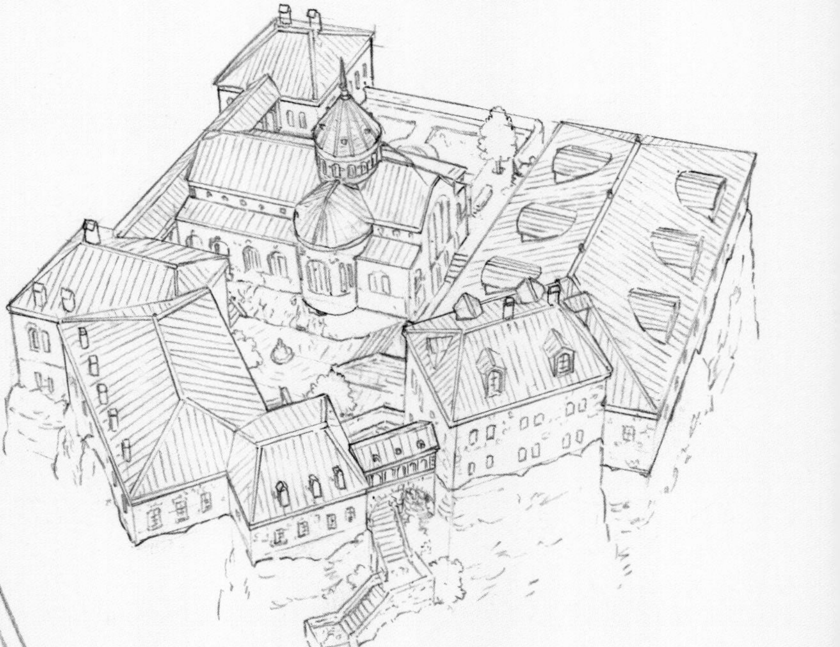

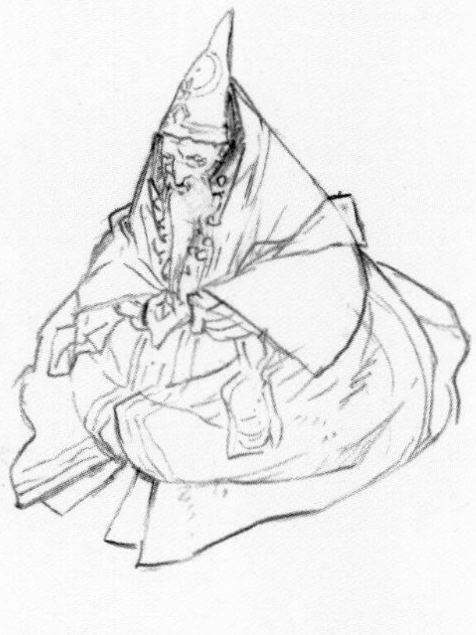

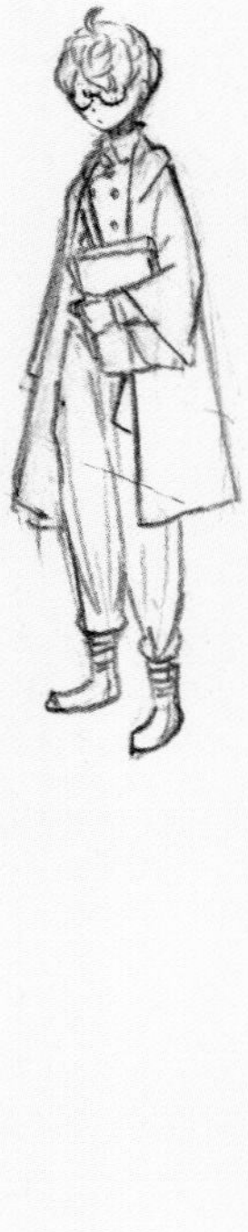

Place: Tibet
Time period: none
This imaginary setting is connected to another universe that has existed in different forms since long before Earth. Though I referenced temples in Tibet for the aesthetic and the atmosphere, I've also incorporated features of the Greek Meteora and Chinese temples into its exterior.

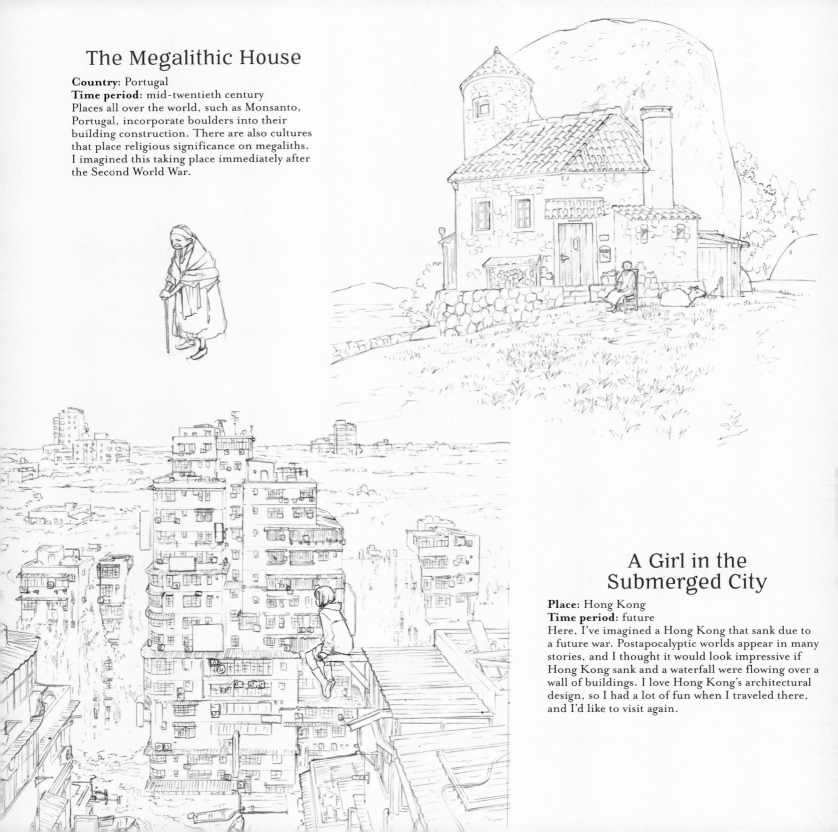

The Megalithic House

Country: Portugal
Time period: mid-twentieth century
Places all over the world, such as Monsanto, Portugal, incorporate boulders into their building construction. There are also cultures that place religious significance on megaliths. I imagined this taking place immediately after the Second World War.

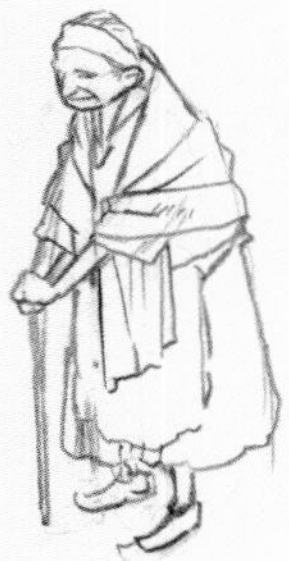

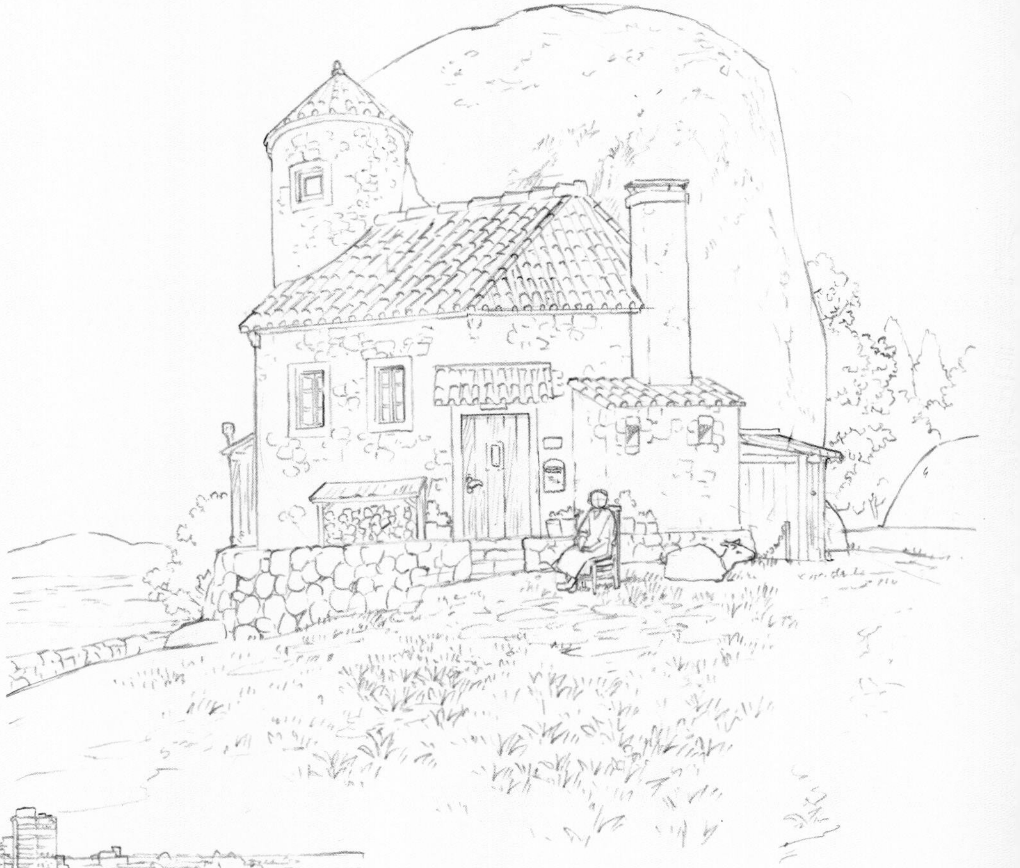

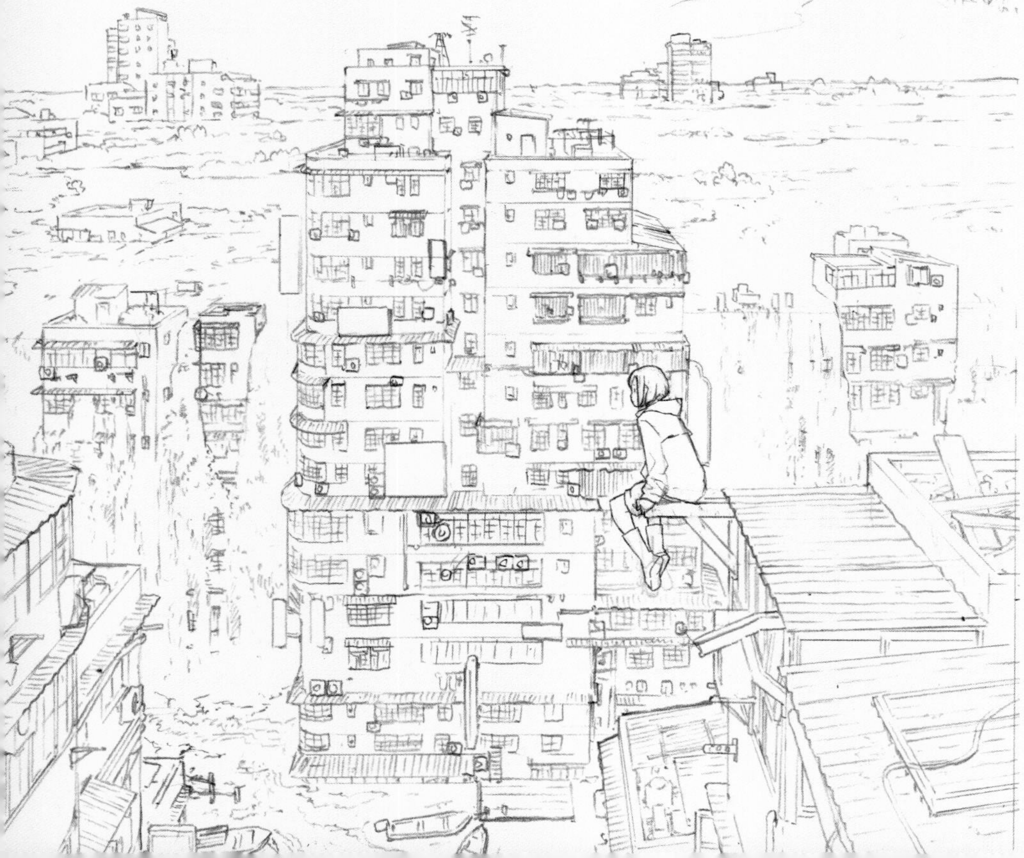

A Girl in the Submerged City

Place: Hong Kong
Time period: future
Here, I've imagined a Hong Kong that sank due to a future war. Postapocalyptic worlds appear in many stories, and I thought it would look impressive if Hong Kong sank and a waterfall were flowing over a wall of buildings. I love Hong Kong's architectural design, so I had a lot of fun when I traveled there, and I'd like to visit again.

Clinic in the Woods

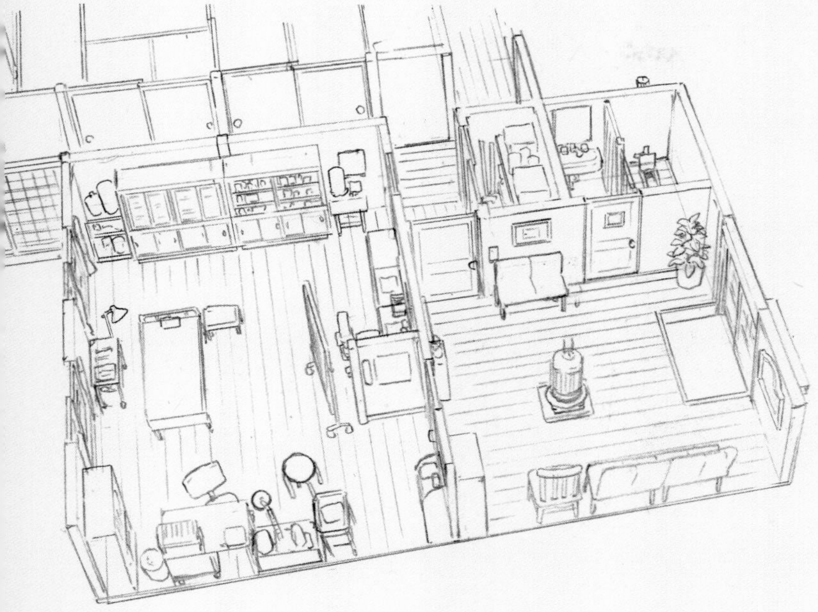

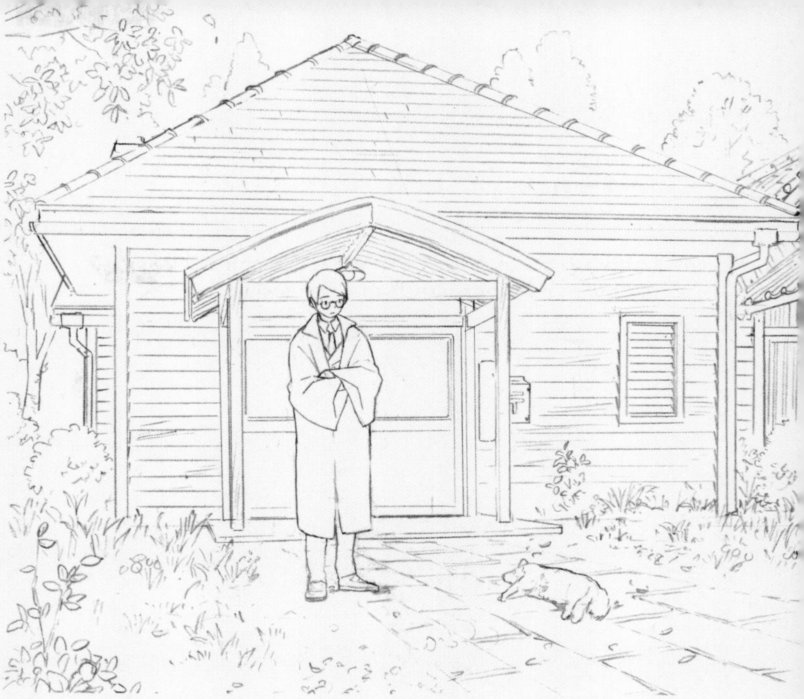

Country: Japan
Time period: early Showa era
A clinic in the early postwar period in the northern Kanto region, where resources were still scarce. This Japanese clinic is one example of old architecture that still exists, similar to old Japanese post offices. Buildings with both Western and Japanese construction in separate areas were especially common from the Meiji era through the early Showa period. In many cases, the guest areas were Western style while the living space was Japanese.

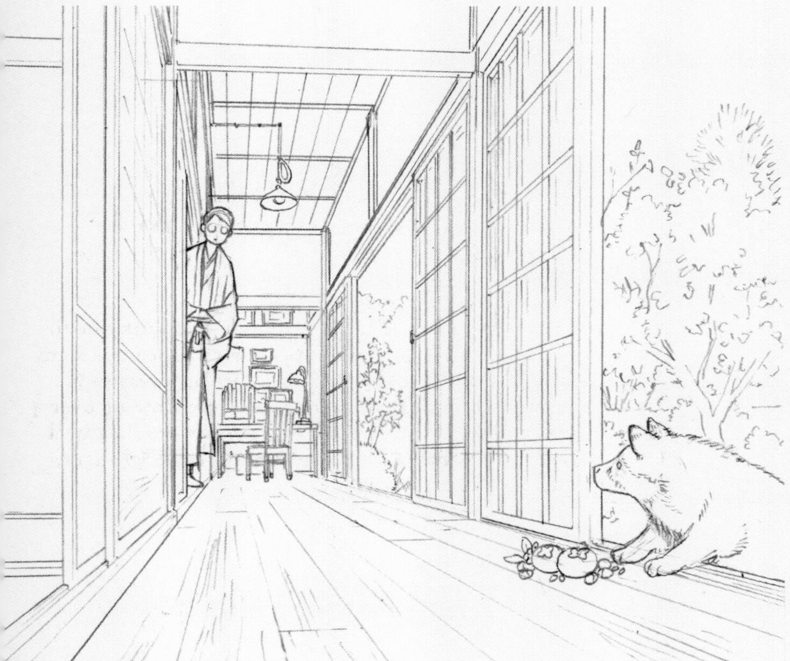

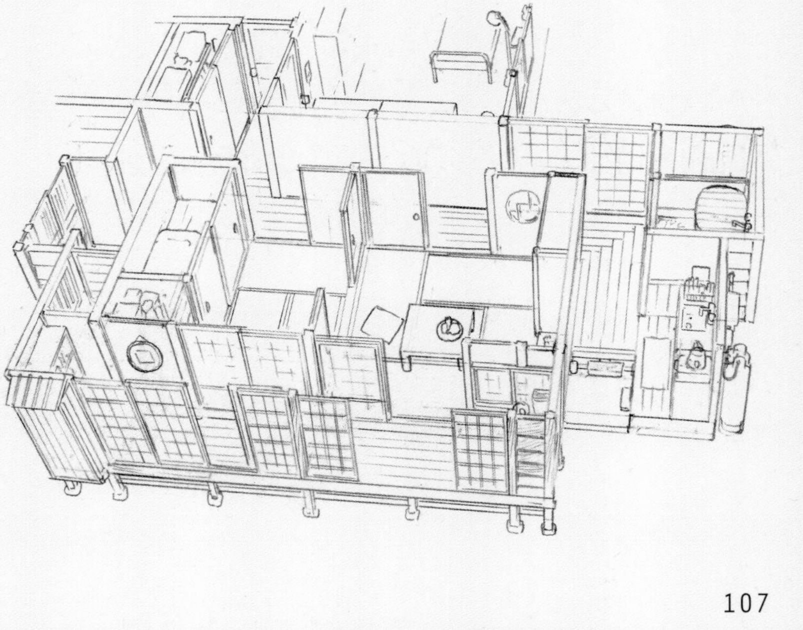

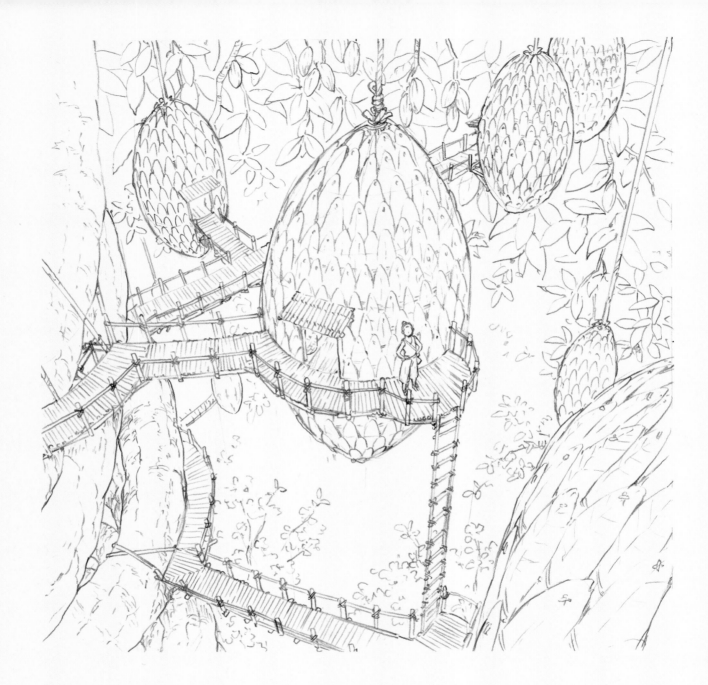

Cacao Tree Houses

Country: Honduras
Time period: none
Cocoa production is widespread in Honduras, and there is a vast belt of tropical rainforest near the Plátano River where cacao trees can be cultivated. It is said that the ancient Mayans had a city in this area, and so I thought it would be a fitting place for a fictional gigantic cacao tree.

A Timid Ogre's Hideout

Country: Japan
Time period: early fifteenth century
This is how I imagine an ogre would actually hide in Japan. He lives in a pit house that he has repaired. I've imagined this occurring around the Muromachi period (1336–1573 CE), but I think it could be anytime between Kamakura (1185–1333 CE) and Showa.

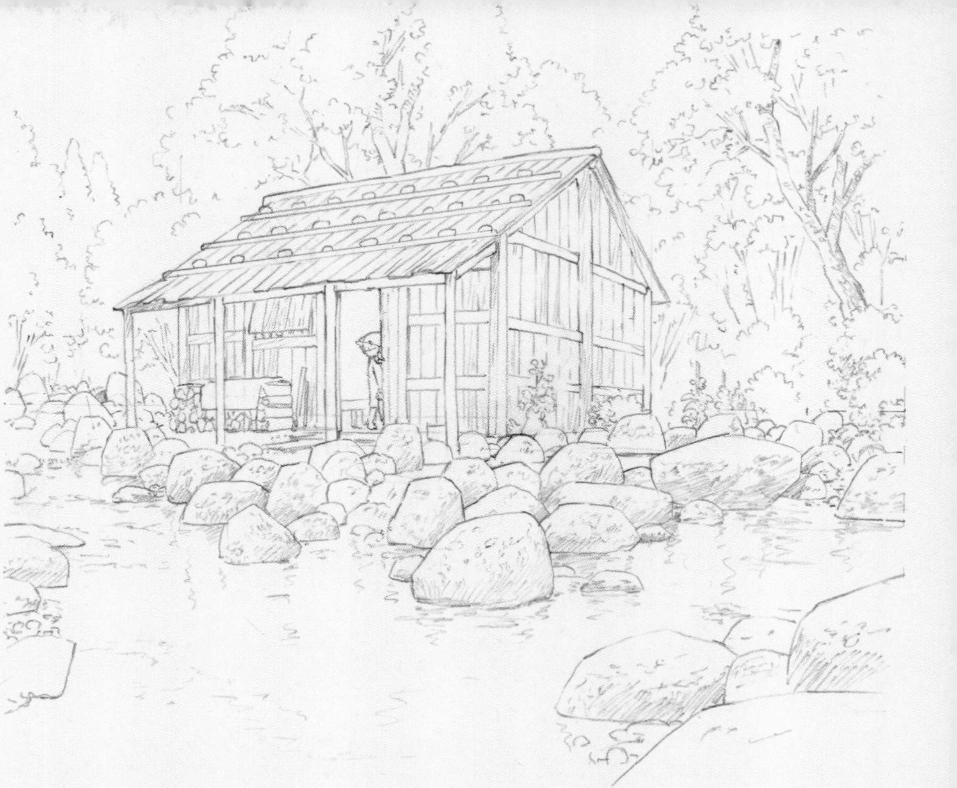

A Tower House Near the Border

Country: Georgia
Time period: nineteenth century
In the northern part of Georgia, at the base of the Caucasus Mountains near the border of Russia, there are several hamlets with tower houses. When aggressors invade, the residents actually do shut themselves into the tower parts of their homes to protect themselves.

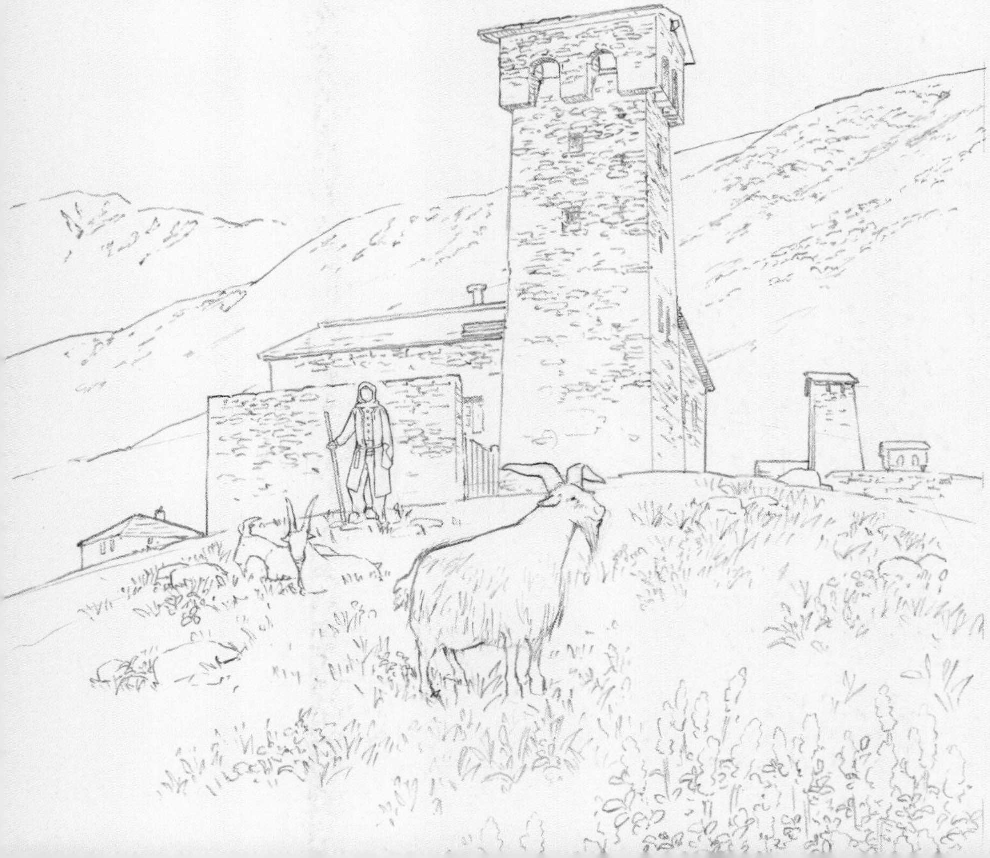

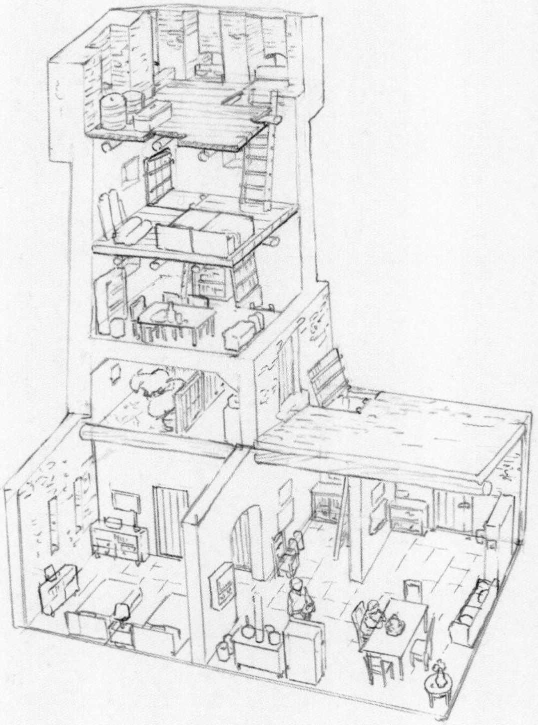

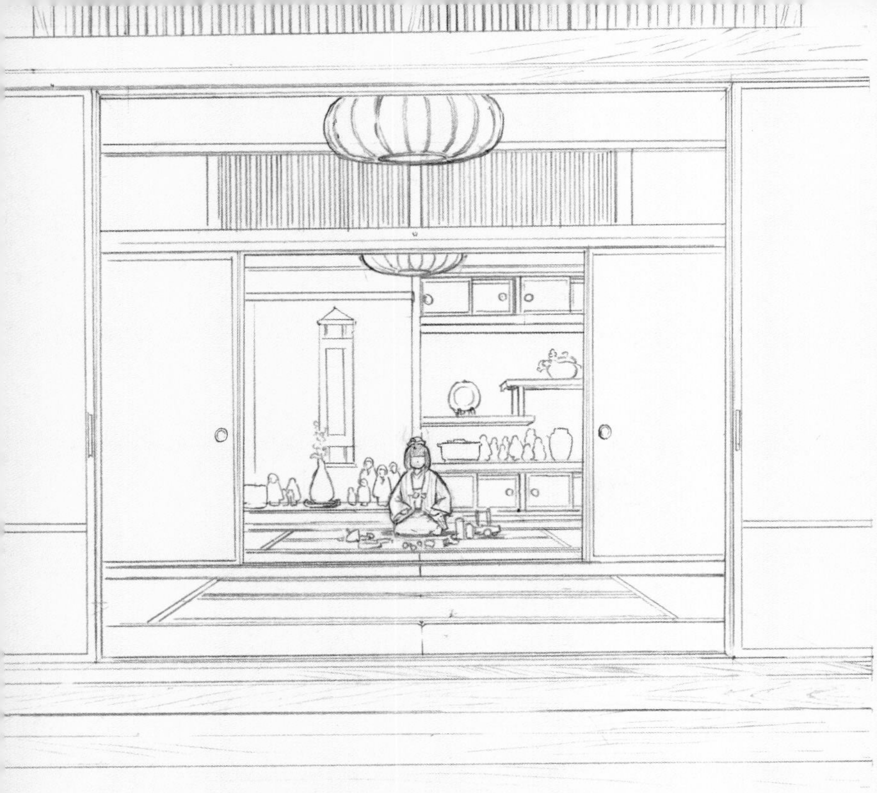

An Outbuilding Inhabited by a Poltergeist

Country: Japan
Time period: modern day
The zashiki-warashi legend is most common in Iwate prefecture, where you can stay at traditional Japanese-style inns that supposedly have these ghosts. They generally appear in the rooms farthest back in the building, so in this drawing, the ghost lives in an outbuilding.

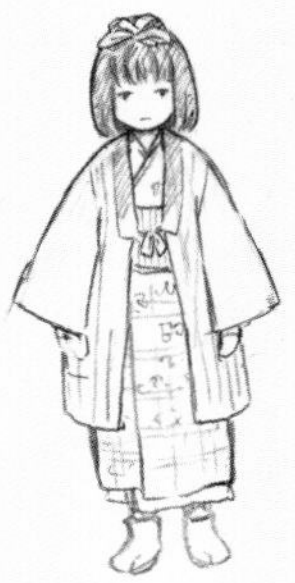

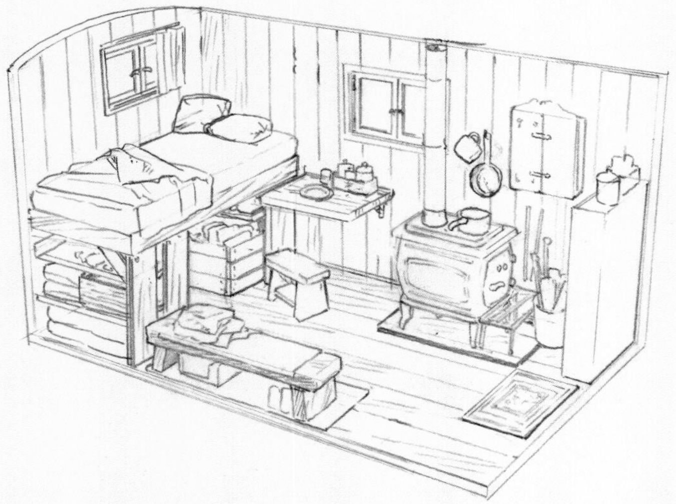

A Shepherd's Hut

Country: Switzerland
Time period: nineteenth century
Shepherding is an old occupation and plays a large part in religion and art. There actually were lookout huts for shepherds, but they are not used much these days.

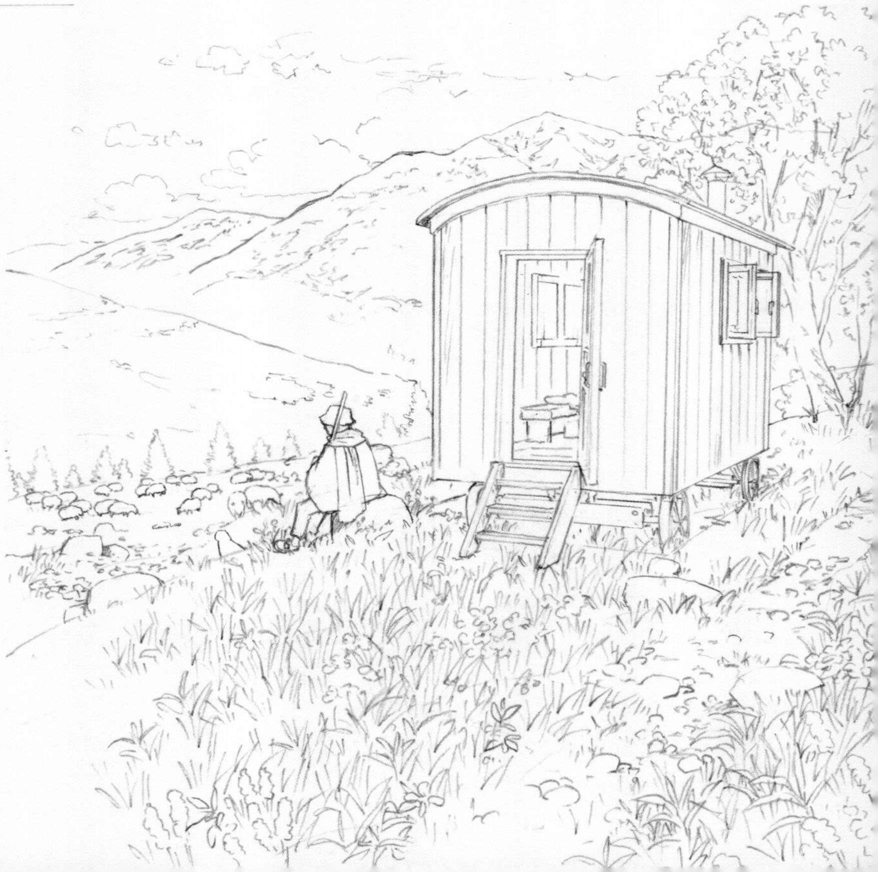

An Eccentric Botanist's Laboratory

Country: France
Time period: early twentieth century
Since the outer walls of European buildings were usually sturdy, it was common for the exteriors to be left intact and for the interiors to be remodeled. Based on this, I thought it would be interesting if someone turned a whole building into an atrium for plants. If someone were to actually do this, I think the heat and humidity would cause issues.

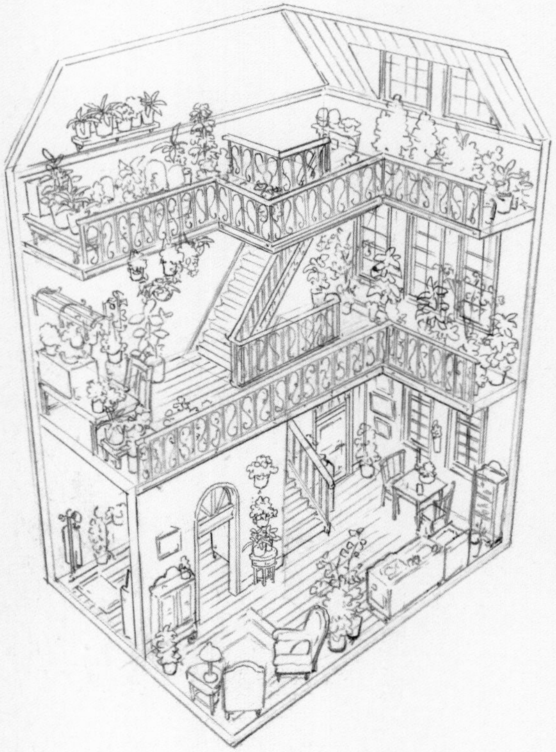

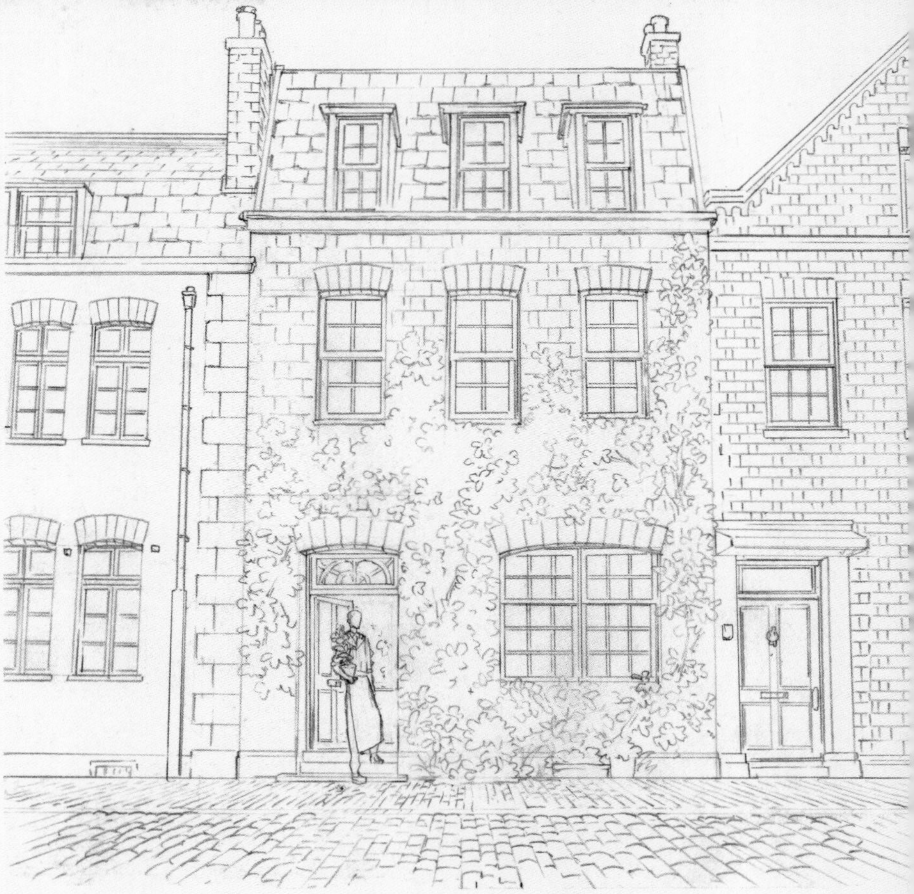

A Wanted Man's Sod House

Country: United States
Time period: late nineteenth century
I learned about sod houses by watching a lot of movies and playing games that dealt with the American frontier, so I drew one. I think you can tell from the unsecured doors and windows that there was a lack of materials in the pioneering era, which I like very much.

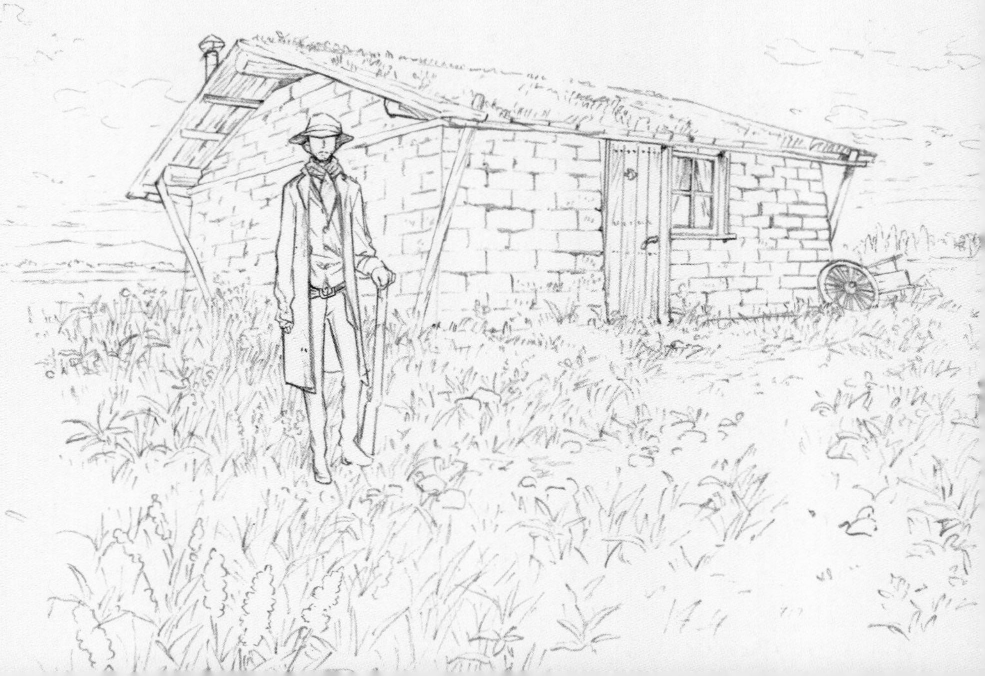

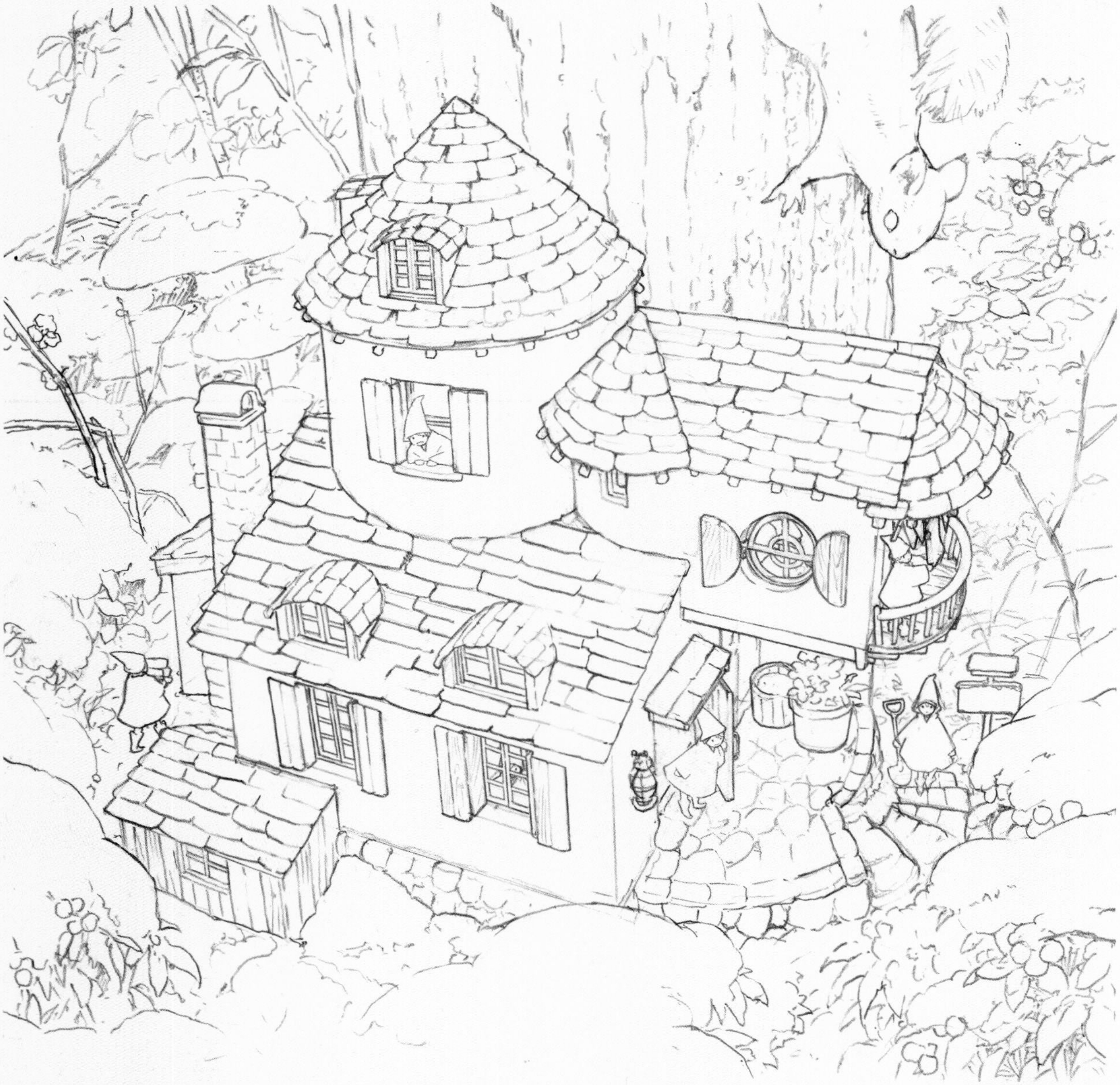

The Seven Dwarfs' House

Country: Germany
Time period: eighteenth century
I wanted this to feel like a fairy tale, so I made the dwarves' clothes and the slatted shutters a highly saturated color and then worked backward from there to design the house. This was an illustration I was commissioned to make for the Comic Market 97 paper bags (small size).

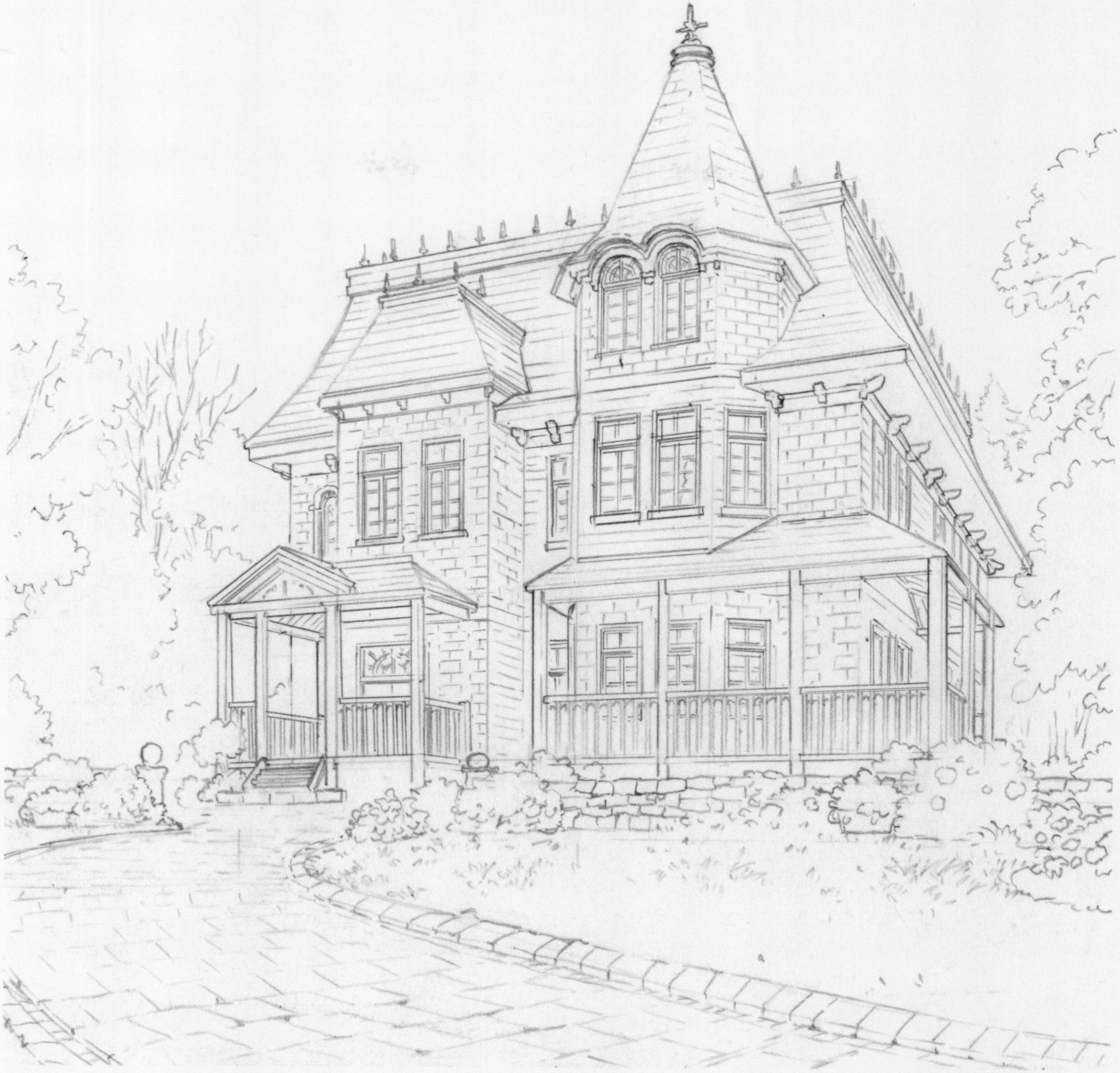

A Lonely Ghost's Mansion

Country: United States
Time period: early 1900s
This is based on a mansion that might show up in a slightly dated movie with horror elements, such as *The Addams Family*. I've packed in many details, such as the lattices around the building, complex silhouettes, entryway atrium, and stairs leading to the basement, that could be useful in a horror scenario.

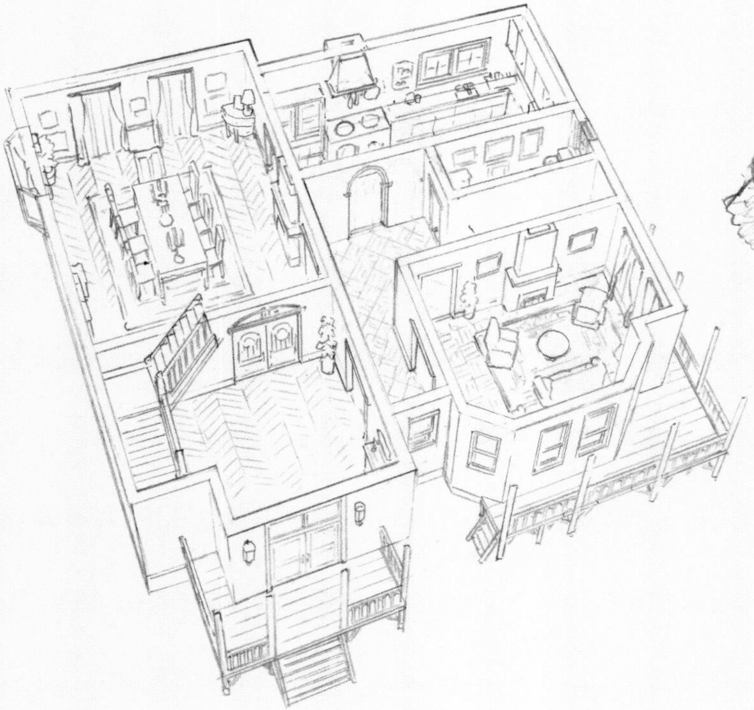

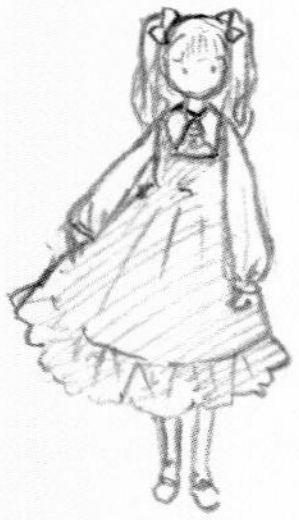

A Lonely Ghost's Mansion

(continued from previous page)

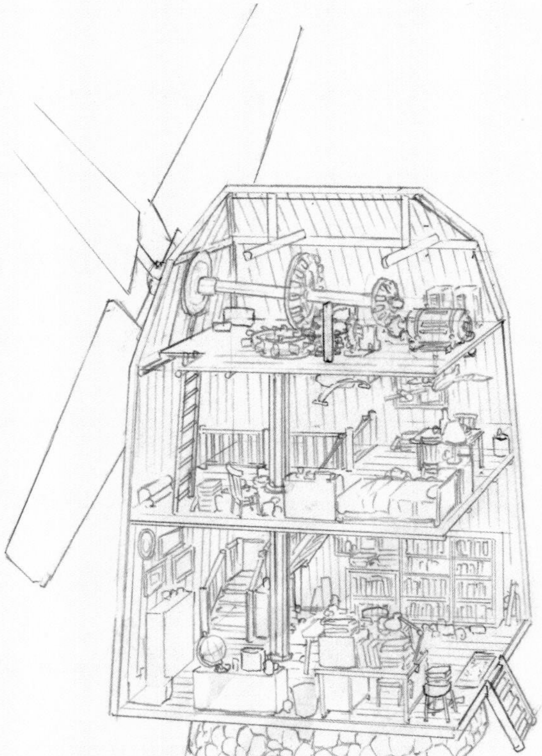

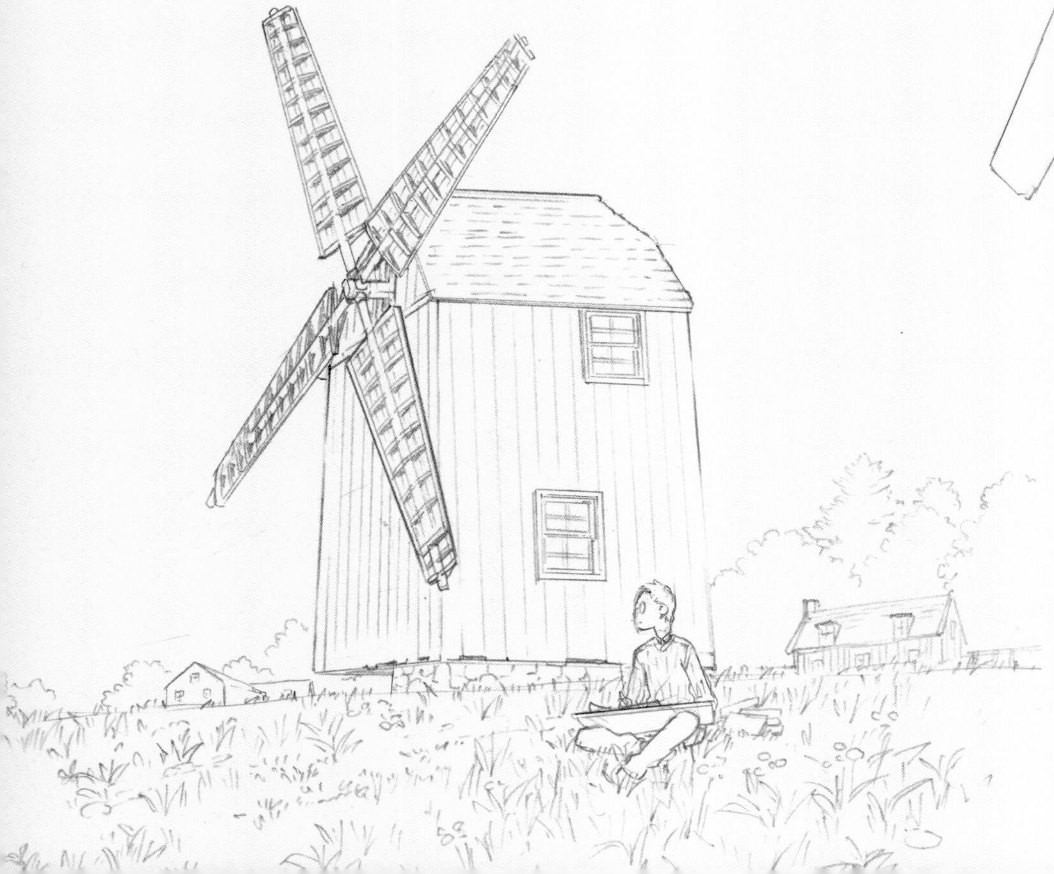

A Young Inventor's Windmill

Country: Netherlands
Time period: 1970s
I associate windmills with the Netherlands, but lately they have stopped using windmills, so I thought up a scenario in which a young inventor has set up shop in one. He finds the place quite useful in many ways. In actuality, I think placing this much furniture in one would create problems because of the weight.

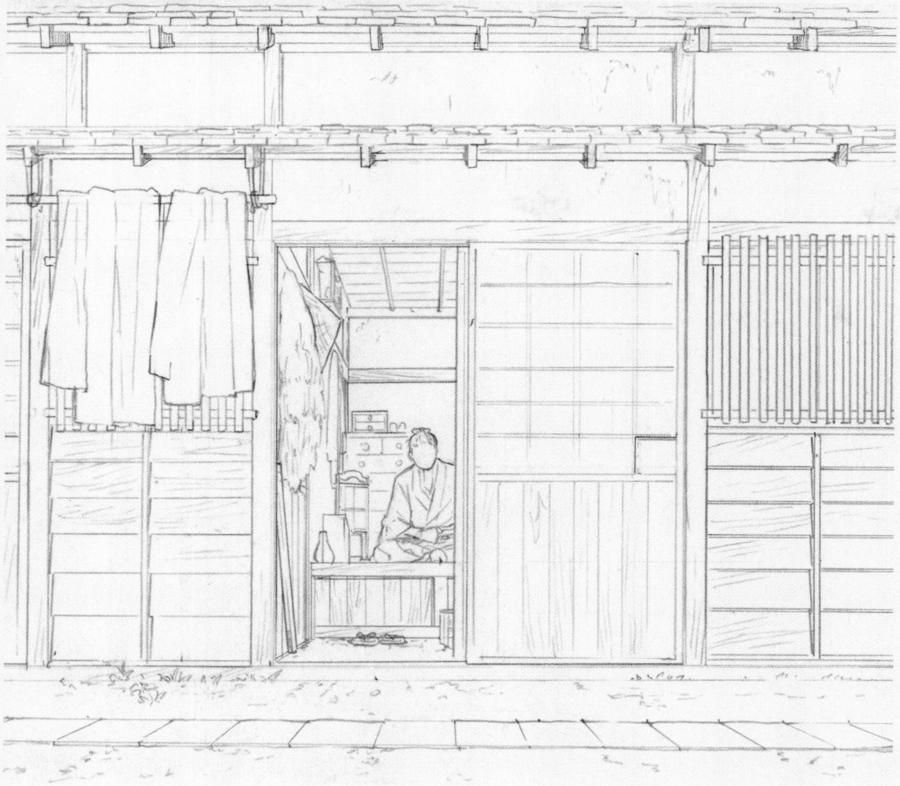

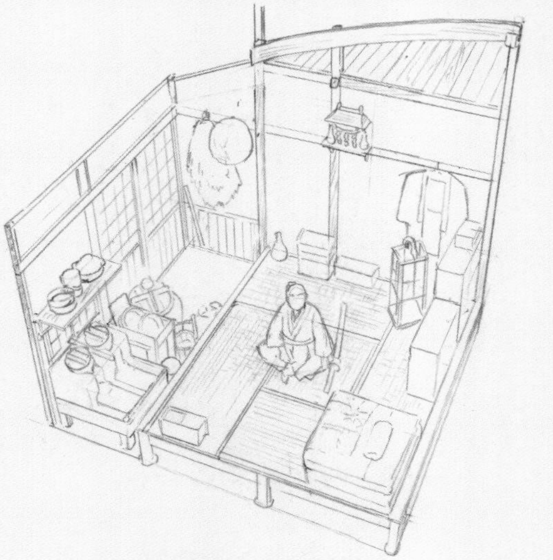

A Ronin's Tenement House

Country: Japan
Time period: Edo period
I enjoy period novels, and after reading many that featured tenement houses, the architecture of these buildings drew my attention. When I looked into it, I found that the residents lived in very cramped quarters. Thanks to that, I will appreciate their context and impact in the next novel I read about them.

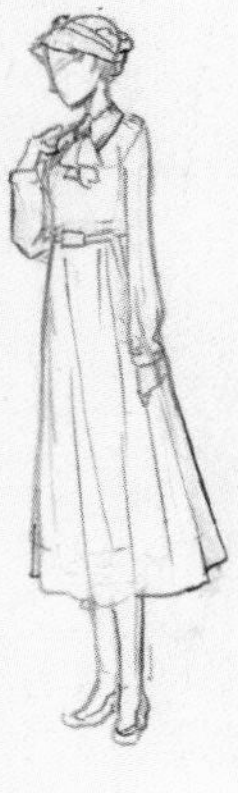

The House of a Woman Fascinated by Dolls

Country: Japan
Time period: early Showa era
I enjoy Edogawa Ranpo's novels, especially the bizarre atmosphere and setting that so embodies the early Showa era, so I used that as the basis for this illustration. I've fancied the ball-jointed dolls of the artist Katan Amano for a long time, so I imagined those here.

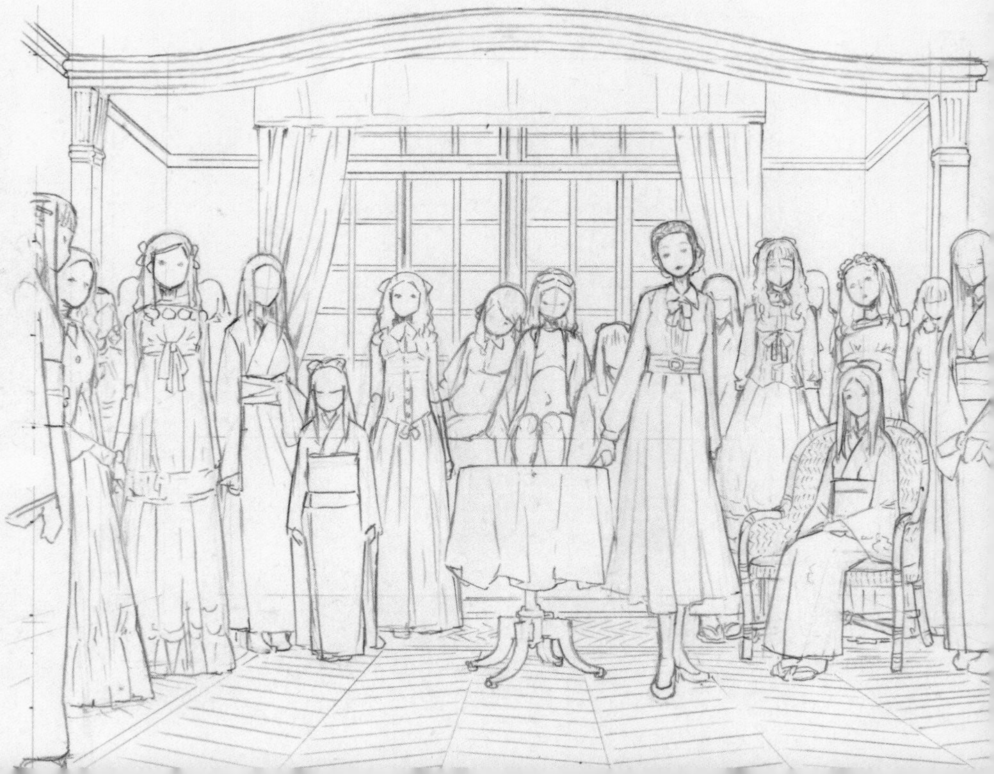

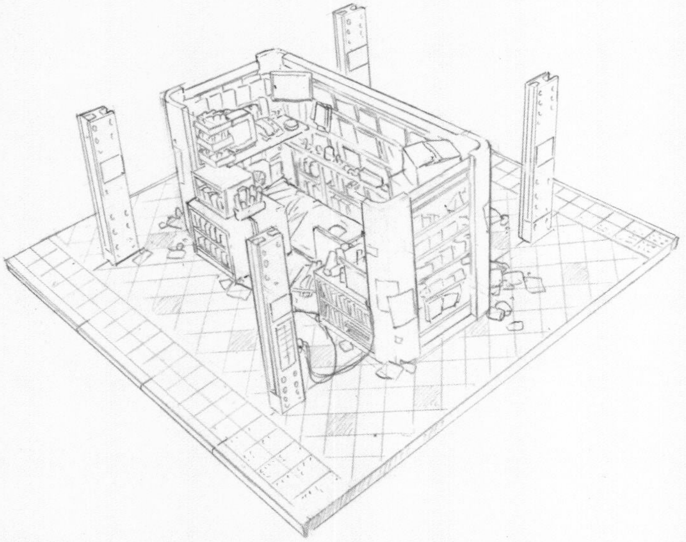

A Man in an Abandoned Subway Station

Country: United States
Time period: 1960s
Many unused "ghost" subway stations exist worldwide. They seem to have gotten their name because they can be seen for a brief moment in the pitch-black subway tunnels as a train hurtles past.

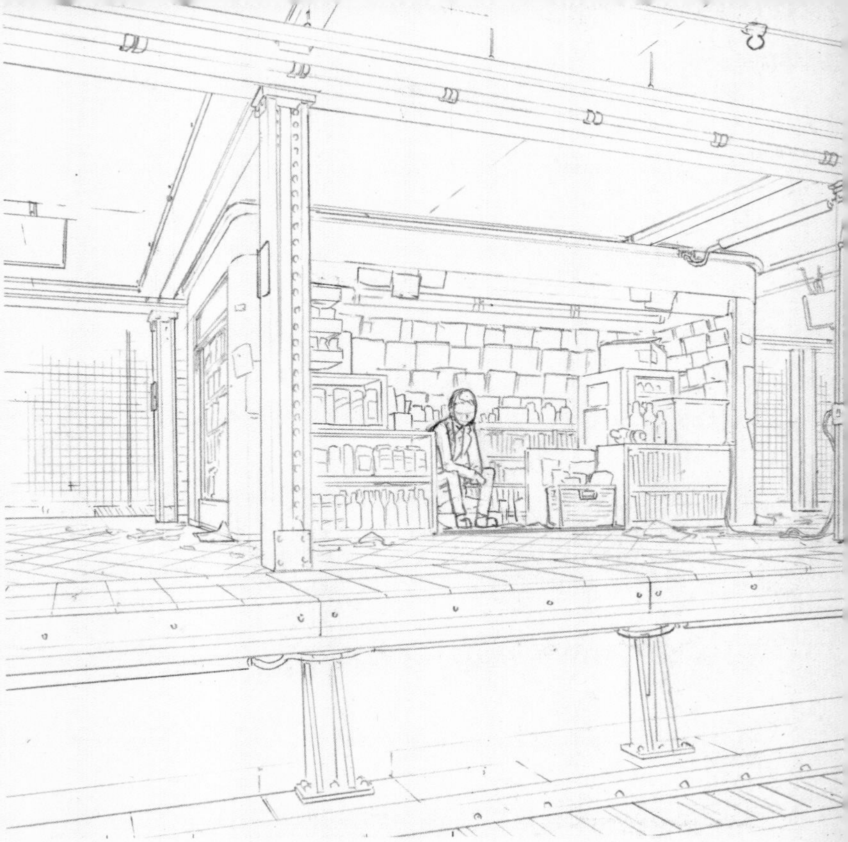

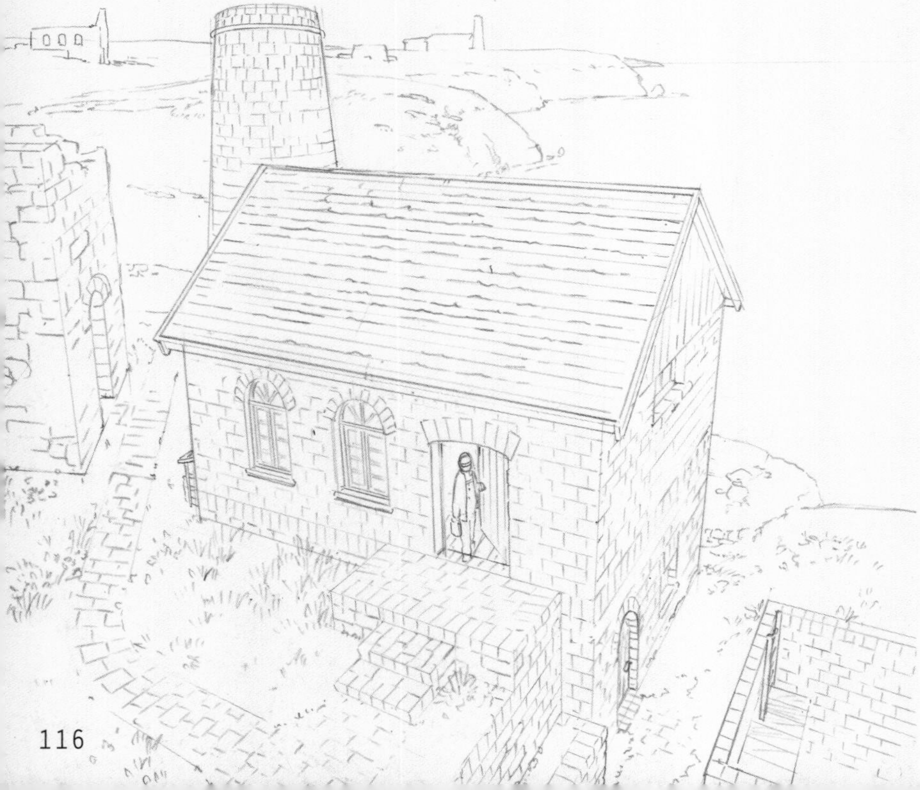

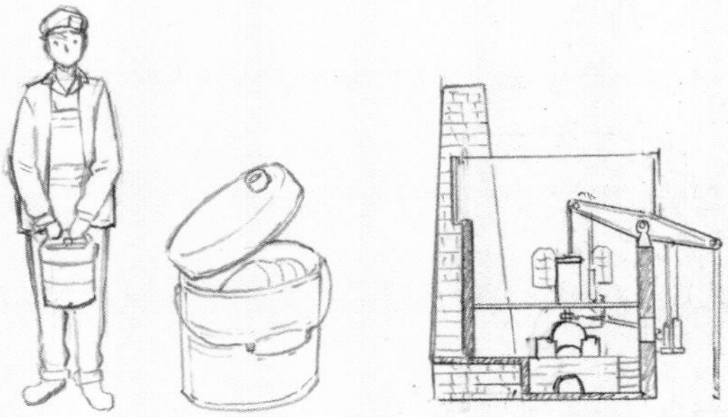

A Miner's Engine House

Country: England (Cornwall)
Time period: early twentieth century
The coal mines in the Cornwall region have been named a World Heritage site, and their remains can be seen even now. The house of Pazul from *Laputa: Castle in the Sky* was probably based on this area.

MAKING OF

a Miner's Engine House

1. Creating the Rough Drafts and Sketches

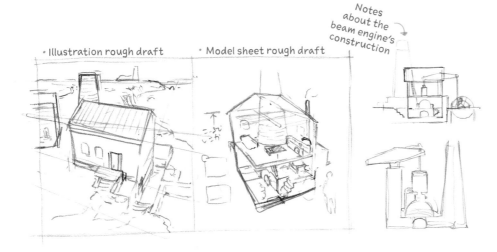

• Illustration rough draft • Model sheet rough draft

Notes about the beam engine's construction

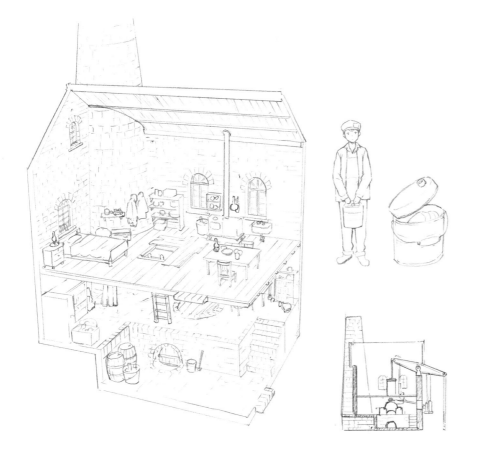

Since *Houses with a Story* is meant to delight through both its illustrations and its model sheets, the drawing process was more complex and time-consuming than usual. Here, I use A Miner's Engine House as an example to present the creation process.

First, I imagine what types of buildings I would like to draw. Since I want readers to get a sense that there's a story behind each illustration, the houses cannot simply look charming on the surface. I contemplate the settings in order to create houses that evoke their origins and seem like they've come straight from works of fiction.

For this illustration, I decided to use ore mines, which appear in many stories, as a theme. I start by researching what a mine is like, what kinds of people might live there, and what their lives might be like. Since I've learned through my research that the mechanisms behind a beam engine and the buildings that housed them led to English mines being named as World Heritage sites, I let my imagination go from there. I then come up with my character: a young laborer living in a former engine house.

Next I create a small rough sketch. For the model sheet sketch, I imagine how an engine house would have to be remodeled to make the dwelling habitable. For example, I've placed a ladder in the boiler hole and drawn a newly installed stove. I also note the boiler construction (upper left figure). I imagine what kind of composition would be most effective and draw up notes on the rough sketch.

I proceed with the model sheet's draft (left figure). Since the structure of the home is difficult to see in the rough sketch, I change the angle of the composition. First I draw the silhouette of the building and the outlines of its distinctive characteristics, and then I draw the large furniture, steadily progressing to smaller details. To make sure the size of the furniture matches the heights of the window frames and ceilings, I occasionally look at the drawing as a whole. When I was at the rough sketch stage, I established the details, so I don't need to pause and think as I draw. Since I've already done the research, I also draw the lunch box.

The same fundamentals apply to the illustration's draft. I reference the rough sketch and start with the large silhouettes, then steadily draw the smaller components. Finally, I finish by drawing the patterns, such as the joints between the bricks.

I pay special attention to the aspect ratios in the model sheet and match the illustration's large silhouettes to them when I first draw the outlines. Next I draw the window frames and determine the height of the ceiling on each floor. I continue checking that everything looks consistent as I move on to smaller details.

In this drawing, one vanishing point is on the screen, so I've drawn it right into the illustration, but because the second vanishing point is offscreen, I've had to draw the perspective paths, as shown in the above drawing. The drawing is an overlooking shot and should be a loose three-point perspective, but I haven't included the lower vanishing point and draw all my vertical lines based on intuition. That should be fine as long as it doesn't look off.

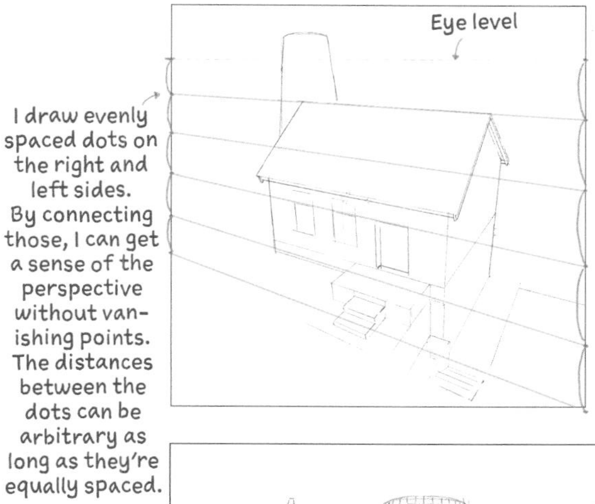
Eye level
I draw evenly spaced dots on the right and left sides. By connecting those, I can get a sense of the perspective without vanishing points. The distances between the dots can be arbitrary as long as they're equally spaced.

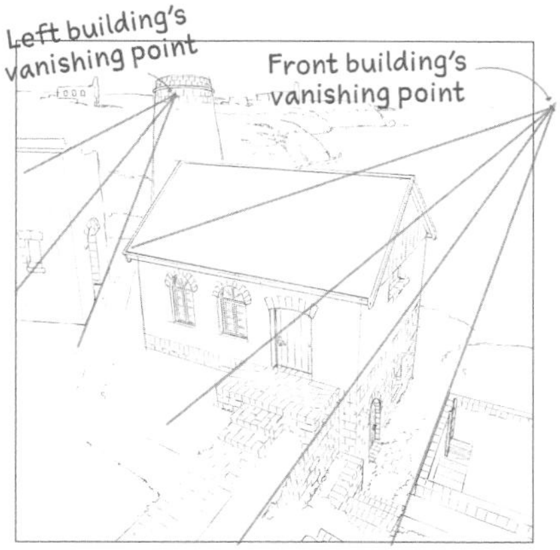
Left building's vanishing point
Front building's vanishing point

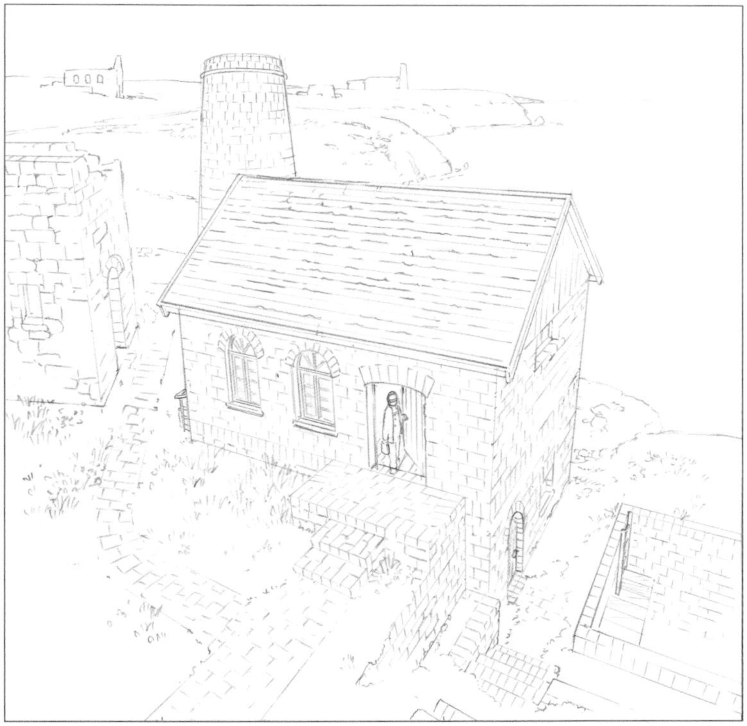

I've offset the corner of the building on the left to keep the drawing from looking flat, so it has separate vanishing points. I've drawn a line based on the building's depth up to where it intersects with eye level, which shows me where one vanishing point is. This helps with the basic layout of the drawing (top right figure).

I draw the rest of the details while referencing many materials. I revise the design of the window frame, door, and roof as well as the buildings in the distance to match the mood of the illustration.

2. Color the Model Sheet

MAKING OF A MINER'S ENGINE HOUSE

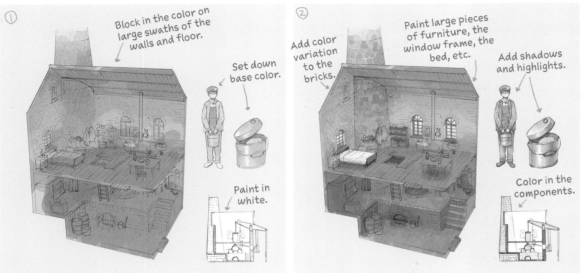

① Block in the color on large swaths of the walls and floor.

Set down base color.

Paint in white.

② Paint large pieces of furniture, the window frame, the bed, etc.

Add color variation to the bricks.

Add shadows and highlights.

Color in the components.

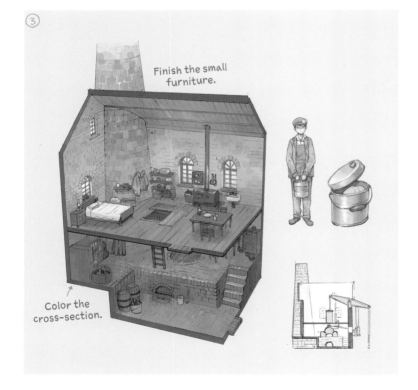

③ Finish the small furniture.

Color the cross-section.

When I start coloring, I use layers only for the building on the left side of the model sheet. First I block in the colors of the larger components. After that, I steadily add color to the details and finally add shadows and highlights.

If I draw too many details, less will be left to the imagination, so I don't use layers when I color in the people and instead draw in the colors broadly overtop. I also take care not to include too many details of the furniture. Since I want to make this look like a watercolor, I've chosen bright shades and don't pay as much attention to light sources as I might usually. I also make sure to slightly emphasize the shadows from wrinkles in cloth.

Once I've finished painting, I make adjustments, such as correcting the tones and adding watercolor textures. It can be useful to have a watercolor texture on hand, but even taking a photo of store-bought watercolor paper and using that in the illustration can make a big difference.

Once the drawing is done, I add the hand-written notes, and the illustration is complete.

3. Color the Illustration

It's important for the illustration to stand on its own, so I draw it with slightly more detail than the model sheet. However, I want it to look like a light watercolor, so I don't draw as much of the background as I would if this were being used for a game.

I add the colors in the same order I did for the model sheet. First I color the ground, then add color to each component. Finally I color the details and add highlights and shadows. (I draw in any large shadows at the start.) This first general blocking of color is called the underpainting. In this stage, I try out different shades for the main colors of the illustration and determine the general impression the illustration should give off.

Once the underpainting is done, I paint in distant objects like the clouds and ocean. To give the illustration a hand-drawn look, it's most efficient to layer the colors starting with the most distant objects.

I've adopted a watercolor style for *Houses with a Story* because I like the design of foreign picture books, which often use this technique. That makes the illustrations look different from the impasto style I normally use, but it has the warmth of a picture book. That meant I would need the coloring to be simple, so the initial planning was important.

Underpainting

The clouds closer to the horizon are denser.

Draw the waves

In shadow

Light hits here

Because of the atmospheric layers, objects in the distance aren't very dark, even in the shadows.

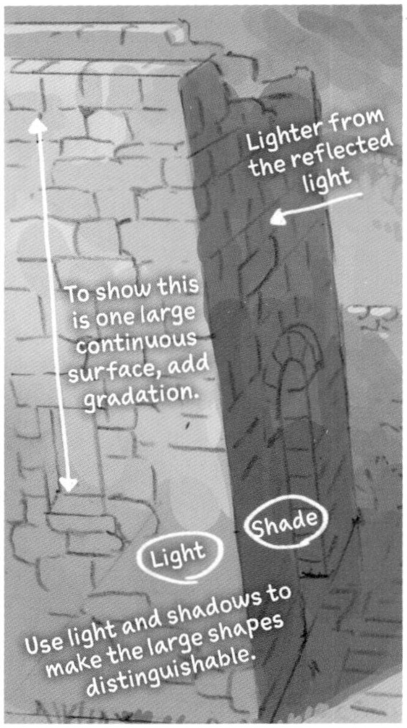
Lighter from the reflected light
To show this is one large continuous surface, add gradation.
Shade
Light
Use light and shadows to make the large shapes distinguishable.

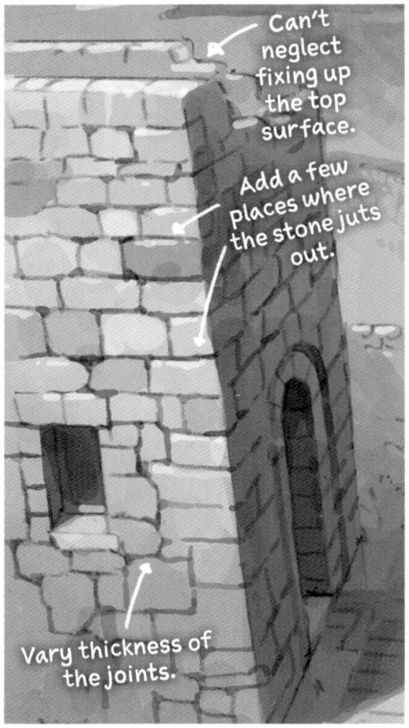
Can't neglect fixing up the top surface.
Add a few places where the stone juts out.
Vary thickness of the joints.

I steadily paint in the foreground. I determine the palette from the underpainting colors and color in the building and silhouettes. Then I add color variation and grime as well as detailed shadows and highlights.

The paving stones and bricks need to look rugged and have a lot of details, so painting the subtle color variations requires patience, but I enjoy it, so I take care with them. For material where each piece should differ slightly, I block in one color, then strategically add bolder color variations. I vary the thickness of the joints between the materials; sometimes I don't draw some parts at all or create places where it looks like there are large gaps. By putting consideration into the balance of the piece, I make the illustration more appealing.

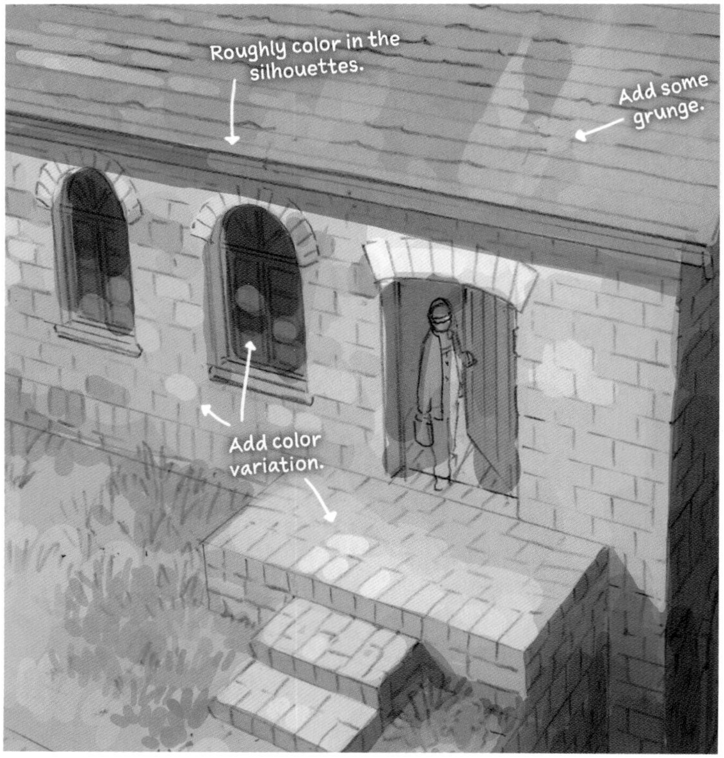
Roughly color in the silhouettes.
Add some grunge.
Add color variation.

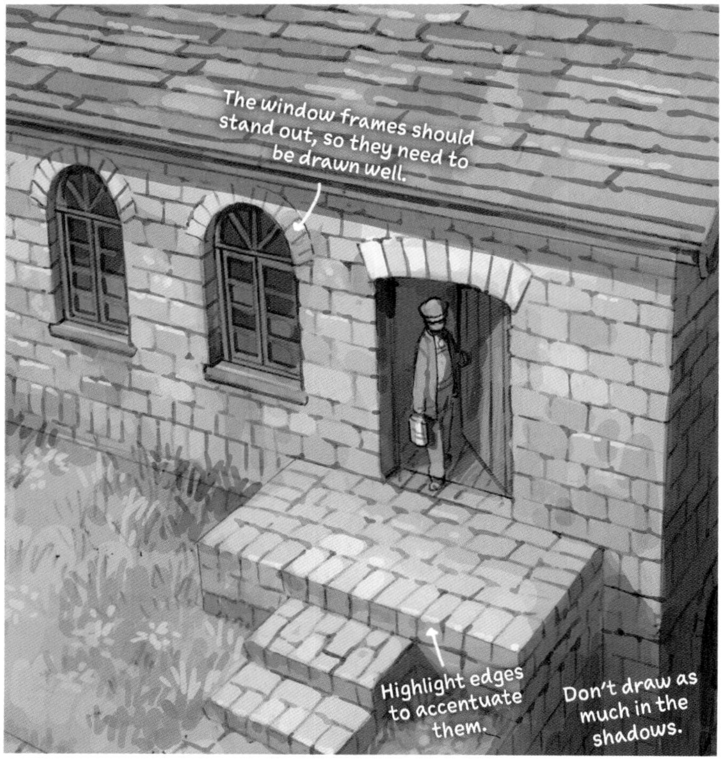
The window frames should stand out, so they need to be drawn well.
Highlight edges to accentuate them.
Don't draw as much in the shadows.

When I draw human-made structures, though the walls and floors need to have small uneven bits, the structures as a whole need to look flat. To achieve this effect, I take care to add gradation to the surfaces during the underpainting stage. Though as a rule of thumb, closer objects should be brighter, this can vary based on reflections, shapes, and other conditions, and I try to keep those things in mind during the underpainting as well.

When I actually experience the importance of these adjustments as I finish a painting, I'm reminded to pay attention to those details the next time I make an underpainting. This feedback loop allows me to create more precise underpaintings, which is important for achieving a hand-drawn look and feel.

Once the buildings are complete, I finish the ground. Instead of drawing the grass in the distance one blade at a time, I draw only large clumps that would cast shadows and avoid detail so they will look natural. To keep the grass from looking monotonous, I use multiple silhouettes and add flowers as well (upper right figure).

Finally I correct the tones, add watercolor-paper texture, and check whether there are any areas that lack color. Once I am done with the fine-tuning, the illustration is complete.

The right figure shows the illustration before I applied the final effects. Compared to the underpainting, the colors, light, and shadows haven't changed much. Imagining the mood of the illustration during the initial rough sketch leads most quickly to the piece's completion.

Color variation
Yellow can be strong here.

Pay special attention to the clumps of grass.
Draw different silhouettes in the grass.

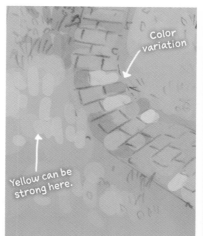

Cataloging-in-Publication Data has been applied for and may be obtained from the Library of Congress.

ISBN 978-1-4197-6124-9

© 2020 Seiji Yoshida / PIE International
English translation © 2023 Abrams
Translated by Jan Mitsuko Cash
Edited by Howard W. Reeves
English language edition design by Madeline Morales

Original Japanese Edition Creative Staff:
Author: Seiji Yoshida
Designer: Yagi Takae
Editor: Kinefuchi Keiko

Originally published in Japan in 2020 by PIE International, under the title ものがたりの家―吉田誠治 美術設定集― (Houses with a Story—Yoshida Seiji Art Works—). English translation rights arranged through PIE International, Japan. Published in English in 2023 by Amulet Books, an imprint of ABRAMS. All rights reserved. No portion of this book may be reproduced, stored in a retrieval system, or transmitted in any form or by any means, mechanical, electronic, photocopying, recording, or otherwise, without written permission from the publisher.

Printed and bound in Malaysia
10 9 8 7 6 5 4 3

Amulet Books are available at special discounts when purchased in quantity for premiums and promotions as well as fundraising or educational use. Special editions can also be created to specification. For details, contact specialsales@abramsbooks.com or the address below.

Amulet Books® is a registered trademark of Harry N. Abrams, Inc

ABRAMS The Art of Books
195 Broadway, New York, NY 10007
abramsbooks.com

FIRST APPEARANCES

The illustration on page 70 was originally drawn for the 97th Comic Market, 2019. The illustration on page 73 was originally drawn for the Dragon Society.

SELECT BIBLIOGRAPHY

Altarriba, Eduard, and Berta Bardí i Milà. *Discovering Architecture*. Lewes, England: Button Books, 2019.

Construction Information December 2018 issue: *A Lifetime Sized Encyclopedia*. X-Knowledge. (Not available in English.)

Ghibli 3-D Architecture Art Book. Studio Ghibli, 2021. (Not available in English.)

Hopkins, Owen. *Reading Architecture: A Visual Lexicon*. London: Laurence King, 2012.

Japan Federation of Construction Contractors. *The Japanese Building Process Illustrated*. Tokyo, Japan: Shokokusha Publishing Company, 2017.

Macaulay, David. *Castle*. Boston: Houghton Mifflin Company, 1977.

Macaulay, David. *Cathedral: The Story of Its Construction*. Boston: Houghton Mifflin Company, 1973.

Tokyo Metropolitan Foundation for History and Culture. *Edo-Tokyo Open Air Architectural Museum Commentary Book*. (Not available in English.)